MY SIDE OF THE MOUNTAIN
TRILOGY

My Side *of the* Mountain

On *the* Far Side *of the* Mountain

Frightful's Mountain

written and illustrated by

JEAN
CRAIGHEAD
GEORGE

DUTTON CHILDREN'S BOOKS ✦ *New York*

CIP Data is available.

Published in the United States by Dutton Children's Books,
a division of Penguin Young Readers Group
345 Hudson Street, New York, New York 10014
www.penguin.com
Printed in U.S.A.
10 9 8
ISBN 0-525-46269-4

Everyone asks me why forty years passed between the writing of *My Side of the Mountain*, *On the Far Side of the Mountain*, and *Frightful's Mountain*. There are two reasons. My mother disapproved of sequels. "Those are trashy books," she told me when I was a child. So I grew up and did not write them.

But kids are wiser than adults, I learned. Letters kept arriving from schools and homes, saying: "We want to know more about Sam, Frightful, and the wilderness." "Sequels," they said, "are important." They were right.

The second reason is that I did not know enough. I have to live and feel everything I write about, and that takes a long time. After *My Side of the Mountain*, it took years of camping, studying falcons and the ecology, and living outdoors to find Sam's voice again.

As I look at this beautiful collection today, I think how pleased my mother would have been. She might not have liked sequels, but she loved trilogies. Thank you, Dutton Children's Books.

Gorge

tree

Mountain
meadow

Gribley Beech

apple tree

house site

walnut tree

cattail supply

My Side of the Mountain
signed S. Gribley

My Side
of the Mountain

written and illustrated by

JEAN
CRAIGHEAD
GEORGE

DUTTON

CHILDREN'S

BOOKS

New York

This book is dedicated to many people—

*to that gang of youngsters who
inhabited the trees and waters of the
Potomac River so many years ago, and
to the bit of Sam Gribley in the
children and adults around me now.*

Library of Congress Cataloging-in-Publication Data

George, Jean Craighead, date
My side of the mountain/written and illustrated by
Jean Craighead George.
p. cm.
Summary: A young boy relates his adventures during the year he
spends living alone in the Catskill Mountains, including his struggle
for survival, his dependence on nature, his animal friends, and his
ultimate realization that he needs human companionship.
ISBN: 0-525-46346-1
[1. Survival—Fiction. 2. Self-reliance—Fiction.
3. Mountain life—Fiction.] I. Title 87-27556 CIP AC
PZ7.G2933My   1988
[Fic]—dc19

Published in the United States by Dutton Children's Books,
a division of Penguin Young Readers Group
345 Hudson Street, New York, New York 10014
Printed in the U.S.A.
Original edition: 38th printing
This edition:
22 21 20 19 18 17 16 15

Contents

AUTHOR'S PREFACE

When I was in elementary school, I packed my suitcase and told my mother I was going to run away from home. As I envisioned it, I would live by a waterfall in the woods and catch fish on hooks made from the forks of tree limbs, as I had been taught by my father. I would walk among the wildflowers and trees, listen to the birds, read the weather report in the clouds and the wind, and stride down mountainsides independent and free. Wisely, my mother did not try to dissuade me. She had been through this herself. She checked my bag to see if I had my toothbrush and a postcard to let her know how I was getting along, and kissed me good-by. Forty minutes later I was home.

When my daughter, Twig, was in elementary school, she told me she was going to run away to the woods. I checked her backpack for her toothbrush and watched her go down the front steps, her shoulders squared confidently. I blew her a kiss and sat down to wait. Presently, she was back.

Although wishing to run to the woods and live on our own seems to be an inherited characteristic in our family, we are not unique. Almost everyone I know has dreamed at some time of running away to a distant mountain or island, castle or sailing ship, to live there in beauty and peace. Few of us make it, however.

It is one thing to wish to go, and another matter to do it. I might have been able to do what Sam Gribley does in this book—live off the land, make a home, survive by wits and library research, for I had the knowledge. My father, who was a naturalist and scientist, taught me the plants and animals of eastern forests and showed me where the wild edible fruits and tubers grew. On weekends along the Potomac River near Washington, D.C., where I was born and grew up, he and I boiled water in leaves and made rabbit traps. Together we made tables and chairs out of saplings bound with the braided inner bark of the basswood tree. My brothers, two of the first falconers in the United States, helped me in the training of a falcon. I had the know-how for surviving in the woods; and yet I came home.

"But not Sam," I said to myself when I sat down at my typewriter and began putting on paper this story, one that I had been writing in my head for many, many years.

The writing came easily—Sam needed a home. I remembered a huge tree my brothers had camped in on an island in the Potomac River. A tree would be Sam's home. And I knew how he would survive when foraging became tough. "A falcon will be his provider," I said to myself.

With ideas coming fast, the first draft was done in two weeks. Five revisions later, it was finished and off to the publisher. Back came a phone call from Sharon Bannigan, the editor of E. P. Dutton's children's book department at that time.

"Elliott Macrae, the publisher," she said, "won't print the book. He says parents should not encourage their kids to leave home."

Discouraged, I hung up the phone and walked out into the woods behind the house. As always when I am in the wildwood, I very quickly forgot what was troubling me. A sentinel crow was protecting its flock by watching the sky for hawks; a squirrel was building a nest of leaves for the winter; a spider was tapping out a message to his mate on a line of her web.

Better to run to the woods than the city, I thought. Here, there is the world to occupy the mind.

The telephone rang. Sharon Bannigan was back on the wire, and she was almost singing. Elliott Macrae had changed his mind. And what, I asked her, had worked the miracle?

"I simply told him it is better to have children run to the woods than the city," she said. "He thought about that. Since he has a home in the wilds of the Adirondack Mountains and goes off there alone himself, he suddenly understood your book. *My Side of the Mountain* will be published in the spring of '59."

From that date to this, I have been answering children's letters about Sam. Most want to know if he is a real person. Some, convinced that he is, have biked to Delhi, New York, from as far away as Long Island, New York, to find his tree, his falcon, weasel, and raccoon. To these and all others who ask, I say, "There is no real Sam, except inside me." His adventures are the fulfillment of that day long ago when I told my mother I was going to run away, got as far as the edge of the woods, and came back. Perhaps Sam will fulfill your dreams, too. Be you writer or reader, it is very pleasant to run away in a book.

My Side of the Mountain

IN WHICH
I Hole Up in a Snowstorm

I am on my mountain in a tree home that people have passed without ever knowing that I am here. The house is a hemlock tree six feet in diameter, and must be as old as the mountain itself. I came upon it last summer and dug and burned it out until I made a snug cave in the tree that I now call home.

"My bed is on the right as you enter, and is made of ash slats and covered with deerskin. On the left is a small fireplace about knee high. It is of clay and stones. It has a chimney that leads the smoke out through a knothole. I chipped out three other knotholes to let fresh air in. The air coming in is bitter cold. It must be below zero outside, and yet I can sit here inside my tree and write with bare hands. The fire is small, too. It doesn't take much fire to warm this tree room.

"It is the fourth of December, I think. It may be the fifth. I am not sure because I have not recently counted the notches in the aspen pole that is my calendar. I have been just too busy gathering nuts and berries, smoking venison, fish, and small game to keep up with the exact date.

"The lamp I am writing by is deer fat poured into a turtle shell with a strip of my old city trousers for a wick.

"It snowed all day yesterday and today. I have not been outside since the storm began, and I am bored for the first time since I ran away from home eight months ago to live on the land.

"I am well and healthy. The food is good. Sometimes I eat turtle soup, and I know how to make acorn pancakes. I keep my supplies in the wall of the tree in wooden pockets that I chopped myself.

"Every time I have looked at those pockets during the last two days, I have felt just like a squirrel, which reminds me: I didn't see a squirrel one whole day before that storm began. I guess they are holed up and eating their stored nuts, too.

"I wonder if The Baron, that's the wild weasel who lives behind the big boulder to the north of my tree, is also denned up. Well, anyway, I think the storm is dying down because the tree is not crying so much. When the wind really blows, the whole tree moans right down to the roots, which is where I am.

"Tomorrow I hope The Baron and I can tunnel out into the sunlight. I wonder if I should dig the snow. But that would mean I would have to put it somewhere, and the only place to put it is in my nice snug tree.

Maybe I can pack it with my hands as I go. I've always dug into the snow from the top, never up from under.

"The Baron must dig up from under the snow. I wonder where he puts what he digs? Well, I guess I'll know in the morning."

When I wrote that last winter, I was scared and thought maybe I'd never get out of my tree. I had been scared for two days—ever since the first blizzard hit the Catskill Mountains. When I came up to the sunlight, which I did by simply poking my head into the soft snow and standing up, I laughed at my dark fears.

Everything was white, clean, shining, and beautiful. The sky was blue, blue, blue. The hemlock grove was laced with snow, the meadow was smooth and white, and the gorge was sparkling with ice. It was so beautiful and peaceful that I laughed out loud. I guess I laughed because my first snowstorm was over and it had not been so terrible after all.

Then I shouted, "I did it!" My voice never got very far. It was hushed by the tons of snow.

I looked for signs from The Baron Weasel. His footsteps were all over the boulder, also slides where he had played. He must have been up for hours, enjoying the new snow.

Inspired by his fun, I poked my head into my tree and whistled. Frightful, my trained falcon, flew to my fist, and we jumped and slid down the mountain, making big

holes and trenches as we went. It was good to be whistling and carefree again, because I was sure scared by the coming of that storm.

I had been working since May, learning how to make a fire with flint and steel, finding what plants I could eat, how to trap animals and catch fish—all this so that when the curtain of blizzard struck the Catskills, I could crawl inside my tree and be comfortably warm and have plenty to eat.

During the summer and fall I had thought about the coming of winter. However, on that third day of December when the sky blackened, the temperature dropped, and the first flakes swirled around me. I must admit that I wanted to run back to New York. Even the first night that I spent out in the woods, when I couldn't get the fire started, was not as frightening as the snowstorm that gathered behind the gorge and mushroomed up over my mountain.

I was smoking three trout. It was nine o'clock in the morning. I was busy keeping the flames low so they would not leap up and burn the fish. As I worked, it occurred to me that it was awfully dark for that hour of the morning. Frightful was leashed to her tree stub. She seemed restless and pulled at her tethers. Then I realized that the forest was dead quiet. Even the woodpeckers that had been tapping around me all morning were silent. The squirrels were nowhere to be seen. The juncos and chickadees and nuthatches were gone. I looked to see what The Baron Weasel was doing. He was not around. I looked up.

From my tree you can see the gorge beyond the meadow. White water pours between the black wet boulders and cascades into the valley below. The water that day was as dark as the rocks. Only the sound told me it was still falling. Above the darkness stood another darkness. The clouds of winter, black and fearsome. They looked as wild as the winds that were bringing them. I grew sick with fright. I knew I had enough food. I knew everything was going to be perfectly all right. But knowing that didn't help. I was scared. I stamped out the fire and pocketed the fish.

I tried to whistle for Frightful, but couldn't purse my shaking lips tight enough to get out anything but *pfffff*. So I grabbed her by the hide straps that are attached to her legs and we dove through the deerskin door into my room in the tree.

I put Frightful on the bedpost, and curled up in a ball on the bed. I thought about New York and the noise and the lights and how a snowstorm always seemed very friendly there. I thought about our apartment, too. At that moment it seemed bright and lighted and warm. I had to keep saying to myself: There were eleven of us in it! Dad, Mother, four sisters, four brothers, and me. And not one of us liked it, except perhaps little Nina, who was too young to know. Dad didn't like it even a little bit. He had been a sailor once, but when I was born, he gave up the sea and worked on the docks in New York. Dad didn't like the land. He liked the sea, wet and big and endless.

Sometimes he would tell me about Great-grandfather Gribley, who owned land in the Catskill Mountains and

felled the trees and built a home and plowed the land—
only to discover that he wanted to be a sailor. The farm
failed, and Great-grandfather Gribley went to sea.

As I lay with my face buried in the sweet greasy smell
of my deerskin, I could hear Dad's voice saying, "That
land is still in the family's name. Somewhere in the
Catskills is an old beech with the name *Gribley* carved
on it. It marks the northern boundary of Gribley's
folly—the land is no place for a Gribley."

"The land is no place for a Gribley," I said. "The
land is no place for a Gribley, and here I am three
hundred feet from the beech with *Gribley* carved on it."

I fell asleep at that point, and when I awoke I was
hungry. I cracked some walnuts, got down the acorn
flour I had pounded, with a bit of ash to remove the bite,
reached out the door for a little snow, and stirred up
some acorn pancakes. I cooked them on a top of a tin
can, and as I ate them, smothered with blueberry jam,
I knew that the land was just the place for a Gribley.

IN WHICH
I Get Started on This Venture

I left New York in May. I had a penknife, a ball of cord,
an ax, and $40, which I had saved from selling maga-
zine subscriptions. I also had some flint and steel which

I had bought at a Chinese store in the city. The man in the store had showed me how to use it. He had also given me a little purse to put it in, and some tinder to catch the sparks. He had told me that if I ran out of tinder, I should burn cloth, and use the charred ashes.

I thanked him and said, "This is the kind of thing I am not going to forget."

On the train north to the Catskills I unwrapped my flint and steel and practiced hitting them together to make sparks. On the wrapping paper I made these notes.

"A hard brisk strike is best. Remember to hold the steel in the left hand and the flint in the right, and hit the steel with the flint.

"The trouble is the sparks go every which way."

And that *was* the trouble. I did not get a fire going that night, and as I mentioned, this was a scary experience.

I hitched rides into the Catskill Mountains. At about four o'clock a truck driver and I passed through a beautiful dark hemlock forest, and I said to him, "This is as far as I am going."

He looked all around and said, "You live here?"

"No," I said, "but I am running away from home, and this is just the kind of forest I have always dreamed I would run to. I think I'll camp here tonight." I hopped out of the cab.

"Hey, boy," the driver shouted. "Are you serious?"

"Sure," I said.

"Well, now, ain't that sumpin'? You know, when I was your age, I did the same thing. Only thing was, I was a farm boy and ran to the city, and you're a city boy running to the woods. I was scared of the city—do you think you'll be scared of the woods?"

"Heck, no!" I shouted loudly.

As I marched into the cool shadowy woods, I heard the driver call to me, "I'll be back in the morning, if you want to ride home."

He laughed. Everybody laughed at me. Even Dad. I told Dad that I was going to run away to Great-grandfather Gribley's land. He had roared with laughter and told me about the time he had run away from home. He got on a boat headed for Singapore, but when the whistle blew for departure, he was down the gangplank and home in bed before anyone knew he was gone. Then he told me, "Sure, go try it. Every boy should try it."

I must have walked a mile into the woods until I found a stream. It was a clear athletic stream that rushed and ran and jumped and splashed. Ferns grew along its bank, and its rocks were upholstered with moss.

I sat down, smelled the piney air, and took out my penknife. I cut off a green twig and began to whittle. I have always been good at whittling. I carved a ship once that my teacher exhibited for parents' night at school.

whittle angles · sharpen · string · wooden fishhook

First I whittled an angle on one end of the twig. Then I cut a smaller twig and sharpened it to a point. I whittled an angle on that twig, and bound the two angles face to face with a strip of green bark. It was supposed to be a fishhook.

According to a book on how to survive on the land that I read in the New York Public Library, this was the way to make your own hooks. I then dug for worms. I had hardly chopped the moss away with my ax before I hit frost. It had not occurred to me that there would be frost in the ground in May, but then, I had not been on a mountain before.

This did worry me, because I was depending on fish to keep me alive until I got to my great-grandfather's mountain, where I was going to make traps and catch game.

I looked into the stream to see what else I could eat, and as I did, my hand knocked a rotten log apart. I remembered about old logs and all the sleeping stages of insects that are in it. I chopped away until I found a cold white grub.

I swiftly tied a string to my hook, put the grub on, and walked up the stream looking for a good place to fish. All the manuals I had read were very emphatic about where fish lived, and so I had memorized this: "In streams, fish usually congregate in pools and deep calm water. The heads of riffles, small rapids, the tail of a pool, eddies below rocks or logs, deep undercut banks, in the shade of overhanging bushes—all are very likely places to fish."

This stream did not seem to have any calm water, and I must have walked a thousand miles before I found a pool by a deep undercut bank in the shade of overhanging bushes. Actually, it wasn't that far, it just seemed that way because as I went looking and finding nothing, I was sure I was going to starve to death.

I squatted on this bank and dropped in my line. I did so want to catch a fish. One fish would set me upon my way, because I had read how much you can learn from one fish. By examining the contents of its stomach you can find what the other fish are eating or you can use the internal organs as bait.

The grub went down to the bottom of the stream. It swirled around and hung still. Suddenly the string came

to life, and rode back and forth and around in a circle. I pulled with a powerful jerk. The hook came apart, and whatever I had went circling back to its bed.

Well, that almost made me cry. My bait was gone, my hook was broken, and I was getting cold, frightened, and mad. I whittled another hook, but this time I cheated and used string to wind it together instead of bark. I walked back to the log and luckily found another grub. I hurried to the pool, and I flipped a trout out of the water before I knew I had a bite.

The fish flopped, and I threw my whole body over it. I could not bear to think of it flopping itself back into the stream.

I cleaned it like I had seen the man at the fish market do, examined its stomach, and found it empty. This horrified me. What I didn't know was that an empty stomach means the fish are hungry and will eat about anything. However, I thought at the time that I was a goner. Sadly, I put some of the internal organs on my hook, and before I could get my line to the bottom I had another bite. I lost that one, but got the next one. I stopped when I had five nice little trout and looked around for a place to build a camp and make a fire.

It wasn't hard to find a pretty spot along that stream. I selected a place beside a mossy rock in a circle of hemlocks.

I decided to make a bed before I cooked. I cut off some boughs for a mattress, then I leaned some dead limbs against the boulder and covered them with hemlock limbs. This made a kind of tent. I crawled in, lay down, and felt alone and secret and very excited.

But ah, the rest of this story! I was on the northeast side of the mountain. It grew dark and cold early. Seeing the shadows slide down on me, I frantically ran around gathering firewood. This is about the only thing

a couple of good shelters - make sure your fire is on scraped earth - also be sure to put it out!

I did right from that moment until dawn, because I remembered that the driest wood in a forest is the dead limbs that are still on the trees, and I gathered an enormous pile of them. That pile must still be there, for I never got a fire going.

I got sparks, sparks, sparks. I even hit the tinder with the sparks. The tinder burned all right, but that was as far as I got. I blew on it, I breathed on it, I cupped it in my hands, but no sooner did I add twigs than the whole thing went black.

Then it got too dark to see. I clicked steel and flint together, even though I couldn't see the tinder. Finally, I gave up and crawled into my hemlock tent, hungry, cold, and miserable.

I can talk about that first night now, although it is still embarrassing to me because I was so stupid, and scared, that I hate to admit it.

I had made my hemlock bed right in the stream valley where the wind drained down from the cold mountaintop. It might have been all right if I had made it on the other side of the boulder, but I didn't. I was right on the main highway of the cold winds as they tore down upon the valley below. I didn't have enough hemlock boughs under me, and before I had my head down, my stomach was cold and damp. I took some boughs off the roof and stuffed them under me, and then my shoulders were cold. I curled up in a ball and was almost asleep when a whippoorwill called. If you have ever been within forty feet of a whippoorwill, you will understand why I couldn't even shut my eyes. They are deafening!

Well, anyway, the whole night went like that. I don't think I slept fifteen minutes, and I was so scared and tired that my throat was dry. I wanted a drink but didn't dare go near the stream for fear of making a misstep and falling in and getting wet. So I sat tight,

and shivered and shook—and now I am able to say—I cried a little tiny bit.

Fortunately, the sun has a wonderfully glorious habit of rising every morning. When the sky lightened, when the birds awoke, I knew I would never again see anything so splendid as the round red sun coming up over the earth.

I was immediately cheered, and set out directly for the highway. Somehow, I thought that if I was a little nearer the road, everything would be all right.

I climbed a hill and stopped. There was a house. A house warm and cozy, with smoke coming out the chimney and lights in the windows, and only a hundred feet from my torture camp.

Without considering my pride, I ran down the hill and banged on the door. A nice old man answered. I told him everything in one long sentence, and then said, "And so, can I cook my fish here, because I haven't eaten in years."

He chuckled, stroked his whiskery face, and took the fish. He had them cooking in a pan before I knew what his name was.

When I asked him, he said Bill something, but I never heard his last name because I fell asleep in his rocking chair that was pulled up beside his big hot glorious wood stove in the kitchen.

I ate the fish some hours later, also some bread, jelly, oatmeal, and cream. Then he said to me, "Sam Gribley, if you are going to run off and live in the woods, you better learn how to make a fire. Come with me."

We spent the afternoon practicing. I penciled these notes on the back of a scrap of paper, so I wouldn't forget.

"When the tinder glows, keep blowing and add fine dry needles one by one—and keep blowing, steadily, lightly, and evenly. Add one inch dry twigs to the needles and then give her a good big handful of small dry stuff. Keep blowing."

THE MANNER IN WHICH
I Find Gribley's Farm

The next day I told Bill good-by, and as I strode, warm and fed, onto the road, he called to me, "I'll see you tonight. The back door will be open if you want a roof over your head."

I said, "Okay," but I knew I wouldn't see Bill again. I knew how to make fire, and that was my weapon. With fire I could conquer the Catskills. I also knew how to fish. To fish and to make a fire. That was all I needed to know, I thought.

Three rides that morning took me to Delhi. Somewhere around here was Great-grandfather's beech tree with the name *Gribley* carved on it. This much I knew from Dad's stories.

By six o'clock I still had not found anyone who had even heard of the Gribleys, much less Gribley's beech, and so I slept on the porch of a schoolhouse and ate chocolate bars for supper. It was cold and hard, but I was so tired I could have slept in a wind tunnel.

At dawn I thought real hard: Where would I find out about the Gribley farm? Some old map, I said. Where would I find an old map? The library? Maybe. I'd try it and see.

The librarian was very helpful. She was sort of young, had brown hair and brown eyes, and loved books as much as I did.

The library didn't open until ten-thirty. I got there at nine. After I had lolled and rolled and sat on the steps for fifteen or twenty minutes, the door whisked open, and this tall lady asked me to come on in and browse around until opening time.

All I said to her was that I wanted to find the old Gribley farm, and that the Gribleys hadn't lived on it for maybe a hundred years, and she was off. I can still hear her heels click, when I think of her, scattering herself around those shelves finding me old maps, histories of the Catskills, and files of letters and deeds that must have come from attics around Delhi.

Miss Turner—that was her name—found it. She found Gribley's farm in an old book of Delaware County. Then she worked out the roads to it, and drew me maps and everything. Finally she said, "What do you want to know for? Some school project?"

"Oh, no, Miss Turner, I want to go live there."

"But, Sam, it is all forest and trees now. The house is probably only a foundation covered with moss."

"That's just what I want. I am going to trap animals and eat nuts and bulbs and berries and make myself a house. You see, I am Sam Gribley, and I thought I would like to live on my great-grandfather's farm."

Miss Turner was the only person that believed me. She smiled, sat back in her chair, and said, "Well, I declare."

The library was just opening when I gathered the notes we had made and started off. As I pushed open the door, Miss Turner leaned over and said to me, "Sam, we have some very good books on plants and trees and animals, in case you get stuck."

I knew what she was thinking, and so I told her I would remember that.

With Miss Turner's map, I found the first stone wall that marked the farm. The old roads to it were all grown up and mostly gone, but by locating the stream at the bottom of the mountain I was able to begin at the bridge and go north and up a mile and a half. There, caterpillaring around boulders, roller-coastering up ravines and down hills, was the mound of rocks that had once been Great-grandfather's boundary fence.

And then, do you know, I couldn't believe I was there. I sat on the old gray stones a long time, looking through the forest, up that steep mountain, and saying to myself, "It must be Sunday afternoon, and it's rain-ing, and Dad is trying to keep us all quiet by telling us about Great-grandfather's farm; and he's telling it so real that I can see it."

And then I said, "No. I am here, because I was never this hungry before."

I wanted to run all the way back to the library and tell Miss Turner that I had found it. Partly because she would have liked to have known, and partly because Dad had said to me as I left, "If you find the place, tell someone at Delhi. I may visit you someday." Of course, he was kidding, because he thought I'd be home the next day, but after many weeks, maybe he would think I meant what I said, and he might come see me.

However, I was too hungry to run back. I took my hook and line and went back down the mountain to the stream.

I caught a big old catfish. I climbed back to the stone wall in great spirits.

It was getting late and so I didn't try to explore. I went right to work making a fire. I decided that even if I didn't have enough time to cut boughs for a bed, I was going to have cooked fish and a fire to huddle around during those cold night hours. May is not exactly warm in the Catskills.

By firelight that night I wrote this:

"Dear Bill [that was the old man]:
"After three tries, I finally got a handful of dry grass on the glow in the tinder. Grass is even better than pine

needles, and tomorrow I am going to try the outside bark of the river birch. I read somewhere that it has combustible oil in it that the Indians used to start fires. Anyway, I did just what you showed me, and had cooked catfish for dinner. It was good.

                              Your friend,
                              Sam."

After I wrote that I remembered I didn't know his last name, and so I stuffed the note in my pocket, made myself a bed of boughs and leaves in the shelter of the stone wall, and fell right to sleep.

I must say this now about that first fire. It was magic. Out of dead tinder and grass and sticks came a live warm light. It cracked and snapped and smoked and filled the woods with brightness. It lighted the trees and made them warm and friendly. It stood tall and bright and held back the night. Oh, this was a different night than the first dark frightful one. Also I was stuffed on catfish. I have since learned to cook it more, but never have I enjoyed a meal as much as that one, and never have I felt so independent again.

IN WHICH
I Find Many Useful Plants

The following morning I stood up, stretched, and looked about me. Birds were dripping from the trees, little birds, singing and flying and pouring over the limbs.

"This must be the warbler migration," I said, and I laughed because there were so many birds. I had never seen so many. My big voice rolled through the woods, and their little voices seemed to rise and answer me.

They were eating. Three or four in a maple tree near me were darting along the limbs, pecking and snatching at something delicious on the trees. I wondered if there was anything there for a hungry boy. I pulled a limb down, and all I saw were leaves, twigs, and flowers. I ate a flower. It was not very good. One manual I had read said to watch what the birds and animals were eating in order to learn what is edible and nonedible in the forest. If the animal life can eat it, it is safe for humans. The book did suggest that a raccoon had tastes more nearly like ours. Certainly the birds were no example.

Then I wondered if they were not eating something I couldn't see—tiny insects perhaps; well, anyway, whatever it was, I decided to fish. I took my line and hook and walked down to the stream.

I lay on a log and dangled my line in the bright water. The fish were not biting. That made me hungrier. My stomach pinched. You know, it really does hurt to be terribly hungry.

A stream is supposed to be full of food. It is the easiest place to get a lot of food in a hurry. I needed something in a hurry, but what? I looked through the clear water and saw the tracks of mussels in the mud. I ran along the log back to shore, took off my clothes, and plunged into that icy water.

I collected almost a peck of mussels in very little time at all, and began tying them in my sweater to carry them back to camp.

But I don't have to carry them anywhere, I said to myself. I have my fire in my pocket, I don't need a table. I can sit right here by the stream and eat. And so I did. I wrapped the mussels in leaves and sort of steamed them in coals. They are not quite as good as clams—a little stronger, I would say—but by the time I had eaten three, I had forgotten what clams tasted like and knew only how delicious freshwater mussels were. I actually got full.

I wandered back to Great-grandfather's farm and began to explore. Most of the acreage was maple and beech, some pine, dogwoods, ash; and here and there a glorious hickory. I made a sketch of the farm on my road map, and put x's where the hickories were. They were gold trees to me. I would have hickory nuts in the fall. I could also make salt from hickory limbs. I cut off one and chopped it into bits and scraps. I stuck them in my sweater.

The land was up and down and up and down, and I wondered how Great-grandfather ever cut it and plowed it. There was one stream running through it, which I was glad to see, for it meant I did not have to go all the way down the mountain to the big creek for fish and water.

Around noon I came upon what I was sure was the old foundation of the house. Miss Turner was right. It was ruins—a few stones in a square, a slight depression for the basement, and trees growing right up through what had once been the living room. I wandered around to see what was left of the Gribley home.

After a few looks I saw an apple tree. I rushed up to it, hoping to find an old apple. No apples beneath it. About forty feet away, however, I found a dried one in the crotch of a tree, stuck there by a squirrel and forgotten. I ate it. It was pretty bad—but nourishing, I hoped. There was another apple tree and three walnuts. I scribbled x's. These were wonderful finds.

I poked around the foundations, hoping to uncover some old iron implements that I could use. I found nothing. Too many leaves had fallen and turned to loam, too many plants had grown up and died down over the old home site. I decided to come back when I had made myself a shovel.

Whistling and looking for food and shelter, I went on up the mountain, following the stone walls, discovering many things about my property. I found a marsh. In it were cattails and arrow-leaf—good starchy foods.

At high noon I stepped onto a mountain meadow. An enormous boulder rose up in the center of it. At the top of the meadow was a fringe of white birch. There were maples and oaks to the west, and a hemlock forest to the right that pulled me right across the sweet grasses, into it.

Never, never have I seen such trees. They were giants—old, old giants. They must have begun when the world began.

I started walking around them. I couldn't hear myself step, so dense and damp were the needles. Great boulders covered with ferns and moss stood among them. They looked like pebbles beneath those trees.

Standing before the biggest and the oldest and the most kinglike of them all, I suddenly had an idea.

THIS IS ABOUT
The Old, Old Tree

I knew enough about the Catskill Mountains to know that when the summer came, they were covered with people. Although Great-grandfather's farm was somewhat remote, still hikers and campers and hunters and fishermen were sure to wander across it.

Therefore I wanted a house that could not be seen. People would want to take me back where I belonged if they found me.

I looked at that tree. Somehow I knew it was home, but I was not quite sure how it was home. The limbs were high and not right for a tree house. I could build a bark extension around it, but that would look silly. Slowly I circled the great trunk. Halfway around the whole plan became perfectly obvious. To the west, between two of the flanges of the tree that spread out to be roots, was a cavity. The heart of the tree was rotting away. I scraped at it with my hands; old, rotten insect-ridden dust came tumbling out. I dug on and on, using my ax from time to time as my excitement grew.

With much of the old rot out, I could crawl in the tree and sit cross-legged. Inside I felt as cozy as a turtle in its shell. I chopped and chopped until I was hungry and exhausted. I was now in the hard good wood, and chopping it out was work. I was afraid December would come before I got a hole big enough to lie in. So I sat down to think.

You know, those first days, I just never planned right. I had the beginnings of a home, but not a bite to eat, and I had worked so hard that I could hardly move forward to find that bite. Furthermore, it was discouraging to feed that body of mine. It was never satisfied, and gathering food for it took time and got it hungrier. Trying to get a place to rest it took time and got it more tired, and I really felt I was going in circles

and wondered how primitive man ever had enough time and energy to stop hunting food and start thinking about fire and tools.

I left the tree and went across the meadow looking for food. I plunged into the woods beyond, and there I discovered the gorge and the white cascade splashing down the black rocks into the pool below.

I was hot and dirty. I scrambled down the rocks and slipped into the pool. It was so cold I yelled. But when I came out on the bank and put on my two pairs of trousers and three sweaters, which I thought was a better way to carry clothes than in a pack, I tingled and burned and felt coltish. I leapt up the bank, slipped, and my face went down in a patch of dogtooth violets.

You would know them anywhere after a few looks at them at the Botanical Gardens and in colored flower books. They are little yellow lilies on long slender stems with oval leaves dappled with gray. But that's not all. They have wonderfully tasty bulbs. I was filling my pockets before I got up from my fall.

"I'll have a salad type lunch," I said as I moved up the steep sides of the ravine. I discovered that as late as it was in the season, the spring beauties were still blooming in the cool pockets of the woods. They are all right raw, that is if you are as hungry as I was. They taste a little like lima beans. I ate these as I went on hunting food, feeling better and better, until I worked my way back to the meadow where the dandelions were blooming. Funny I hadn't noticed them earlier. Their greens are good, and so are their roots—a little strong and milky, but you get used to that.

A crow flew into the aspen grove without saying a

word. The little I knew of crows from following them in Central Park, they always have something to say. But this bird was sneaking, obviously trying to be quiet. Birds are good food. Crow is certainly not the best, but I did not know that then, and I launched out to see where it was going. I had a vague plan to try to noose it. This is the kind of thing I wasted time on in those days when time was so important. However, this venture turned out all right, because I did not have to noose that bird.

I stepped into the woods, looked around, could not see the crow, but noticed a big stick nest in a scrabbly pine. I started to climb the tree. Off flew the crow. What made me keep on climbing in face of such discouragement, I don't know, but I did, and that noon I had crow eggs and wild salad for lunch.

At lunch I also solved the problem of carving out my tree. After a struggle I made a fire. Then I sewed a big skunk cabbage leaf into a cup with grass strands. I had read that you can boil water in a leaf, and ever since then I had been very anxious to see if this were true. It seems impossible, but it works. I boiled the eggs in a leaf. The water keeps the leaf wet, and although the top dries up and burns down to the water level, that's as far as the burning goes. I was pleased to see it work.

Then here's what happened. Naturally, all this took a lot of time, and I hadn't gotten very far on my tree, so I was fretting and stamping out the fire when I stopped with my foot in the air.

good cooking fireplace
with leaf bucket

The fire! Indians made dugout canoes with fire. They burned them out, an easier and much faster way of getting results. I would try fire in the tree. If I was very careful, perhaps it would work. I ran into the hemlock forest with a burning stick and got a fire going inside the tree.

Thinking that I ought to have a bucket of water in case things got out of hand, I looked desperately around me. The water was far across the meadow and down the ravine. This would never do. I began to think the whole inspiration of a home in the tree was no good. I really did have to live near water for cooking and drinking and comfort. I looked sadly at the magnificent hemlock and was about to put the fire out and desert it when I said something to myself. It must have come out of some book: "Hemlocks usually grow around mountain streams and springs."

I swirled on my heel. Nothing but boulders around

me. But the air was damp, somewhere—I said—and darted around the rocks, peering and looking and sniffing and going down into pockets and dales. No water. I was coming back, circling wide, when I almost fell in it. Two sentinel boulders, dripping wet, decorated with flowers, ferns, moss, weeds—everything that loved water—guarded a bathtub-sized spring.

"You pretty thing," I said, flopped on my stomach, and pushed my face into it to drink. I opened my eyes. The water was like glass, and in it were little insects with oars. They rowed away from me. Beetles skittered like bullets on the surface, or carried a silver bubble of air with them to the bottom. Ha, then I saw a crayfish.

I jumped up, overturned rocks, and found many crayfish. At first I hesitated to grab them because they can pinch. I gritted my teeth, thought about how much more it hurts to be hungry, and came down upon them. I did get pinched, but I had my dinner. And that was the first time I had planned ahead! Any planning that I did in those early days was such a surprise to me and so successful that I was delighted with even a small plan. I wrapped the crayfish in leaves, stuffed them in my pockets, and went back to the burning tree.

Bucket of water, I thought. Bucket of water? Where was I going to get a bucket? How did I think, even if I found water, I could get it back to the tree? That's how citified I was in those days. I had never lived without a bucket before—scrub buckets, water buckets—and so when a water problem came up, I just thought I could run to the kitchen and get a bucket.

"Well, dirt is as good as water," I said as I ran back to my tree. "I can smother the fire with dirt."

Days passed working, burning, cutting, gathering food, and each day I cut another notch on an aspen pole that I had stuck in the ground for a calendar.

IN WHICH
I Meet One of My Own Kind and
Have a Terrible Time Getting Away

Five notches into June, my house was done. I could stand in it, lie down in it, and there was room left over for a stump to sit on. On warm evenings I would lie on my stomach and look out the door, listen to the frogs and nighthawks, and hope it would storm so that I could crawl into my tree and be dry. I had gotten soaked during a couple of May downpours, and now that my house was done, I wanted the chance to sit in my hemlock and watch a cloudburst wet everything but me. This opportunity didn't come for a long time. It was dry.

One morning I was at the edge of the meadow. I had cut down a small ash tree and was chopping it into lengths of about eighteen inches each. This was the beginning of my bed that I was planning to work on after supper every night.

With the golden summer upon me, food was much easier to get, and I actually had several hours of free time after supper in which to do other things. I had been eating frogs' legs, turtles, and best of all, an occasional rabbit. My snares and traps were set now. Furthermore, I had a good supply of cattail roots I had dug in the marsh.

If you ever eat cattails, be sure to cook them well, otherwise the fibers are tough and they take more chewing to get the starchy food from them than they are worth. However, they taste just like potatoes after you've been eating them a couple of weeks, and to my way of thinking are extremely good.

Well, anyway, that summer morning when I was gathering material for a bed, I was singing and chopping and playing a game with a raccoon I had come to know. He had just crawled in a hollow tree and had gone to bed for the day when I came to the meadow. From time to time I would tap on his tree with my ax. He would hang his sleepy head out, snarl at me, close his eyes, and slide out of sight.

The third time I did this, I knew something was happening in the forest. Instead of closing his eyes, he pricked up his ears and his face became drawn and tense. His eyes were focused on something down the mountain. I stood up and looked. I could see nothing.

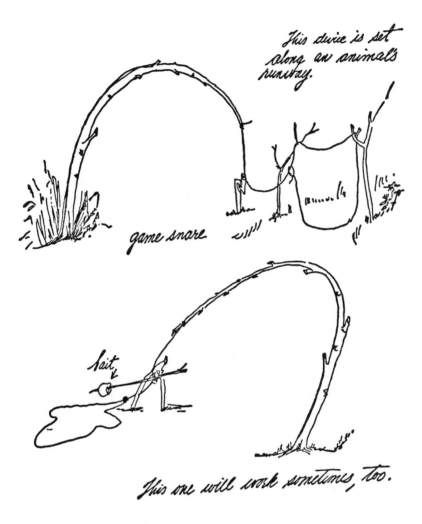

This device is set along an animal's runway.

game snare

This one will work sometimes, too.

I squatted down and went back to work. The raccoon dove out of sight.

"Now what's got you all excited?" I said, and tried once more to see what he had seen.

I finished the posts for the bed and was looking around for a bigger ash to fell and make slats for the springs when I nearly jumped out of my shoes.

"Now what are you doing up here all alone?" It was a human voice. I swung around and stood face to face with a little old lady in a pale blue sunbonnet and a loose brown dress.

"Oh! Gosh!" I said. "Don't scare me like that. Say one word at a time until I get used to a human voice." I must have looked frightened because she chuckled, smoothed down the front of her dress, and whispered, "Are you lost?"

"Oh, no, ma'am," I stuttered.

"Then a little fellow like you should not be all alone way up here on this haunted mountain."

"Haunted?" said I.

"Yes, indeed. There's an old story says there are little men up here who play ninepins right down in that gorge in the twilight." She peered at me. "Are you one of them?"

"Oh, no, no, no, no," I said. "I read that story. It's just make-believe." I laughed, and she puckered her forehead.

"Well, come on," she said, "make some use of yourself and help me fill this basket with strawberries."

I hesitated—she meant *my* strawberry supply.

"Now, get on with you. A boy your age should be doing something worthwhile, 'stead of playing mumbly peg with sticks. Come on, young man." She jogged me out into the meadow.

We worked quite a while before we said any more. Frankly, I was wondering how to save my precious, precious strawberries, and I may say I picked slowly. Every time I dropped one in her basket, I thought how good it would taste.

"Where do ye live?" I jumped. It is terribly odd to hear a voice after weeks of listening only to birds and raccoons, and what is more, to hear the voice ask a question like that.

"I live here," I said.

"Ye mean Delhi. Fine. You can walk me home."

Nothing I added did any good. She would not be shaken from her belief that I lived in Delhi. So I let it go.

We must have reaped every last strawberry before she stood up, put her arm in mine and escorted me down the mountain. I certainly was not escorting her. Her wiry little arms were like crayfish pinchers. I couldn't have gotten away if I had tried. So I walked and listened.

She told me all the local and world news, and it was rather pleasant to hear about the National League, an atom bomb test, and a Mr. Riley's three-legged dog that chased her chickens. In the middle of all this chatter she said, "That's the best strawberry patch in the entire Catskill range. I come up here every spring. For forty years I've come to that meadow for my strawberries. It gits harder every year, but there's no jam can beat the jam from that mountain. I know. I've been around here all my life." Then she went right into the New York Yanks without putting in a period.

As I helped her across the stream on big boulders, I heard a cry in the sky. I looked up. Swinging down the valley on long pointed wings was a large bird. I was struck by the ease and swiftness of its flight.

"Duck hawk," she said. "Nest around here every year. My man used to shoot 'em. He said they killed chickens, but I don't believe it. The only thing that kills chickens is Mr. Riley's three-legged dog."

She tipped and teetered as she crossed the rocks, but kept right on talking and stepping as if she knew that no matter what, she would get across.

We finally reached the road. I wasn't listening to her very much. I was thinking about the duck hawk. This bird, I was sure, was the peregrine falcon, the king's hunting bird.

"I will get one. I will train it to hunt for me," I said to myself.

Finally I got the little lady to her brown house at the edge of town.

She turned fiercely upon me. I started back.

"Where are you going, young man?"

I stopped. Now, I thought, she is going to march me into town. Into town? Well, that's where I'll go then, I said to myself. And I turned on my heel, smiled at her, and replied, "To the library."

The King's Provider

Miss Turner was glad to see me. I told her I wanted some books on hawks and falcons, and she located a few, although there was not much to be had on the subject. We worked all afternoon, and I learned enough. I departed when the library closed. Miss Turner whispered to me as I left, "Sam, you need a haircut."

I hadn't seen myself in so long that this had not occurred to me. "Gee, I don't have any scissors."

She thought a minute, got out her library scissors, and sat me down on the back steps. She did a fine job, and I looked like any other boy who had played hard all day, and who, with a little soap and water after supper, would be going off to bed in a regular house.

I didn't get back to my tree that night. The May apples were ripe, and I stuffed on those as I went through the woods. They taste like a very sweet banana, are earthy and a little slippery. But I liked them.

At the stream I caught a trout. Everybody thinks a trout is hard to catch because of all the fancy gear and flies and lines sold for trout fishing, but, honestly, they are easier to catch than any other fish. They have big mouths and snatch and swallow whole anything they see when they are hungry. With my wooden hook in its mouth, the trout was mine. The trouble is that trout are not hungry when most people have time to fish. I knew they were hungry that evening because the creek was swirling, and minnows and everything else were jumping out of the water. When you see that, go fish. You'll get them.

I made a fire on a flat boulder in the stream, and cooked the trout. I did this so I could watch the sky. I wanted to see the falcon again. I also put the trout head on the hook and dropped it in the pool. A snapping turtle would view a trout head with relish.

I waited for the falcon patiently. I didn't have to go anywhere. After an hour or so, I was rewarded. A slender speck came from the valley and glided above the stream. It was still far away when it folded its wings and bombed the earth. I watched. It arose, clumsy and big—carrying food—and winged back to the valley.

I sprinted down the stream and made myself a lean-to near some cliffs where I thought the bird had disappeared. Having learned that day that duck hawks prefer to nest on cliffs, I settled for this site.

Early the next morning, I got up and dug the tubers of the arrow-leaf that grew along the stream bank. I baked these and boiled mussels for breakfast, then I curled up behind a willow and watched the cliff.

The falcons came in from behind me and circled the stream. They had apparently been out hunting before I had gotten up, as they were returning with food. This was exciting news. They were feeding young, and I was somewhere near the nest.

I watched one of them swing in to the cliff and disappear. A few minutes later it winged out empty-footed. I marked the spot mentally and said, "Ha!"

After splashing across the stream in the shallows, I stood at the bottom of the cliff and wondered how on earth I was going to climb the sheer wall.

I wanted a falcon so badly, however, that I dug in with my toes and hands and started up. The first part was easy; it was not too steep. When I thought I was stuck, I found a little ledge and shinnied up to it.

I was high, and when I looked down, the stream spun. I decided not to look down anymore. I edged up to another ledge, and lay down on it to catch my breath. I was shaking from exertion and I was tired.

I looked up to see how much higher I had to go when my hand touched something moist. I pulled it back and saw that it was white—bird droppings. Then I saw them. Almost where my hand had been sat three fuzzy whitish gray birds. Their wide-open mouths gave them a startled look.

"Oh, hello, hello," I said. "You are cute."

When I spoke, all three blinked at once. All three heads turned and followed my hand as I swung it up and toward them. All three watched my hand with opened mouths. They were marvelous. I chuckled. But I couldn't reach them.

I wormed forward, and *wham!*—something hit my shoulder. It pained. I turned my head to see the big female. She had hit me. She winged out, banked, and started back for another strike.

Now I was scared, for I was sure she would cut me wide open. With sudden nerve, I stood up, stepped forward, and picked up the biggest of the nestlings. The females are bigger than the males. They are the "falcons." They are the pride of kings. I tucked her in my sweater and leaned against the cliff, facing the bulletlike dive of the falcon. I threw out my foot as she struck, and the sole of my tennis shoe took the blow.

The female was now gathering speed for another attack, and when I say speed, I mean 50 to 60 miles an hour. I could see myself battered and torn, lying in the valley below, and I said to myself, "Sam Gribley, you had better get down from here like a rabbit."

I jumped to the ledge below, found it was really quite wide, slid on the seat of my pants to the next ledge, and stopped. The hawk apparently couldn't count. She did not know I had a youngster, for she checked her nest, saw the open mouths, and then she forgot me.

I scrambled to the riverbed somehow, being very careful not to hurt the hot fuzzy body that was against my own. However, Frightful, as I called her right then and there because of the difficulties we had had in getting together, did not think so gently of me. She dug her talons into my skin to brace herself during the bumpy ride to the ground.

I stumbled to the stream, placed her in a nest of buttercups, and dropped beside her. I fell asleep.

When I awoke my eyes opened on two gray eyes in a white stroobly head. Small pinfeathers were sticking out of the stroobly down, like feathers in an Indian quiver. The big blue beak curled down in a snarl and up in a smile.

"Oh, Frightful," I said, "you are a raving beauty."

Frightful fluffed her nubby feathers and shook. I picked her up in the cup of my hands and held her

under my chin. I stuck my nose in the deep warm fuzz.
It smelled dusty and sweet.

I liked that bird. Oh, how I liked that bird from that
smelly minute. It was so pleasant to feel the beating life
and see the funny little awkward movements of a young
thing.

The legs pushed out between my fingers, I gathered
them up, together with the thrashing wings, and tucked
the bird in one piece under my chin. I rocked.

"Frightful," I said. "You will enjoy what we are
going to do."

I washed my bleeding shoulder in the creek, tucked
the torn threads of my sweater back into the hole they
had come out of, and set out for my tree.

A BRIEF ACCOUNT OF
*What I Did About
the First Man Who Was After Me*

At the edge of the meadow, I sensed all was not well at
camp. How I knew there was a human being there was
not clear to me then. I can only say that after living so
long with the birds and animals, the movement of a
human is like the difference between the explosion of a
cap pistol and a cannon.

I wormed toward camp. When I could see the man

I felt to be there, I stopped and looked. He was wearing a forester's uniform. Immediately I thought they had sent someone out to bring me in, and I began to shake. Then I realized that I didn't have to go back to meet the man at all. I was perfectly free and capable of settling down anywhere. My tree was just a pleasant habit.

I circled the meadow and went over to the gorge. On the way I checked a trap. It was a deadfall. A figure four under a big rock. The rock was down. The food was rabbit.

I picked a comfortable place just below the rim of the gorge where I could pop up every now and then and watch my tree. Here I dressed down the rabbit and fed Frightful some of the more savory bites from a young falcon's point of view: the liver, the heart, the brain. She ate in gulps. As I watched her swallow I sensed a great pleasure. It is hard to explain my feelings at that moment. It seemed marvelous to see life pump through that strange little body of feathers, wordless noises, milk eyes—much as life pumped through me.

The food put the bird to sleep. I watched her eyelids close from the bottom up, and her head quiver. The fuzzy body rocked, the tail spread to steady it, and the little duck hawk almost sighed as she sank into the leaves, sleeping.

I had lots of time. I was going to wait for the man to leave. So I stared at my bird, the beautiful details of the new feathers, the fernlike lashes along the lids, the saucy bristles at the base of the beak. Pleasant hours passed.

Frightful would awaken, I would feed her, she would fall back to sleep, and I would watch the breath rock her body ever so slightly. I was breathing the same way, only not as fast. Her heart beat much faster than mine. She was designed to her bones for a swifter life.

It finally occurred to me that I was very hungry. I stood up to see if the man were gone. He was yawning and pacing.

The sun was slanting on him now, and I could see him quite well. He was a fire warden. Of course, it has not rained, I told myself, for almost three weeks, and the fire planes have been circling the mountains and valleys, patrolling the mountains. Apparently the smoke from my fire was spotted, and a man was sent to check it. I recalled the bare trampled ground around the tree, the fireplace of rocks filled with ashes, the wood chips from the making of my bed, and resolved hereafter to keep my yard clean.

So I made rabbit soup in a tin can I found at the bottom of the gorge. I seasoned it with wild garlic and jack-in-the-pulpit roots.

Jack-in-the-pulpits have three big leaves on a stalk and are easily recognized by the curly striped awning above a stiff, serious preacher named Jack. The jack-in-the-pulpit root, or corm, tastes and looks like potato. It should never be eaten raw.

The fire I made was only of the driest wood, and I made it right at the water's edge. I didn't want a smoky fire on this particular evening.

After supper I made a bough bed and stretched out with Frightful beside me. Apparently, the more you stroke and handle a falcon, the easier they are to train.

I had all sorts of plans for hoods and jesses, as the straps on a falcon are called, and I soon forgot about the man.

Stretched on the boughs, I listened to the wood pewees calling their haunting good nights until I fell sound asleep.

IN WHICH
I Learn to Season My Food

The fire warden made a fire some time in the colder hours of the night. At dawn he was asleep beside white smoldering ashes. I crawled back to the gorge, fed Frightful rabbit bites, and slipped back to the edge of the meadow to check a box trap I had set the day before. I made it by tying small sticks together like a log cabin. This trap was better than the snares or deadfalls. It had caught numerous rabbits, several squirrels, and a groundhog.

I saw, as I inched toward it, that it was closed. The sight of a closed trap excites me to this day. I still can't believe that animals don't understand why delicious food is in such a ridiculous spot.

Well, this morning I pulled the trap deep into the woods to open it. The trapped animal was light. I couldn't guess what it was. It was also active, flipping and darting from one corner to the next. I peeked in to locate it, so that I could grab it quickly behind the head without getting bitten. I was not always successful at this, and had scars to prove it.

I put my eye to the crack. A rumpus arose in the darkness. Two bright eyes shone, and out through that hole that was no wider than a string bean came a weasel. He flew right out at me, landed on my shoulder, gave me a lecture that I shall never forget, and vanished under the scant cover of trillium and bloodroot leaves.

He popped up about five feet away and stood on his hind feet to lecture me again. I said, "Scat!" so he darted right to my knee, put his broad furry paws on my pants, and looked me in the face. I shall never forget the fear and wonder that I felt at the bravery of that weasel. He stood his ground and berated me. I could see by the flashing of his eyes and the curl of his lip that he was furious at me for trapping him. He couldn't talk, but I knew what he meant.

Wonder filled me as I realized he was absolutely un-afraid. No other animal, and I knew quite a few by now, had been so brave in my presence. Screaming, he jumped on me. This surprised and scared me. He leapt from my lap to my head, took a mouthful of hair and wrestled it. My goose bumps rose. I was too frightened to move. A good thing, too, because I guess he figured I was not going to fight back and his scream of anger changed to a purr of peace. Still, I couldn't move.

Presently, down he climbed, as stately as royalty, and off he marched, never looking back. He sank beneath the leaves like a fish beneath the water. Not a stem rippled to mark his way.

And so The Baron and I met for the first time, and it was the beginning of a harassing but wonderful friendship.

Frightful had been watching all this. She was tense with fright. Although young and inexperienced, she knew an enemy when she saw one. I picked her up and whispered into her birdy-smelling neck feathers.

"You wild ones know."

Since I couldn't go home, I decided to spend the day in the marsh down the west side of the mountain. There were a lot of cattails and frogs there.

Frightful balanced on my fist as we walked. She had learned that in the short span of one afternoon and a night. She is a very bright bird.

On our way we scared up a deer. It was a doe. I watched her dart gracefully away, and said to Frightful, "That's what I want. I need a door for my house, tethers for you, and a blanket for me. How am I going to get a deer?"

This was not the first time I had said this. The forest was full of deer, and I already had drawn plans on a piece of birch bark for deadfalls, pit traps, and snares. None seemed workable.

The day passed. In the early evening we stole home, tree by tree, to find that the warden had gone. I cleaned up my front yard, scattered needles over the bare spots, and started a small fire with very dry wood that would not smoke much. No more wardens for me. I liked my tree, and although I could live somewhere else, I certainly did not want to.

Once home, I immediately started to work again. I had a device I wanted to try, and put some hickory sticks in a tin can and set it to boiling while I fixed dinner. Before going to bed, I noted this on a piece of birch bark:

"This night I am making salt. I know that people in the early days got along without it, but I think some of these wild foods would taste better with some flavoring. I understand that hickory sticks, boiled dry, leave a salty residue. I am trying it."

In the morning I added:

"It is quite true. The can is dry, and thick with a black substance. It is very salty, and I tried it on frogs' legs for breakfast. It is just what I have needed."

And so I went into salt production for several days, and chipped out a niche inside the tree in which to store it.

*"June 19

"I finished my bed today. The ash slats work very well, and are quite springy and comfortable. The bed just fits in the right-hand side of the tree. I have hem-

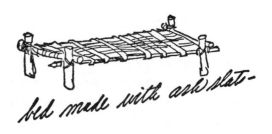

bed made with ash slat—

lock boughs on it now, but hope to have deer hide soon. I am making a figure-four trap as tall as me with a log on it that I can barely lift. It doesn't look workable. I wish there was another way of getting a deer.

"June 20

"I decided today to dig a pit to trap a deer, so I am whittling a shovel out of a board I found in the stream this morning. That stream is very useful. It has given me tin cans for pots, and now an oaken board for a shovel.

"Frightful will hop from the stump to my fist. She still can't fly. Her wing feathers are only about an inch long. I think she likes me."

How a Door Came to Me

One morning before the wood pewees were up, I was smoking a mess of fish I had caught in the stream. When I caught more than I could eat, I would bone them, put them on a rack of sticks, and slowly smoke them until they dried out. This is the best way to preserve extra food. However, if you try it, remember to use a hard wood—hickory is the best. I tried pine on the first batch, and ruined them with black tarry smoke. Well, it was very silent—then came a scream. I jumped into my tree. Presently I had enough nerve to look out.

"Baron Weasel!" I said in astonishment. I was sure it was the same weasel I had met in the trap. He was on the boulder in front of the hemlock, batting the ferns with his front feet and rearing and staring at me.

"Now, you stay right there," I said. Of course, he flipped and came off the rock like a jet stream. He was at the door before I could stop him, and loping around my feet like a bouncing ball.

"You look glad all over, Baron. I hope all that frisking means joy," I said. He took my pants leg in his teeth, tugged it, and then rippled softly back to the boulder. He went down a small hole. He popped up again, bit a fern near by, and ran around the boulder. I crept out to look for him—no weasel. I poked a stick in the hole at the base of the rock trying to provoke him. I felt a little jumpy, so that when a shot rang out through the woods I leapt a foot in the air and dove into my hole. A cricket chirped, a catbird scratched the leaves. I waited. One enormous minute later a dark form ran onto the meadow. It stumbled and fell.

I had the impression that it was a deer. Without

waiting to consider what I might be running toward, I burst to the edge of the meadow.

No one was in sight, I ran into the grass. There lay a dead deer! With all my strength I dragged the heavy animal into the woods. I then hurried to my tree, gathered up the hemlock boughs on my bed, rushed back and threw them over the carcass. I stuck a few ferns in them so they would look as if they were growing there and ran back to camp, breathless.

Hurriedly I put out the fire, covered it with dirt, hid my smoking rack in the spring, grabbed Frightful and got in my tree.

Someone was poaching, and he might be along in a minute to collect his prize. The shot had come from the side of the mountain, and I figured I had about four minutes to clean up before the poacher arrived.

Then when I was hidden and ready, Frightful started her cry of hunger. I had not fed her yet that morning. Oh, how was I going to explain to her the awful need to be quiet? How did a mother falcon warn her young of danger? I took her in my hands and stroked her stomach. She fought me and then she lay still in my hand, her feet up, her eyes bright. She stiffened and drooped. I kept on stroking her. She was hypnotized. I would stop for a few moments, she would lie still, then pop to her feet. I was sure this wasn't what her mother did to keep her quiet, but it worked.

Bushes cracked, leaves scuttled, and a man with a rifle came into the meadow. I could just see his head and shoulders. He looked around and banged toward the hemlock forest. I crawled up on my bed and stroked the hungry Frightful.

I couldn't see the man from my bed, but I could hear him.

I heard him come to the tree. I could see his boots. He stopped by the ashes of the fire; and then went on. I could see my heart lift my sweater. I was terrified.

I stayed on the bed all morning, telling the fierce little bundle of feathers in my hand that there was deer meat in store for her if she would just wait with me.

Way down the other side of the mountain, I heard another shot. I sure hoped that deer dropped on the poacher's toes and that he would now go home.

At noon I went to my prize. Frightful sat beside me as I skinned and quartered it. She ate deer until she was misshapen.

I didn't make any notes as to how long it took me to do all the work that was required to get the deer ready for smoking and the hide scraped and ready for tanning, but it was many, many days.

However, when I sat down to a venison steak, that was a meal! All it was, was venison. I wrote this on a piece of birch bark. "I think I grew an inch on venison!" Frightful and I went to the meadow when the meal was done, and I flopped in the grass. The stars came up, the ground smelled sweet, and I closed my eyes. I heard, *"Pip, pop, pop, pop."*

"Who's making that noise?" I said sleepily to Frightful. She ruffled her feathers.

I listened. *"Pop, pip."* I rolled over and stuck my face in the grass. Something gleamed beneath me, and in the fading light I could see an earthworm coming out of its hole.

Nearby another one arose and there was a *pop.* Little bubbles of air snapped as these voiceless animals of the earth came to the surface. That got me to smiling. I was glad to know this about earthworms. I don't know why, but this seemed like one of the nicest things I had learned in the woods—that earthworms, lowly, confined to the darkness of the earth, could make just a little stir in the world.

IN WHICH
Frightful Learns Her ABC's

Free time was spent scraping the fur off the deer hide to get it ready for tanning. This much I knew: in order to tan hide, it has to be steeped in tannic acid. There is tannic acid in the woods in oak trees, but it took me several weeks to figure out how to get it. You need a lot of oak chips in water. Water and oak give off tannic acid. My problem was not oak or water but getting a vessel big enough to put the deer hide in.

Coming home from the stream one night I had an inspiration.

It had showered the day before, and as Frightful and I passed an old stump, I noticed that it had collected the rain. "A stump, an oak stump, would be perfect," I said right out loud to that pretty bird.

So I felled an oak over by the gorge, burned a hole in it, carried water to it, and put my deerskin in it. I let it steep, oh, maybe five days before I took it out and dried it. It dried stiff as a board, and I had to chew, rub, jump on it, and twist it to get it soft. When this was done, however, I had my door. I hung it on pegs inside my entrance, and because it was bigger than it had to be, I would cut off pieces now and then when I needed them. I cut off two thin strips to make jesses, or leg straps, for Frightful. All good falcons wear jesses and leashes so they can be tethered for their training.

I smoked the meat I couldn't eat and stored it. I used everything I could on that animal. I even used one of its bones for a spearhead. I was tired of catching frogs by the jump-and-miss system. I made two sharp points, and strapped them to the end of a long stick, one on each side, to make a kind of fork. It worked beautifully. Frogs were one of my favorite meals, and I found I could fix them many ways; however, I got to like frog soup fixed in this way: "Clean, skin, and boil until tender. Add wild onions, also water lily buds and wild carrots. Thicken with acorn flour. Serve in turtle shell."

perch

jesses or leg straps

leash

By now my two pairs of pants were threadbare and my three sweaters were frayed. I dreamed of a deerskin suit, and watched my herd with clothes in mind.

The deer for my suit did not come easily. I rigged up a figure-four trap under the log, and baited it with elderberries rolled into a ball. That just mushed up and didn't work. Then I remembered that deer like salt. I made a ball of hickory salt with turtle fat to hold it together.

Every evening Frightful and I, sometimes accompanied by The Baron Weasel, would go to the edge of the meadow and look toward the aspen grove to see if the great log had fallen. One night we saw three deer standing around it quietly, reaching toward the smell of salt. At that moment, The Baron jumped at my pants leg, but got my ankle with an awful nip. I guess I had grown some; my pants and socks did not meet anymore. I screamed, and the deer fled.

I chased The Baron home. I had the uneasy feeling that he was laughing as he darted, flipped, buckled, and disappeared.

The Baron was hard to understand. What did he want from me? Occasionally I left him bites of turtle or venison, and although he smelled the offerings, he never ate them. The catbird would get them. Most animals stick around if you feed them. But The Baron did not eat anything. Yet he seemed to like me. Gradually it occurred to me that he didn't have a mate or a family. Could he be a lonely bachelor, taking up with odd company for lack of an ordinary life? Well, whatever, The Baron liked me for what I was, and I appreciated that. He was a personable little fellow.

Every day I worked to train Frightful. It was a long process. I would put her on her stump with a long leash and step back a few feet with some meat in my hand. Then I would whistle. The whistle was supposed eventually to mean food to her. So I would whistle, show her the meat, and after many false flaps she would finally fly to my hand. I would pet her and feed her. She could fly fairly well, so now I made sure that she never ate unless she flew to my fist.

One day at breakfast I whistled for Frightful. I had no food, she wasn't even hungry, but she came to me anyway. I was thrilled. She had learned a whistle meant "come."

I looked into her steely eyes that morning and thought I saw a gentle recognition. She puffed up her feathers as she sat on my hand. I call this a "feather word." It means she is content.

Now each day I stepped farther and farther away from Frightful to make her fly greater and greater distances. One day she flew a good fifty feet, and we packed up and went gathering seeds, bark, and tubers to celebrate.

I used my oldest sweater for gathering things. It was not very convenient, and each time I filled it I mentally designed bigger and better pockets on my deer-hide suit-to-be.

The summer was wonderful. There was food in abundance and I gathered it most of the morning, and stored it away in the afternoon. I could now see that my niches were not going to be big enough for the amount of food I would need for the winter, so I began burning out another tree. When the hickory nuts, walnuts, and acorns appeared, I was going to need a bin. You'd be surprised what a pile of nuts it takes to make one turtle shell full of nut meats—and not a snapping-turtle shell either, just a box-turtle shell!

With the easy living of the summer also came a threat. Hikers and vacationers were in the woods, and more than once I pulled inside my tree, closed my deer-flap door, and hid while bouncing noisy people crossed the meadow on their way to the gorge. Apparently the gorge was a sight for those who wanted a four-mile hike up the mountain.

One morning I heard a group arriving. I whistled for Frightful. She came promptly. We dove into the tree. It was dark inside the tree with the flap closed, and I realized that I needed a candle. I planned a lamp of a turtle shell with a deer-hide wick, and as I was cutting off a piece of hide, I heard a shrill scream.

The voices of the hikers became louder. I wondered if one of them had fallen into the gorge. Then I said to Frightful, "That was no cry of a human, pretty bird. I'll bet you a rabbit for dinner that our deer trap worked. And here we are stored in a tree like a nut and unable to claim our prize."

We waited and waited until I couldn't be patient any more, and I was about to put my head out the door when a man's voice said, "Look at these trees!"

A woman spoke. "Harold, they're huge. How old do you think they are?"

"Three hundred years old, maybe four hundred," said Harold.

They tramped around, actually sat on The Baron's boulder, and were apparently going to have lunch, when things began to happen out there and I almost gave myself away with hysterics.

"Harold, what's the matter with that weasel? It's running all over this rock." A scream! A scuttering and scraping of boots on the rocks.

"He's mad!" That was the woman.

"Watch it, Grace, he's coming at your feet." They ran.

By this time I had my hand over my mouth to keep back the laughter. I snorted and choked, but they never heard me. They were in the meadow—run right out of the forest by that fiery Baron Weasel.

I still laugh when I think of it.

It was not until dark that Frightful and I got to the deer, and a beauty it was.

The rest of June was spent smoking it, tanning it, and finally, starting on my deerskin suit. I made a bone needle, cut out the pants by ripping up one pair of old city pants for a pattern. I saved my city pants and burned them bit by bit to make charred cloth for the flint and steel.

rack for smoking fish and meat

"Frightful," I said while sewing one afternoon. She was preening her now silver-gray, black, and white feathers. "There is no end to this. We need another deer. I can't make a blouse."

We didn't get another deer until fall, so with the scraps I made big square pockets for food gathering. One hung in front of me, and the other down my back. They were joined by straps. This device worked beautifully.

Sometime in July I finished my pants. They fit well, and were the best-looking pants I had ever seen. I was terribly proud of them.

With pockets and good tough pants I was willing to pack home many more new foods to try. Daisies, the bark of a poplar tree that I saw a squirrel eating, and puffballs. They are mushrooms, the only ones I felt were safe to eat, and even at that, I kept waiting to die the first night I ate them. I didn't, so I enjoyed them from that night on. They are wonderful. Mushrooms are dangerous and I would not suggest that one eat them from the forest. The mushroom expert at the Botanical Gardens told me that. He said even he didn't eat wild ones.

The inner bark of the poplar tree tasted like wheat kernels, and so I dried as much as I could and powdered it into flour. It was tedious work, and in August when the acorns were ready, I found that they made better flour and were much easier to handle.

I would bake the acorns in the fire, and grind them between stones. This was tedious work, too, but now that I had a home and smoked venison and did not have to hunt food every minute, I could do things like make flour. I would simply add spring water to the flour and bake this on a piece of tin. When done, I had the best pancakes ever. They were flat and hard, like I imagined Indian bread to be. I liked them, and would carry the leftovers in my pockets for lunch.

One fine August day I took Frightful to the meadow. I had been training her to the lure. That is, I now tied her meat on a piece of wood, covered with hide and feathers. I would throw it in the air and she would swoop out of the sky and catch it. She was absolutely free during these maneuvers, and would fly high into the air and hover over me like a leaf. I made sure she was very hungry before I turned her loose. I wanted her back.

After a few tries she never missed the lure. Such marksmanship thrilled me. Bird and lure would drop to the earth, I would run over, grab her jesses, and we would sit on the big boulder in the meadow while she ate. Those were nice evenings. The finest was the night I wrote this:

"Frightful caught her first prey. She is now a trained falcon. It was only a sparrow, but we are on our way. It happened unexpectedly. Frightful was climbing into the sky, circling and waiting for the lure, when I stepped forward and scared a sparrow.

"The sparrow flew across the meadow. Out of the sky came a black streak—I've never seen anything drop so fast. With a great backwatering of wings, Frightful broke her fall, and at the same time seized the sparrow. I took it away from her and gave her the lure. That sounds mean, but if she gets in the habit of eating what she catches, she will go wild."

IN WHICH
I Find a Real Live Man

One of the gasping joys of summer was my daily bath in the spring. It was cold water, I never stayed in long, but it woke me up and started me into the day with a vengeance.

I would tether Frightful to a hemlock bough above me and splash her from time to time. She would suck in her chest, look startled, and then shake. While I bathed and washed, she preened. Huddled down in the water between the ferns and moss, I scrubbed myself with the bark of the slippery elm. It gets soapy when you rub it.

The frogs would hop out and let me in, and the

woodthrush would come to the edge of the pool to see
what was happening. We were a gay gathering—me
shouting, Frightful preening, the woodthrush cocking
its pretty head. Occasionally The Baron Weasel would
pop up and glance furtively at us. He didn't care for
water. How he stayed glossy and clean was a mystery

to me, until he came to the boulder beside our bath pool one day, wet with the dew from the ferns. He licked himself until he was polished.

One morning there was a rustle in the leaves above. Instantly, Frightful had it located. I had learned to look where Frightful looked when there were disturbances in the forest. She always saw life before I could focus my eyes. She was peering into the hemlock above us. Finally I too saw it. A young raccoon. It was chittering and now that all eyes were upon it, began coming down the tree.

And so Frightful and I met Jessie Coon James, the bandit of the Gribley farm.

He came headfirst down to our private bath, a scrabbly, skinny young raccoon. He must have been from a late litter, for he was not very big, and certainly not well fed. Whatever had been Jessie C. James's past, it was awful. Perhaps he was an orphan, perhaps he had been thrown out of his home by his mother, as his eyes were somewhat crossed and looked a little peculiar. In any event he had come to us for help, I thought, and so Frightful and I led him home and fed him.

In about a week he fattened up. His crumply hair smoothed out, and with a little ear scratching and back rubbing, Jessie C. James became a devoted friend. He also became useful. He slept somewhere in the dark tops of the hemlocks all day long, unless he saw us start for the stream. Then, tree by tree, limb by limb, Jessie followed us. At the stream he was the most useful mussel digger that any boy could have. Jessie could find mussels where three men could not. He would start to eat them, and if he ate them, he got full and wouldn't dig anymore, so I took them away from him until he found me all I wanted. Then I let him have some.

Mussels are good. Here are a few notes on how to fix them.

"Scrub mussels in spring water. Dump them into boiling water with salt. Boil five minutes. Remove and cool in the juice. Take out meat. Eat by dipping in acorn paste flavored with a smudge of garlic, and green apples."

Frightful took care of the small game supply, and now that she was an expert hunter, we had rabbit stew, pheasant potpie, and an occasional sparrow, which I generously gave to Frightful. As fast as we removed the rabbits and pheasants new ones replaced them.

Beverages during the hot summer became my chore, largely because no one else wanted them. I found some sassafras trees at the edge of the road one day, dug up a good supply of roots, peeled and dried them. Sassafras tea is about as good as anything you want to drink. Pennyroyal makes another good drink. I dried great bunches of this, and hung them from the roof of the tree room together with the leaves of winterberry. All these fragrant plants I also used in cooking to give a new taste to some not-so-good foods.

The room in the tree smelled of smoke and mint. It was the best-smelling tree in the Catskill Mountains.

Life was leisurely. I was warm, well fed. One day while I was down the mountain, I returned home by way of the old farmhouse site to check the apple crop. They were summer apples, and were about ready to be picked. I had gathered a pouchful and had sat down under the tree to eat a few and think about how I would dry them for use in the winter when Frightful dug her talons into my shoulder so hard I winced.

"Be gentle, bird!" I said to her.

I got her talons out and put her on a log, where I watched her with some alarm. She was as alert as a high tension wire, her head cocked so that her ears, just membranes under her feathers, were pointed east. She evidently heard a sound that pained her. She opened her beak. Whatever it was, I could hear nothing, though I strained my ears, cupped them, and wished she would speak.

Frightful was my ears as well as my eyes. She could hear things long before I. When she grew tense, I listened or looked. She was scared this time. She turned round and round on the log, looked up in the tree for a perch, lifted her wings to fly, and then stood still and listened.

Then I heard it. A police siren sounded far down the road. The sound grew louder and louder, and I grew afraid. Then I said, "No, Frightful, if they are after me there won't be a siren. They'll just slip up on me quietly."

No sooner had I said this than the siren wound down, and apparently stopped on the road at the foot of the mountain. I got up to run to my tree, but had not gotten past the walnut before the patrol cars started up and screamed away.

We started home although it was not late in the afternoon. However, it was hot, and thunderheads were building up. I decided to take a swim in the spring and work on the moccasins I had cut out several days ago.

With the squad car still on my mind, we slipped quietly into the hemlock forest. Once again Frightful almost sent me through the crown of the forest by digging her talons into my shoulder. I looked at her. She was staring at our home. I looked, too. Then I stopped, for I could make out the form of a man stretched between the sleeping house and the store tree.

Softly, tree by tree, Frightful and I approached him. The man was asleep. I could have left and camped in the gorge again, but my enormous desire to see another human being overcame my fear of being discovered.

We stood above the man. He did not move, so Frightful lost interest in my fellow being. She tried to hop to her stump and preen. I grabbed her leash however, as I wanted to think before awakening him. Frightful flapped. I held her wings to her body as her flapping was noisy to me. Apparently not so to the man. The man did not stir. It is hard to realize that the rustle of a falcon's wings is not much of a noise to a man from the city, because by now, one beat of her wings and I would awaken from a sound sleep as if a shot had gone off. The stranger slept on. I realized how long I'd been in the mountains.

Right at that moment, as I looked at his unshaven face, his close-cropped hair, and his torn clothes, I thought of the police siren, and put two and two together.

"An outlaw!" I said to myself. "Wow!" I had to think what to do with an outlaw before I awoke him.

Would he be troublesome? Would he be mean? Should I go live in the gorge until he moved on? How I wanted to hear his voice, to tell him about The Baron and Jessie C. James, to say words out loud. I really did not want to hide from him; besides, he might be hungry, I thought. Finally I spoke.

"Hi!" I said. I was delighted to see him roll over, open his eyes, and look up. He seemed startled, so I reassured him. "It's all right, they've gone. If you don't tell on me I won't tell on you." When he heard this, he sat up and seemed to relax.

"Oh," he said. Then he leaned against the tree and added, "Thanks." He evidently was thinking this over, for he propped his head on his elbow and studied me closely.

"You're a sight for sore eyes," he said, and smiled. He had a nice smile—in fact, he looked nice and not like

an outlaw at all. His eyes were very blue and, although tired, they did not look scared or hunted.

However, I talked quickly before he could get up and run away.

"I don't know anything about you, and I don't want to. You don't know anything about me, and don't want to, but you may stay here if you like. No one is going to find you here. Would you like some supper?" It was still early, but he looked hungry.

"Do you have some?"

"Yes, venison or rabbit?"

"Well . . . venison." His eyebrows puckered in question marks. I went to work.

He arose, turned around and around, and looked at his surroundings. He whistled softly when I kindled a spark with the flint and steel. I was now quite quick at this, and had a tidy fire blazing in a very few minutes. I was so used to myself doing this that it had not occurred to me that it would be interesting to a stranger.

"Desdemondia!" he said. I judged this to be some underworld phrase. At this moment Frightful, who had been sitting quietly on her stump, began to preen. The outlaw jumped back, then saw she was tied and said, "And who is this ferocious-looking character?"

"That is Frightful; don't be afraid. She's quite wonderful and gentle. She would be glad to catch you a rabbit for supper if you would prefer that to venison."

"Am I dreaming?" said the man. "I go to sleep by a campfire that looked like it was built by a boy scout, and I awaken in the middle of the eighteenth century."

I crawled into the store tree to get the smoked venison and some cattail tubers. When I came out again, he was speechless.

"My storehouse," I explained.

"I see," he answered. From that moment on he did not talk much. He just watched me. I was so busy cooking the best meal that I could possibly get together that I didn't say much either. Later I wrote down that menu, as it was excellent.

"Brown puffballs in deer fat with a little wild garlic, fill pot with water, put venison in, boil. Wrap tubers in leaves and stick in coals. Cut up apples and boil in can with dogtooth violet bulbs. Raspberries to finish meal."

dogtooth violet

When the meal was ready, I served it to the man in my nicest turtle shell. I had to whittle him a fork out of the crotch of a twig, as Jessie Coon James had gone off with the others. He ate and ate and ate, and when he was done he said, "May I call you Thoreau?"

"That will do nicely," I said. Then I paused—just to let him know that I knew a little bit about him too. I smiled and said, "I will call you Bando."

His eyebrows went up, he cocked his head, shrugged his shoulders and answered, "That's close enough."

With this he sat and thought. I felt I had offended him, so I spoke. "I will be glad to help. I will teach you how to live off the land. It is very easy. No one need find you."

His eyebrows gathered together again. This was characteristic of Bando when he was concerned, and so I was sorry I had mentioned his past. After all, outlaw or no outlaw, he was an adult, and I still felt unsure of myself around adults. I changed the subject.

"Let's get some sleep," I said.

"Where do you sleep?" he asked. All this time sitting and talking with me, and he had not seen the entrance to my tree. I was pleased. Then I beckoned, walked a few feet to the left, pushed back the deer-hide door, and showed Bando my secret.

"Thoreau," he said. "You are quite wonderful." He went in. I lit the turtle candle for him, he explored, tried the bed, came out and shook his head until I thought it would roll off.

We didn't say much more that night. I let him sleep on my bed. His feet hung off, but he was comfortable, he said. I stretched out by the fire. The ground was dry, the night warm, and I could sleep on anything now.

I got up early and had breakfast ready when Bando

came stumbling out of the tree. We ate crayfish, and he really honestly seemed to like them. It takes a little time to acquire a taste for wild foods, so Bando surprised me the way he liked the menu. Of course he was hungry, and that helped.

That day we didn't talk much, just went over the mountain collecting foods. I wanted to dig up the tubers of the Solomon's seal from a big garden of them on the other side of the gorge. We fished, we swam a little, and I told him I hoped to make a raft pretty soon, so I could float into deeper water and perhaps catch bigger fish.

When Bando heard this, he took my ax and immediately began to cut young trees for this purpose. I watched him and said, "You must have lived on a farm or something."

At that moment a bird sang.

"The wood pewee," said Bando, stopping his work. He stepped into the woods, seeking it. Now I was astonished.

"How would you know about a wood pewee in your business?" I grew bold enough to ask.

"And just what do you think my business is?" he said as I followed him.

"Well, you're not a minister."

"Right!"

"And you're not a doctor or a lawyer."

"Correct."

"You're not a businessman or a sailor."

"No, I am not."

"Nor do you dig ditches."

"I do not."

"Well . . ."

"Guess."

Suddenly I wanted to know for sure. So I said it.

"You are a murderer or a thief or a racketeer; and you are hiding out."

Bando stopped looking for the pewee. He turned and stared at me. At first I was frightened. A bandit might do anything. But he wasn't mad, he was laughing. He had a good deep laugh and it kept coming out of him. I smiled, then grinned and laughed with him.

"What's funny, Bando?" I asked.

"I like that," he finally said. "I like that a lot." The tickle deep inside him kept him chuckling. I had no more to say, so I ground my heel in the dirt while I waited for him to get over the fun and explain it all to me.

"Thoreau, my friend, I am just a college English teacher lost in the Catskills. I came out to hike around the woods, got completely lost yesterday, found your fire and fell asleep beside it. I was hoping the scoutmaster and his troop would be back for supper and help me home."

"Oh, no." My comment. Then I laughed. "You see, Bando, before I found you, I heard squad cars screaming up the road. Occasionally you read about bandits that hide out in the forest, and I was just so sure that you were someone they were looking for."

We gave up the pewee and went back to the raft-making, talking very fast now, and laughing a lot. He was fun. Then something sad occurred to me.

"Well, if you're not a bandit, you will have to go home very soon, and there is no point in teaching you how to live on fish and bark and plants."

"I can stay a little while," he said. "This is summer vacation. I must admit I had not planned to eat crayfish on my vacation, but I am rather getting to like it.

"Maybe I can stay until your school opens," he went on. "That's after Labor Day, isn't it?"

I was very still, thinking how to answer that.

Bando sensed this. Then he turned to me with a big grin.

"You really mean you are going to try to winter it out here?"

"I think I can."

"Well!" He sat down, rubbed his forehead in his hands, and looked at me. "Thoreau, I have led a varied life—dishwasher, sax player, teacher. To me it has been an interesting life. Just now it seems very dull." He sat awhile with his head down, then looked up at the mountains and the rocks and trees. I heard him sigh.

"Let's go fish. We can finish this another day."

That is how I came to know Bando. We became very good friends in the week or ten days that he stayed with me, and he helped me a lot. We spent several days gathering white oak acorns and groundnuts, harvesting the blueberry crop and smoking fish.

We flew Frightful every day just for the pleasure of lying on our backs in the meadow and watching her mastery of the sky. I had lots of meat, so what she caught those days was all hers. It was a pleasant time, warm, with occasional thundershowers, some of which we stayed out in. We talked about books. He did know a lot of books, and could quote exciting things from them.

One day Bando went to town and came back with five pounds of sugar.

"I want to make blueberry jam," he announced. "All those excellent berries and no jam."

He worked two days at this. He knew how to make jam. He'd watched his pa make it in Mississippi, but we got stuck on what to put it in.

I wrote this one night:

"August 29

"The raft is almost done. Bando has promised to stay until we can sail out into the deep fishing holes.

"Bando and I found some clay along the stream bank. It was as slick as ice. Bando thought it would make good pottery. He shaped some jars and lids. They look good—not Wedgwood, he said, but containers. We dried them on the rock in the meadow, and later Bando made a clay oven and baked them in it. He thinks they might hold the blueberry jam he has been making.

"Bando got the fire hot by blowing on it with some homemade bellows that he fashioned from one of my skins that he tied together like a balloon. A reed is the nozzle.

"August 30

"It was a terribly hot day for Bando to be firing clay jars, but he stuck with it. They look jam-worthy, as he says, and he filled three of them tonight. The jam is good, the pots remind me of crude flower pots without the hole in the bottom. Some of the lids don't fit. Bando says he will go home and read more about pottery making so that he can do a better job next time.

"We like the jam. We eat it on hard acorn pancakes.

"Later. Bando met The Baron Weasel today for the first time. I don't know where The Baron has been this past week, but suddenly he appeared on the rock, and nearly jumped down Bando's shirt collar. Bando said he liked The Baron best when he was in his hole.

"September 3

"Bando taught me how to make willow whistles today. He and I went to the stream and cut two fat twigs about eight inches long. He slipped the bark on them. That means he pulled the wood out of the bark, leaving a tube. He made a mouthpiece at one end, cut a hole beneath it, and used the wood to slide up and down like a trombone.

"We played music until the moon came up. Bando could even play jazz on the willow whistles. They are wonderful instruments, sounding much like the wind in

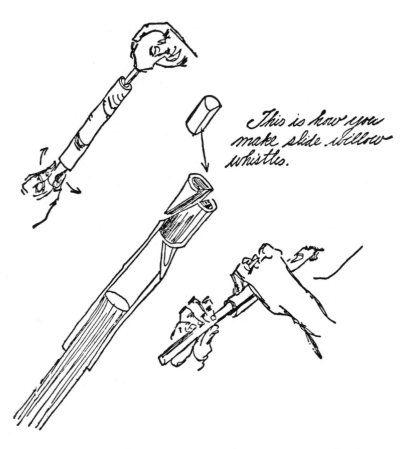

This is how you make slide willow whistles.

the top of the hemlocks. Sad tunes are best suited to willow whistles. When we played 'The Young Voyageur' tears came to our eyes, it was so sad."

There were no more notes for many days. Bando had left me saying: "Good-by, I'll see you at Christmas." I was so lonely that I kept sewing on my moccasins to keep myself busy. I sewed every free minute for four days, and when they were finished, I began a glove to protect my hand from Frightful's sharp talons.

One day when I was thinking very hard about being alone, Frightful gave her gentle call of love and contentment. I looked up.

"Bird," I said. "I had almost forgotten how we used to talk." She made tiny movements with her beak and fluffed her feathers. This was a language I had forgotten since Bando came. It meant she was glad to see me and hear me, that she was well fed, and content. I picked her up and squeaked into her neck feathers. She moved her beak, turned her bright head, and bit my nose very gently.

Jessie Coon James came down from the trees for the first time in ten days. He finished my fish dinner. Then just before dusk, The Baron came up on his boulder and scratched and cleaned and played with a fern leaf.

I had the feeling we were all back together again.

IN WHICH
The Autumn Provides Food and Loneliness

September blazed a trail into the mountains. First she burned the grasses. The grasses seeded and were harvested by the mice and the winds.

Then she sent the squirrels and chipmunks running boldly through the forest, collecting and hiding nuts.

Then she frosted the aspen leaves and left them sunshine yellow.

Then she gathered the birds together in flocks, and the mountaintop was full of songs and twitterings and flashing wings. The birds were ready to move to the south.

And I, Sam Gribley, felt just wonderful, just wonderful.

I pushed the raft down the stream and gathered arrowleaf bulbs, cattail tubers, bulrush roots, and the nut-like tubers of the sedges.

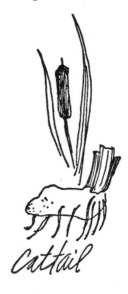

Cattail

And then the crop of crickets appeared and Frightful hopped all over the meadow snagging them in her great talons and eating them. I tried them, because I had heard they are good. I think it was another species of cricket that was meant. I think the field cricket would taste excellent if you were starving. I was not starving, so I preferred to listen to them. I abandoned the crickets and went back to the goodness of the earth.

I smoked fish and rabbit, dug wild onions by the pouchful, and raced September for her crop.

wild onion

"October 15

"Today The Baron Weasel looked moldy. I couldn't get near enough to see what was the matter with him, but it occurs to me that he might be changing his summer fur for his white winter mantle. If he is, it is an itchy process. He scratches a lot."

Seeing The Baron changing his mantle for winter awoke the first fears in me. I wrote that note on a little birch bark, curled up on my bed, and shivered.

The snow and the cold and the long lifeless months are ahead, I thought. The wind was blowing hard and cool across the mountain. I lit my candle, took out the rabbit and squirrel hides I had been saving, and began rubbing and kneading them to softness.

The Baron was getting a new suit for winter. I must have one too. Some fur underwear, some mittens, fur-lined socks.

Frightful, who was sitting on the foot post of the bed, yawned, fluffed, and thrust her head into the slate gray feathers of her back. She slept. I worked for several hours.

I must say here that I was beginning to wonder if I should not go home for the winter and come back again in the spring. Everything in the forest was getting prepared for the harsh months. Jessie Coon James was as fat as a barrel. He came down the tree slowly, his fat falling in a roll over his shoulders. The squirrels were working and storing food. They were building leaf nests. The skunks had burrows and plugged themselves in at dawn with bunches of leaves. No drafts could reach them.

As I thought of the skunks and all the animals preparing themselves against the winter, I realized suddenly that my tree would be as cold as the air if I did not somehow find a way to heat it.

"NOTES:

"Today I rafted out into the deep pools of the creek to fish. It was a lazy sort of autumn day, the sky clear, the leaves beginning to brighten, the air warm. I stretched out on my back because the fish weren't biting, and hummed.

"My line jerked and I sat up to pull, but was too late. However, I was not too late to notice that I had drifted into the bank—the very bank where Bando had dug the clay for the jam pots.

"At that moment I knew what I was going to do. I was going to build a fireplace of clay, even fashion a little chimney of clay. It would be small, but enough to warm the tree during the long winter.

"Next Day

"I dragged the clay up the mountain to my tree in my second best pair of city pants. I tied the bottoms of the legs, stuffed them full, and as I looked down on my strange cargo, I thought of scarecrows and Halloween. I thought of the gang dumping ashcans on Third Avenue and soaping up the windows. Suddenly I was terribly lonely. The air smelled of leaves and the cool wind from the stream hugged me. The warblers in the trees above me seemed gay and glad about their trip south. I stopped halfway up the mountain and dropped my head. I was lonely and on the verge of tears. Suddenly there was a flash, a pricking sensation on my leg, and

I looked down in time to see The Baron leap from my pants to the cover of fern.

"He scared the loneliness right out of me. I ran after him and chased him up the mountain, losing him from time to time in the ferns and crowfeet. We stormed into camp an awful sight, The Baron bouncing and screaming ahead of me, and me dragging that half scarecrow of clay.

"Frightful took one look and flew to the end of her leash. She doesn't like The Baron, and watches him—well, like a hawk. I don't like to leave her alone. End notes. Must make fireplace."

It took three days to get the fireplace worked out so that it didn't smoke me out of the tree like a bee. It was an enormous problem. In the first place, the chimney sagged because the clay was too heavy to hold itself up, so I had to get some dry grasses to work into it so it could hold its own weight.

I whittled out one of the old knotholes to let the smoke out, and built the chimney down from this. Of course when the clay dried, it pulled away from the tree, and all the smoke poured back in on me.

So I tried sealing the leak with pine pitch, and that worked all right, but then the funnel over the fire bed cracked, and I had to put wooden props under that.

The wooden props burned, and I could see that this wasn't going to work either; so I went down the mountain to the site of the old Gribley farmhouse and looked around for some iron spikes or some sort of metal.

I took the wooden shovel that I had carved from the board and dug around what I thought must have been the back door or possibly the woodhouse.

I found a hinge, old handmade nails that would come in handy, and finally, treasure of treasures, the axle of an old wagon. It was much too big. I had no hacksaw to cut it into smaller pieces, and I was not strong enough to heat it and hammer it apart. Besides, I didn't have anything but a small wooden mallet I had made.

I carried my trophies home and sat down before my tree to fix dinner and feed Frightful. The evening was cooling down for a frost. I looked at Frightful's warm feathers. I didn't even have a deer hide for a blanket. I had used the two I had for a door and a pair of pants. I wished that I might grow feathers.

I tossed Frightful off my fist and she flashed through the trees and out over the meadow. She went with a determination strange to her. "She is going to leave," I cried. "I have never seen her fly so wildly." I pushed the smoked fish aside and ran to the meadow. I whistled and whistled and whistled until my mouth was dry and no more whistle came.

I ran onto the big boulder. I could not see her. Wildly I waved the lure. I licked my lips and whistled again. The sun was a cold steely color as it dipped below the mountain. The air was now brisk, and Frightful was gone. I was sure that she had suddenly taken off on the migration; my heart was sore and pounding. I had enough food, I was sure. Frightful was not absolutely necessary for my survival; but I was now so fond of her. She was more than a bird. I knew I must have her back to talk to and play with if I was going to make it through the winter.

I whistled. Then I heard a cry in the grasses up near the white birches.

In the gathering darkness I saw movement. I think I flew to the spot. And there she was; she had caught herself a bird. I rolled into the grass beside her and clutched her jesses. She didn't intend to leave, but I was going to make sure that she didn't. I grabbed so swiftly that my hand hit a rock and I bruised my knuckles.

The rock was flat and narrow and long; it was the answer to my fireplace. I picked up Frightful in one hand and the stone in the other; and I laughed at the cold steely sun as it slipped out of sight, because I knew I was going to be warm. This flat stone was what I needed to hold up the funnel and finish my fireplace.

And that's what I did with it. I broke it into two pieces, set one on each side under the funnel, lit the fire, closed the flap of the door and listened to the wind bring the first frost to the mountain. I was warm.

Then I noticed something dreadful. Frightful was sitting on the bedpost, her head under her wings. She was toppling. She jerked her head out of her feathers. Her eyes looked glassy. She is sick, I said. I picked her up and stroked her, and we both might have died there if I had not opened the tent flap to get her some water.

The cold night air revived her. "Air," I said. "The fireplace used up all the oxygen. I've got to ventilate this place."

We sat out in the cold for a long time because I was more than a little afraid of what our end might have been.

I put out the fire, took the door down and wrapped up in it. Frightful and I slept with the good frost nipping our faces.

"NOTES:

"I cut out several more knotholes to let air in and out of the tree room. I tried it today. I have Frightful on my fist watching her. It's been about two hours and she hasn't fainted and I haven't gone numb. I can still write and see clearly.

"Test: Frightful's healthy face."

IN WHICH
We All Learn About Halloween

"*October 28*

"I have been up and down the mountain every day for a week, watching to see if walnuts and hickory nuts are ripe. Today I found the squirrels all over the trees, harvesting them furiously, and so I have decided that ripe or not, I must gather them. It's me or the squirrels.

"I tethered Frightful in the hickory tree while I went to the walnut tree and filled pouches. Frightful protected the hickory nuts. She keeps the squirrels so busy scolding her that they don't have time to take the nuts. They are quite terrified by her. It is a good scheme. I shout and bang the tree and keep them away while I gather.

"I have never seen so many squirrels. They hang from the slender branches, they bounce through the limbs, they seem to come from the whole forest. They must pass messages along to each other—messages that tell what kind of nuts and where the trees are."

A few days later, my storehouse rolling with nuts, I began the race for apples. Entering this race were squirrels, raccoons, and a fat old skunk who looked as if he could eat not another bite. He was ready to sleep his autumn meal off, and I resented him because he did not need my apples. However, I did not toy with him.

I gathered what apples I could, cut some in slices, and dried them on the boulder in the sun. Some I put in the storeroom tree to eat right away. They were a little wormy, but it was wonderful to eat an apple again.

Then one night this was all done, the crop was gathered. I sat down to make a few notes when The Baron came sprinting into sight.

He actually bounced up and licked the edges of my turtle-shell bowl, stormed Frightful, and came to my feet.

"Baron Weasel," I said. "It is nearing Halloween. Are you playing tricks or treats?" I handed him the remains of my turtle soup dinner, and, fascinated, watched him devour it.

"NOTES:

"The Baron chews with his back molars, and chews with a ferocity I have not seen in him before. His eyes gleam, the lips curl back from his white pointed teeth, and he frowns like an angry man. If I move toward him, a rumble starts in his chest that keeps me back. He flashes glances at me. It is indeed strange to be looked in the eye by this fearless wild animal. There is something human about his beady glance. Perhaps because that glance tells me something. It tells me he knows who I am and that he does not want me to come any closer."

The Baron Weasel departed after his feast. Frightful, who was drawn up as skinny as a stick, relaxed and fluffed her feathers, and then I said to her, "See, he got his treats. No tricks." Then something occurred to me. I reached inside the door and pulled out my calendar stick. I counted 28, 29, 30, 31.

"Frightful, that old weasel knows. It is Halloween. Let's have a Halloween party."

Swiftly I made piles of cracked nuts, smoked rabbit, and crayfish. I even added two of my apples. This food was an invitation to the squirrels, foxes, raccoons, opossums, even the birds that lived around me to come have a party.

When Frightful is tethered to her stump, some of the animals and birds will only come close enough to scream at her. So bird and I went inside the tree, propped open the flap, and waited.

Not much happened that night. I learned that it takes a little time for the woodland messages to get around. But they do. Before the party I had been very careful about leaving food out because I needed every mouthful. I took the precaution of rolling a stone in front of my store tree. The harvest moon rose. Frightful and I went to sleep.

At dawn, we abandoned the party. I left the treats out, however. Since it was a snappy gold-colored day, we went off to get some more rabbit skins to finish my winter underwear.

We had lunch along the creek—stewed mussels and wild potatoes. We didn't get back until dusk because I discovered some wild rice in an ox bow of the stream. There was no more than a handful.

Home that night, everything seemed peaceful enough. A few nuts were gone, to the squirrels, I thought. I baked a fish in leaves, and ate a small, precious amount of wild rice. It was marvelous! As I settled

wild potato

down to scrape the rabbit skins of the day, my neighbor the skunk marched right into the campground and set to work on the smoked rabbit. I made some Halloween notes:

"The moon is coming up behind the aspens. It is as big as a pumpkin and as orange. The winds are cool, the stars are like electric light bulbs. I am just inside the doorway, with my turtle-shell lamp burning so that I can see to write this.

"Something is moving beyond the second hemlock. Frightful is very alert, as if there are things all around us. Halloween was over at midnight last night, but for us it is just beginning. That's how I feel, anyhow, but it just may be my imagination.

"I wish Frightful would stop pulling her feathers in and drawing herself up like a spring. I keep thinking that she feels things.

"Here comes Jessie C. James. He will want the venison.

"He didn't get the venison. There was a snarl, and a big raccoon I've never seen walked past him, growling and looking ferocious. Jessie C. stood motionless—I might say, scared stiff. He held his head at an angle and let the big fellow eat. If Jessie so much as rolled his eyes that old coon would sputter at him."

It grew dark, and I couldn't see much. An eerie yelp behind the boulder announced that the red fox of the meadow was nearing. He gave me goose bumps. He stayed just beyond my store tree, weaving back and forth on silent feet. Every now and then he would cry— a wavery owllike cry. I wrote some more.

"The light from my turtle lamp casts leaping shadows. To the beechnuts has come a small gray animal. I can't make out what—now, I see it. It's a flying squirrel. That surprises me, I've never seen a flying squirrel around here, but of course I haven't been up much after sunset."

When it grew too dark to see, I lit a fire, hoping it would not end the party. It did not, and the more I watched, the more I realized that all these animals were familiar with my camp. A white-footed mouse walked over my woodpile as if it were his.

I put out the candle and fell asleep when the fire turned to coals. Much later I was awakened by screaming. I lifted my head and looked into the moonlit forest. A few guests, still lingering at the party, saw me move, and dashed bashfully into the ground cover. One was big and slender. I thought perhaps a mink. As I slowly came awake, I realized that screaming was coming from behind me. Something was in my house. I jumped up and shouted, and two raccoons skittered under my feet. I reached for my candle, slipped on hundreds of nuts, and fell. When I finally got a light and looked about me, I was dismayed to see what a mess my guests had made of my tree house. They had found the cache of acorns and beechnuts and had tossed them all over my bed and floor. The party was getting rough.

I chased the raccoons into the night and stumbled over a third animal and was struck by a wet stinging spray. It was skunk! I was drenched. As I got used to the indignity and the smell, I saw the raccoons cavort around my fireplace and dodge past me. They were back in my tree before I could stop them.

A bat winged in from the darkness and circled the tallow candle. It was Halloween and the goblins were at work. I thought of all the ash cans I had knocked over on the streets of New York. It seemed utterly humorless.

Having invited all these neighbors, I was now faced with the problem of getting rid of them. The raccoons were feeling so much at home that they snatched up beechnuts, bits of dried fish and venison and tossed them playfully into the air. They were too full to eat any more, but were having a marvelous time making toys out of my hard-won winter food supply.

I herded the raccoons out of the tree and laced the door. I was breathing "relief" when I turned my head to the left, for I sensed someone watching me. There in the moonlight, his big ears erect on his head, sat the red fox. He was smiling—I know he was. I shouted, "Stop laughing!" and he vanished like a magician's handkerchief.

All this had awakened Frightful, who was flopping in the dark in the tree. I reached in around the deer flap to stroke her back to calmness. She grabbed me so hard I yelled—and the visitors moved to the edge of my camp at my cry.

Smelling to the sky, bleeding in the hand, and robbed of part of my hard-won food, I threw wood on the fire and sent an enormous shaft of light into the night. Then I shouted. The skunk moved farther away. The raccoons galloped off a few feet and galloped back. I snarled at them. They went to the edge of the darkness and stared at me. I had learned something that night from that very raccoon bossing Jessie C. James—to animals, might is right. I was biggest and I was oldest, and I was going to tell them so. I growled and snarled and hissed and snorted. It worked. They understood and moved away. Some looked back and their eyes glowed. The red eyes chilled me. Never had there been a more real Halloween night. I looked up, expecting to see a witch. The last bat of the season darted in the moonlight. I dove on my bed, and tied the door. There are no more notes about Halloween.

IN WHICH
I Find Out What to Do with Hunters

That party had a moral ending. Don't feed wild animals! I picked up and counted my walnuts and hickory nuts. I was glad to discover there was more mess than loss. I decided that I would not only live until spring but that I still had more nuts than all the squirrels on Gribley's (including flying squirrels).

In early November I was awakened one morning by a shot from a rifle. The hunting season had begun! I had forgotten all about that. To hide from a swarm of hunters was truly going to be a trick. They would be behind every tree and on every hill and dale. They would be shooting at everything that moved, and here was I in deerskin pants and dirty brown sweater, looking like a deer.

I decided, like the animals, to stay holed up the first

day of the season. I whittled a fork and finished my rabbit-skin winter underwear. I cracked a lot of walnuts.

The second day of the hunting season I stuck my head out of my door and decided my yard was messy. I picked it up so that it looked like a forest floor.

The third day of the hunting season some men came in and camped by the gorge. I tried to steal down the other side of the mountain to the north stream, found another camp of hunters there, and went back to my tree.

By the end of the week both Frightful and I were in need of exercise. Gunshots were still snapping around the mountain. I decided to go see Miss Turner at the library. About an hour later I wrote this:

"I got as far as the edge of the hemlock grove when a shot went off practically at my elbow. I didn't have Frightful's jesses in my hand and she took off at the blast. I climbed a tree. There was a hunter so close to me he could have bitten me, but apparently he was busy watching his deer. I was able to get up into the high branches without being seen. First, I looked around for Frightful. I could see her nowhere. I wanted to whistle for her but didn't think I should. I sat still and looked and wondered if she'd go home.

"I watched the hunter track his deer. The deer was still running. From where I was I could see it plainly, going toward the old Gribley farm site. Quietly I climbed higher and watched. Then of all things, it jumped the stone fence and fell dead.

"I thought I would stay in the tree until the hunter quartered his kill and dragged it out to the road. Ah, then, it occurred to me that he wasn't even going to find that deer. He was going off at an angle, and from what I could see, the deer had dropped in a big bank of dry ferns and would be hard to find.

"It got to be nerve-racking at this point. I could see my new jacket lying in the ferns, and the hunter looking for it. I closed my eyes and mentally steered him to the left.

"Then, good old Frightful! She had winged down the mountain and was sitting in a sapling maple not far from the deer. She saw the man and screamed. He looked in her direction; heaven knows what he thought she was, but he turned and started toward her. She rustled her wings, climbed into the sky, and disappeared over my head. I did want to whistle to her, but feared for my deer, myself, and her.

"I hung in the tree and waited about a half an hour. Finally the man gave up his hunt. His friends called, and he went on down the mountain. I went down the tree.

"In the dry ferns lay a nice young buck. I covered it carefully with some of the stones from the fence, and more ferns, and rushed home. I whistled, and down from the top of my own hemlock came Frightful. I got a piece of birch bark to write all this on so I wouldn't get too anxious and go for the deer too soon.

"We will wait until dark to go get our dinner and my new jacket. I am beginning to think I'll have all the deer hide and venison I can use. There must be other lost game on this mountain."

I got the deer after dark, and I was quite right. Before the season was over I got two more deer in the same way. However, with the first deer to work on, the rest of the season passed quickly. I had lots of scraping and preparing to do. My complaint was that I did not dare light a fire and cook that wonderful meat. I was afraid of being spotted. I ate smoked venison, nut meats, and hawthorn berries. Hawthorn berries taste a little bit like apples. They are smaller and drier than apples. They also have big seeds in them. The hawthorn bush is easy to tell because it has big red shiny thorns on it.

Each day the shooting lessened as the hunters left the hills and went home. As they cleared out, Frightful and I were freer and freer to roam.

The air temperature now was cold enough to preserve the venison, so I didn't smoke the last two deer, and about two weeks after I heard that first alarming shot, I cut off a beautiful steak, built a bright fire, and when the embers were glowing, I had myself a real dinner. I soaked some dried puffballs in water, and when they were big and moist, I fried them with wild onions and skimpy old wild carrots and stuffed myself until I felt kindly toward all men. I wrote this:

"November 26

"Hunters are excellent friends if used correctly. Don't let them see you; but follow them closely. Preferably use the tops of trees for this purpose, for hunters don't look up. They look down and to the right and left and straight ahead. So if you stay in the trees, you can not only see what they shoot, but where it falls, and if you are extremely careful, you can sometimes get to it before they do and hide it. That's how I got my third deer."

I had a little more trouble tanning these hides because the water in my oak stump kept freezing at night. It was getting cold. I began wearing my rabbit-fur underwear most of the morning. It was still too warm at noon to keep it on, but it felt good at night. I slept in it until I got my blanket made. I did not scrape the deer hair off my blanket. I liked it on. Because I had grown, one deerskin wouldn't cover me. I sewed part of another one to it.

The third hide I made into a jacket. I just cut a rectangle with a hole in it for my head and sewed on straight wide sleeves. I put enormous pockets all over

it, using every scrap I had, including the pouches I had made last summer. It looked like a cross between a Russian military blouse and a carpenter's apron, but it was warm, roomy and, I thought, handsome.

IN WHICH
Trouble Begins

I stood in my doorway the twenty-third of November dressed from head to toe in deerskins. I was lined with rabbit fur. I had mittens and squirrel-lined moccasins. I was quite excited by my wardrobe.

I whistled and Frightful came to my fist. She eyed me with her silky black eyes and pecked at my suit.

"Frightful," I said, "this is not food. It is my new suit. Please don't eat it." She peeped softly, fluffed her feathers, and looked gently toward the meadow.

"You are beautiful, too, Frightful," I said, and I touched the slate gray feathers of her back. Very gently I stroked the jet black ones that came down from her eyes. Those beautiful marks gave her much of her superb dignity. In a sense she had also come into a new suit. Her plumage had changed during the autumn, and she was breathtaking.

I walked to the spring and we looked in. I saw us quite clearly, as there were no longer any frogs to plop in the water and break the mirror with circles and ripples.

"Frightful," I said as I turned and twisted and looked. "We would be quite handsome if it were not for my hair. I need another haircut."

I did the best job I was able to do with a penknife.

I made a mental note to make a hat to cover the stray ends.

Then I did something which took me by surprise. I smelled the clean air of November, turned once more to see how the back of my suit looked, and walked down the mountain. I stepped over the stream on the stones. I walked to the road.

Before I could talk myself out of it, I was on my way to town.

As I walked down the road, I kept pretending I was going to the library; but it was Sunday, and I knew the library was closed.

I tethered Frightful just outside town on a stump. I didn't want to attract any attention. Kicking stones as I went, and whistling, I walked to the main intersection of town as if I came every Sunday.

I saw the drugstore and began to walk faster, for I was beginning to sense that I was not exactly what everybody saw every day. Eyes were upon me longer than they needed to be.

By the time I got to the drugstore, I was running. I slipped in and went to the magazine stand. I picked up a comic book and began to read.

Footsteps came toward me. Below the bottom pictures I saw a pair of pants and saddle shoes. One shoe went *tap, tap.* The feet did a kind of hop step, and I watched them walk to the other side of me. *Tap, tap, tap,* again; a hop step and the shoes and pants circled me. Then came the voice. "Well, if it isn't Daniel Boone!"

I looked into a face about the age of my own—but a little more puppyish—I thought. It had about the same coloring—brown eyes, brown hair—a bigger nose than mine, and more ears, but a very assured face. I said, "Well?" I grinned, because it had been a long time since I had seen a young man my age.

The young man didn't answer, he simply took my sleeve between his fingers and examined it closely. "Did you chew it yourself?" he asked.

I looked at the spot he was examining and said, "Well, no, I pounded it on a rock there, but I did have to chew it a bit around the neck. It stuck me."

We looked at each other then. I wanted to say something, but didn't know where to begin. He picked at my sleeve again.

"My kid brother has one that looks more real than that thing. Whataya got that on for anyway?"

I looked at his clothes. He had on a nice pair of gray slacks, a white shirt opened at the neck, and a leather jacket. As I looked at these things, I found my voice.

"Well, I'd rip anything like you have on all to pieces in about a week."

He didn't answer; he walked around me again.

"Where did you say you came from?"

"I didn't say, but I come from a farm up the way."

"Whatja say your name was?"

"Well, you called me Daniel Boone."

"Daniel Boone, eh?" He walked around me once more, and then peered at me.

"You're from New York. I can tell the accent." He leaned against the cosmetic counter. "Come on, now, tell me, is this what the kids are wearing in New York now? Is this gang stuff?"

"I am hardly a member of a gang," I said. "Are you?"

"Out here? Naw, we bowl." The conversation went to bowling for a while, then he looked at his watch.

"I gotta go. You sure are a sight, Boone. Whatja doing anyway, playing cowboys and Indians?"

"Come on up to the Gribley farm and I'll show you what I'm doing. I'm doing research. Who knows when we're all going to be blown to bits and need to know how to smoke venison."

"Gee, you New York guys can sure double talk. What does that mean, burn a block down?"

"No, it means smoke venison," I said. I took a piece out of my pocket and gave it to him. He smelled it and handed it back.

"Man," he said, "whataya do, eat it?"

"I sure do," I answered.

"I don't know whether to send you home to play with my kid brother or call the cops." He shrugged his shoulders and repeated that he had to go. As he left, he called back, "The Gribley farm?"

"Yes. Come on up if you can find it."

I browsed through the magazines until the clerk got anxious to sell me something and then I wandered out. Most of the people were in church. I wandered around the town and back to the road.

It was nice to see people again. At the outskirts of town a little boy came bursting out of a house with his shoes off, and his mother came bursting out after him. I caught the little fellow by the arm and I held him until his mother picked him up and took him back. As she went up the steps, she stopped and looked at me. She stepped toward the door, and then walked back a few steps and looked at me again. I began to feel conspicuous and took the road to my mountain.

I passed the little old strawberry lady's house. I almost went in, and then something told me to go home.

I found Frightful, untied her, stroked her creamy breast feathers, and spoke to her. "Frightful, I made a friend today. Do you think that is what I had in mind all the time?" The bird whispered.

I was feeling sad as we kicked up the leaves and started home through the forest. On the other hand, I was glad I had met Mr. Jacket, as I called him. I never asked his name. I had liked him although we hadn't even had a fight. All the best friends I had, I always fought, then got to like them after the wounds healed.

The afternoon darkened. The nuthatches that had been clinking around the trees were silent. The chickadees had vanished. A single crow called from the edge of the road. There were no insects singing, there were no catbirds, or orioles, or vireos, or robins.

"Frightful," I said. "It is winter. It is winter and I have forgotten to do a terribly important thing—stack up a big woodpile." The stupidity of this sent Mr. Jacket right out of my mind, and I bolted down the valley to my mountain. Frightful flapped to keep her balance. As I crossed the stones to my mountain trail, I said to that bird, "Sometimes I wonder if I will make it to spring."

IN WHICH
I Pile Up Wood and Go on with Winter

Now I am almost to that snowstorm. The morning after I had the awful thought about the wood, I got up early. I was glad to hear the nuthatches and chickadees. They gave me the feeling that I still had time to chop. They were bright, busy, and totally unworried about storms. I shouldered my ax and went out.

I had used most of the wood around the hemlock house, so I crossed to the top of the gorge. First I took all the dry limbs off the trees and hauled them home. Then I chopped down dead trees. With wood all around me, I got in my tree and put my arm out. I made an *x* in the needles. Where the *x* lay, I began stacking wood. I wanted to be able to reach my wood from the tree when the snow was deep. I piled a big stack at this point. I reached out the other side of the door and made another *x*. I piled wood here. Then I stepped around my piles and had a fine idea. I decided that if I used up one pile, I could tunnel through the snow to the next and the next. I made many woodpiles leading out into the forest.

I watched the sky. It was as blue as summer, but ice was building up along the waterfall at the gorge. I knew winter was coming, although each day the sun would rise in a bright sky and the days would follow cloudless. I piled more wood. This is when I realized that I was scared. I kept cutting wood and piling it like a nervous child biting his nails.

It was almost with relief that I saw the storm arrive.

Now I am back where I began. I won't tell it again, I shall go on now with my relief and the fun and wonderfulness of living on a mountaintop in winter.

The Baron Weasel loved the snow, and was up and about in it every day before Frightful and I had had our breakfast. Professor Bando's jam was my standby on those cold mornings. I would eat mounds of it on my hard acorn pancakes, which I improved by adding hickory nuts. With these as a bracer for the day, Frightful and I would stamp out into the snow and reel down the mountain. She would fly above my head as I slid and plunged and rolled to the creek.

The creek was frozen. I would slide out onto it and break a little hole and ice fish. The sun would glance off the white snow, the birds would fly through the trees, and I would come home with a fresh meal from the valley. I found there were still plants under the snow, and I would dig down and get teaberry leaves and wintergreen. I got this idea from the deer, who found a lot to eat under the snow. I tried some of the mosses that they liked, but decided moss was for the deer.

Around four o'clock we would all wander home. The nuthatches, the chickadees, the cardinals, Frightful, and me. And now came the nicest part of wonderful days. I would stop in the meadow and throw Frightful off my fist. She would wind into the sky and wait above me as I kicked the snow-bent grasses. A rabbit would pop up, or sometimes a pheasant. Out of the sky, from a pinpoint of a thing, would dive my beautiful falcon. And, oh, she was beautiful when she made a strike—all power and beauty. On the ground she would cover her quarry. Her perfect feathers would stand up on her body and her wings would arch over the food. She never touched it until I came and picked her up. I would go home and feed her, then crawl into my tree room, light a little fire on my hearth, and Frightful and I would begin the winter evening.

I had lots of time to cook and try mixing different plants with different meats to make things taste better— and I must say I originated some excellent meals.

When dinner was done, the fire would blaze on; Frightful would sit on the foot post of the bed and preen and wipe her beak and shake. Just the fact that she was alive was a warming thing to know.

I would look at her and wonder what made a bird a bird and a boy a boy. The forest would become silent. I would know that The Baron Weasel was about, but I would not hear him.

Then I would get a piece of birch bark and write, or I would make new things out of deer hide, like a hood for Frightful, and finally I would take off my suit and my moccasins and crawl into my bed under the sweet-smelling deerskin. The fire would burn itself out and I would be asleep.

Those were nights of the very best sort.

One night I read some of my old notes about how to pile wood so I could get to it under the snow, and I laughed until Frightful awoke. I hadn't made a single tunnel. I walked on the snow to get wood like The Baron Weasel went for food or the deer went for moss.

IN WHICH
I Learn About Birds and People

Frightful and I settled down to living in snow. We went to bed early, slept late, ate the mountain harvest, and explored the country alone. Oh, the deer walked with us, the foxes followed in our footsteps, the winter birds flew over our heads, but mostly we were alone in the white wilderness. It was nice. It was very, very nice. My deerskin rabbit-lined suit was so warm that even when my breath froze in my nostrils, my body was snug and comfortable. Frightful fluffed on the coldest days, but a good flight into the air around the mountain would warm her, and she would come back to my fist with a thump and a flip. This was her signal of good spirits.

I did not become lonely. Many times during the summer I had thought of the "long winter months ahead" with some fear. I had read so much about the loneliness of the farmer, the trapper, the woodsman during the bleakness of winter that I had come to believe it. The winter was as exciting as the summer—maybe more so. The birds were magnificent and almost tame. They talked to each other, warned each other, fought for food, for kingship, and for the right to make the most noise. Sometimes I would sit in my doorway, which became an entrance to behold—a portico of pure white snow, adorned with snowmen—and watch them with endless interest. They reminded me of Third Avenue, and I gave them the names that seemed to fit.

There was Mr. Bracket. He lived on the first floor of our apartment house, and no one could sit on his step or even make a noise near his door without being chased. Mr. Bracket, the chickadee, spent most of his time chasing the young chickadees through the woods. Only his mate could share his favorite perches and feeding places.

Then there were Mrs. O'Brien, Mrs. Callaway, and Mrs. Federio. On Third Avenue they would all go off to the market together first thing in the morning, talking and pushing and stopping to lecture to children in gutters and streets. Mrs. Federio always followed Mrs. O'Brien, and Mrs. O'Brien always followed Mrs. Callaway in talking and pushing and even in buying an apple. And there they were again in my hemlock; three busy chickadees. They would flit and rush around and click and fly from one eating spot to another. They were noisy, scolding and busily following each other. All the other chickadees followed them, and they made way only for Mr. Bracket.

The chickadees, like the people on Third Avenue, had their favorite routes to and from the best food supplies. They each had their own resting perches and each had a little shelter in a tree cavity to which they would fly when the day was over. They would chatter and call good night and make a big fuss before they parted; and then the forest would be as quiet as the apartment house on Third Avenue when all the kids were off the streets and all the parents had said their last words to each other and everyone had gone to their own little hole.

Sometimes when the wind howled and the snows blew, the chickadees would be out for only a few hours. Even Mr. Bracket, who had been elected by the chickadees to test whether or not it was too stormy for good hunting, would appear for a few hours and disappear. Sometimes I would find him just sitting quietly on a limb next to the bole of a tree, all fluffed up and doing nothing. There was no one who more enjoyed doing nothing on a bad day than Mr. Bracket of Third Avenue.

Frightful, the two Mr. Brackets, and I shared this feeling. When the ice and sleet and snow drove down through the hemlocks, we all holed up.

I looked at my calendar pole one day, and realized that it was almost Christmas. Bando will come, I thought. I'll have to prepare a feast and make a present for him. I took stock of the frozen venison and decided that there were enough steaks for us to eat nothing but venison for a month. I scooped under the snow for teaberry plants to boil down and pour over snowballs for dessert.

I checked my cache of wild onions to see if I had enough to make onion soup, and set aside some large firm groundnuts for mashed potatoes. There were still piles of dogtooth violet bulbs and Solomon's seal roots and a few dried apples. I cracked walnuts, hickory nuts, and beechnuts, then began a pair of deer-hide moccasins to be lined with rabbit fur for Bando's present. I finished these before Christmas, so I started a hat of the same materials.

Two days before Christmas I began to wonder if Bando would come. He had forgotten, I was sure—or he was busy, I said. Or he thought that I was no longer here and decided not to tramp out through the snows to find out. On Christmas Eve Bando still had not arrived, and I began to plan for a very small Christmas with Frightful.

About four-thirty Christmas Eve I hung a small red cluster of teaberries on the deerskin door. I went in my tree room for a snack of beechnuts when I heard a faint "halloooo" from far down the mountain. I snuffed out my tallow candle, jumped into my coat and moccasins, and plunged out into the snow. Again a "halloooo" floated over the quiet snow. I took a bearing on the sound and bounced down the hill to meet Bando. I ran into him just as he turned up the valley to follow the stream bed. I was so glad to see him that I hugged him and pounded him on the back.

"Never thought I'd make it," he said. "I walked all the way from the entrance of the State Park; pretty good, eh?" He smiled and slapped his tired legs. Then he grabbed my arm, and with three quick pinches, tested the meat on me.

"You've been living well," he said. He looked closely at my face. "But you're gonna need a shave in a year or two." I thanked him and we sprang up the mountain, cut across through the gorge and home.

"How's the Frightful?" he asked as soon as we were inside and the light was lit.

I whistled. She jumped to my fist. He got bold and stroked her. "And the jam?" he asked.

"Excellent, except the crocks are absorbent and are sopping up all the juice."

"Well, I brought you some more sugar; we'll try next year. Merry Christmas, Thoreau!" he shouted, and looked about the room.

"I see you have been busy. A blanket, new clothes, and an ingenious fireplace—with a real chimney—and say, you have silverware!" He picked up the forks I had carved.

We ate smoked fish for dinner with boiled dogtooth violet bulbs. Walnuts dipped in jam were dessert. Bando was pleased with his jam.

When we were done, Bando stretched out on my bed. He propped his feet up and lit his pipe.

"And now, I have something to show you," he said. He reached in his coat pocket and took out a newspaper clipping. It was from a New York paper, and it read:

WILD BOY SUSPECTED LIVING OFF DEER
AND NUTS IN WILDERNESS OF CATSKILLS

I looked at Bando and leaned over to read the headline myself.

"Have you been talking?" I asked.

"Me? Don't be ridiculous. You have had several visitors other than me."

"The fire warden—the old lady!" I cried out.

"Now, Thoreau, this could only be a rumor. Just because it is in print, doesn't mean it's true. Before you get excited, sit still and listen." He read:

" 'Residents of Delhi, in the Catskill Mountains, report that a wild boy, who lives off deer and nuts, is hiding out in the mountains.

" 'Several hunters stated that this boy stole deer from them during hunting season.' "

"I did not!" I shouted. "I only took the ones they had wounded and couldn't find."

"Well, that's what they told their wives when they came home without their deer. Anyway, listen to this:

" 'This wild boy has been seen from time to time by Catskill residents, some of whom believe he is crazy!' "

"Well, that's a terrible thing to say!"

"Just awful," he stated. "Any normal red-blooded American boy wants to live in a tree house and trap his own food. They just don't do it, that's all."

"Read on," I said.

" 'Officials say that there is no evidence of any boy living alone in the mountains, and add that all abandoned houses and sheds are routinely checked for just such events. Nevertheless, the residents are sure that such a boy exists!' End story."

"That's a lot of nonsense!" I leaned back against the bedstead and smiled.

"Ho, ho, don't think that ends it," Bando said, and reached in his pocket for another clipping. "This one is dated December fifth, the other was November twenty-third. Shall I read?"

"Yes."

OLD WOMAN REPORTS MEETING WILD BOY
WHILE PICKING STRAWBERRIES IN CATSKILLS

" 'Mrs. Thomas Fielder, ninety-seven, resident of Delhi, N.Y., told this reporter that she met a wild boy on Bitter Mountain last June while gathering her annual strawberry jelly supply.

" 'She said the boy was brown-haired, dusty, and wandering aimlessly around the mountains. However, she added, he seemed to be in good flesh and happy.

" 'The old woman, a resident of the mountain resort town for ninety-seven years, called this office to report her observation. Local residents report that Mrs. Fielder is a fine old member of the community, who only occasionally sees imaginary things.' "

Bando roared. I must say I was sweating, for I really did not expect this turn of events.

"And now," went on Bando, "and now the queen of

the New York papers. This story was buried on page nineteen. No sensationalism for this paper.

BOY REPORTED LIVING OFF LAND IN CATSKILLS

" 'A young boy of seventeen or eighteen, who left home with a group of boy scouts, is reported to be still scouting in that area, according to the fire warden of the Catskill Mountains.

" 'Evidence of someone living in the forest—a fireplace, soup bones, and cracked nuts—was reported by Warden Jim Handy, who spent the night in the wilderness looking for the lad. Jim stated that the young man had apparently left the area, as there was no evidence of his camp upon a second trip—' "

"What second trip?" I asked.

Bando puffed his pipe, looked at me wistfully and said, "Are you ready to listen?"

"Sure," I answered.

"Well, here's the rest of it. '. . . there was no trace of his camp on a second trip, and the warden believes that the young man returned to his home at the end of the summer.'

"You know, Thoreau, I could scarcely drag myself away from the newspapers to come up here. You make a marvelous story."

I said, "Put more wood on the fire, it is Christmas. No one will be searching these mountains until May Day."

Bando asked for the willow whistles. I got them for him, and after running the scale several times, he said, "Let us serenade the ingenuity of the American newspaperman. Then let us serenade the conservationists who have protected the American wilderness, so that a boy can still be alone in this world of millions of people."

I thought that was suitable, and we played "Holy Night." We tried "The Twelve Days of Christmas," but the whistles were too stiff and Bando too tired.

"Thoreau, my body needs rest. Let's give up," he said after two bad starts. I banked the fire and blew out the candle and slept in my clothes.

It was Christmas when we awoke. Breakfast was light—acorn pancakes, jam, and sassafras tea. Bando went for a walk, I lit the fire in the fireplace and spent the morning creating a feast from the wilderness.

I gave Bando his presents when he returned. He liked them. He was really pleased; I could tell by his eyebrows. They went up and down and in and out. Furthermore, I know he liked the presents because he wore them.

The onion soup was about to be served when I heard a voice shouting in the distance, "I know you are there! I know you are there! Where are you?"

"Dad!" I screamed, and dove right through the door onto my stomach. I all but fell down the mountain shouting, "Dad! Dad! Where are you?" I found him resting in a snowdrift, looking at the cardinal pair that

lived near the stream. He was smiling, stretched out on his back, not in exhaustion, but in joy.

"Merry Christmas!" he whooped. I ran toward him. He jumped to his feet, tackled me, thumped my chest, and rubbed snow in my face.

Then he stood up, lifted me from the snow by the pockets on my coat, and held me off the ground so that we were eye to eye. He sure smiled. He threw me down in the snow again and wrestled with me for a few minutes. Our formal greeting done, we strode up the mountain.

"Well, son," he began. "I've been reading about you in the papers and I could no longer resist the temptation to visit you. I still can't believe you did it."

His arm went around me. He looked real good, and I was overjoyed to see him.

"How did you find me?" I asked eagerly.

"I went to Mrs. Fielder, and she told me which mountain. At the stream I found your raft and ice-fishing holes. Then I looked for trails and footsteps. When I thought I was getting warm, I hollered."

"Am I that easy to find?"

"You didn't have to answer, and I'd probably have frozen in the snow." He was pleased and not angry at me at all. He said again, "I just didn't think you'd do it. I was sure you'd be back the next day. When you weren't, I bet on the next week; then the next month. How's it going?"

"Oh, it's a wonderful life, Dad!"

When we walked into the tree, Bando was putting the final touches on the venison steak.

"Dad, this is my friend, Professor Bando; he's a teacher. He got lost one day last summer and stumbled onto my camp. He liked it so well that he came back for Christmas. Bando, meet my father."

Bando turned the steak on the spit, rose, and shook my father's hand.

"I am pleased to meet the man who sired this boy," he said grandly. I could see that they liked each other and that it was going to be a splendid Christmas. Dad stretched out on the bed and looked around.

"I thought maybe you'd pick a cave," he said. "The papers reported that they were looking for you in old sheds and houses, but I knew better than that. However, I never would have thought of the inside of a tree. What a beauty! Very clever, son, very, very clever. This is a comfortable bed."

He noticed my food caches, stood and peered into them. "Got enough to last until spring?"

"I think so," I said. "If I don't keep getting hungry visitors all the time." I winked at him.

"Well, I would wear out my welcome by a year if I could, but I have to get back to work soon after Christmas."

"How's Mom and all the rest?" I asked as I took down the turtle-shell plates and set them on the floor.

"She's marvelous. How she manages to feed and

clothe those eight youngsters on what I bring her, I don't know; but she does it. She sends her love, and says that she hopes you are eating well-balanced meals."

The onion soup was simmering and ready. I gave Dad his.

"First course," I said.

He breathed deeply of the odor and downed it boiling hot.

"Son, this is better onion soup than the chef at the Waldorf can make."

Bando sipped his, and I put mine in the snow to cool.

"Your mother will stop worrying about your diet when she hears of this."

Bando rinsed Dad's soup bowl in the snow, and with great ceremony and elegance—he could really be elegant when the occasion arose—poured him a turtle shell of sassafras tea. Quoting a passage from one of Dickens's food-eating scenes, he carved the blackened steak. It was pink and juicy inside. Cooked to perfection. We were all proud of it. Dad had to finish his tea before he could eat. I was short on bowls. Then I filled his shell. A mound of sort of fluffy mashed cattail tubers, mushrooms, and dogtooth violet bulbs, smothered in gravy thickened with acorn powder. Each plate had a pile of soaked and stewed honey locust beans—mixed with hickory nuts. The beans are so hard it took three days to soak them.

It was a glorious feast. Everyone was impressed, including me. When we were done, Bando went down to the stream and cut some old dried and hollow reeds. He came back and carefully made us each a flute with the tip of his penknife. He said the willow whistles were too old for such an occasion. We all played Christmas carols until dark. Bando wanted to try some complicat-

ed jazz tunes, but the late hour, the small fire dancing and throwing heat, and the snow insulating us from the winds made us all so sleepy that we were not capable of more than a last slow rendition of taps before we put ourselves on and under skins and blew out the light.

Before anyone was awake the next morning, I heard Frightful call hungrily. I had put her outside to sleep, as we were very crowded. I went out to find her. Her Christmas dinner had been a big piece of venison, but the night air had enlarged her appetite. I called her to

my fist and we went into the meadow to rustle up breakfast for the guests. She was about to go after a rabbit,
but I thought that wasn't proper fare for a post-Christ-
mas breakfast, so we went to the stream. Frightful
caught herself a pheasant while I kicked a hole in the
ice and did a little ice fishing. I caught about six trout
and whistled Frightful to my hand. We returned to the
hemlock. Dad and Bando were still asleep, with their
feet in each other's faces, but both looking very content.

I built the fire and was cooking the fish and making
pancakes when Dad shot out of bed.

"Wild boy!" he shouted. "What a sanguine smell.
What a purposeful fire. Breakfast in a tree. Son, I toil
from sunup to sundown, and never have I lived so well!"

I served him. He choked a bit on the acorn pancakes—they are a little flat and hard—but Bando got
out some of his blueberry jam and smothered the pancakes with an enormous portion. Dad went through the
motions of eating this. The fish, however, he enjoyed,
and he asked for more. We drank sassafras tea, sweet-
ened with some of the sugar Bando had brought me,
rubbed our turtle shells clean in the snow, and went out
into the forest.

Dad had not met Frightful. When she winged down
out of the hemlock, he ducked and flattened out in the
snow shouting, "Blast off."

He was very cool toward Frightful until he learned
that she was the best provider we had ever had in our
family, and then he continually praised her beauty

and admired her talents. He even tried to pet her, but Frightful was not to be won. She snagged him with her talons.

They stayed away from each other for the rest of Dad's visit, although Dad never ceased to admire her from a safe distance.

Bando had to leave two or three days after Christmas. He had some papers to grade, and he started off reluctantly one morning, looking very unhappy about the way of life he had chosen. He shook hands all around and then turned to me and said, "I'll save all the newspaper clippings for you, and if the reporters start getting too hot on your trail, I'll call the New York papers and give them a bum steer." I could see he rather liked the idea, and departed a little happier.

Dad lingered on for a few more days, ice fishing, setting my traps and snares, and husking walnuts. He whittled some cooking spoons and forks.

On New Year's Day he announced that he must go.

"I told your mother I would only stay for Christmas. It's a good thing she knows me or she might be worried."

"She won't send the police out to look for you?" I asked hurriedly. "Could she think you never found me?"

"Oh, I told her I'd call her Christmas night if I didn't." He poked around for another hour or two, trying to decide just how to leave. Finally he started down the mountain. He had hardly gone a hundred feet before he was back.

"I've decided to leave by another route. Somebody might backtrack me and find you. And that would be too bad." He came over to me and put his hand on my shoulder. "You've done very well, Sam." He grinned and walked off toward the gorge.

I watched him bound from rock to rock. He waved from the top of a large rock and leaped into the air. That was the last I saw of Dad for a long time.

IN WHICH
*I Have a Good Look at Winter
and Find Spring in the Snow*

With Christmas over, the winter became serious. The snows deepened, the wind blew, the temperatures dropped until the air snapped and talked. Never had humanity seemed so far away as it did in those cold still months of January, February, and March. I wandered the snowy crags, listening to the language of the birds by day and to the noises of the weather by night. The wind howled, the snow avalanched, and the air creaked.

I slept, ate, played my reed whistle, and talked to Frightful.

To be relaxed, warm, and part of the winter wilderness is an unforgettable experience. I was in excellent condition. Not a cold, not a sniffle, not a moment of fatigue. I enjoyed the feeling that I could eat, sleep and be warm, and outwit the storms that blasted the mountains and the subzero temperatures that numbed them.

It snowed on. I plowed through drifts and stamped paths until eventually it occurred to me that I had all the materials to make snowshoes for easier traveling.

Here are the snowshoe notes:

"I made slats out of ash saplings, whittling them thin enough to bow. I soaked them in water to make them bend more easily, looped the two ends together, and wound them with hide.

"With my penknife I made holes an inch apart all around the loop.

"I strung deer hide crisscross through the loops. I made a loop of hide to hold my toe and straps to tie the shoes on.

"When I first walked in these shoes, I tripped on my toes and fell, but by the end of the first day I could walk from the tree to the gorge in half the time."

I lived close to the weather. It is surprising how you watch it when you live in it. Not a cloud passed unnoticed, not a wind blew untested. I knew the moods of the storms, where they came from, their shapes and colors. When the sun shone, I took Frightful to the meadow and we slid down the mountain on my snapping-turtle-shell sled. She really didn't care much for this.

When the winds changed and the air smelled like snow, I would stay in my tree, because I had gotten lost in a blizzard one afternoon and had had to hole up in a rock ledge until I could see where I was going. That day the winds were so strong I could not push against them, so I crawled under the ledge; for hours I wondered if I would be able to dig out when the storm blew on. Fortunately I only had to push through about a foot of snow. However, that taught me to stay home when the air said "snow." Not that I was afraid of being caught far from home in a storm, for I could find food and shelter and make a fire anywhere, but I had become as attached to my hemlock house as a brooding bird to her nest. Caught out in the storms and weather, I had an urgent desire to return to my tree, even as The Baron Weasel returned to his den, and the deer to their copse. We all had our little "patch" in the wilderness. We all fought to return there.

I usually came home at night with the nuthatch that roosted in a nearby sapling. I knew I was late if I tapped the tree and he came out. Sometimes when the weather was icy and miserable, I would hear him high in the tree near the edge of the meadow, yanking and yanking and flicking his tail, and then I would see him wing to bed early. I considered him a pretty good barometer, and if he went to his tree early, I went to mine early too. When you don't have a newspaper or radio to give you weather bulletins, watch the birds and animals. They can tell when a storm is coming. I called the nuthatch "Barometer," and when he holed up, I holed up, lit my light, and sat by my fire whittling or learning new tunes on my reed whistle. I was now really into the teeth of winter, and quite fascinated by its activity. There is no such thing as a "still winter night." Not only are many animals running around in the creaking cold, but the trees cry out and limbs snap and fall, and the wind gets caught in a ravine and screams until it dies. One noisy night I put this down:

"There is somebody in my bedroom. I can hear small exchanges of greetings and little feet moving up the wall. By the time I get to my light all is quiet.

"Next Day

"There was something in my room last night, a small tunnel leads out from my door into the snow. It is a marvelous tunnel, neatly packed, and it goes from a dried fern to a clump of moss. Then it turns and disappears. I would say mouse.

"That Night

"I kept an ember glowing and got a light fast before the visitor could get to the door. It *was* a mouse—a perfect little white-footed deer mouse with enormous black eyes and tidy white feet. Caught in the act of intruding, he decided not to retreat, but came toward me a few steps. I handed him a nut meat. He took it in his fragile paws, stuffed it in his cheek, flipped, and went out his secret tunnel. No doubt the tunnel leads right over to my store tree, and this fellow is having a fat winter."

There were no raccoons or skunks about in the snow, but the mice, the weasels, the mink, the foxes, the shrews, the cottontail rabbits were all busier than Coney Island in July. Their tracks were all over the mountain, and their activities ranged from catching each other to hauling various materials back to their dens and burrows for more insulation.

By day the birds were a-wing. They got up late, after I did, and would call to each other before hunting. I would stir up my fire and think about how much food it must take to keep one little bird alive in that fierce cold. They must eat and eat and eat, I thought.

Once, however, I came upon a male cardinal sitting in a hawthorn bush. It was a miserable day, gray, damp, and somewhere around the zero mark. The cardinal wasn't doing anything at all—just sitting on a twig, all fluffed up to keep himself warm. Now there's a wise bird, I said to myself. He is conserving his energy, none of this flying around looking for food and wasting effort. As I watched him, he shifted his feet twice, standing on one and pulling the other up into his warm feathers. I had often wondered why birds' feet didn't freeze, and there was my answer. He even sat down on both of them and let his warm feathers cover them like socks.

"January 8

"I took Frightful out today. We went over to the meadow to catch a rabbit for her; as we passed one of the hemlocks near the edge of the grove, she pulled her feathers to her body and looked alarmed. I tried to find out what had frightened her, but saw nothing.

"On the way back we passed the same tree and I noticed an owl pellet cast in the snow. I looked up. There were lots of limbs and darkness, but I could not see the owl. I walked around the tree; Frightful stared at one spot until I thought her head would swivel off. I looked, and there it was, looking like a broken limb—a great horned owl. I must say I was excited to have such a neighbor. I hit the tree with a stick and he flew off. Those great wings—they must have been five feet across—beat the wind, but there was no sound. The owl steered down the mountain through the tree limbs, and somewhere not far away he vanished in the needles and limbs.

"It is really very special to have a horned owl. I guess I feel this way because he is such a wilderness bird. He needs lots of forest and big trees, and so his presence means that the Gribley farm is a beautiful place indeed."

One week the weather gave a little to the sun, and snow melted and limbs dumped their loads and popped up into the air. I thought I'd try to make an igloo. I was cutting big blocks of snow and putting them in a circle. Frightful was dozing with her face in the sun, and the tree sparrows were raiding the hemlock cones. I worked and hummed, and did not notice the gray sheet of cloud that was sneaking up the mountain from the northwest. It covered the sun suddenly. I realized the air was damp enough to wring. I could stay as warm as a bug if I didn't get wet, so I looked at the drab mess in the sky, whistled for Frightful, and started back to the tree. We holed up just as Barometer was yanking his way home, and it was none too soon. It drizzled, it misted, it sprinkled, and finally it froze. The deer-hide door grew stiff with ice as darkness came, and it rattled like a piece of tin when the wind hit it.

I made a fire, the tree room warmed, and I puttered around with a concoction I call possum sop. A meal of frozen possum stewed with lichens, snakeweed, and lousewort. It is a different sort of dish. Of course what I really like about it are the names of all the plants with the name possum. I fooled for an hour or so brewing this dish, adding this and that, when I heard the mouse in his tunnel. I realized he was making an awful fuss, and decided it was because he was trying to gnaw through ice to get in. I decided to help him. Frightful was on her post, and I wanted to see the mouse's face when he found he was in a den with a falcon. I pushed the deerskin door. It wouldn't budge. I kicked it. It gave a little, cracking like china, and I realized that I was going to be iced in if I didn't keep that door open.

I finally got it open. There must have been an inch and a half of ice on it. The mouse, needless to say, was gone. I ate my supper and reminded myself to awaken and open the door off and on during the night. I put more wood on the fire, as it was damp in spite of the flames, and went to bed in my underwear and suit.

I awoke twice and kicked open the door. Then I fell into a sound sleep that lasted hours beyond my usual rising time. I overslept, I discovered, because I was in a block of ice, and none of the morning sounds of the forest penetrated my glass house to awaken me. The first thing I did was try to open the door; I chipped and kicked and managed to get my head out to see what had happened. I was sealed in. Now, I have seen ice storms, and I know they can be shiny and glassy and treacherous, but this was something else. There were sheets of ice binding the aspens to earth and cementing the tops of the hemlocks in arches. It was inches thick! Frightful winged out of the door and flew to a limb, where she tried to perch. She slipped, dropped to the ground, and skidded on her wings and undercoverts to a low spot where she finally stopped. She tried to get to her feet, slipped, lost her balance, and spread her wings. She finally flapped into the air and hovered there until she could locate a decent perch. She found one close against the bole of the hemlock. It was ice free.

I laughed at her, and then I came out and took a step. I landed with an explosion on my seat. The jolt splintered the ice and sent glass-covered limbs clattering to earth like a shopful of shattering crystal. As I sat there, and I didn't dare to move because I might get hurt, I heard an enormous explosion. It was followed by splintering and clattering and smashing. A maple at the edge of the meadow had literally blown up. I feared now for my trees—the ice was too heavy to bear. While down, I chipped the deer flap clean, and sort of swam back into my tree, listening to trees exploding all over the mountain. It was a fearful and dreadful sound. I lit a fire, ate smoked fish and dried apples, and went out again. I must say I toyed with the idea of making ice skates. However, I saw the iron wagon axle iced against a tree, and crawled to it. I de-iced it with the butt of my ax, and used it for a cane. I would stab it into the ground and inch along. I fell a couple of times but not as hard as that first time.

Frightful saw me start off through the woods, for I had to see this winter display, and she winged to my shoulder, glad for a good perch. At the meadow I looked hopefully for the sun, but it didn't have a chance. The sky was as thick as Indiana bean soup. Out in the open I watched one tree after another splinter and break under the ice, and the glass sparks that shot into the air and the thunder that the ice made as it shattered were something to remember.

At noon not a drip had fallen, the ice was as tight as it had been at dawn. I heard no nuthatches, the chickadees called once, but were silent again. There was an explosion near my spring. A hemlock had gone. Frightful and I crept back to the tree. I decided that if my house was going to shatter, I would just as soon be in it. Inside, I threw sticks to Frightful and she caught them in her talons. This is a game we play when we are tense and bored. Night came and the ice still lay in sheets. We slept to the occasional boom of breaking trees, although the explosions were not as frequent. Apparently the most rotted and oldest trees had collapsed first. The rest were more resilient, and unless a wind came up, I figured the damage was over.

At midnight a wind came up. It awakened me, for the screech of the iced limbs rubbing each other and the snapping of the ice were like the sounds from a madhouse. I listened, decided there was nothing I could do, buried my head under the deer hide, and went back to sleep.

Around six or seven I heard Barometer, the nuthatch. He yanked as he went food hunting through the hemlock grove. I jumped up and looked out. The sun had come through, and the forest sparkled and shone in cruel splendor.

That day I heard the *drip, drip* begin, and by evening some of the trees had dumped their loads and were slowly lifting themselves to their feet, so to speak. The aspens and birch trees, however, were still bent like Indian bows.

Three days later, the forest arose, the ice melted, and for about a day or so we had warm, glorious weather.

The mountain was a mess. Broken trees, fallen limbs were everywhere. I felt badly about the ruins until I thought that this had been happening to the mountain for thousands of years and the trees were still there, as were the animals and birds. The birds were starved, and many had died. I found their cold little bodies under bushes and one stiff chickadee in a cavity. Its foot was drawn into its feathers, its feathers were fluffed.

Frightful ate old frozen muskrat during those days, We couldn't kick up a rabbit or even a mouse. They were in the snow under the ice, waiting it out. I suppose the mice went right on tunneling to the grasses and the mosses and had no trouble staying alive, but I did wonder how The Baron Weasel was doing. I needn't have. Here are some notes about him.

"I should not have worried about The Baron Weasel; he appeared after the ice storm, looking sleek and pleased with himself. I think he dined royally on the many dying animals and birds. In any event, he was full of pep and ran up the hemlock to chase Frightful off her perch. That Baron! It's a good thing I don't have to tie Frightful much anymore, or he would certainly try to kill her. He still attacks me, more for the fun of being sent sprawling out into the snow than for food, for he hasn't put his teeth in my trousers for months."

January was a fierce month. After the ice storm came more snow. The mountaintop was never free of it, the gorge was blocked; only on the warmest days could I hear, deep under the ice, the trickle of water seeping over the falls. I still had food, but it was getting low. All the fresh-frozen venison was gone, and most of the bulbs and tubers. I longed for just a simple dandelion green.

dandelion

Toward the end of January I began to feel tired, and my elbows and knees were a little stiff. This worried me. I figured it was due to some vitamin I wasn't getting, but I couldn't remember which vitamin it was or even where I would find it if I could remember it.

One morning my nose bled. It frightened me a bit, and I wondered if I shouldn't hike to the library and reread the material on vitamins. It didn't last long, however, so I figured it wasn't too serious. I decided I would live until the greens came to the land, for I was of the opinion that since I had had nothing green for months, that was probably the trouble.

On that same day Frightful caught a rabbit in the meadow. As I cleaned it, the liver suddenly looked so tempting that I could hardly wait to prepare it. For the next week, I craved liver and ate all I could get. The tiredness ended, the bones stopped aching and I had no more nosebleeds. Hunger is a funny thing. It has a kind of intelligence all its own. I ate liver almost every day until the first plants emerged, and I never had any more trouble. I have looked up vitamins since. I am not surprised to find that liver is rich in vitamin C. So are citrus fruits and green vegetables, the foods I lacked. Wild plants like sorrel and dock are rich in this vitamin. Even if I had known this at that time, it would have done me no good, for they were but roots in the earth. As it turned out, liver was the only available source of vitamin C—and on liver I stuffed, without knowing why.

So much for my health. I wonder now why I didn't have more trouble than I did, except that my mother worked in a children's hospital during the war, helping to prepare food, and she was conscious of what made up a balanced meal. We heard a lot about it as kids, so I was not unaware that my winter diet was off balance.

After that experience, I noticed things in the forest

that I hadn't paid any attention to before. A squirrel had stripped the bark off a sapling at the foot of the meadow, leaving it gleaming white. I pondered when I saw it, wondering if he had lacked a vitamin or two and had sought them in the bark. I must admit I tried a little of the bark myself, but decided that even if it was loaded with vitamins, I preferred liver.

I also noticed that the birds would sit in the sun when it favored our mountain with its light, and I, being awfully vitamin minded at the time, wondered if they were gathering vitamin D. To be on the safe side, in view of this, I sat in the sun too when it was out. So did Frightful.

My notes piled up during these months, and my journal of birch bark became a storage problem. I finally took it out of my tree and cached it under a rock ledge nearby. The mice made nests in it, but it held up even when it got wet. That's one thing about using the products of the forest. They are usually weatherproof. This is important when the weather is as near to you as your skin and as much a part of your life as eating.

I was writing more about the animals now and less about myself, which proves I was feeling pretty safe. Here is an interesting entry.

"February 6

"The deer have pressed in all around me. They are hungry. Apparently they stamp out yards in the valleys where they feed during the dawn and dusk, but many

of them climb back to the hemlock grove to hide and sleep for the day. They manage the deep snows so effortlessly on those slender hooves. If I were to know that a million years from today my children's children's children were to live as I am living in these mountains, I should marry me a wife with slender feet and begin immediately to breed a race with hooves, that the Catskill children of the future might run through the snows and meadows and marshes as easily as the deer."

I got to worrying about the deer, and for many days I climbed trees and cut down tender limbs for them. At first only two came, then five, and soon I had a ring of large-eyed white-tailed deer waiting at my tree at twilight for me to come out and chop off limbs. I was astonished to see this herd grow, and wondered what signals they used to inform each other of my services. Did they smell fatter? Look more contented? Somehow they were able to tell their friends that there was a free lunch on my side of the mountain, and more and more arrived.

One evening there were so many deer that I decided to chop limbs on the other side of the meadow. They were cutting up the snow and tearing up the ground around my tree with their pawing.

Three nights later they all disappeared. Not one deer came for limbs. I looked down the valley, and in the dim light could see the open earth on the land below. The deer could forage again. Spring was coming to the land! My heart beat faster. I think I was trembling. The valley also blurred. The only thing that can do that is tears, so I guess I was crying.

That night the great horned owls boomed out across the land. My notes read:

"February 10

"I think the great horned owls have eggs! The mountain is white, the wind blows, the snow is hard packed, but spring is beginning in their hollow maple. I will climb it tomorrow.

"February 12

"Yes, yes, yes, yes. It is spring in the maple. Two great horned owl eggs lie in the cold snow-rimmed cavity in the broken top of the tree. They were warm to my touch. Eggs in the snow. Now isn't that wonderful? I didn't stay long, for it is bitter weather and I wanted the female to return immediately. I climbed down, and as I ran off toward my tree I saw her drift on those muffled wings of the owl through the limbs and branches as she went back to her work. I crawled through the tunnel of ice that leads to my tree now, the wind beating at my back. I spent the evening whittling and thinking about the owl high in the forest with the first new life of the spring."

And so with the disappearance of the deer, the hoot of the owl, the cold land began to create new life. Spring is terribly exciting when you are living right in it.

I was hungry for green vegetables, and that night as I went off to sleep, I thought of the pokeweeds, the dandelions, the spring beauties that would soon be pressing up from the earth.

MORE ABOUT
*The Spring in the Winter
and the Beginning of My Story's End*

The owl had broken the spell of winter. From that time on, things began to happen that you'd have to see to believe. Insects appeared while the snow was on the ground. Birds built nests, raccoons mated, foxes called to each other, seeking again their lifelong mates. At the end of February, the sap began to run in the maple trees. I tapped some trees and boiled the sap to syrup. It takes an awful lot of sap to make one cup of syrup, I discovered—thirty-two cups, to be exact.

All this and I was still in my winter fur-lined underwear. One or two birds returned, the ferns by the protected spring unrolled—very slowly, but they did. Then the activity gathered momentum, and before I was aware of the change, there were the skunk cabbages poking their funny blooms above the snow in the marsh. I picked some and cooked them, but they aren't any good. A skunk cabbage is a skunk cabbage.

From my meadow I could see the valleys turning green. My mountain was still snow-capped, so I walked into the valleys almost every day to scout them for edible plants. Frightful rode down with me on my

marsh marigold

shoulder. She knew even better than I that the season had changed, and she watched the sky like radar. No life traveled that sky world unnoticed by Frightful. I thought she wanted to be free and seek a mate, but I could not let her. I still depended upon her talents and company. Furthermore, she was different, and if I did let her go, she probably would have been killed by another female, for Frightful had no territory other than the hemlock patch, and her hunting instincts had been trained for man. She was a captive, not a wild bird, and that is almost another kind of bird.

milkweed

One day I was in the valley digging tubers and collecting the tiny new dandelion shoots when Frightful saw another duck hawk and flew from my shoulder like a bolt, pulling the leash from my hand as she went.

"Frightful!" I called. "You can't leave me now!" I whistled, held out a piece of meat, and hoped she would not get her leash caught in a treetop. She hovered above my head, looked at the falcon and then at my hand, folded her wings, and dropped to my fist.

"I saw that!" a voice said. I spun around to see a young man about my own age, shivering at the edge of the woods.

"You're the wild boy, aren't you?"

I was so astonished to see a human being in all this cold thawing silence that I just stood and looked at him. When I gathered my wits I replied. "No, I'm just a citizen."

"Aw, gee," he said with disappointment. Then he gave in to the cold and shivered until the twigs around him rattled. He stepped forward.

"Well, anyway, I'm Matt Spell. I work after school on the Poughkeepsie *New Yorker,* a newspaper. I read all the stories about the wild boy who lives in the Catskills, and I thought that if I found him and got a good story, I might get to be a reporter. Have you ever run across him? Is there such a boy?"

"Aw, it's all nonsense," I said as I gathered some dry wood and piled it near the edge of the woods. I lit it swiftly, hoping he would not notice the flint and steel. He was so cold and so glad to see the flames that he said nothing.

I rolled a log up to the fire for him and shoved it against a tree that was blocked from the raw biting wind by a stand of hawthorns. He crouched over the flames for a long time, then practically burnt the soles off his shoes warming his feet. He was that miserable.

"Why didn't you dress warmer for this kind of a trip?" I asked. "You'll die up here in this damp cold."

"I think I am dying," he said, sitting so close to the fire, he almost smothered it. He was nice looking, about thirteen or fourteen, I would have said. He had a good bold face, blue eyes, hair about the color of my stream in the thaw. Although he was big, he looked like the kind of fellow who didn't know his own strength. I liked Matt.

"I've still got a sandwich," he said. "Want half?"

"No, thanks," I said. "I brought my lunch." Frightful had been sitting on my shoulder through all this, but now the smoke was bothering her and she hopped to a higher perch. I still had her on the leash.

"There was a bird on your shoulder," Matt said. "He had nice eyes. Do you know him?"

"I'm sort of an amateur falconer," I replied. "I come up here to train my bird. It's a she—Frightful is her name."

"Does she catch anything?"

"Now and then. How hungry are you?" I asked as his second bite finished the sandwich.

"I'm starved; but don't share your lunch. I have some money, just tell me which road takes you toward Delhi."

I stood up and whistled to Frightful. She flew down. I undid her leash from her jesses. I stroked her head for a moment; then threw her into the air and walked out into the field, kicking the brush as I went.

I had noticed a lot of rabbit tracks earlier, and followed them over the muddy earth as best I could. I kicked up a rabbit and with a twist Frightful dropped out of the sky and took it.

Roast rabbit is marvelous under any conditions, but when you're cold and hungry it is superb. Matt enjoyed every bite. I worked on a small portion to be sociable, for I was not especially hungry. I dared not offer him the walnuts in my pocket, for too much had been written about that boy living off nuts.

"My whole circulatory system thanks you," Matt

said. He meant it, for his hands and feet were now warm, and the blue color had left his lips and was replaced by a good warm red.

"By the way, what's your name?"

"Sam. Sam Gribley," I said.

"Sam, if I could borrow a coat from you, I think I could make it to the bus station without freezing to death. I sure didn't think it would be so much colder in the mountains. I could mail it back to you."

"Well," I hesitated, "my house is pretty far from here. I live on the Gribley farm and just come down here now and then to hunt with the falcon; but maybe we could find an old horse blanket or something in one of the deserted barns around here."

"Aw, never mind, Sam. I'll run to keep warm. Have you any ideas about this wild boy—seen anyone that you think the stories might be referring to?"

"Let's start toward the road," I said as I stamped out the fire. I wound him through the forest until I was dizzy and he was lost, then headed for the road. At the edge of the woods I said, "Matt, I have seen that boy."

Matt Spell stopped.

"Gee, Sam, tell me about him." I could hear paper rattle, and saw that Matt's cold hands were not too stiff to write in his notebook.

We walked down the road a bit and then I said, "Well, he ran away from home one day and never went back."

"Where does he live? What does he wear?"

We sat down on a stone along the edge of the road. It was behind a pine tree, and out of the ripping wind.

"He lives west of here in a cave. He wears a bearskin coat, has long hair—all matted and full of burrs—and according to him he fishes for a living."

"You've talked to him?" he asked brightly.

"Oh, yes, I talk to him."

"Oh, this is great!" He wrote furiously. "What color are his eyes?"

"I think they are bluish gray, with a little brown in them."

"His hair?"

"Darkish—I couldn't really tell under all those coon tails."

"Coon tails? Do you suppose he killed them himself?"

"No. It looked more like one of those hats you get with cereal box tops."

"Well, I won't say anything about it then; just, coontail hat."

"Yeah, coon-tail hat's enough," I agreed. "And I think his shoes were just newspapers tied around his feet. That's good insulation, you know."

"Yeah?" Matt wrote that down.

"Did he say why he ran away?"

"I never asked him. Why does any boy run away?"

Matt put down his pencil and thought. "Well, I ran

away once because I thought how sorry everybody would be when I was gone. How they'd cry and wish they'd been nicer to me." He laughed.

Then I said, "I ran away once because . . . well, because I wanted to do something else."

"That's a good reason," said Matt. "Do you suppose that's why . . . by the way, what is his name?"

"I never asked him," I said truthfully.

"What do you suppose he really eats and lives on?" asked Matt.

"Fish, roots, berries, nuts, rabbits. There's a lot of food around the woods if you look for it, I guess."

"Roots? Roots wouldn't be good."

"Well, carrots are roots."

"By golly, they are; and so are potatoes, sort of. Fish?" pondered Matt, "I suppose there are lots of fish around here."

"The streams are full of them."

"You've really seen him, huh? He really is in these mountains?"

"Sure, I've seen him," I said. Finally I stood up.

"I gotta get home. I go the other way. You just follow this road to the town, and I think you can get a bus from there."

"Now, wait," he said. "Let me read it back to you to check the details."

"Sure."

Matt stood up, blew on his hands and read: "The wild

boy of the Catskills does exist. He has dark brown hair, black eyes, and wears a handsome deerskin suit that he apparently made himself. He is ruddy and in excellent health and is able to build a fire with flint and steel as fast as a man can light a match.

"His actual dwelling is a secret, but his means of support is a beautiful falcon. The falcon flies off the boy's fist, and kills rabbits and pheasants when the boy needs food. He only takes what he needs. The boy's name is not known, but he ran away from home and never went back."

"No, Matt, no," I begged.

I was about to wrestle it out with him when he said furtively, "I'll make a deal with you. Let me spend my spring vacation with you and I won't print a word of it. I'll write only what you've told me."

I looked at him and decided that it might be nice to have him. I said, "I'll meet you outside town any day you say, providing you let me blindfold you and lead you to my home and providing you promise not to have a lot of photographers hiding in the woods. Do you know what would happen if you told on me?"

"Sure, the newsreels would roll up, the TV cameras would arrive, reporters would hang in the trees, and you'd be famous."

"Yes, and back in New York City."

"I'll write what you said and not even your mother will recognize you."

"Make it some other town, and it's a deal," I said. "You might say I am working for Civil Defense doing research by learning to live off the land. Tell them not to be afraid, that crayfish are delicious and caves are warm."

Matt liked that. He sat down again. "Tell me some of the plants and animals you eat so that they will know what to do. We can make this informative."

I sat down, and listed some of the better wild plants and the more easily obtainable mammals and fish. I gave him a few good recipes and told him that I didn't recommend anyone trying to live off the land unless they liked oysters and spinach.

Matt liked that. He wrote and wrote. Finally he said, "My hands are cold. I'd better go. But I'll see you on April twelfth at three-thirty outside of town. Okay? And just to prove that I'm a man of my word, I'll bring you a copy of what I write."

"Well, you better not give me away. I have a scout in civilization who follows all these stories."

We shook hands and he departed at a brisk pace.

I returned to my patch on the mountain, talking to myself all the way. I talk to myself a lot, but everyone does. The human being, even in the midst of people, spends nine-tenths of his time alone with the private voices of his own head. Living alone on a mountain is not much different, except that your speaking voice gets rusty. I talked inside my head all the way home, think-

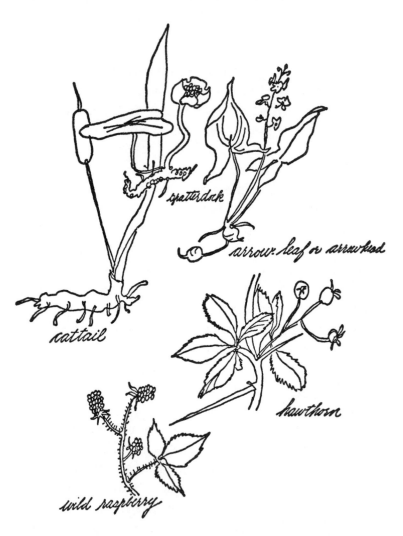

spatterdock

arrow-leaf or arrowhead

cattail

hawthorn

wild raspberry

ing up schemes, holding conversations with Bando and Dad and Matt Spell. I worded the article for Matt after discussing it with Bando, and made it sound very convincing without giving myself up. I kind of wanted to write it down and send it to Matt, but I didn't.

I entered my tree, tied Frightful to the bedpost, and there was Jessie Coon James. It had been months since I'd seen him. He was curled up on my bed, asleep. A turtle shell that had been full of cracked walnuts was empty beside him. He awoke, jumped to the floor, and walked slowly between my legs and out the door. I had the feeling Jessie was hoping I had departed for good and that he could have my den. He was a comfort-loving creature. I was bigger and my hands were freer than his, so he conceded me the den. I watched him climb over The Baron's rock and shinny up a hemlock. He moved heavily into the limbs, and it occurred to me that Jessie was a she-Jessie, not a he-Jessie.

I cooked supper, and then sat down by my little fire and called a forum. It is very sociable inside my head, and I have perfected the art of getting a lot of people arguing together in silence or in a forum, as I prefer to call it. I can get four people all talking at once, and a fifth can be present, but generally I can't get him to talk. Usually these forums discuss such things as a storm and whether or not it is coming, how to make a spring suit, and how to enlarge my house without destroying the life in the tree. Tonight, however, they discussed what to do about Matt Spell. Dad kept telling me to go right down to the city and make sure he published nothing, not even a made-up story. Bando said, no, it's all right, he still doesn't know where you live; and then Matt walked into the conversation and said that he wanted to spend his spring vacation with me, and that he promised not to do anything untoward. Matt kept using "untoward"—I don't know where he got that expression, but he liked it and kept using it—that's how I knew Matt was speaking; everything was "untoward."

That night I fell asleep with all these people discussing the probability of my being found and hauled back to the city. Suddenly Frightful broke into the conversation. She said, "Don't let that Matt come up here. He eats too much." That was the first time that Frightful had ever talked in a forum. I was delighted, for I was always sure that she had more to say than a few cries. She had not missed Matt's appetite.

The forum dissolved in a good humor, everyone being delighted with Frightful. I lifted my head to look at her. She had her beak in the feathers of her back, sound asleep.

She spoke in my head, however, and said, "You really want to be found, or you would not have told Matt all you did."

"I like you better when you don't talk," I said, pulled the deer hide over me, and fell into a deep sleep.

IN WHICH
I Cooperate with the Ending

By the middle of March I could have told you it was
spring without looking. Jessie did not come around anymore, she was fishing the rewarding waters of the open
stream, she was returning to a tree hollow full of babies.
The Baron Weasel did not come by. There were sala-
manders and frogs to keep him busy. The chickadees
sang alone, not in a winter group, and the skunks and
minks and foxes found food more abundant in the forest
than at my tree house. The circumstances that had
brought us all together in the winter were no more.
There was food on the land and the snow was slipping
away.

watercress

By April I was no longer living off my storehouse.
There were bulbs, tubers, and greens to be had. Meals
were varied once more. There were frogs' legs, eggs, and
turtle soup on my table.

I took my baths in the spring again rather than in the
turtle shell with warmed-over snow. I plunged regularly

into the ice water of the spring—shouting as my breath was grabbed from my lungs. I scrubbed, ran for my tree, and dried myself before the fire, shouting as I stepped into my clothes. Then I would sing. I made up a lot of nice songs after my bath, one of which I taught to a man who was hiking along the top of the gorge one day.

He said his name was Aaron, and he was quiet and tall. I found him sitting on the edge of the cliff, looking across the valley. He was humming little tunes. He had a sad smile that never went away. I knew I would not have to hide from him just by looking at him, so I walked up and sat down beside him. I taught him my "cold water song."

I learned he wrote songs and that he was from New York. He had come to the Catskills for the Passover festivities and had wandered off for the day. He was about to go back when I sat down and said, "I heard you humming."

"Yes," he said. "I hum a good deal. Can you hum?"

"Yes," I replied, "I can hum. I hum a good deal, too, and even sing, especially when I get out of the spring in the morning. Then I really sing aloud."

"Let's hear you sing aloud."

So I said, feeling very relaxed with the sun shining on my head, "All right, I'll sing you my cold water song."

"I like that," Aaron said. "Sing it again." So I did.

"Let me suggest a few changes." He changed a few words to fit the tune and the tune to fit the words, and then we both sang it.

"Mind if I use the hum hum hum dee dee part?" he asked presently.

"You can use it all," I said. "Tunes are free up here. I got that from the red-eyed vireo."

He sat up and said, "What other songs are sung up here?"

I whistled him the "hi-chickadee" song of the black-capped Mr. Bracket; and the waterfall song of the wood thrush. He took out a card, lined it with five lines, and wrote in little marks. I stretched back in the sun and hummed the song of the brown thrasher and of Barometer, the nuthatch. Then I boomed out the song of the great horned owl and stopped.

"That's enough, isn't it?" I asked.

"I guess so." He lay back and stretched, looked into the leaves, and said, "If I do something with this, I'll come back and play it to you. I'll bring my portable organ."

"Fine," I said.

Then, after a drowsy pause, he said, "Will you be around these parts this summer?"

"I'll be around," I said. Aaron fell asleep, and I rolled over in the sun. I liked him. He hadn't asked me one personal question. Oddly enough, I wasn't sure whether that made me glad or not. Then I thought of the words Frightful had spoken in my head. "You want to be found," and I began to wonder. I had sought out a human being. This would not have happened a year ago.

I fell asleep. When I awoke, Aaron was gone and

Frightful was circling me. She saw me stir, swooped in, and sat on a rock beside me. I said, "Hi," but did not get up, just lay still listening to the birds, the snips and sputs of insects moving in the dry leaves, and the air stirring the newly leafing trees. Nothing went on in my head. It was comfortably blank. I knew the pleasures of the lizard on the log who knows where his next meal is coming from. I also knew his boredom. After an hour I did have a thought. Aaron had said that he was up in the Catskills for Passover. Then it must also be near Easter, and Matt would be coming soon. I had not counted notches in weeks.

A cool shadow crossed my face and I arose, whistled for Frightful to come to my hand, and wandered slowly home, stuffing my pockets with spring beauty bulbs as I went.

Several days later I met Matt on Route 27 at three-thirty. I tied his handkerchief around his eyes and led him, stumbling and tripping, up the mountain. I went almost directly home. I guess I didn't much care if he remembered how to get there or not. When I took off the blindfold, he looked around.

"Where are we? Where's your house?" I sat down and motioned him to sit. He did so with great willingness—in fact, he flopped.

"What do you sleep on, the ground?"

I pointed to the deerskin flaps moving in the wind in the hemlock.

"Whatdaya do, live in a tree?"

"Yep."

Matt bounced to his feet and we went in. I propped the door open so that the light streamed in, and he shouted with joy. I lit the tallow candle and we went over everything, and each invention he viewed with a shout.

While I prepared trout baked in wild grape leaves, Matt sat on the bed and told me the world news in brief. I listened with care to the trouble in Europe, the trouble in the Far East, the trouble in the south, and the trouble in America. Also to a few sensational murders, some ball scores, and his report card.

"It all proves my point," I said sagely. "People live too close together."

"Is that why you are here?"

"Well, not exactly. The main reason is that I don't like to be dependent, particularly on electricity, rails, steam, oil, coal, machines, and all those things that can go wrong."

"Well, is that why you are up here?"

"Well, not exactly. Some men climbed Mount Everest because it was there. Here is a wilderness."

"Is that why?"

"Aw, come on, Matt. See that falcon? Hear those white-throated sparrows? Smell that skunk? Well, the falcon takes the sky, the white-throated sparrow takes the low bushes, the skunk takes the earth, you take the newspaper office, I take the woods."

"Don't you get lonely?"

"Lonely? I've hardly had a quiet moment since arriving. Stop being a reporter and let's eat. Besides, there are people in the city who are lonelier than I."

"Okay. Let's eat. This is good, darned good; in fact, the best meal I've ever eaten." He ate and stopped asking questions.

We spent the next week fishing, hunting, trapping, gathering greens and bulbs. Matt talked less and less, slept, hiked, and pondered. He also ate well, and kept Frightful very busy. He made himself a pair of moccasins out of deer hide, and a hat that I can't even describe. We didn't have a mirror so he never knew how it looked, but I can say this: when I happened to meet him as we came fishing along a stream bed, I was always startled. I never did get used to that hat.

Toward the end of the week, who should we find sleeping in my bed after returning from a fishing trip, but Bando! Spring vacation, he said. That night we played our reed whistles for Matt, by an outdoor fire. It was that warm. Matt and Bando also decided to make a guest house out of one of the other trees. I said "Yes, let's" because I felt that way, although I knew what it meant.

A guest house meant I was no longer a runaway. I was no longer hiding in the wilderness. I was living in the woods like anyone else lives in a house. People drop by, neighbors come for dinner, there are three meals to get, the shopping to do, the cleaning to accomplish. I felt exactly as I felt when I was home. The only differ-

ence was that I was a little harder to visit out here, but
not too hard. There sat Matt and Bando.

We all burned and dug out another hemlock. I worked
with them, wondering what was happening to me. Why

didn't I cry "No"? What made me happily build a city in the forest—because that is what we were doing.

When the tree was done, Bando had discovered that the sap was running in willow trees and the limbs were just right for slide whistles. He spent the evening making us trombones. We played them together. That word *together*. Maybe that was the answer to the city.

Matt said rather uncomfortably just before bedtime, "There may be some photographers in these hills."

"Matt!" I hardly protested. "What did you write?"

It was Bando who pulled out the article.

He read it, a few follow-ups, and comments from many other papers. Then he leaned back against his leaning tree, as it had come to be, and puffed silently on his pipe.

"Let's face it, Thoreau; you can't live in America today and be quietly different. If you are going to be different, you are going to stand out, and people are going to hear about you; and in your case, if they hear about you, they will remove you to the city or move to you and you won't be different anymore." A pause.

"Did the owls nest, Thoreau?"

I told him about the owls and how the young played around the hemlock, and then we went to bed a little sad—all of us. Time was running out.

Matt had to return to school, and Bando stayed on to help burn out another tree for another guest house. We chopped off the blackened wood, made one bed, and started the second before he had to return to his teaching.

I wasn't alone long. Mr. Jacket found me.

I was out on the raft trying to catch an enormous snapping turtle. It would take my line, but when I got its head above water, it would eye me with those cold ancient eyes and let go. Frightful was nearby. I was making a noose to throw over the turtle's head the next time it surfaced when Frightful lit on my shoulder with a thud and a hard grip. She was drawn up and tense, which in her language said "people," so I wasn't surprised to hear a voice call from across the stream, "Hi, Daniel Boone. What are you doing?" There stood Mr. Jacket.

"I am trying to get this whale of a snapper," I said in such an ordinary voice that it was dull.

I went on with the noose making, and he called to me, "Hit it with a club."

I still couldn't catch the old tiger, so I rafted to shore and got Mr. Jacket. About an hour later we had the turtle, had cleaned it, and I knew that Mr. Jacket was Tom Sidler.

"Come on up to the house," I said, and he came on up to the house, and it was just like after school on Third Avenue. He wanted to see everything, of course, and he did think it unusual, but he got over it in a hurry and settled down to helping me prepare the meat for turtle soup.

He dug the onions for it while I got it boiling in a tin can. Turtle is as tough as rock and has to be boiled for hours before it gets tender. We flavored the soup with hickory salt, and cut a lot of Solomon's seal tubers into it. Tom said it was too thin, and I thickened it with mashed up nuts—I had run out of acorn flour. I tried some orris root in it—pretty fair.

"Wanta stay and eat it and spend the night?" I asked him somewhere along the way. He said, "Sure," but added that he had better go home and tell his mother. It took him about two hours to get back and the turtle was still tough, so we went out to the meadow to fly Frightful. She caught her own meal, we tied her to her perch, and climbed in the gorge until almost dark. We ate turtle soup. Tom slept in the guest tree.

I lay awake wondering what had happened. Everything seemed so everyday.

I liked Tom and he liked me, and he came up often, almost every weekend. He told me about his bowling team and some of his friends, and I began to feel I knew a lot of people in the town below the mountain. This made my wilderness small. When Tom left one weekend I wrote this down:

"Tom said that he and Reed went into an empty house, and when they heard the real estate man come in, they slid down the laundry chute to the basement and crawled out the basement window. He said a water main broke and flooded the school grounds and all the kids took off their shoes and played baseball in it."

I drew a line through all this and then I wrote:

"I haven't seen The Baron Weasel. I think he has deserted his den by the boulder. A catbird is nesting nearby. Apparently it has learned that Frightful is tied some of the time, because it comes right up to the fireplace for scraps when the leash is snapped."

I drew a line through this too, and filled up the rest of the piece of bark with a drawing of Frightful.

I went to the library the next day and took out four books.

Aaron came back. He came right to the hemlock forest and called. I didn't ask him how he knew I was there. He stayed a week, mostly puttering around with the willow whistles. He never asked what I was doing on the mountain. It was as if he already knew. As if he had talked to someone, or read something, and there was nothing more to question. I had the feeling that I was an old story somewhere beyond the foot of the mountain. I didn't care.

Bando got a car and he came up more often. He never mentioned any more newspaper stories, and I never asked him. I just said to him one day, "I seem to have an address now."

He said, "You do."

I said, "Is it Broadway and Forty-second Street?"

He said, "Almost." His eyebrows knitted and he looked at me sadly.

"It's all right, Bando. Maybe you'd better bring me a shirt and some blue jeans when you come next time. I was thinking, if they haven't sold that house in town, maybe Tom and I could slide down the laundry chute."

Bando slowly turned a willow whistle over in his hands. He didn't play it.

IN WHICH
The City Comes to Me

The warblers arrived, the trees turned summer green, and June burst over the mountain. It smelled good, tasted good, and was gentle to the eyes.

I was stretched out on the big rock in the meadow one morning. Frightful was jabbing at some insect in the grass below me when suddenly a flashbulb exploded and a man appeared.

"Wild boy!" he said, and took another picture. "What are you doing, eating nuts?"

I sat up. My heart was heavy. It was so heavy that I posed for him holding Frightful on my fist. I refused to take him to my tree, however, and he finally left. Two other photographers came, and a reporter. I talked a little. When they left, I rolled over on my stomach and wondered if I could get in touch with the Department of Interior and find out more about the public lands in the West. My next thought was the baseball game in the flooded school yard.

Four days passed, and I talked to many reporters and photographers. At noon of the fifth day a voice called from the glen: "I know you are there!"

"Dad!" I shouted, and once again burst down the mountainside to see my father.

As I ran toward him, I heard sounds that stopped me. The sound of branches and twigs breaking, of the flowers being crushed. Hordes were coming. For a long moment I stood wondering whether to meet Dad or run forever. I was self-sufficient, I could travel the world over, never needing a penny, never asking anything of anyone. I could cross to Asia in a canoe via the Bering Strait. I could raft to an island. I could go around the world on the fruits of the land. I started to run. I got as far as the gorge and turned back. I wanted to see Dad.

I walked down the mountain to greet him and to face the people he had brought from the city to photograph me, interview me, and bring me home. I walked slowly, knowing that it was all over. I could hear the voices of the other people. They filled my silent mountain.

Then I jumped in the air and laughed for joy. I recognized my four-year-old brother's pleasure song. The family! Dad had brought the family! Every one of them. I ran, twisting and turning through the trees like a Cooper's hawk, and occasionally riding a free fifty feet downhill on an aspen sapling.

"Dad! Mom!" I shouted as I came upon them along the streambed, carefully picking their way through raspberry bushes. Dad gave me a resounding slap and Mother hugged me until she cried.

John jumped on me. Jim threw me into the rushes. Mary sat on me. Alice put leaves in my hair. Hank pulled Jim off. Joan pulled me to my feet, and Jake bit my ankle. That cute little baby sister toddled away from me and cried.

"Wow! All of New York!" I said. "This is a great day for the Katerskills."

I led them proudly up the mountain, thinking about dinner and what I had that would go around. I knew how Mother felt when we brought in friends for dinner.

As we approached the hemlock grove, I noticed that Dad was carrying a pack. He explained it as food for the first few days, or until I could teach John, Jim, Hank, and Jake how to live off the land. I winked at him.

"But, Dad, a Gribley is not for the land."

"What do you mean?" he shouted. "The Gribleys have had land for three generations. We pioneer, we open the land." He was almost singing.

"And then we go to sea," I said.

"Things have changed. Child labor laws; you can't take children to sea."

I should have glowed over such a confession from Dad had I not been making furious plans as we climbed; food, beds, chores. Dad, however, had had since Christmas to outplan me. He strung up hammocks for everyone all through the forest, and you never heard a happier bunch of kids. The singing and shouting and giggling sent the birds and wildlife deeper into the shadows. Even little Nina had a hammock, and though she was only a toddler, she cooed and giggled all by herself as she rocked between two aspens near the meadow. We ate Mother's fried chicken. Chicken is good, it tastes like chicken.

I shall never forget that evening.

And I shall never forget what Dad said, "Son, when I told your mother where you were, she said, 'Well, if he doesn't want to come home, then we will bring home to him.' And that's why we are all here."

I was stunned. I was beginning to realize that this was not an overnight camping trip, but a permanent arrangement. Mother saw my expression and said, "When you are of age, you can go wherever you please. Until then, I still have to take care of you, according to all the law I can find." She put her arm around me, and we rocked ever so slightly. "Besides, I am not a Gribley. I am a Stuart, and the Stuarts loved the land." She looked at the mountain and the meadow and the gorge, and

I felt her feet squeeze into the earth and take root.

The next day I took John, Jim, and Hank out into the mountain meadows with Frightful to see if we could not round up enough food to feed this city of people. We did pretty well.

When we came back, there was Dad with four four-by-fours, erected at the edge of my meadow, and a pile of wood that would have covered a barn.

"Gosh, Dad," I cried, "what on earth are you doing?"

"We are going to have a house," he said.

I was stunned and hurt.

"A house! You'll spoil everything!" I protested. "Can't we all live in trees and hammocks?"

"No. Your mother said that she was going to give you a decent home, and in her way of looking at it, that means a roof and doors. She got awfully mad at those newspaper stories inferring that she had not done her duty."

"But she did." I was almost at the point of tears. "She's a swell mother. What other boy has a mother who would let him do what I did?"

"I know. I know. But a woman lives among her neighbors. Your mother took all those editorials personally, as if they were Mr. Bracket and Mrs. O'Brien speaking. The nation became her neighbors, and no one, not even—" He hesitated. A catbird meowed. "Not even that catbird is going to think that she neglected you."

I was about to protest in a loud strong voice when Mother's arm slipped around my shoulder.

"That's how it is until you are eighteen, Sam," she said. And that ended it.

On the Far Side of the Mountain

adirondack mountains

Helderberg mountains

The far side of
my mountain

batskill
mountains

tree
mill
+ garden

meadow

Bando

mrs. Strawberry's
farm
(mrs. Fielder)

On *the* Far Side
of the Mountain

written and illustrated by

JEAN
CRAIGHEAD
GEORGE

DUTTON

CHILDREN'S

BOOKS

New York

Library of Congress Cataloging-in-Publication Data

George, Jean Craighead, date
On the far side of the mountain/by Jean Craighead George.
—1st ed.   p. cm.
Summary: Sam's peaceful existence in his wilderness home
is disrupted when his sister runs away and his pet falcon is
confiscated by a conservation officer.
ISBN: 0-525-46348-8
[1. Wilderness survival—Fiction.   2. Brothers and sisters—Fiction.
3. Falcons—Fiction.]   I. Title   89-25988   CIP   AC
PZ7.G29330n   1990
[Fic]—dc20

Published in the United States by Dutton Children's Books,
a division of Penguin Young Readers Group
345 Hudson Street, New York, New York 10014
Printed in the U.S.A.   First edition
10 9 8 7 6

Contents

IN WHICH
A Storm Breaks

This June morning is hot and humid with a haze so dense I can barely see the huge hemlock tree in which I live. I like the haze. It has erased all but the great tree trunks, making my mountaintop home as simple as it was when I first came here more than two years ago.

I lean back in the lounging chair I constructed from bent saplings held together with rope made from the inner bark of the basswood tree, and enjoy the primitive forest.

A wind rises as the sun warms the earth. The haze moves off, and I see my pond, my millhouse, and the root cellar. The first year I lived here I had only a tree, a bed, and a fireplace. But one idea led to another, and the next thing I knew, I had built myself a habitat. Things just kept evolving. Take this lounging chair, for instance. One day I replaced the old stump I sat on with a three-legged stool, and then I replaced the three-legged stool with this comfortable chair.

The people changed, too. At first I was alone. Then

my family arrived and—except for my lively sister, Alice—departed. I don't know where Alice is this morning. She was going to go strawberry picking, but the haze is too dense for that. Maybe she's sitting on the porch of her tree house talking to herself just as I am. A haze mutes not only the birds and beasts, but people, too.

As a hot dry wind clears the air, I can see Frightful, my peregrine falcon, sitting in front of the six-foot-in-diameter hemlock tree that I hollowed out for a home. Unlike the chairs and people, Frightful has not changed. She still holds her body straight up and down and her head high in the manner of the peregrine falcon. Her tawny breast is decorated with black marks; her back is gray blue; her head black. When she flies, she is still a crossbow in the sky, and she still "waits on" above my head until I kick up a pheasant or a rabbit. Then she stoops, speeding toward her prey at two hundred miles an hour, the fastest animal on earth. She almost never misses.

"Hello, Frightful," I say.

"Creee, creee, creee, car-reet," she answers. That is her name for me, "Creee, creee, creee, car-reet." All peregrine falcons call the high-pitched *creees,* but when Frightful sees me in the morning or when I return from the forest, even when she is flying high above my head, she adds "car-reet." "Hello, Sam," she is saying.

She is perched on a T-block that I covered with deer-hide to protect her feet. She lifts a broad foot and scratches her head with a curved claw on the end of a long, narrow toe.

"Creee, creee, creee, car-reet."

I call her name in her own language; I whistle three notes—low, high, low. She responds by lifting the feathers on her body, then shaking them. This is called *rousing*, which is feather talk meaning "I like you." I can't speak in feathers so I answer by imitating her love notes. I do this by pulling air through my two front teeth to make a soft, cozy sound.

Sometimes I have nightmares that she has left me. I awake in a sweat and try to reason with myself. Frightful will not leave me, I say. If she were going to do that, she would have departed last spring when I was flying her free. A wild tercel, the male peregrine falcon, passed overhead. The last of the vanishing eastern peregrine falcons breed in Greenland and Canada, and a few winter as far south as the Catskills. This one was on his way to his home in the north. Frightful playfully joined him. Together they performed the peregrine courtship dance, swooping low, zooming high, then spiralling earthward. I was scared. I thought Frightful was going to leave me. I whistled. She instantly pulled deeply on her wings and sped back. Within a few feet of my outstretched hand, she braked and alighted on my glove as softly as the fluff from a dandelion seed. "Creee, creee, creee, car-reet," she said. "Hello, Frightful," I answered happily.

Now, I whistle her name again. She turns her head and looks at me. Her curved, flesh-ripping beak looks sweet and demure when you see her head on. Her over-hanging brow shades large black eyes that are outlined in white feathers. She is a gorgeous creature.

At peace with me and herself, she bobs her head as she follows the flight of a bird. I cannot see it, but I know it's a bird because Frightful's feathers tell me so. She has flattened most of them to her body while lifting those between her shoulders. "Bird," that means. "Human" is feathers flattened, eyes wide, neck pulled in, wings drooped to fly.

I get to my feet. I have daydreamed enough. While the last of the haze burns off, I weed the meadow garden and split kindling before returning to my tree.

A hot sun now filters down through the lacy needles of the hemlocks in my grove. I look for Alice, wonder-ing what she's up to. That's how one thinks of Alice—what is she up to? She's probably gone downmountain to the farm to see that pig she talks to.

Sticks snap in the distance. Someone is coming. Frightful has clamped her feathers to her body to say that whoever it is is not a friend. Her feathers read "danger." The phoebe clicks out his alarm cry and I tense. I have learned to heed these warning signals. The birds and animals see, hear, smell, and feel approaching danger long before I do. I press my ear to the ground and hear footsteps. They are heavy: possibly a black bear.

I smell the musky scent of warning from my friend
Baron Weasel. The Baron, who was living here when I
arrived, considers himself the real owner of the mountaintop, but because he finds me interesting, he lets me
stay.

Right now he doesn't like what's coming and dives into his den under the boulder. I glance at Frightful again.

Her feathers are flattened to her body, her eyes wide, neck stretched, and her wings are lowered for flight. "Human," she is saying. I wait.

A man in a green uniform rounds the bend, sees me, and hesitates as if uncertain.

"Hello," I say aloud, and to myself: Here it comes. He's some official. I've got to go to school this fall. Dad didn't pay the taxes on the farm. Alice is up to something again.

"Do you know where Sam Gribley lives?" he asks.

"Here," I answer. "I'm Sam Gribley."

"Oh," he says and glances at my face, then my berry-dyed T-shirt, and finally, my moccasins. These seem to confuse him. Apparently he is not expecting a teenager.

Suddenly he looks over my shoulder and walks past me. I spin around to see him standing before Frightful.

"My name is Leon Longbridge," he says with his back to me. "I'm the conservation officer. You're harboring an endangered species—a peregrine falcon."

I am unable to speak.

"Keeping an endangered species carries a fine and a year's imprisonment."

"I didn't know that." He faces me.

"You should have, but since you didn't, I won't arrest you. But I will have to confiscate the bird."

I can't believe what I am hearing.

"I'll let her go," I say. "I'll turn her free." I step between my bird and the man. "Won't everything be all right if she's free?"

"No," he snaps. "I'm a falconer, too. You set her loose, and as soon as I'm gone, you'll whistle and she'll come right back." He walks up to her and places his gloved hand under her breast. She steps up on it as she has been trained to do.

With a twist of his wrist he slips a hood over her head and tightens the drawstrings with his teeth and free hand. He is a falconer, I see, and a good one. My knees feel rubbery.

Frightful sits quietly. She cannot see, so she does not move, which is the reason for a hood. If a falcon is hooded she will not bate, that is, she won't fly off your fist and hang head down by her jesses, beating her wings and hurting herself.

"What will you do with her?" I ask.

"How old was she when you got her?"

"About ten days."

"Then I can't let her go. She's imprinted on you. If you raise a bird from a chick, it thinks you're its mother and that it looks like you. Such a bird won't mate with its kind, because it sees people as its kind. Set free it is worthless as far as the perpetuation of the species is concerned. And perpetuation of the species is what protecting endangered animals is all about—to let them breed and increase their kind.

"No hunger streaks," he comments as he turns

Frightful on his fist and looks her over. "I must say, you take good care of your bird for a kid." Hunger streaks appear in tail and wing feathers if a bird does not get the right food during the time the feathers are growing in.

I am thinking what to do. Mr. Longbridge has wrapped the leash tightly around his hand and now begins to move.

I walk beside him, desperately working out a plan to save her.

I try pity. "Sir, I need that bird badly. I hunt with her. She provides food for my table."

"There's a supermarket in Delhi," he says, hurrying along. I hurry along, too.

I try politeness. "Please, sir, let her go."

"You heard me."

The sun now shines out of a hazeless sky, and I can see his face more clearly. He has bony cheeks, a long nose, and heavy brows. Dark crow's-feet mark the corners of his eyes.

I try reason. "Sir, you say you can't let her go because she won't breed. If she is useless, I might as well keep her. She's useful to me."

"She'll be bred in captivity."

"But how, if she won't mate?"

"Artificial insemination. The university has a very successful artificial breeding program for endangered birds of prey." He is holding Frightful out from his body; I reach out to grab her. He sees me move and draws Frightful against his chest. I can't reach her.

I try philosophy. "But captive birds are not really birds. A bird must be part of the landscape and sky to be complete."

"Her young will be returned to the wild," he replies. "The juveniles are hacked to freedom."

He really is a falconer. *Hack* is an old falconry term. Trainers put young unleashed birds who are just learning to fly and hunt on a hack board, a sort of artificial nest. They leave them there with food, just as the parents do at the nest. The youngsters, falconers say, are "at hack"—free to fly and hunt. If they miss their prey, they come back to the board to eat. After a juvenile makes its first kill, the falconers leash and train it. I guess Frightful's young would be put at hack, but not jessed and leashed when they learned to hunt. Instead, they would fly on and live out their lives in the wild. I ask the officer if that is so.

He ignores me, so I get in front of him and walk backwards while trying to think what to do next.

Pity didn't work. Politeness didn't work. Reason and philosophy failed. I try compassion. "I love that bird. She knows me. We are bonded. She'll die without me."

"She'll adjust. All she needs is the right food."

Walking backwards, I see the color of the officer's eyes. One is brown and the other is blue. I am so fascinated that I lose the perfect opportunity to cut Frightful free, because, in spite of the hood, she bated and hung down, exposing her jesses. But I saw too late.

The officer puts his hand under Frightful's breast and returns her to his fist.

I move closer.

About three inches of leash is exposed. I whip my hunting knife from my pocket and lunge to cut it.

A karate blow to my wrist doubles me over and I stagger backwards.

"You're stealing my property," I shout.

"It's not yours."

"She is." Once I had the idea conservation officers were gentle people—not this one.

"You are harassing and talking back to an officer of the law," he shouts. "I can book you for that, *and* for harboring an endangered species."

We have come to the edge of my meadow, where a trail leads to the bottom of the mountain and the county road where he must have parked his car. He trots down it. I run after him.

Then I think of Alice. I'll call her. If he sees her yellow tufts of hair, her large eyes and bony arms and legs, and if I tell him her life depends on the falcon's catching food, he might make an exception of me and my bird. He would see that I need Frightful to fatten Alice. Adults always want to fatten Alice, even mean adults.

I don't call her. I know her well. If she saw what the officer was doing, she would dive and bite him as she bit the man who was stealing eggs from my old friend Mrs.

Fielder's chicken house. Then we'd really be in trouble, as we were that time. I can only threaten.

"I'm getting a lawyer," I call out.

Mr. Longbridge stops and comes up the mountain a few paces.

"You get a lawyer into this, and you'll go to jail for sure. You're violating the law. I really should arrest you, you know."

He turns and hurries down the trail. I run after him a short distance and give up. The law is the law.

I sink into my lounging chair and put my arms and head on my knees. I'm glad Alice isn't here. I don't have to tell her about Frightful. I need time to be alone.

IN WHICH
The Population Shrinks

Pushing back the deerskin door of my hemlock home, I enter the smoke and minty smelling tree hollow and slump to the pile of furs that replaces my outgrown sapling bed. I put my face down to cry, but no tears come.

After a long while I get up. I have to provide for Alice and myself. I should be making a box trap to catch rabbits, or a deadfall to take a deer. I don't move to do either, for I have no spirit for the jobs. It's almost as if

I am completely helpless without Frightful. I guess I am, so I had better do something to keep myself going.

Walking to my desk, I sit down at the table I built for writing. I look at my clay fireplace, which I now use only for heat and cheeriness, not cooking. I made an elaborate stone stove and oven outside where I bake, grill, and boil.

Stoves, tables, clay fireplace—I keep filling my head with thoughts about these things so I won't think about Frightful.

Reading always clears my mind; I'll try that.

I open my journal, a handsome leather-bound note-book Miss Turner gave me last summer. She said the birch-bark scrolls I used when I first came to the wilderness were too fragile for notes, but I still have them and they are as good as ever.

I thumb through the first pages hoping to find something to distract me, like a sketch of a snare, when I notice gaps in the June entries of last year. Wondering why, I begin reading the June 27 entry.

"Alice, my sister who is two years younger than I am, is going to live on the mountain with me—for better or worse.

"The way I look at it, she's here by default. Mom; Dad; my four brothers, John, Jim, Hank, and Jake; and my four sisters, Alice, Mary, Joan, and Nina climbed up my mountain three weeks ago and announced they were here to stay. Dad was going to plow the abandoned fields, sow seeds, and reap the grain. The boys said they would help build the house from the planks and two-by-fours Dad brought up here for that purpose. Mom and the girls were eager to grow a garden and keep a cow.

"Well, the house never got built. Mrs. Fielder, whom I always call Mrs. Strawberry because she and I gathered wild strawberries the spring I arrived on the mountain, was kind to my family. She offered them rooms in her large old farmhouse until they got started. She's alone and said they would be company for her.

"Hardly had my father borrowed Mrs. Strawberry's horse, Slats, and the plow, and taken them up one side of my meadow and down again, than he knew why his grandfather had abandoned this land. He was not plowing soil. He was plowing rocks. Mrs. Strawberry put it this way. 'If you want to grow stones, Mr. Gribley, this is the place for you. Here in these mountains, stones are our best crop.'

"Next Dad tried to put in a garden. After hours of digging to find soil in my meadow, he gave up. As a last resort he called in a soil conservation officer and conferred with him.

" 'The land's good for trees and wildlife,' he told Dad, 'and maybe a few wild plants that like poor soil—and that's about all.'

"June seventeenth he and Mother climbed the long, hard mountain trail to my home. One look at their faces told me they had not come for sumac tea."

I chuckle as I remember Dad asking me where Alice was—she spent most of her time up here with me—and I told him she was at the spring fiddling with a gadget she had been working on for days.

"Children," Dad said when Alice came down from the spring, "pack up your things. We're going to leave. It's impossible to farm this mountain. Men more skilled than I have tried and failed. If they couldn't do it, it's insane for me to think I can. I'm going back to what I am good at—working on the docks near the sea."

"Well, I'm not going," Alice replied nicely but firmly.

The irises in Alice's eyes look as if they are made of little pieces of blue and white crystal. When she's excited, each piece sparkles. They flashed until I thought they would splinter and crack when she told Dad she wasn't going back to the city.

"I love it here!" she said. "I'm going to stay."

"Indeed, you're not," he answered, much to my relief. I really didn't want to be responsible for a thirteen-year-old. "You're coming back to the city with Sam and the rest of us."

"Is Sam going back?" She turned to me incredulously.

"Of course," Dad answered without thinking. He hesitated. "You will, won't you, Sam?"

"No, sir," I answered. "I don't think I will. I'm doing very well here and love it."

Alice ran to Mother. "Please, let me stay," she whined like a lost puppy.

Mom walked off to think, made up her mind, and came back to me.

"Alice can stay, Sam," she said, "if you think you can support another person. She is far safer here than in the city."

My heart plunged to my toes. This is my home, my mountain, the world I had created all by myself. I needed a little sister like Frightful needed vegetables.

"What about Alice's education?" my father asked, not liking the idea either.

"She can go to correspondence school." Mother answered so promptly that it seemed that she had given this more thought than was apparent at first.

"If kids can live on sailboats going around the world," she said, "and get a good education through correspondence schools, so can Alice."

Dad could not come up with another objection. When Mother had said Alice would be safer in the woods with me than out on the mean streets, she had won.

"But for one year only," he said. Then he winked at me. "Don't worry," he whispered behind his hand. "She won't be here long. Alice gets homesick. She'll be crying like a lamb by tomorrow, and you can bring her home."

In a louder voice he said, "I'm leaving my toolbox and tools at Mrs. Strawberry's for you. I won't be needing them."

"Neither will I," I answered. Tools meant change to me, and I liked my home the way it was.

I should have been proud and happy to know my parents had so much confidence in me that they would leave Alice in my charge, but the truth was that I was peeved. Alice is not your ordinary kid. She can be wonderful company, but—she can also be Alice.

Then Mother and Dad hugged us and promised to write. As I watched them go, I felt a pang of sorrow. Not Alice. They were hardly out of sight before she blew out a breath so long it sounded as if she had been holding it for a year.

With Mom and Dad's farewells still resounding in our ears, Alice took out her Swiss Army knife, with all the gadgets on it—from screwdriver to scissors—and clipped a broken nail. Next, she pulled her socks over her knotty calves, straightened up, and smiled at me.

"Thanks, Sam," she said. "You've just made me the happiest girl in the world." Her eyes crackled.

"And now to finish my plumping mill."

"Your what?"

"I'm making a plumping mill."

"And what is *that*?"

"A plumping mill is a mechanical device run by water power. It lifts a hammer and drops it."

"And?"

"And pounds grains and nuts into flour. I'm tired of grinding acorns, Sam, I really am. So I'm making a machine that will do it for me."

"Where did you learn about a plumping mill?"

"From your librarian friend, Miss Turner, where else? I told her how hard it was to pound acorns into flour for our pancakes; she told me that the first settlers ground their grains with plumping mills."

I was intrigued. "Go on."

"She found a diagram of a plumping mill in one of her books, and I copied it down on paper then made it—come here—I'll show you."

We climbed to the cascade that spills out of the spring, and Alice picked up a four-foot sapling. On one end she had tied a rock, on the other end, a wooden box cut low on one side like a scoop. Two forked limbs, cut and trimmed, had been pounded into the ground near the cascade. A heavy stick lay across them. On top of this Alice laid the sapling on which the box and stone were fastened. She pushed the box under the cascade and arranged the stone so that it was resting on a disc of wood.

The box filled with water, became heavier than the stone, fell, and the stone went up in the air. The box emptied and, now lighter than the stone, went up. The stone plunged down and hit the wood with a thump.

"This is stupendous," I said. But Alice was not smiling, in fact, she was nearly in tears.

"No, it isn't," she wailed. "The sapling creeps off the stick all the time. I have to sit here and hold it on. I might as well pound the acorns myself for all the time it saves."

I kneeled down by the plumping mill and studied it.

"This'll work," I said, seeing the problem. "It'll work just fine." I took out my knife.

While Alice sniffed and wiped tears, I carefully bored a hole through the sapling to which the stone and hammer were attached, then slipped the cross stick into the hole half way. When it balanced, I put the stick in the forks.

"Oh, Sam, that's it. You've done it," Alice said, clapping her hands. "Of course, I remember now. The sapling had a hole in it." She put a handful of boiled acorns on the disc of wood into which she had chipped a bowl. I waded into the stream and stacked the rocks on the cascade to direct the water more forcibly into the box. It filled quickly. The stone went up, the box went down, emptied, and went up. The stone crashed down. The acorns smashed. We had a plumping mill.

Alice and I sat on the bank leisurely watching as the contraption went up and down, up and down, turning acorns into flour.

"Alice," I said. "You've given me a great idea. I'm going to make a water mill. The spring puts out gallons and gallons of water an hour. If I make a dam here," I walked off a line downhill of the spring, "it will fill up this dip in the hill and we'll have a pond almost a quarter-acre big. Water from it would turn a waterwheel. The waterwheel would turn gears. Gears would run saws up and down, and I wouldn't have to cut wood an hour every day.

Alice's plumping mill

"Come on," I said, jumping to my feet. "Let's make a water mill!" I started off to get the lumber once meant for Dad's house, but Alice was not budging. She stood still with her hands on her hips.

"Don't you want to?" I asked.

"First of all I want a house."

"A house?" I said.

This young lady, I realized, was not planning to cry and go home tomorrow.

"Yes," she answered, "a house. I need a place to live. There's not enough room in your tree for me."

"I can sleep outside."

"No, I want a house up in a tree—a tree house, and I want windows and a mirror."

"A mirror?" I said incredulously and wondered how far my parents had gotten.

"I've already put some of Dad's boards up in the big oak tree on the other side of the knoll."

"You've what?"

"I've shoved some of his two-by-fours and a few planks into the white oak. Come see."

She led me past The Baron Weasel's den and down through the woods about fifty yards to the enormous old white oak. It had grown up in the open, probably when that side of the mountain was an Indian field, for its limbs grow horizontally to the ground, not up, as they do when a white oak grows in a forest reaching for the sun. I say Indian field, not great-grandfather's field, because the white oak, like my hemlock, is at least three hundred years old, maybe four. No Gribleys tilled the soil in those days.

As I pushed aside the mountain laurel, I saw three two-by-fours and some planks lying across several of the lower limbs of the tree. The oak, I saw, was a perfect foundation for a tree house.

Alice shinnied up a rope she had made of basswood bark, and I followed.

"It's not very safe," I said as the boards shifted under my feet. "But with Dad's tools, I can fix that."

With that statement, I was committed to change.

I made a few calculations. "With a few more planks, I can make a sturdy platform."

"And then," Alice said. "We'll do like the Ojibway Indians. We'll bend saplings from one side to the other to form a dome—a wigwam—and we'll cover it with bark, just like they did."

I stared at my young sister.

Alice's
tree house

"And," she went on, drawing pictures in the air, "we'll make windows out of glass jars like the first settlers did, and carpet the floor with all those rabbit skins you have so I'll be warm in the winter."

"Anything else?" I asked sarcastically.

"Yes, a porch. And I'd love to have a weather vane on the roof."

"This kid," I had written then, "is definitely not going home soon."

IN WHICH
I Start Over

I turn the pages to find a blank page in my journal for today's events.

"June 17

"It's just a year since Alice moved in and stayed.

"And it's somewhere around three o'clock in the afternoon according to my sundial." I doodle with my pencil for a moment, then go on.

"Frightful was consficated today by the—"

I stop. Putting my arms on the desk and my head on my arms, I see my falcon going down the mountain on the conservation officer's fist.

Presently, I hear the leather hinges on the door of the root cellar squeak as Alice goes in. She doesn't seem to have noticed that Frightful is gone or she would be calling me. I am grateful. I just want to be by myself.

As I listen to Alice's footsteps pass my tree and fade along the path to her tree house, Leon Longbridge comes vividly back to mind. I hear his voice, see his blue eye and brown eye, and suddenly I think of something. Why didn't he show me his badge or some identification? I should think a person confiscating an endangered species would certainly have to show a person his authority to take the bird. Maybe he's not even a conservation officer.

"I'm going to Delhi and ask the sheriff," I say, hoping he isn't and that I can get her back.

I make preparations for the trip by filling my belt pouch with nuts and smoked venison. I never leave my mountaintop without food. Anything can happen to delay me—a twisted ankle, a storm, a trout waiting to be caught.

As I close the root cellar door, I find a piece of paper tucked in one of the leather hinges I made from my brother Jake's old belt. It's a note from Alice. She's always leaving me messages, usually not on paper but in the mud, written in pine needles, or scratched on a leaf. Once she floated a birch-bark note downstream to me while I was fishing.

"I'm thinking waterfalls," this one reads.

That's Alice—tantalizing—"thinking waterfalls." I'm sure she is. Ever since she set foot in the Catskills, she has talked about, and gone out of her way to find, cascades, cataracts, waterfalls, rills, riffles and niagaras.

For whatever reason she's thinking about waterfalls now, I'm glad she is. She's preoccupied and I don't have to tell her about Frightful yet.

I'll tell her in a note. That won't be as difficult as saying it to her face. I won't have to see the sorrow in her eyes or be witness to what she might do.

I return to my desk and tear a sheet out of my journal.

"Dear Alice," I begin.

"It is easier for me to write this than tell it to you. Frightful has been confiscated by the conservation officer. She's an endangered species, and the laws concerning her are rigid. I'm going to Delhi to see if there is anything I can do to get her back. I don't think there is, but it will make me feel better.

"Keep the charcoal going under the fish on the smoking rack. Turn them once more. They ought to be done by late afternoon. Wrap them in maple leaves and store them in the grape vine basket in the root cellar.

Hastily, Sam."

I leave the note on the path to her tree house, check the door on the sluice that carries the water to the waterwheel to make sure it's tightly closed, and depart.

The course I run is straight down the mountain to the county road, where I leave the cool shelter of the woods and trot over the hot asphalt to town. The traffic increases as I near the bridge over Delhi Creek, so I slow down. The heat and stench of exhaust from the cars is almost unbearable and I want to turn back. I don't. I have to know.

Walking here on the streets, I feel conspicuous in my mountain clothes, but I guess I'm not. The summer visitors in Delhi are dressed in old pants and T-shirts, too. I look no stranger than any of them in my moccasins and the jeans my brother Jake gave me when he left. Once I was laughed at when I wore my deerskin clothes to town, but in these clothes no one even notices me. And I wouldn't care if they did. I want to find Leon Longbridge.

I round a corner and pause. The library is to the left, the Delaware county courthouse and sheriff's office are to the right. I strike out for the sheriff's office.

Inside a woman is working at a typewriter. Above the door to another room is a sign reading COUNTY SHERIFF'S OFFICE, and under it is a card saying *Conservation Officer on duty today.* I'll soon know the truth.

"Madam?" My voice squeaks and I clear my throat. "Madam."

"Excuse me a minute," she answers and types on.

Presently, the typing stops. The woman takes off her glasses and smiles.

"I was wondering, madam," I begin, then hesitate as I try to word this just right. "I was wondering, is Mr.— Do you have a conservation officer by the name of Leon Longbridge?"

"Leon Longbridge?" She is scratching a mosquito bite on her neck, and my heart skips a beat, for she looks as if she has never heard of him.

"Oh, yes," she says. "Leon Longbridge is the environmental conservation officer. He just happens to be here today. He has a big territory to cover, so he's usually in the field. You're lucky."

"Can he confiscate an endangered species if somebody has one?"

"Yes, indeed, he can. He can even make arrests. Do you want to see him?"

I swallow hard in disappointment.

"No, thank you."

I walk slowly out the door.

Back on the sidewalk, I move fast, weaving in and out of the strolling people, barely noticing them. I am thinking over and over and over again: There is nothing I can do to get Frightful back. She is gone. She is gone.

Sam, I say to myself as I start across the bridge, you must stop these thoughts and start thinking about what to do now that you have no falcon.

Life, my friend Bando once said, is meeting problems and solving them whether you are an amoeba or a space traveller. I have a problem. I have to provide Alice and myself with meat. Fish, nuts, and vegetables are good and necessary, but they don't provide enough fuel for the hard physical work we do. Although we have venison now, I can't always count on getting it. So far this year, our venison has been only road kill from in front of Mrs. Strawberry's farm.

I decide to take the longest way home, down the flood plain of the West Branch of the Delaware to Spillkill, my own name for a fast stream that cascades down the south face of the mountain range I'm on. I need time to think. Perhaps Alice and I should be like the early Eskimos. We should walk, camp and hunt, and when the seasons change, walk on to new food sources. But I love my tree and my mountaintop.

Another solution would be to become farmers, like the people of the Iroquois Confederacy who once lived here. They settled in villages and planted corn and squash, bush beans and berries. We already grow groundnuts in the damp soil and squash in the poor land. But the Iroquois also hunted game. I can't do that anymore.

I'm back where I started from.

Slowly I climb the Spillkill. As I hop from rock to rock beneath shady basswoods and hemlocks, I hear the cry of the red-tailed hawk who nests on the mountain crest. I am reminded of Frightful and my heart aches. I can almost hear her call my name, Creee, creee, creee, car-reet.

Maybe I can get her back if I plead with the man who is in charge of the peregrines at the university. "But it's the law," he would say. I could write to the president of the United States and ask him to make an exception of

Alice and me. That won't work. The president swore to uphold the Constitution and laws of the United States when he took office.

I climb on. I must stop thinking about the impossible and solve the problem of what to do now. I must find a new way to provide for us. Frightful is going to be in good hands at the university, and she will have young.

I smile at the thought of little Frightfuls and lift my reluctant feet.

When I am far above the river, I take off my clothes and moccasins and bathe in a deep, clear pool until I am refreshed and thinking more clearly. Climbing up the bank, I dress and sit down. I breathe deeply of the mountain air and try to solve my problem more realistically.

Alice and I could raise chickens—no, they're domestic birds and wouldn't look right in the wilderness—pheasant and quail would be better. I put my elbows on my knees and hold my head in both hands. I don't like that idea either. Alice would undoubtedly name them and then we couldn't eat them. You can't eat pets. Alice named that pig she talks to, and now the man who owns it can't butcher it.

Across the rushing stream grows a carpet of dark moss. I wade over to it and lie down in its cool greenery. I can't go back to Alice just yet. I'm not ready to talk about Frightful. I'm just not. I close my eyes.

The leaves above me jangle like wind chimes. The vireos twitter as they carry food to their nestlings. A squirrel family scampers over the leaves, rattling them noisily, which is one of the ways squirrels communicate with each other. It means "I've found a nut crop."

The birdcalls grow more frenzied as twilight approaches. The males are making their last territorial annoucements before darkness falls. The tree frogs start singing, and I open my eyes. I am looking up into the trees.

A limb just above me resembles a shotgun.

"I would never use a gun," I say out loud. I would be forever tied to stores for bullets, and the friendly spirit of my mountaintop would be violated. The birds would not come and sit on my hand, Baron Weasel would move out, and Jessie Coon James would no longer trust me. Something happens to a person when he picks up a gun, and the animals sense it. They depart.

"No guns," I say.

In frustration I pick up a stone and throw it. It flies down the rocky stream bed and forcibly cracks against a boulder.

"Stones," I say. "I'll make a sling."

A sling is the answer. I jump to my feet. Ammunition lies everywhere, and the birds and beasts are not afraid of stones.

No sooner do I solve one problem than I face another. How do you make a sling? Not a slingshot, the forked stick with an elastic band attached to it, but the powerful sling with which David killed Goliath.

I try to remember the pictures I've seen of huge Goliath falling to earth with little David standing beneath him, his sling at his side. I see a short strap with two long cords fastened to both ends. That's all there was to it, I think, also recalling the sling my uncle made when I was a kid. To operate it, a stone is put in the strap; the ends of the strings are held and whirled above the head. When the stone is speeding, it is aimed, one string is released, and the stone zings to its mark.

I should go to the library and ask Miss Turner for a book on how to make a sling, but I can't. I don't want to tell her about Frightful. I don't want to tell anyone.

I find a basswood tree, take out my knife, and cut off several branches. Peeling off the inner bark, I braid it into a tough but slender rope. When I get home, I'll replace the bark rope with rawhide, as that will be more durable. Meanwhile I can practice.

It's almost dark when I fasten two cords to a strap of leather I cut from one of my moccasins. I swing the sling, aim at a tree, and let go. The stone misses by yards.

I think about Alice. I really should get back and tell her; she is the one who will be affected the most by Frightful's confiscation. She may even have to go home to our parents. I get to my feet and start out but sit down again. Alice will cry, or worse, she'll run down the mountain to find Leon Longbridge—and who knows what she'll do then. I think of the merchant who took Slats, the horse, because Mrs. Strawberry hadn't

paid a bill. Alice followed him to the county road and called "Kidnapper!" to the driver of a car that came along. The driver pulled over and stopped. While the merchant was trying to explain himself, Alice got on the horse and rode him back to Mrs. Strawberry.

But I can't face Alice. I'll just spend the night out here. She'll be all right even if I don't come back for days. She has enough food in the root cellar to last a long time, and if she doesn't want to eat smoked fish or venison, she can catch a fresh fish in the millpond. I caught and released some largemouth bass and a batch of bluegills in the pond shortly after it was built. They are big fish now, and Alice is good at fishing. She also knows where the yellowdock and mustard greens grow in case she wants fresh vegetables. I really don't worry about her; she's very resourceful.

As a matter of fact, she probably won't even miss me. When she's working on a project, she gets so involved she doesn't bother to come to my tree for meals. Instead she takes food from the root cellar to her tree house and works while she eats. I didn't see her for two days when she was making a mirror out of a windowpane and some mercury. When I realized she had not bought the mercury but gotten it out of a thermometer she had taken from Mr. Reilly's barn, I made her buy a new one for him with some of the forty dollars I had brought with me from the city and never spent.

When she took it back, she was so embarrassed she could hardly lift her head. Mr. Reilly was very nice about it. He said that he had done something like that when he was a kid.

"Unfortunately," he had said, "most of us have to learn from mistakes. But we do learn. I'll bet you never do this again."

"I won't," Alice had said softly. And I know she never will.

Come to think about it, if anyone is all right tonight, Alice is. Frightful must be terrified and I am miserable, but Alice, I'll bet, is humming and working and probably hasn't even read my note.

I focus on a tree trunk across the stream, twirl the sling over my head, and let a stone fly. I miss again. Discouraged, I lie down on the leafy ground and look up through the foliage at the silent moon.

IN WHICH

A Trade Comes My Way

"*Midday, June 20*

"I'm back. I stayed on the Spillkill three nights practicing with the sling and grieving for Frightful. I got one squirrel, which I brought home to eat. I missed forty times. Not good."

"Hall-oo, the tree! Hall-oo the house!"

It's Bando. I blow out my deer-fat candle and run outside to meet this old friend who is trudging up the trail.

"Hall-ooooo," I shout. I am always glad to see Bando. He's a wonderful guy. During my first year on the mountain he would hike up the steep trail and spend holidays with me. He teaches English in a college near the Hudson River, and during the long school vacations he helped me with difficult chores, like making clay pots and blueberry jam. During those days I got to know and admire him. Furthermore, he understood that I wanted to live on my own in the wilderness to test my skills and to learn. He also understood that I didn't want anyone to know where I was, because I would undoubtedly be shipped home. He never told anyone. And he was always encouraging, especially when I thought I could not make it through the blizzards of winter to spring.

Bando fell in love with this mountain that year and last spring he bought a cabin on the dirt road about two miles down the mountain from here. Three weeks later he married. His wife, Zella, is a lawyer. She's a pretty lady and I like her. She's not crazy about the cabin, however. It has no electricity or running water. The only heat comes from the fireplace. The log walls are chinked with bark and clay to keep out the cold, but they don't do the job when the wind blows hard.

When they moved in, the floor was earthen. It's one of the original cabins of the Westward Movement and, like the Iroquois Indians, the pioneers put furs down for floors, not boards. One day after Zella had swept the floor to make it look neat and clean, she picked up a stick and drew a rug of flowers, deer, and butterflies in the earth. Bando was so pleased that he told her he wasn't going to make the oak-plank floor he was planning.

That afternoon he came up the mountain to tell me he didn't understand Zella. "Her rug drawing was so wonderful," he said, "that I didn't want to cover it with a wooden floor. I thought I was complimenting her, but she turned on her heel and walked out the door. Did I miss a point?"

"Yes," I said. "She wants a floor."

Smiling as I recall that day, I join him at the top of the last steep ascent.

"Sam, I'm glad you're home." At the water mill door he drops several small logs on top of others he apparently carried up earlier. "I came by this morning, but no one was here."

"Not even Alice?" I realize I haven't seen her since I came home.

"Not even Alice."

"Maybe she's down at the library reading about waterfalls," I say. "The last I heard from her she said she was 'thinking waterfalls.'" Bando raises an eyebrow.

"Watch out, Sam. When Alice is thinking, things happen."

I smile, but not wholeheartedly.

"Sam," Bando says, pointing to the logs, "I need to saw these lengthwise—down the middle from tip to base."

"What are you making?"

"You know those two chairs I put together when you were making your chaise longue?" I nod. He and I had a good time finding limbs that were twisted and bent by the wind, the sun, and the ice. And we had a good time fashioning them into arms and legs for chairs.

"Listen to this," Bando says. "A man saw them in front of my cabin and offered me so much money for them, I couldn't refuse. He said they were fine examples of Adirondack furniture."

"What's Adirondack furniture?"

"Furniture made with the unpeeled branches and crooked forks of trees. The bark is kept on to give them that rustic look. We left it on for the same reason, but we didn't know we were stylish. Adirondack furniture was very popular at the turn of the century when people were passionate nature lovers. And, suddenly, now it is popular again."

"A man bought them, you say? Paid money for our twisted armrests and crooked chair legs?"

"Yes, and he paid a lot. I thought I'd make some more."

Bando has just showed me another solution to my problem. I can make Adirondack furniture and sell it. If I can't get enough meat with my sling, I can, and may have to, earn money. I cringe at the thought of shopping, then remember Alice likes stores.

"Want to join me in this trade?" he asks.

"I'll help you, Bando. It would be fun," I say. "But I don't want a business."

I think of Frightful and pick up one of Bando's sapling logs and concentrate on it to erase her from my mind.

"Open the sluice gate," I tell him. "I'll take the pins out of the wheel and get the saw lined up."

"Good," he says. "The sooner we get going the better. Zella wants an outdoor chair again so she can sit and look at the mountains. She's somewhat miffed that I sold her chair out from under her, as she puts it." He winks and both of his black eyebrows rise to meet his cap of white hair.

I carry a log inside the millhouse and place it against the saw, which is held in place vertically by a strong wooden frame that Bando and I made after he visited a waterwheel sawmill on the other side of the Hudson.

With a jerk of my wrist, I pull out the pins that keep the wheel from turning when not in use. It's balanced so well that when Jessie Coon James climbed up on it one day, she was carried around twice before she let go and fell in the water. After that, I locked it with pins.

"Let her roll!" I shout and look out the window.

Bando is coming down the pond hill. He passes Frightful's empty perch without noticing she's gone. I am grateful. I still can't bring myself to talk about her.

In minutes I hear the water gushing down the sluice-way, bubbling and chortling along until it spills out the end and strikes the paddles of the wheel just forward of its highest point.

It turns. I grin as I always do when I start up the mill. Water is so wonderful. It takes such a very little flow to build up enough weight to turn a big wheel and generate enormous power.

I put my elbows on the windowsill while Bando saws. Not seeing any sign of Alice, I begin to wonder seriously what she's doing. Maybe she's working on another one of her "great ideas." I hope not. They can be humdingers. Last autumn when the waterwheel was still under construction, Alice came to my tree while I was trying to figure out where to dig an irrigation ditch to carry the water from the millpond to the squash and groundnuts in the rocky meadow. I was concentrating on one of the maps the correspondence school had sent her for a course in map reading and mapmaking. My mountain and all its elevations were on it, so I was studying the contours for the waterway when she stuck her head in the door.

"Sam," she said. "Look at this."

"Alice, please. I'm working."

"But this is important. Really important. The correspondence school is offering a science course."

I lost my concentration and irritably put down my pencil and stepped outside. "Alice, what *do* you want?"

"Sam, the first lesson is how to convert a water mill to electricity. Let's make electricity when we finish the mill."

"I don't want electricity, Alice."

"We could have electric heaters. I can't write well with mittens on."

"I don't want electric heaters. I like the fire."

"Sam, you're just an old fogy. I'm going to take that course. I'll make electricity if you won't."

"No, Alice, no. I will not have electricity on my mountain."

"Sam," her eyes crackled. "This is my mountain, too. The farm belongs to Mr. and Mrs. Charles Gribley, who happen to be my parents as well as yours." She looked right into my eyes and clamped her jaws tightly. "You have no right to stop me from doing what I want to do in my own home!"

"Maybe not," I said. "But nevertheless, I don't want electricity and all that it will bring—radios, TV, vacuum cleaners, hair dryers, washing machines—noise. I want to hear the birds."

In her disgust Alice pulled off her rabbit-lined hat so fast it created static electricity in her hair. The yellow wisps stood up on end like a circus clown's, and I wondered how I ever thought she was cute.

"Sam?" Bando's voice snaps me out of my daydream. He is staring at me. "Are you all right? You're glassy-eyed."

"I'm not all right, Bando," I answer, the image of my regal bird flashing into my mind. "Frightful was confiscated by the conservation officer three days ago." I almost break down but regain my composure and go on. "I should have told you when I first saw you, but I just couldn't."

He sits down on a block of wood.

"Is that really true?"

"Yes, it is."

"That's dreadful." Bando runs his fingers through his hair. "I've been afraid of this. Zella brought me a copy of the Endangered Species Act not long ago. I should have told you about it, but I thought the conservation officer understood your needs."

I am fighting back tears now. "It's all right." I bite my lower lip. After a while I am able to tell him about Leon Longbridge and how he is taking Frightful to the university to be bred. He listens.

"I think she'll die without you, Sam."

"Oh, no," I say, trying to be convincing. "She's a bird. She'll eat and thrive."

We saw Bando's logs without any more words.

"What are you going to do, Sam?" he asks when we are done. "I mean how are you going to live?"

"I made a sling." I take it from my pocket.

"Are you any good at it? That's a tough martial art to master."

"I'm not very good at it."

Bando puts most of the slats in his packbasket and stacks the others in the corner of the millhouse, to collect later.

"If you ever want a job in my furniture factory . . ." he says, but stops in mid-sentence. He has no heart for facetiousness.

Shouldering his packbasket, he leaves the millhouse.

I climb to the millpond, close the gate, and watch the water slow down, trickle, and then stop. I finger the sling in my pocket.

IN WHICH
I Go Backwards in Order to Go Forwards

When Bando left, I opened my journal again. Since reading about the old days keeps my mind off Frightful, I flip to last summer and the days when we were building the dam and water mill. Those were wonderful times.

The water mill was begun soon after the plumping mill.

The dam came first. After I had gathered enough roots and bulbs and smoked enough fish to last Alice and me for a couple of months, I began it. Then I waded into the stream that comes from the spring and began to stack logs, stones, and mud where I had planned the dam the day our folks left. Little did I know it wouldn't last.

"*July 29*

"A big storm dumped so much water on the mountain the last three days that the dam washed out—logs, rocks, and mud.

" 'Now what do we do?' " I asked Alice.

" 'The beaver dam didn't wash out,' she said. 'I saw it this morning when I was picking raspberries. Let's go see what they do right.' "

"Later That Night

"At twilight I climbed a tree and watched a pair of young beavers begin a new dam. They started it not with the big logs and rocks I had used but with shrubs and saplings placed butt-ends upstream. As soon as a low spot developed and the water ran out, they blocked the flow with sticks. This gradually raised the height and raised it evenly."

"August 15

"Alice and I did as the beavers did and we have a dam.

"Right away, our dam leaked, so down the mountain I went to see how the beavers made theirs watertight. They carried mud on their flat tails and plastered it on the upstream side of the dam. The current washed the mud in among the sticks and stones and sealed the leaks. I had been plastering holes on the downstream side of the dam where I saw the leaks. Naturally, this mud washed out. So back I went and mended my dam like the beavers did. It worked.

"When I was finished, we had an extraordinarily strong dam, which, like the beavers', was much wider at the base than the top. This counteracts the immense pressure on the bottom of the dam. Today we have a quarter-acre pond which already has frogs and little fish. I'm going to stock it with bass and bluegills."

The millhouse came next.

"August 21

"There are stones everywhere on this mountain, as Dad well knows, and so it seemed sensible to make the millhouse out of stones. The rocks are sandstone and shale, which were laid down layer upon layer in an ancient sea that existed before the mountains rose. The shale, in particular, breaks into perfect building blocks with the tap of the hammer in the right place. I got real good at this and, within the week, had a pile of stones ready to be stacked into a millhouse.

"I met Miss Turner one day while I was hunting Frightful and told her about the project. The next day she came up the mountain with a book on how to build dry walls—no mortar—just stones."

I wrote this in my journal.

"Lay the stones level, that's the first principle in keeping a wall from shifting and falling down.

"The second is to lay the stones one on two, two on one.

"Our great grandfathers built stone walls and buildings that are standing today. In Europe some have been standing since the year 1000."

"*September 14*

"The millhouse is done. It stands below the dam on that flat spot the stream carved before it took its present course down the mountain. It looks very natural there, and as soon as the mosses take hold, it will look even more so. One door, one window, and a hole for the shaft are all the openings we built, because they are very difficult to make. The window, however, lets in lots of light, and I'll be able to see just fine when I work.

"The millhouse looks very professional thanks to Miss Turner. She read the how-to books carefully and was very fussy about which stones she put where. She took her vacation up here so that she could supervise the laying of the walls. She also gave all of us work gloves. Stones are hard on your hands.

"Mrs. Strawberry came up one day and tapped stones. She was a master at it, breaking them into almost perfect blocks. She got way ahead of the builders—Alice, Miss Turner, and me—so we got Bando and Zella and they gladly pitched in.

"This is the first time I've seen Zella happy on the mountain. She had been taught by her grandfather, a bricklayer, how to make corners when she was a kid, and she was delighted to see how much she remembered. The corners, as well as the walls, are very professional and strong because of Miss Turner and Zella."

"September 15

"Zella went off on a law case, and Bando stayed here to help with the millhouse roof. We decided not to put on a gabled roof right now, because we want to make the sluice, the trough that carries the water from the pond to the mill. So the roof is just logs covered with bark to keep out the rain."

"September 28

"The sluice is in place. Getting it there was fairly easy, for I simply felled the big hemlock at the edge of the pond. Mrs. Strawberry showed me how to drop the tree right where I wanted it.

"She notched it with Dad's axe in the direction I had marked for it to fall—from the dam to the millhouse—and then she told me to saw on the opposite side. After an hour or so I heard the tree snap. It tilted, began to fall slowly, then faster and faster until it crashed down with a splintering of limbs to lie exactly where Mrs. Strawberry had said it would. She wiped her hands, saying she should have been a lumberjack.

"I knew I had to burn and chip out the inside of the tree to make a trough, like the pioneers made water pipes. It was not hard work, but it was a tedious chore I could do when I didn't have help, so Bando and I started on the waterwheel."

"October 10

"Bando had a Columbus Day vacation and helped collect the last of Dad's house lumber. Then we borrowed Slats to haul the planks from the collapsed barn on Bando's property. With a carpentry compass, I drew a huge circle on the ground. This was our pattern for the wheel.

"For three days we fitted boards into the circle, and when we were finished, we had two doughnut-shaped structures six feet in diameter and fourteen inches deep. Bando will come back next weekend to help build the shaft and spokes.

"Meanwhile I'm nailing the paddleboard between the two wheels while Alice and Miss Turner are building a wall outside the millhouse on which to lay the wheel shaft. Bando had a carpenter make two bearings—large blocks of wood, each with a U in them—in which the shaft will lie and turn. One will be on the wall Alice and Miss Turner are working on, the other will be inside."

"November 25

"It's taken until today to get the waterwheel in place. Bando and Zella were too busy to come to the mountain during most of November, and Miss Turner's mother was sick, so she couldn't work. I did finish the sluice but stopped working on the wheel because Alice and I had to gather the nut crop. The beechnuts are abundant this year, and so are the hickory and butter nuts, but the acorn crop is poor. Alice did find one productive tree, and we have enough to last until spring.

"Work was further delayed when Mrs. Strawberry came up to tell us that another deer had been killed on the county road and I went down to butcher that prize and haul it up here.

"Then the smoking of the venison took more time. While I was working at that, Alice decided to make a smokehouse, and before I knew it, she had me tapping and stacking stones again. Although it delayed the mill, I'm glad we made it. The venison is much better when smoked in a building where the fire can be controlled.

"I was delayed even further because Alice wanted rabbit skins tacked on the floor and walls of her tree house before the cold set in. To get enough, I spent extra hours hunting with Frightful each afternoon. I was almost finished with the job when, at the end of the day, I met a cousin of Mrs. Strawberry walking along the dirt road with his sheep. He's a sheepherder, and when he learned I was making my sister a carpet with the rabbit I was carrying, he offered me two sheepskins. I didn't refuse them, but Alice and I didn't use them for rugs, we made them into parkas for the winter. More time from the wheel.

"Alice has her weather vane. One day she fussed because I hadn't made her one, and so I stopped shaping the shaft for the waterwheel and went to work on the weather vane.

"All I did was fit a narrow-necked bottle snugly in a wooden box. Into the bottle I put a stick with a slit at the top, and into the slit I shoved an arrow-shaped board. I held it in place with pegs. The pegs are square. I read that if you put square pegs in round holes the wood welds and stays tight for years.

"When it was done, I climbed up on her roof and secured it with deer tendon. Then we stood on her porch admiring it.

" 'The wind is blowing from the north northwest,' said Alice clapping her hands. 'Tomorrow will be a beautiful day.'

"Actually, the weather vane has proved to be very useful, but a barometer I made has been even more so. It's a wide-mouthed Mason jar with a piece of a rubber glove Zella gave me tied securely over it. I picked a clear day to tie it on because, when you seal the jar, the air is trapped inside at the pressure of the day on which you make it. If it's a rainy day, your reading will always be low.

"When a storm is coming, the rubber cap indents to say that the barometric pressure is low. One day I saw that it was indented severely, and cancelled a foraging trip. The storm turned out to be a cloudburst, and an island where we were going to spend the night was flooded.

"So it wasn't until yesterday that Bando and I got the wheel in place with the help of Mrs. Strawberry, Slats, Alice, Zella, and Miss Turner.

"We threw a rope over a limb, tied one end to the wheel and the other to Slats. Then Mrs. Strawberry led him slowly away from the tree. The wheel rose into the air until we could push and guide it. With everyone helping, we eased the wheel to the mill and carefully directed the shaft through the hole in the streamside wall made for this purpose. Inside we laid it to rest on the bearing. Mrs. Strawberry backed up Slats, lowering the outside end of the shaft on Alice and Miss Turner's stone wall. With that, the waterwheel was in place.

"Alice ran to the pond and opened the sluice gate. The water rolled down the hollowed tree, hit the wheel blades—and the darn thing turned. We cheered and clapped and danced. We had a rolling waterwheel!"

"November 29

"We had wonderful feast day on Thanksgiving. Miss Turner brought up a turkey, and Mrs. Strawberry and Zella made salad and pumpkin pie. Alice and I baked acorn bread in my stone oven. The day was warm, and we ate outside watching the waterwheel turn. We all felt great pride and satisfaction."

"November 30

"But a turning wheel does not do anyone much good. The shaft has to turn something to be useful. So I made a cog wheel or gear out of a disc of oak by putting pegs around the edge.

"I fitted the cog wheel onto the shaft and made a smaller cog wheel to fit into the pegs of the first. Into the smaller one I inserted a bent iron to which I attached Dad's saw in the frame. I would sure like to try to run the saw, but I'll wait for my friends. They're all coming next weekend for the big moment."

"*December 6*

"Everybody gathered for the opening of the sawmill. Miss Turner made the bread this time, Bando and Zella brought cheese, and Mrs. Strawberry made corn pudding. Alice had brewed some tea with wild peppermint

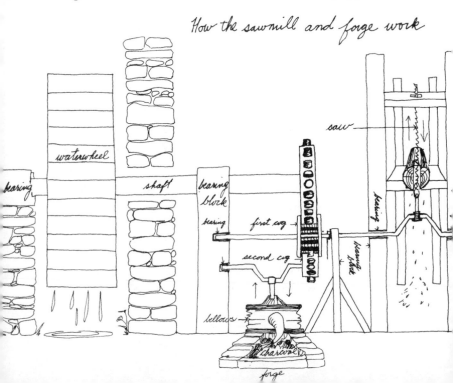

How the sawmill and forge work

leaves, and I contributed two nice bass. They grow fast in ponds.

"At high noon I held a log in front of the saw. Alice opened the sluice gate and ran back to join us faster than the water flowed.

"We cheered as it rushed forward, hit the blades, turned the wheel and shaft which turned the first cog which turned the second cog which sent the saw up and down!

"We made so much noise cheering that Frightful bated and I had to rescue her to keep her from breaking her pinions. Hearing the noise, the crows came in to see if we were harassing an owl."

I stop reading my journal and look up. The water mill was a big change. I sawed wood and made a gable for the millhouse roof and shingles to cover it. I had leaped from the Stone Age into the beginning of the Industrial Revolution without any pain, in fact, with a lot of joy.

A few days after the mill was running, Alice poked her head in the door of my tree while I was writing.

"You're not going to have acorn pancakes, Sam Gribley," she said, "unless you make a waterfall for my plumping mill."

I had forgotten all about her mill in the excitement of building the dam and sawmill. The cascade that ran her mill was now underwater. So that very day I made a staircase of stones under the pond overflow. The water splashed down, filled her wooden box and lifted the stone, and she was back in business again. The falls are attractive and sound nice in the evening. I can understand why Alice likes waterfalls.

I go back to my journal.

"Christmas Eve

"I added another cog wheel with a bent iron. To the iron I attached a bellows. I cut boards from Bando's barn siding into two heart shapes. A wide strip of deerskin pegged to each allowed them to move up and down. A cow horn made a perfect nozzle through which the air rushed when the bellows was pumped. I laid the bellows on a low table made of stones and directed the stream of air onto the charcoal in a stone fire bin. When the wheel turned, the third cog wheel pushed the bellows up and down, and I had a forge.

"Now I can bend and shape pieces of iron I find around the ruins of the Gribley house and barn. Eventually I'll forge them into shovels, ladles, and even nails."

"Christmas Day

"This is the day of our annual Christmas party. Bando, Zella, and Miss Turner were going to join us for a wild turkey Frightful caught, but a big snowstorm struck last night, and no one got up the mountain.

"In the morning Alice fed the wild birds and I dug down to Baron Weasel's den to see what he was up to. As I was tunneling in to him, he was tunneling out to me. He burst out of the snow and slid down the hill on his belly.

"One fellow I don't have to worry about in a snow-storm is The Baron Weasel. Later he arrived at my tree for Christmas dinner. I gave him the liver and giblets from the turkey."

"December 26

"The pond is a white muffin, the millhouse has disap-peared under a snowdrift, and Alice and I are playing checkers with groundnuts and dried apples. Winter is here."

IN WHICH

I Am in for a Surprise

I hear the latch on the root cellar door thump and close my journal. Alice must be getting something for supper. I have put off talking to her about Frightful long enough. I get to my feet.

Stepping out of the darkness of my tree into the bright light, I squint, then walk to the cellar. No one is there.

The door is closed, and the lock, which is a board that lies across two brackets, is tilted and is almost out at one end. Someone was here, but it wasn't Alice. She's too protective of our hard-won supplies to leave the lock ajar. It must have been Jessie Coon James. She's always fiddling with this lock. In fact, I made it because Jessie once opened the door with her little handlike paws and helped herself to venison and nuts. From the looks of things, I had best make a better lock. She has this one all but figured out.

As I open the door, the clean scent of apples greets me. They came from the trees Great-grandfather Gribley planted. Even though they're now old and choked by forest, they produce plenty of apples for Alice and me.

I decide to bake a squash for supper. I feel my way to the back of this cave, which I dug into the side of the hill to keep our food dark and cool. The cattail rush basket in which we store the hickory nuts is almost empty. That's funny. Although I took some to Delhi with me, I didn't think I'd taken that many. I wonder if that raccoon of mine did get in here after all. There might be a hole in the stone wall that I faced the cave with.

I check the other supplies. The basket of groundnuts is almost empty. It couldn't be Jessie. She makes a complete shambles of the cellar when she gets in. So it must be Alice. She brought back a wild-food cookbook from the library last week and mentioned that one of the recipes called for lots of nuts.

I step over the jars of maple syrup that Alice and I made last February and pick up a squash. Alice planted squash seeds a year ago, and they grew as big as pumpkins—some plants like our poor soil.

After locking the door securely by wedging a stone in the brace, I carry the vegetable to my outdoor kitchen and start off for the tree house and Alice.

The trail to her house is bordered with stones she gathered and put there. She wanted to edge all the paths, but I objected. Bordered trails get too much use. The wildflowers can't push up, and when they don't grow, the soil erodes and is carried into the streams by the rain. The best thing to do, I told Alice, is to take different routes from place to place, or put a log across an old path and let it rest. I kick leaves onto her trail to protect it. Jessie Coon James walks up to me.

"Hello there, Jessie," I say as my old friend greets me with a chittering purr. Gathering her up in my arms, I give her a big hug. Gently she sticks her black paws in my ears, feels my cheek, then turns around, and, hanging onto my neck with her hind legs, reaches down into my pocket with her front paws. She finds the venison.

"You're real hungry, Jessie," I say. "How come? Hasn't Alice fed you today?"

Jessie moved in with Alice when the cold weather arrived last fall and never moved out. Raccoons sleep in dens in the winter. Alice's dimly lit tree house was snug and better than a hollow tree because, when she awoke on warm days, Alice fed her. In February she left to find a mate, but hardly had a week passed before she was back in her tree house. In March she had four babies.

She and Alice took care of them until they were on their own.

It's unusual for Jessie to be so hungry. One thing Alice does not do is neglect animals.

As I mull all this, Jessie climbs up on my shoulder and eats the venison.

"Hey," I say, "I know what's the matter with you. Alice isn't here. And she hasn't been for several days, by your appetite."

I put her down and run up the steps, notched in a log, to Alice's front porch and push back her blanket door. The light from the Mason-jar window falls on a note lying in plain view on the furs. I have a hunch this is not one of her ordinary notes. I snatch it up. It's not dated.

"Dear Sam,
"I'm leaving. Don't worry about me. I'll be just fine thanks to all you have taught me.
                                        Love, Alice."

I read the note twice more.

Alice has left.

I can't believe it, so I read it a fourth time, then walk out on her porch and sit down, dangling my legs in the air. She must be mad at me for not converting to electricity, or because I don't like her stone-lined paths. She might be angry about the irrigation ditch. We argued about it. She claimed it took water from her cascade and plumping mill. I insisted, in fact I thought I proved, that it didn't.

Why is she leaving? I ask myself. She can't just walk off this way.

Hey, Sam Gribley, I admonish. Didn't you pack up a few belongings, tell your father you were going to leave, and take off for the adventure of your life?

"Okay, Alice," I say out loud. "It's your turn."

In fact, Alice is better prepared to take care of herself than I was when I left home. I didn't know anything about the wilderness. She can catch fish with a thorn hook and a line of braided basswood, and she knows the wild edible plants.

I back down the steps and pick up Jessie. I am feeling very sorry for myself. Frightful has been confiscated— and now Alice is gone. Even if we did argue a lot, she was good company.

"Hall-oo, the tree!"

Bando's here! And just in time.

I run up the path, trot along the edge of the pond, then, placing my two feet together, leap goatlike down the slope to the millhouse.

"Bando!" I cry eagerly and put Jessie down.

"What's the matter with you, Sam? You act as if you haven't seen me for years. I was just here." He throws some fine crooked limbs on the ground, reaches into a pocket on his vest, and hands me a pamphlet.

"Zella sent this. Alice told her you wanted it."

"Making Electricity with Water Mills," I read. "Alice said *I* wanted this?"

"Yes," Bando answers. "And Zella said to tell you that if you do get the mill generating electricity, please bring a wire down to her." He looks at me hopelessly. "She wants electric lights and an electric stove."

I barely hear him. That Alice can fight with me even when she's not here. I don't want electricity, Alice.

I stuff the pamphlet under a stone in the corner of the mill, thinking as I do so that it *is* good Alice has gone off on her own.

Bando walks to the pond and opens the sluice gate. The water gushes forward, the wheel turns, and he joins me, whistling some obscure tune. Running the water-wheel always puts him in high spirits. He picks up a contorted sapling.

"How do you like this piece for an arm?"

"It's okay," I say without much interest, for I am still arguing with Alice.

Leaving Bando at the saw, I walk back to my tree. After washing the squash in the pond, I build a fire in the stone oven I built not long after the millhouse was completed. When the fire is roaring hot, I rake the burning coals to one side, put the squash on the large sandstone slab at the bottom of the oven, and close the door. The door is another slab of sandstone.

I've decided to barbeque the squirrel to go with the squash, so I light a second fire in the pit under the grill.

This is made from long, narrow pieces of shale laid on the top of a stone-lined pit like slats on an orange crate. There's a reflector at the far end, which is another stone slab propped to throw heat on the grill. In winter it also throws heat into my tree. Tonight it's too hot for that, so I lift the reflector and lay it on the ground.

While supper cooks and the waterwheel turns, I spade the ditch that will carry the pond water to the plants in the meadow. Now and then I run back to the grill and turn the squirrel. I don't look at the path to Alice's tree house or Frightful's empty perch.

Eventually Bando climbs the hill, closes the sluice

gate, and comes to my outdoor kitchen. He sits down on a section of stump at my table, which is a huge sandstone slab laid on three big boulders. I sit across from him.

I want to tell him about Alice. I don't. She has a right to her privacy. When she's ready, she'll tell me what she's been up to.

Bando folds his hands on the table and clears his throat.

"I'm so sorry about Frightful," he says.

I can't think of what to say, so I walk over to the squirrel and turn it again. Bando sees I'm not ready to talk.

"I'll leave you to your thoughts, Sam," he says and gets to his feet.

Shouldering his packbasket, now filled with future chair arms and legs, he leaves.

Just before sundown the squash is cooked and the squirrel is juicy and tender. I serve myself on one of the wooden plates I carved when we were snowed in last winter.

Funny thing, I skipped breakfast and lunch today, but I'm not hungry. I think people have better appetites when they eat with someone, even if they argue. I give the squirrel to Jessie and put the squash in the root cellar for tomorrow.

When night comes, I do not go to bed in my tree but stretch out on my lounging chair and listen for Alice.

I thought she might get frightened and come home. I should have known better than that.

At midnight, I walk to the head of the trail that leads to the bottom of the mountain. An owl hoots; a bird sleeping in a laurel bush awakes and flutters its wings.

As I amble back, I wonder if Mrs. Strawberry knows what Alice is up to. They talk a lot, so she just might. It's not that I want to pry, but maybe Alice is not going off to find her own home. Maybe she's just down the mountain with that pig.

As I finally crawl into my tree, I wonder what she took with her. If I knew I might figure out where she's going. I light my deer-fat candle and go down the trail to Alice's tree house once more. It's a very warm night and I'm glad for that. Alice can sleep on the bare ground and be perfectly comfortable.

Inside her wigwam I see that her deerskin pants we made last spring are missing, as well as the denim jacket she came here with. Two of the four T-shirts that hung on the pegs by the door are gone. Her tennis shoes are here, but not her boots. She must be expecting rough terrain. She's not talking to a pig, then.

She's left all her books, as far as I can see, but has taken the maps from the orienteering, or map reading, course. Also gone are her backpack and our water carrier, a square of hide folded in fourths. It's a great device, because it can also be used for a pillow or a hat— all of which means she will not be back soon.

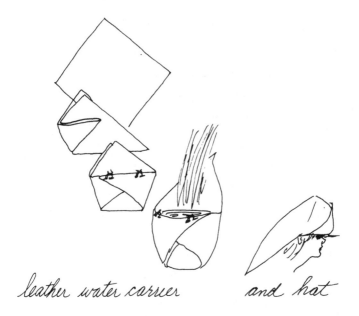

leather water carrier *and hat*

I recall the nearly empty hickory nut and groundnut baskets. I didn't notice if any of the smoked venison or fish was gone, but I'll bet they are.

Her Swiss Army knife's not here, which I would expect no matter where she was going. She takes it everywhere. But why aren't her gloves on the peg? Bando said the temperature has been in the eighties by day and seventies by night. Maybe she's going to build a stone house at her new home site and needs her gloves.

As I wander back to my tree, I think of Alice alone in the forest, as I once was. I remember my frustration as I tried to start a fire the first night, and my fear when I couldn't catch a fish to eat. Then I remember the triumphs of making a fire, catching a fish, and sleeping on a bed of pine boughs all alone in the wilderness. I'm a bit envious of Alice. I'm also a whole lot curious. Tomorrow I'll ask Mrs. Strawberry if she knows where Alice went. Not that I would try to find her, but I would like to know what she's up to.

IN WHICH
I Am Sent East by Northeast

Just before sunrise I strike out across the field to Mrs. Strawberry's weatherworn farmhouse. Tucked in a grove of old lilacs, it is surrounded by barns and outbuildings that are sagging toward the ground. These mountains do not love a farm.

At the gate, Slats trots up and tries to shove his way into the yard with me.

"Phbbbbbb," I say, blowing through my lips. According to Mrs. Strawberry, this is horse talk for "You're annoying." Frightful doesn't have such a word in her vocabulary, but then her ancestors were never pestered by flies as were Slats's.

I lift the latch and push him back. He paws the ground.

"You can't come in," I say. "So stop begging." Pawing the ground is a horse's way of begging.

As I step into the yard, I glance up at my mountain. It's strong and beautiful, with the sun rising behind it.

The view from here is its western side. No matter from which direction you look, it's an inspiring sight. Why on earth would Alice want to leave?

A green frog pipes, a star shoots, and a light comes on in Mrs. Strawberry's farm kitchen. I knock.

"Sam!" she says, opening the door. "What are you doing here?" She is wearing the brown felt hat she always wears in and out of doors and is smiling her I'm-REALLY-glad-to-see-you smile. It softens the lines around her sharp nose and pointed chin.

"Come in," she says. "Have some breakfast."

Slats grabs the gate in his teeth and rattles it, then thrashes his head up and down.

"No, you can't come in, Slats!" Mrs. Strawberry calls.

"He's annoyed," she says to me. "Alice hasn't been around to ride him since she started her new project."

I hold my breath—she knows.

"Does Alice have a new project?"

"Yes, indeedy, she's up to something again."

"Do you know what it is?" I try to sound as if I were asking if Alice were in the barn pitching hay.

"Don't you?" she asks.

"No."

"I don't either. Never asked."

"She's left home—to find a new one, I think."

"My goodness," she replies. "That's quite a project."

My face must look troubled because the next thing Mrs. Strawberry says is, "Don't you worry, Sam. Whatever Alice is up to, she's all right. Go on home and do your chores."

"I'm not worried—just curious. She took her maps."

"Hmm. Sounds like she's going far."

"That's what I think. And she's got a good start. The last time I saw her was five days ago. The first day the haze rolled in. The next day I left for Delhi without seeing her. When I returned, she was gone."

"I saw her three days ago," Mrs. Strawberry says. She steps over to a flowerpot to pick off dead geraniums.

Three days ago—that means she started the day after Frightful was confiscated. I make a quick calculation. Alice and I can walk about twenty miles a day. That could put her sixty miles from here. Sixty miles, which way? in what direction?

If I knew in which direction she was going, I might be able to look at a map and figure out her destination. I'd sure like to know where she's headed.

She should have told me. At least I told Dad that I was going to run away to Great-grandfather Gribley's farm. He didn't believe me, but he should have. Alice hasn't even given me a hint—at least I don't recognize one if she has.

I linger, hoping Mrs. Strawberry's memory will keep clearing and she will remember more about "what Alice is up to," as we all say.

Slats takes the gate in his teeth and shakes it again.

"Ee-he-eeeeeeee," squeals Mrs. Strawberry. She's imitating the cry of a challenging horse, like western cowboys do to discipline their steeds. Hearing a threat in his own language, Slats trots off.

"You just have to be stern with that horse," she says. "It's like Alice and her pig. She can get that pig to do anything with a stern bit of pig talk."

"*Her* pig," I exclaim. "I knew she had a pig friend, but I didn't know it was hers."

"It is now. Mr. Reilly"—she points to a farm down the road—"who owns Crystal, or who did own her, gave Crystal to her."

"That was very nice of him."

"Not really. Alice gave the pig a name so he didn't have the heart to butcher her. And the pig loves Alice. Crystal won't eat if she isn't around. Pigs are very affectionate, especially to children, and particularly to a child who learns to say, 'I love you' in pig-ese." I keep listening, my picture of Alice and her pig taking on new dimensions.

"Now that I think about it," Mrs. Strawberry goes on, "Alice might have been going off to find her own place." She draws on her memory. "She was leading her pig on a leash."

"Alice took her pig?" I smile. She can't go very fast or far with a pig, and—a pig can be easily tracked.

Of course, I'm not going to follow her, although it would be easier than playing On the Track, the game we made up when went berrying or food gathering. You track the other person by observing broken sticks or footprints or even clues that a person sets out, like an acorn under a pine tree. It's fun.

I'll just find their first few tracks and figure out where Alice is. Then I'll go home.

Mrs. Strawberry is watching me closely.

"Are you worried about her, Sam?"

"Not at all," I answer, thinking how easy it will be to find pig prints and pig droppings. She studies my face again. She doesn't believe me.

"I can't help you very much," she goes on, "but I can tell you this, she and the pig were walking across my fallow field, toward your mountain. I thought they were going home."

"South?" I ask eagerly.

"South and a little bit east." I thank her very much and hurry down the steps to the gate.

Out of sight of Mrs. Strawberry, I veer toward Mr. Reilly's house, leaping mullens and thistles growing in the fallow field. Perhaps *he* knows where Alice is going.

As I approach the lights in the cow barn, I slow down and stop. Alice is a secret-keeper among other things. If Mrs. Strawberry doesn't know, he won't know either.

Making a right-angle turn, I go south and slightly east across the field. I watch for bent grasses and hoofprints.

At the end of Mrs. Strawberry's property, two hills meet in a swamp. Dead trees rise out of the dark water. In them are eight blue heron nests—a rookery. Eight nests, I say. That might mean sixteen more great blue herons if all goes well this summer.

I climb the fence and continue walking south and a bit east, searching for pig tracks among the rushes and trees along the swamp stream. I can't find any. You'd think a pig would leave a beaten trail in this wetland, but Crystal hasn't or, at least, I can't find it.

The haze thickens as the sun warms the land, and I can't see well so I sit on a log by the stream and wait for the air to clear.

A blue jay who flew into a willow when I sat down is right above me, a prisoner of the haze too. He doesn't see me. We both sit still and wait.

At last the wind blows, the whiteness thins, and the blue jay catches sight of me. He screams and flies over a sandy spit.

"Well, look at that!" I exclaim out loud and jump to the spit. "Alice has been here."

A stick is standing upright in the sand. Two rocks have been placed on either side of it, about three feet apart. A line has been drawn between them. Another line intersects the first.

I have found a compass made by Alice. We make these when we're travelling in strange forests. To make one, you pound a stick in the ground and put a stone at the end of its shadow. That is west. After about an hour you put another stone on the end of the new position of the stick's shadow. That is east. You draw an east-west

line between the two stones, then the north-south. Alice
has labeled north.

The compass is a good find, but it doesn't tell me
which way she's going. I get down on all fours and look
more closely to see if she has plotted her direction—and

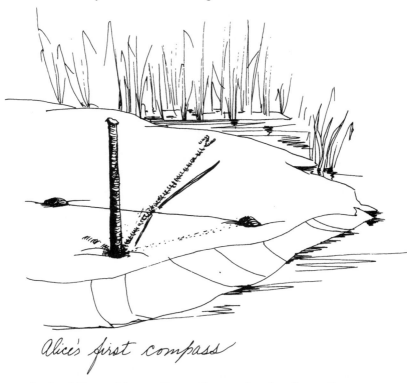

Alice's first compass

she has! Two thin reeds on the sand point from the center of the compass outward. The longest points east by
northeast or about 70 degrees. The other points almost
due south.

I know what she's doing. She and I use long sticks or reeds to indicate our long-range objective, short ones to point out the immediate route. She must be reading one of the maps she took. Although she's headed east by northeast for the long run, she's going almost due south for a short distance.

Alice has plotted her course. This is no exercise for her map-reading teacher; this is serious. She's off on her own—with a pig.

She knows exactly where she is going, and I will, too, before very long.

With a couple of bounds, I leave the stream, run through the woods for a short distance, and climb an embankment to the dirt road that runs along the bottom of my mountain.

IN WHICH
Zella Makes Sense

The answer to where Alice is going is in Bando's cabin. I jog up the dusty road that follows the creek. I'll soon know where she's headed. Then I'll go home and do the chores.

As I climb over the fence into Bando's pasture, a song

sparrow clicks out his alarm note from the raspberry thicket. I assume I am his enemy until I see a crow sneaking toward his nest intent upon eating the eggs. I rush the crow. He flies off, crying his alarm caws.

Bando looks up when he hears the crow and hails me. He's in front of his cabin in the shade of the big slippery elm tree, contemplating a twisted limb. Bando really *is* serious about making Adirondack furniture. He's up and at work, and the sun is hardly over the treetops.

"What brings you here, Sam?" he asks when I join him. His prematurely white hair is cut so short that it looks like a skullcap. Bando is getting a little paunch, but I like it, especially right now. He looks older and wiser, and that makes me feel better. This has been a bad week: first Frightful, then Alice.

"You look like you ate a green persimmon, Sam," he says.

"Alice ran away."

He drops the twisted wood.

"Really? Where did she go?"

"I don't know." Bando looks worried so I quickly add, "She's perfectly all right. She made a sun compass in the sand along the marsh creek to plot her direction. I'll know where she's going if I can look at your maps."

"Sure," he says. "Come on in." Bando has been collecting the same maps Alice got from her school course ever since he bought his cabin. They are the U.S. Geological Survey topographic maps and are a good thing to own in these wild mountains.

"She can't be going far," I say as we step up on a large doorstep of rock and into the cabin. "She has a pig."

"A pig?" he asks incredulously. Bando dislikes pigs as much as I do. A bunch of them from the farm below him got loose this spring and made a mud hole of his garden.

Zella comes in through the back door.

"Did I hear you say Alice ran away?"

"Good morning, Zella," I say. "She sure did. She left me a note saying she was leaving, but she didn't say where she was going or how long she'd be staying."

Zella looks nice this morning in a dark blue jacket and skirt. I guess she's going to work. Her black hair is pulled back from her face with silver combs. Dark-rimmed glasses over her long-lashed eyes make her look very professional and also pretty.

"So, at last she's done it," Zella says with a whimsical smile.

"Done what?" I ask.

"Gone off on her own. She's wanted to do it for a long time."

"She has? She never told me about it."

"Perhaps she didn't want anyone to know where she's gone." She winks at me. I didn't want anyone to know where I was either for fear they'd take me home.

"I think she does want me to know," I say. "She left me a message in the sand along the swamp stream.

She told me she's going east by northeast—to somewhere."

Bando has spread several of the topographical maps
on his big oak table. The maps, which you order
through the United States Department of Interior, U.S.
Geological Survey, are masterpieces of mapmaking.
They reflect the shape of the Earth's surface, portrayed
by contour lines twenty feet apart. These brown lines
are the distinctive characteristic of topographic maps.
They tell you exactly where and how high you are, so
you can never get lost. They also show roads, buildings,
railroads, transmission lines, mines and caves, vegeta-
tion, and towns, cities, rivers, lakes, canals, marshes,
and waterfalls.

Bando leans over the state map.

"You say she's going east by northeast?" he says taking out a compass with a housing that has 360 degrees
marked on it, as well as a clear plastic base-plate with
straight sides that can be used as a ruler. It also has a
directional, or pointer, arrow drawn on it. The compass
is for orienteering—finding your way with a map—and
saves you a lot of time plotting your course. You don't
have to use a protractor to figure out the degrees.

Bando lines up the state map with north and, placing
his compass approximately on the swamp creek, turns
the housing to 70 degrees, or east by northeast.

The directional arrow points to the Helderberg
Mountains.

"Do you suppose she's going there?" I ask.

"That's the most interesting spot on the east by northeast line," Bando says. "Beyond that's Albany, and we know she's not going there.

"But why the Helderbergs?" he muses. "They're not as spectacular as the Catskills or Adirondacks."

"I wouldn't mind going there myself," I say. "Miss Turner said there is a pair of goshawks that nest on the Helderberg Escarpment. I'd sure like to see them."

"Goshawks?" says Bando. "I would, too. I read a book about one. What a remarkable, spirited bird."

"They're the most aggressive of all the birds of prey," I say. "Many of the kings of medieval England preferred them to peregrine falcons—they can capture huge cranes and buzzards. And they're downright ferocious when it comes to defending their young. Miss Turner said the Helderberg pair knocked a man out of their nest tree."

"Let me look at the map of the Helderbergs," Zella says, then picks up the magnifying glass and studies the map Bando spreads out for her.

"I see a lot of waterfalls," she says. On the maps, waterfalls are the blue lines going through brown contour lines drawn closely together, thereby indicating a steep incline or cliff.

"Once Alice told me," Zella goes on, "that her dream was to go on a long hike, clamber beautiful waterfalls, with the water splashing around her, and sleep beside them at night."

"Hey, Bando," I say. "That could be what she's

doing all right. She really does like waterfalls. Remember I told you about the note she left me saying, 'thinking waterfalls'?"

"Yes, I do," Bando says. "But she can't climb waterfalls."

"Why not?" Zella asks.

"Because she's got a pig."

"She's got a pig named Crystal," I explain to Zella.

"How smart of her," Zella says, straightening up from the map. "Pigs are very intelligent. She'll be good company for Alice."

Zella doesn't know much about country life, but she's nice.

"Even an intelligent pig would not be much good on a long hike," I say. "They're no good at all as far as I'm concerned."

"What's wrong with them?" Zella asks.

"You ought to know," Bando says. "They tore up our garden and ate all the carrots and lettuce."

"They rout in the ground," I say and wax into a lecture. "They destroy the ground cover so that the birds and animals of the ferns and mosses have no home. I would never let one on my mountain—never."

"That's exactly why I think a pig would be of help to Alice. The pig—what did you say her name was?"

"Crystal."

"Crystal"—she smiles and her eyes shine—"would dig up tubers and bulbs for Alice to eat."

Bando and I look at each other. Zella is right. A pig

would be helpful to Alice. My thinking is taking a different course now. "Pigs are excellent water diviners, too. I recall reading that somewhere. She could help Alice find waterfalls."

"How?" Bando asks, as if I've lost my mind. "How would a pig know Alice *wanted* her to find waterfalls?"

"She talks to that pig," I answer, looking Bando right straight in the eye. I want him to believe this. Animals communicate with each other, and when you learn their language, you can communicate with them too. Scientists as well as animal lovers do this. Bando looks doubtful, so I try to explain.

"It's like I talk to Frightful with love squeaks and whistles and Mrs. Strawberry talks to Slats by blowing air through her lips."

As I speak of Frightful, I realize that I've been so preoccupied with Alice's adventure that I haven't thought about her for hours and hours.

"Now, then," says Bando, turning back to the map. "Let's sum this up. We know where Alice is going in general—east northeast toward the Helderbergs, and she's going via waterfalls."

"Right," I agree.

"So," Bando goes on, "now all we have to do is figure out her route."

"This much I know. She is starting out by going southeast for a short distance," I say.

He takes out the Delhi quadrangle map, the one with our homes on it. The quadrangle maps, which are literally quadrangles, 16¾ by 22¾ inches, are not like the county maps. These are land not political boundaries. Their scale is three and three-quarter inches to the mile—a lot of space to put down the details. On the Delhi quadrangle map is Bando's cabin, my mountain, Mrs. Strawberry's house and farm, as well as all the buildings in Delhi. My millhouse and tree are not on it, for which I am grateful. I like privacy.

Bando puts the directional arrow of his compass on the swamp creek and pencils a line across the page at 157 degrees, south southeast, the second direction Alice gave us and the first one she took. It intersects Peaks Brook.

"Of course," I say. "That makes sense. She and the pig can walk down the streambed quite comfortably. The water's low. When they get to the West Branch of the Delaware River, Alice can launch out on her east-northeast direction to the nearest waterfall."

"Right," Bando says, straightening up and rubbing his back. "Now, to find her."

"No," I protest. "We don't do that. I feel strongly about not following her. She wants to do this by herself, and I think she has every right to."

Bando is shaking his head no.

"When you found me in my tree," I remind him. "You thought I had every right to be there. You didn't report me."

"But I kept an eye on you, didn't I?"

"Well, I suppose so—sort of."

"I *did* keep an eye on you, and I think we should keep an eye on Alice."

"What do you think, Zella?" I ask.

"Alice is just fine," she replies. "Why don't you two just let her do her thing."

"Zella, love," says Bando. "You know Alice as well as Sam and I do. She's going to get herself in trouble, bite a chicken thief, siphon milk from a farmer's milk can—remember how she put that tube into my cup of hot chocolate and siphoned all my drink into her cup on the floor?" He chuckles. "I didn't mind—but strangers are not so tolerant."

"She'll be just fine," Zella repeats. "And you *did* mind."

Zella slips her arm in Bando's, and he laughs at himself. I don't even smile because I know only too well that Bando is right. Alice has a knack for getting into scrapes.

"Bando," I say. "I agree. I'm going to follow her. I'll keep out of her sight and I won't stop her. But I want to make sure she doesn't yell 'kidnapper' or siphon milk from a farmer's milk can."

"I'll come with you," he says. "Zella is leaving for a trial that's coming up in Poughkeepsie."

"For goodness' sake," Zella says. "Can't that little girl do something on her own? You two just want an excuse to go hiking."

"That's not so," protests Bando unconvincingly.

Zella smiles at him and picks up her suitcase. She

pauses as she walks toward the door and turns to me.

"Sam, I'm so sorry about Frightful. I thought it might happen eventually, but I hoped that those officials who knew you and your way of life would let you keep her."

I look at the floor so she can't see my misty eyes.

"Leon Longbridge is a fine man," she goes on. "We both know him. I worked with him on a legal case and came to admire him. He'll see to it that Frightful is given good care."

I'm really glad to hear that Zella likes Leon Longbridge, because I don't. But her words make me feel a lot better.

Zella gives Bando a hug and a kiss and leaves. We hear the engine of the four-wheel drive start up and listen until it is out of hearing.

"Let's begin where Alice drew her compass in the sand," Bando says as he takes down his packbasket from the wall. In it he puts a bedroll, cup, spoon, some raisins, a collapsible fishing rod and a change of clothes, a raincoat, and a couple of cans of stew. The topographic maps are folded and put in a waterproof holder, then placed in a pocket of the fishing jacket he's wearing.

"I'm ready," he says. "Shall I wait here until you get your equipment?"

"I'm ready," I answer pointing to my belt pack stuffed with the venison and nuts I put there this morning. Then I pat my pockets where I keep fishing lines and my flint and steel, and bring out my sling, now strung with rawhide. "I never leave my mountain without food and gear for a week," I say.

"How far do you think Alice has gotten?" Bando asks.

"Not far," I answer. "She left the mountain three days ago, but she couldn't have made a sun compass the day after Frightful was confiscated because of the haze in the valley. There were no shadows all that day, I recall. I think she started off the next day when the sun was bright. She can't be more than ten or fifteen miles from here with that pig. We can do that in half a day."

Bando checks around the cabin before we leave. Zella has made it cozy with two rocking chairs, a patchwork quilt on the bed, colorful posters, and bright copper pots at the fireplace. I look down at the wood floor.

"You did a nice job here," I say.

"I saved my marriage, that's what I did," he answers and winks at me.

As we walk across Bando's meadow, he whistles; I throw back my head, and, feeling free as the wind, breathe in the fresh mountain air. Although I am heavy-hearted, my spirits are rising. To walk in nature is always good medicine.

Entering the woods, we take a deer trail to the bottom of the mountain, then cut over to Mrs. Strawberry's field. We stop at the sand spit and Alice's sun compass.

The bobolinks are singing in the fields, two herons are flying toward their roost, and grasshoppers are stridulating at our feet.

"Good old Alice," I say to Bando now that I know we are going to find her very soon. "I might have stuck myself on the mountaintop working hard all summer if it hadn't been for her."

IN WHICH

I Learn to Think Like a Pig

Bando stands over the sun compass squinting, scratching his head, and finally grinning as he compares it with his own compass.

"The crazy thing's quite accurate," he says and takes out the quadrangle map of Delhi. Spreading it on the sand, he gets down on his hands and knees and studies it. "Sam, we're going to have to think like Alice to find her. Look here. If you were Alice, where would you go after you got to Peaks Brook?"

I get down beside him and imagine I am Alice as I read the map.

"If I were her," I say, "when I got to the West Branch of the Delaware, I'd follow it to the most powerful stream coming off the highest mountain and go up it to a waterfall."

"Good. That's what I'd do if I were Alice. We're off!"

Walking into the sun, now a hand span over the trees, we follow the slow stream to Peaks Brook. This brook, which starts on the east side of my mountain, is vigorous and so cold it feels as if it were melted snow. I avoid wading in it and stick to its stony edge.

Since it's only two miles to the West Branch, and maybe fifteen miles to Alice, we go slowly, stopping to admire a handsome, almost pure white sycamore and an enormous eastern cottonwood as big or bigger than my tree. Bando lingers over a rock outcrop, and we are happy to see a swatch of rare bluebells. It is a hot day and the icy stream cools the air.

As we go, the brook plays pranks. Here and there it cuts through rocks, leaving no shores to walk on, and we are forced to jump downstream from boulder to boulder. In high spirits, we whoop as we leap. It's wonderful to be out on the trail.

As we zag along, I practice with my sling, missing eighteen times out of twenty. Not good, but not bad. A wolf pack misses its prey sixteen out of twenty tries.

Finally, we go under the highway and railroad bridge and come out on the flats of the West Branch of the Delaware.

"Now, we've got another problem," Bando says, looking around. "Did she go downstream or upstream?"

"She's going east northeast now," I say. "Where does that send her?"

"Upstream," he says after taking a sighting with his compass.

Bando puts the map away and starts off.

"Let's not go yet," I say. "The fishing looks good here. I'll get us some lunch."

I catch three pumpkinseed sunfish and a catfish while Bando gathers tender dandelion leaves, chicory greens, and wild carrots for salad. At the same time, he looks for pig tracks.

"No tracks," he reports. "I hope we are thinking like Alice." He takes a seat on a rock and watches me make a fire with my flint and steel.

"Maybe," he muses, "there are no tracks because Crystal's a little pig and Alice is carrying her."

"I doubt it," I reply. "Alice has been talking to this pig for months, and she wasn't a piglet when they met. Maybe we're just not on their course."

I steam the fish and vegetables in violet leaves, and we eat by the river, admiring the kingfishers who dive into the water and come up with fish every time. Then we push on.

Farther along we come to the confluence of the Little Delaware and the West Branch, and Bando takes out his compass and map again.

"The West Branch will take us right through Delhi. Would you want to go through Delhi with a pig on a leash if you were Alice?"

"No."

"Look at the map, then," he says. "We have a problem ahead."

I see what he means. If we take the Little Delaware

and avoid Delhi, we will be way off course. The only other choice, as far as I can see, is to climb Federal Hill and it's nine hundred feet almost straight up.

"That's awfully steep for a pig," I say, "but I'm no expert on pigs."

"As a matter of fact," Bando says. "It may not be too steep. I read a well-researched book about three pigs who followed cattle drovers across prairies and over mountains on a trek to Montana."

That's Bando for you. He always gets his knowledge from reading.

Nevertheless, before making up my mind to climb Federal Hill, I tell Bando to stand still and I spiral out from him in a wider and wider sweep until I have covered almost the entire delta of the Little Delaware and the West Branch.

"Bando!" I shout.

"What?"

"Pig tracks."

He joins me at a trot.

"Pig tracks?" he asks dubiously as he looks at the cloven prints. "They look like deer to me."

"No. Deer prints are much more pointed and tapered. These are quite rounded."

Bando nods and puts his hand beside the prints. "We can certainly say that Crystal is no baby piglet. Those prints are as big as my palm," he observes, and we start off again.

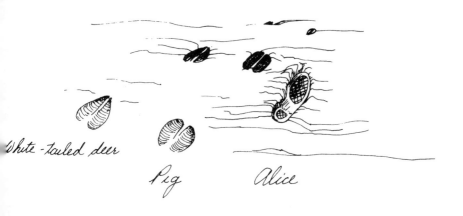

White-tailed deer

Pig   Alice

The tracks lead us through a shallows in the river to the other side, then east by northeast to the bottom of Federal Hill. Near the far edge of the flood plain I find Alice's footsteps in a stretch of muddy sand.

"Hello, little sister," I hoot in excitement. "There you are!"

Grinning with satisfaction, I follow her tracks into the woods where they soon disappear on the leafy trail. But Crystal's do not, and Bando and I follow her up the steep mountain. Then, almost at the top, her tracks disappear.

"The pig took off like a bird," Bando says, studying the last footprint. I spiral again, moving out from that print as I search for another. When I am almost ready to give up, I come upon a trampled and routed garden of May apples.

"I've found her," I call. "She stopped for lunch."

"Let's take five," says Bando and sits down. "That's a steep climb and, besides, we're making good time.

They can't be too far ahead. That pig is hardly a greyhound."

The sunlight filters through lacy hemlock needles and we stretch out on our backs, chewing the tasty twigs of a spicebush and silently admiring the forest.

"You know, Sam," Bando finally says. "I remember something else about pigs from that book."

"Really? What?"

"They bite. They can be as mean and dangerous as a guard dog. They even kill and eat snakes."

"Is that right? I'm glad to hear that." Although Alice is very good at taking care of herself, I'm happy to know pigs can bite. I smile and look at Bando. "I'm beginning to like that pig," I say.

"So am I."

Bando chuckles.

"What's so funny?"

"I'd sure hate to be the one who tries to tackle Alice and her pig."

"So would I," I say, shaking my head. "They both bite."

I spread out the Delhi quadrangle map.

"I figure Alice was sitting right here where we are two days ago," I say. "And at about this time of day. If so, and if I were her, I'd be looking for a waterfall and a campsite right now."

Bando glances at the sun and nods. I take out the map.

"Fitches Brook is it," I say, pointing to a cluster of

brown contour lines drawn close together which indicate a steep hill. There is a blue line through them. Together they say "waterfall."

"It's the only stream with a slope steep enough to make a waterfall and close enough to be reached before evening." I point to a submerged swamp symbol. "The brook begins here." I measure. "We have about four miles to go."

"Let's get along, then," Bando says, rising to his feet. "We'll want to have enough light when we get there to do a little fishing."

It is easy to follow dear old Crystal, as we are now calling her, and at about 4:00 P.M. we arrive at a reed-filled mountain swamp in a dark spruce forest where Fitches Brook starts.

Bando unfolds his collapsible fishing rod, and I gather cattail tubers and catch a mess of frogs for dinner. It's still too early to stop for the night, so we fish and gather May apples for dessert as we follow the splashing stream downhill.

I almost missed Alice's camp. It wasn't by the steepest waterfall, as I thought it would be, but considerably below and under, of all things, a dead oak. I passed that tree with only a quick glance, because it didn't look like anything Alice would pick, and then something occurred to me. I turned back. The leaves and sticks under the tree had been recently placed there. They did not match the colors of the leaves and sticks around them because their wet dark bottoms were up, not down.

Alice and I always cover our campsite with leaves when we depart so that no one will know we have been there. Those displaced leaves have a distinctive look to the knowing eye—jumbled and unnatural.

I kick a few aside, looking for blackened fireplace rocks or wood that would tell me Alice had camped here. Finding none where the strewn leaves are, I search the other side of the oak.

I come upon holes in the ground that could have been made by none other than a pig. They are outlined by rounded hoof prints and have sniff marks in them. Ha, I say to myself.

"Bando," I call. "A pig has been here."

Bando joins me, folding his rod as he contemplates the dead tree and the leaf-strewn ground.

"Alice slept here?" he asks incredulously.

"She did." I pick up a recently fire-blackened stone.

"If she loves beautiful waterfalls so much," he says, "why this unattractive place?"

"It's not unattractive to the pig," I answer. "We're not only going to have to think like Alice, but also like a pig."

"Got it," he says and picks up a half-eaten black-snake. "Pig kill," he says. "It's been thrashed and bitten. The book says that's how pigs kill snakes." He looks around, then points to another snake, soaking up the last sun of the day on a limb of the dead tree. "We're in blacksnake habitat. Another reason for Alice and her pig to stop here."

"Bando," I say, "pigs are omnivores. We've got to think snakes, fungi, grasshoppers, and big juicy moths as well as bulbs and roots." He sighs. I go on. "Here we are among fungi and snakes. It's clear Crystal is making decisions for Alice."

"And us," he mumbles, taking out his bedroll and spreading it under the leafless tree. I gather pine boughs for my bed, cook the frogs legs and cattail tubers, then put out the fire.

After eating we stretch out on the ground. Gradually the sky darkens and fireflies flash their love lights as the males rise through the trees by the brook.

"Bando?"

"Yes?"

"We're doing fine. I think we'll find Alice tomorrow."

"Maybe," he answers. "Trouble is, she knows where she's going. We don't."

"That's true," I reply resignedly.

A screech owl calls from the dead oak, and I look up. There is nothing so magical as a tree with an owl in it. The dead oak has come to life.

The little owl brings Frightful back to mind.

"Bando?"

"Yes, Sam."

"Do you think it's too late in the season for Frightful to breed? We're way into June."

"It probably is, but the geneticists do amazing things today."

Owl tree

I'm glad to hear that, but I still can't go to sleep.
"Bando?"
"Yes?"
"Have you seen the place where they keep the falcons at the university—the peregrine mew?"
"Yes. I have a friend on the staff there. You got me interested in peregrine falcons, and he got me interested in the effort to keep them on the planet with us."
"Tell me about the mew."
"Well, it's an enormous barn that is divided into apartments for paired falcons. Each mew has a high wooden shelf that resembles a cliff where the birds nest in the wilds. The females lay their eggs on these platforms. Some pairs will mate in captivity, others like Frightful, who is imprinted on you, must be artificially inseminated. Once the eggs are laid, the birds incubate them, and when they hatch, the sight of the nestlings triggers a ferocious parental love. The parents tend their young until they fly.

"It's a nice place, Sam, not like a cliff above a wild river, but nice. You'd like it."

I close my eyes and see Frightful incubating her eggs. A hot wind rises out of the valley, rustling the leaves and making me sleepy at last.

IN WHICH

Bando Finds Some Old Adirondack Furniture

At dawn we return our campsite pretty much to its original pristine appearance and walk on down the brook.

Shortly we are out of the forest and standing in a field. A large farm lies in the valley below.

"We've lost Alice's trail somewhere," I say. "If I were her, I would not go down through a farm with a pig on a leash."

"I would," Bando says. "There's a corncrib down there. Pigs like corn, you know."

We look at each other as the same thought strikes us. Alice has already been to the farm. About a hundred yards back we had noticed several corncobs along the shore of Fitches Brook. Still unaccustomed to thinking like a pig, we had agreed that raccoons had been at work on some farmer's crop.

Back we go, avalanching rocks as we scramble up the

shaley streambed and arrive at the embankment where we had seen an ear of corn. It's gone. I am searching upstream for it and any others when Bando calls. He is pointing to the stream bank. Four corncobs have been laid there in the shape of an arrow. Alice has been here. They point to a big flat rock where a squirrel is now stuffing kernels from another ear of corn in his cheeks. You can't leave anything sitting around in the woods or someone will get it. Even hard deer antlers are eaten by white-footed deer mice.

I leap across the stream on the rocks, the squirrel runs, and I pick up his ear of corn. There are broad teeth marks on it which are not squirrel. Could be deer, but it's not. It's pig. Pig droppings nearby clinch the identification, and then, looking around, I see Crystal's tracks in the soft loam. I'm off.

"Not so fast," Bando calls. "Come back. I've found something else."

On bare earth in the sun is another compass. This one is different from the first. Alice has propped up a stick at a 45-degree angle to the ground. On it hangs a stone on a string. Under it is a north-south directional stick. Smiling, I recall how Alice and I made a compass like this last spring. We placed a marker on the shadow that the hanging rock cast in the morning. Then, when the sun passed the meridian, we put another marker on the afternoon stone-shadow. Between the two marks and directly under the suspended rock, we laid a stick. We had a north-south line.

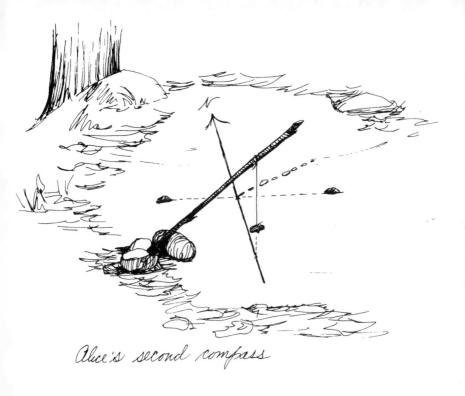

Alice's second compass

"She's checking her direction," I say.

"Well, she's got north, all right," Bando says, looking at his compass. "Her stick points to within 3 degrees of true north."

"And she plotted her directional line too," I say, pointing to the little pebbles lined up there.

"Ah, ha!" Bando lays his compass with the directional arrow lined up with the pebbles. Carefully he turns the compass housing until the arrow and north are lined up. He looks at the bearing marker. "She's going more easterly now—80 degrees."

We spread the county map on the ground and lay a grass blade from our stream location across the page at

80 degrees. The blade crosses the Schoharie Reservoir and intercepts Manorkill Falls.

I count contour lines and multiply by twenty. "Wow," I say. "That waterfall drops almost straight down a hundred feet."

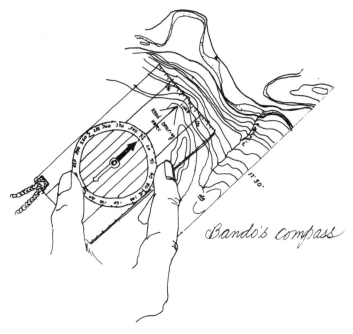

Bando's compass

"Manorkill Falls," Bando says. "I've read it's spectacular. If I were a girl who loved waterfalls, I'd be headed right for it."

"In fact," I say. "I'm so sure she's going there that we should go directly to it without losing any more time following pig tracks."

"Good idea," Bando agrees.

There are no trails or roads up here, so, by lining up trees to keep us going in a straight line, and by reading the quadrangle maps to avoid cliffs and marshes, we strike off across the top of the mountain range.

We traverse fields and forests, walk through barren lands where quails and woodcocks fly up at our feet, and, after twelve miles of bushwhacking, enter the Plattekill State Forest. We are greeted by a flock of wild turkeys, big, noisy, and glorious. They gobble and fly off, miraculously missing limbs and trunks as they zip through the forest. I could never hit one of those with my sling.

Although we're tired, the top of the mountain we're climbing calls to us, and we scramble on to its summit. Here we can see the Catskill, Helderberg, and distant Adirondack Mountains. I understand why people climb mountains. I am an eagle.

Bando sits down. We've been walking hard since 6:00 A.M., almost ten hours, and we're both glad to rest. The trek was rough because we stayed in the forests, where the understory is a jungle of hazelnut, viburnum, and twisted young hardwoods fighting for the sun. Travelling through them was work.

I offer Bando some smoked venison and dried apples. He eats heartily.

"I'm ready to stop for the night," he says. "I don't think we have to hurry now. If I were Alice and had reached Manorkill Falls, I'd stay for at least a day or two, wouldn't you?"

"I sure would," I say, noting the scratches on his arms and the smudges of dirt on his cheeks. "You're right, we don't have to hurry."

While he makes his bed, I practice with my sling. On the trek today, I missed nineteen out of twenty targets. I'm not doing so well. I guess it takes a lot of practice.

Later, Bando sleeps. I watch the stars and think of Frightful.

I wake early, pick a few Labrador tea leaves and brew them in Bando's tin cup. Then I gather a batch of day-lily buds for our breakfast. These I moisten in dew and dip in hazelnuts I pounded to a powder with a stone. I steam them in spicebush leaves.

With a catbird diving at us to chase us away from his nest, we leave the mountaintop on a northeasterly course. Bando is a little stiff and sore this morning, so we walk slowly, enjoying the vistas from the skyline of this mountain range.

We stop frequently to consult the map, whether we need to or not. Map reading gives us a good excuse to rest.

"Sam, look here," Bando says during one of these stops. "There's a power line below us. It leads to the road at the bottom of Manorkill Falls. It'll be a lot easier to walk on the cleared land under those wires than in this dense forest. Shall we take it?"

I agree we should, and within a few miles we break out of the tangled undergrowth into a meadow under the power line. We walk in daylilies, Queen Anne's lace, and the last daisies of June. A few black-eyed Susans bloom to say midsummer is nearly here.

We make good time, and I practice with my sling on the steel tower struts. There are so many that if I don't hit the one I aim at, I hit the one next to it. This is very satisfying, for although I'm not hitting my target, I am hitting something.

As we follow the meadow down the last steep slope of the mountain range, I see a patch of evening primroses near a stone fence. The roots of this flower are very good if you boil them long enough to remove the peppery taste. Taking my hunting knife from its sheath on my belt, I kneel down to dig but whoop instead.

"Bando! Crystal's been here!"

He runs down the hillside. "By golly, she has!"

"We stopped thinking pig," I say. "Crystal must have led Alice to the power lines. All kinds of edible plants grow in this habitat." I point to an uprooted primrose. "Including one of my favorites. Crystal has good taste." Getting to my feet, I glance around. She has also dug up a batch of Jerusalem artichokes, and I pick up one of the potatolike tubers she missed.

"Thank you, Crystal," I say and stuff it in my pouch along with the primrose.

"How do you think Crystal found all of this food?" Bando asks after we have started off again. "And I presume she did find it, not Alice."

"Smelled it, I guess," I say. "We humans will never know how meadows or mountains smell, but deer and

Jerusalem artichoke

horses and pigs do." Bando sniffs deeply and shakes his head.

"We were left out when it comes to smelling things," he says. "I would love to be able to smell a mountain and follow my nose to it."

Crystal's tracks are quite obvious now that we know she has been here, and we are able to trot along as we follow her down the steep slope. Bando veers off to the left and stops.

"Looks like a struggle here," he says pointing to tracks that are dug in deep, as if Crystal were resisting being pulled somewhere.

"Seems Alice is dragging her into those woods," Bando says.

"I wonder why," I ask, trying to think like Alice. I look for an answer in the mountains and rolling terrain but find none.

On we go, following the pig tracks. Presently we enter

a dark woods of very old yellow birches and again lose Crystal. The forest ends, and we are on a steep hillside looking across a valley at the famous profile of White Man Mountain.

"Bando!" I say. "I know what Alice is up to. The summer house of John Burroughs, the nature writer, is somewhere around here. I read parts of his books to Alice last winter. That's the mountain he loved. An artist sketched it for one of his books."

We wind down and around and within a quarter of a mile come upon John Burroughs' grave. It is surrounded by a stone wall and covered with lilies of the valley.

Bando finds some shelled beechnuts and hazelnuts lying at the base of a hollow tree near the grave.

"Could this be Alice?" he asks, bringing the nuts to me. "I'm suspicious of everything now."

I look at the nuts all neatly peeled and recognize the handiwork of a white-footed deer mouse. I put my hand in the hollow and find more.

"Alice has been here," I say. "But she did not shell the nuts. She raided a deer-mouse pantry. Deer mice take the coats off the seeds and nuts before they store them. You're real lucky when you find one. It's like opening a can of cocktail nuts. They're ready to eat." I pop a hazelnut in my mouth.

We take to a country road, where posters advertising the Roxbury Country Fair are nailed to every telephone pole.

"I love fairs," says Bando. "Think we have time to go?"

"No," I answer. "I don't think Alice is going to stay at Manorkill Falls as long as you think she is. There are lots of beautiful cascades in the Helderbergs."

We walk on in silence, round a bend and stop.

"There it is," I exclaim, pointing to a small brown house. "That's Woodchuck Lodge, John Burroughs' summer home."

"It is?" says Bando. "Well, as far as I'm concerned, it's the capital of Adirondack furniture. Look at that house!" Bando takes off his packbasket and gets out a notebook and pencil.

Woodchuck Lodge is small and rustic, with a sharply gabled roof and a porch railing of twisted limbs and branches. The porch furniture looks like my lounging chair, and the trim on the gable is a weaving of gnarled oaks and maple branches.

"Woodchuck Lodge," I read on the door, "is a National Monument supervised by the National Park Service." At this moment no one is here but us.

I start a small fire in the outdoor fireplace, wrap the primrose and artichoke in maple leaves, and clip some young shoots of a pokeweed.

"You know, Sam," Bando says as he sketches and watches me concoct a wild, savory lunch, "I think I'll just open one of the cans of stew."

As I put his food on the fire, I see four stones to my left and recognize a pathfinder's sign. Three stones are stacked one on top of the other, the fourth, on the ground beside them, points the direction the person is taking.

"Bando," I say, squatting beside the sign, "Alice has been here. She's changing course, going in the direction of that stone on the ground."

"How do you know it's Alice?" Bando asks.

"Pig tracks right here and an acorn, her woodland signature."

Bando lays his compass beside the directional stone and adjusts it.

"Seventy degrees," he says. "She's going east by northeast again."

"She's off to Manorkill Falls," I say and remove the hot stew from the fire.

IN WHICH
I Become Royalty

Alice is not at Manorkill Falls. I was certain she would be.

Bando and I climbed the steep gorge to the top, searching every cave and ledge along the ascent, and found no sign of her or her pig, no clues to say that they were here.

"If Alice," Bando says as we stand on the rim of the

gorge, "was in search of a beautiful waterfall, she should be right here where I am." The water roars and tumbles below us, sending up a soft spray that nurtures mosses and maidenhair ferns where it falls.

"But she's not," I say. "And I don't think she will be."

"Why?" he asks.

"Pigs don't care about views and water music. No sensible pig, and Crystal is a sensible pig as we well know, is going to let anyone, not even Alice, lead her up to this place. Federal Hill is one thing, but Crystal would need pitons for this ascent," I say, looking at all the watercress available for dinner.

"That's right. But where is she then?" Bando asks, not really expecting me to answer. Rather, he looks for an answer himself by taking out the map of Schoharie county, which we're in, and the map of Albany county, which we're coming to, and spreading them contiguously. As for me, I've given up trying to think like Alice for the day, and turn to a job I know I can do.

I dig a beetle larva out of a decaying log and put it on a thornbush fishhook I made and tied to a fine cord of deer tendon. Then, taking off my moccasins, I wade into the cold water and cast into a pool below a submerged log. A dragonfly skims over the surface, his crystal wings reflecting the sunlight.

Wop! I yank, and hook a large trout. Playing it carefully so it won't break my line as it darts from side to side, I concentrate on dinner. After a lively battle, I land the fish.

Bando is still bent over the maps. I clean the trout and wrap it in May-apple leaves, then dig a hole in the earth and build a fire. When the coals are hot, I push them into the hole, place the fish on them, and cover all with leaves, then soil.

"There's a farm at the bottom of the gorge," Bando says as I brush the dirt off my hands and sit down beside him. "There aren't many around. The land's too steep."

"Hmmm," I say, trying to think like my sister. "Let's go there and ask the farmer if she's been by for corn."

"Let's not ask people and get them all stirred up. We know she's all right, but they won't. They'll call the police and we don't want that."

"I'm going to ask, anyway," I say. "I think those stones at John Burroughs' home meant change of plans as well as change of direction."

"Why do you think that?"

"Because that's the first time she's used a plain old pathfinder's sign. She wanted to be sure that message was seen. Furthermore, she signed it with an acorn so I'd make no mistake about who laid the stones.

"And," I go on, still trying to think like Alice, "I've got a hunch she's left the change of plans with a person. Once we talked about how we might leave clues with people if we ever got off the mountain. It's like her to try it, so I'm going to take a chance and speak to that farmer. He's the only one around for miles, and since she's not at this falls, she's doing something radically different."

"I still don't think you should," Bando says as I serve him the fish on a nice thin slab of slate, garnished with watercress and crisp daylily roots. "But maybe you're right."

We find a log and sit down. A woodthrush sings. His song sounds like water spilling down the rocks in a cool, dark forest. As I listen, I thank Alice in spite of myself. Were it not for her, I would not be hearing that glorious song on top of this magnificent gorge.

Bando eats and goes back to the maps.

"Look at this, Sam," he says brightly. He is feeling better with sweet trout in his belly. "There's got to be some granddaddy of a waterfall at the Helderberg Escarpment. A large stream runs right off the edge of that eight-hundred-foot cliff." I get down on my knees and look.

"Wow!" I say. "I'll bet Alice is going there." I study the map. "And there are fields and farms nearby for Crystal. I think we're on Alice's brain wave now."

"Let's go," Bando says. "I'd like to see the goshawks." He packs his belongings, and we start the long descent to the bottom of the gorge.

About an hour later we are standing in the enormous rock bowl that holds the reservoir. The sun has just gone down.

"Where's the farm?" I ask.

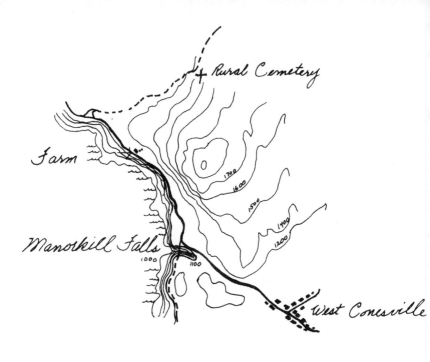

"Up the road about half a mile on the right." I start off.

"Hold on," Bando says. "I really don't like this idea, so I'll let you go alone to ask about Alice."

"You're not coming?"

"I'll meet you later. Zella asked me to give her a call if I got the chance." He shifts his packbasket. "West Conesville is about half a mile from here. Since it'll soon be dark and we can't go on, this looks like a good time to telephone her."

"All right," I say reluctantly. "Where shall we meet?"

"I saw a rural cemetery on the map about a mile beyond the farm. Make camp and I'll meet you there."

"When?"

"I'm not sure. Don't wait up for me."

As I approach the farm, I slow down to study the situation I'm walking into. The land is well tended, the buildings strong and freshly painted. This is reassuring, because these things speak of a hardworking farmer, and hardworking farmers are usually sincere people. The ones I know have no time for pretense. They answer yes or no. I trust this farmer will do likewise when I ask if he's seen Alice.

The farmhouse is very old. It has two small low windows on the second floor, and the clapboard is slightly wider than the boards on houses today. I glance at the corncrib as I pass it and hope that Alice did not help herself to a meal for Crystal. I scold myself for thinking this.

I tuck my shirt in my jeans and, combing my hair with a teasel-weed head I found near the corncrib, I walk up the steps to the house.

As I lift the knocker, I read the Dutch name, Van Sandtford, beneath it. The Dutch were the first settlers in this part of New York, so it could be that this is a pioneer family. Thinking this helps me relax. I understand pioneers. I am one with them.

Footsteps resound and the door is opened by a large, bony gentleman. He has sandy hair, a long nose, and deep-set blue eyes. He looks like one of the portraits of the pioneers on the walls of the Delhi library.

"Sir," I begin. "I'm inquiring about my sister. She

was purchasing corn. Did she by any chance come by here today?"

"Alice, you mean? The pretty girl with the pig?" My heart bangs; I'm on the track.

"Yes, Alice," I say and smile broadly, wondering what to say next. I am saved by Mr. Van Sandtford.

"She stayed here for a few days with her pig," he says. "But she's gone on to the Livingstonville fair with my daughter, Hanni."

"Oh," I say, trying not to cry out in disappointment.

"She and Hanni met at the Roxbury fair, and Hanni invited her to stay here until the 4-H Club fair at Livingstonville started."

So that's why she gave me the change-of-plans sign at John Burroughs' place, I say to myself. She saw the Roxbury fair posters and went down to see it. She wasn't at Manorkill Falls because she got a ride.

"My son, Hendrik," Mr. Van Sandtford goes on, "drove Alice and Hanni to Livingstonville last evening with their hogs. Hanni raises hogs, too. The girls are going to sleep in the barn with their animals." I must look surprised, for he says, "I hope that's all right, and that your family won't object."

"No, no. It's fine," I say.

Mr. Van Sandtford steps out on the porch to join me, and his eyes sweep over his farm as he checks barn, silo, and fields in the manner of a farmer. A cow might be sick or a fox might be in the chicken coop. Apparently all is well. He sits on the railing.

"I love the way these 4-H Club kids take care of their animals," he goes on. "You'd think they were their children."

I walk down the steps, trying to make an exit.

"I hope Alice hasn't been a burden," I say.

"A burden? Alice?" he replies. "She worked very hard. She cleaned the hog barn, swept the porch, and helped Hanni and Hendrick with the cows and horses. She's a great little girl."

"Good," I answer almost too eagerly.

"Clever sow Alice has," her host continues. "Isn't it amazing the way she rolls over?"

"Yes. Yes, it is," I stutter and jump down the stone path, hoping to escape before it becomes evident that I don't know much about Crystal.

Mrs. Van Sandtford has come out on the porch and is looking at me as if she knew something about me that I don't know. I feel uneasy.

"We enjoyed Alice," she says. "I just know she's going to win a blue ribbon with that Spotted Poland China of hers." Spotted Poland China? I am thinking she means dishes, until I realize she is talking about Alice's pig.

"Well, I appreciate your helping her," I repeat awkwardly. "She was so anxious to get to the pig fair that she couldn't wait for me to drive her there." I bite my lips. I am getting myself in trouble. Huck Finn is right—truth is better and actually safer than a lie.

I hurry toward the gate.

"Wouldn't you like a cup of tea before you go, Mr. Van Rensselaer?" Mrs. Van Sandtford asks.

I suck in air. Mr. Van Rensselaer? Now what is Alice up to?

"No, thank you," I say. "I've really got to go." With that empty remark, I smile and leave.

Halfway to the rural cemetery, I think of something, turn around, and run the mile to West Conesville. Bando told me not to wait up for him. I know why.

The full moon is rising over the chimneys and gabled rooftops of the little town as I walk up the steps to the Ruffed Grouse Hotel and enter the lobby. At the registration desk I tap a bell and a tall man appears.

"Sir," I say. "Would you please tell Mr. Zackery that Sam Gribley is here."

"He's in the dining room," he replies and directs me to a large room hung with red drapes and dimly lit with electric sconces.

"Sam!"

"Bando." It's as I suspected. He's eating.

"Sit down, Sam. Have a bite on me."

"I've eaten."

He grins sheepishly.

"Sam, I'm not as young as you are. I just have to get a good meal before I can think like a pig and a girl again."

"Well, you don't have to think like either anymore," I say. "I found Alice and the pig."

"Where?"

"They're at the 4-H Club fair in Livingstonville."

Bando puts down his fork. "A 4-H Club fair? Alice? I wonder what she's up to there?"

He opens the menu to the list of desserts, and I think about my new name but can't make any sense out of it.

"Who are the Van Rensselaers, Bando?" I finally ask.

"The Van Rensselaers? They were the feudal lords of what is now Albany county. Before we were a democracy—in fact, in the 1600s—they were given hundreds of thousands of acres of land by the Dutch king—all of Albany county. They divided this land into 120-acre parcels and rented them to their countrymen who came to the New World. The Van Rensselaers made fortunes and became a powerful and influential family. Why?"

"Meet Sam Van Rensselaer," I say, extending my hand.

"Alice?"

"Alice is calling herself Alice Van Rensselaer, so that makes me Sam Van Rensselaer."

"Well," Bando smiles. "With a name like that you can go to all the fanciest places. The Van Rensselaers were colonial New York's royalty."

This does not help me figure out why she picked that name. She must be trying to tell me something, but what?

Bando finishes his meal, and we leave the dining room, with me dashing ahead for the door.

"Sam," Bando takes my arm. "I've taken a room here."

"Really?"

"I'm tired," he says. "I need a comfortable bed."

He does look tired. I have been very thoughtless.

"I'm sorry," I say. "I didn't know you were *that* exhausted, or I would have stopped earlier."

"One night's good sleep will fix me up," he says, putting his hand on his hip and limping like an old man.

"Sure," I laugh. "Sleep well."

"There are twin beds in my room. You can have one of them. If it's too soft, there's always the floor."

"No, thanks," I say. "I couldn't sleep indoors if I wanted to. I'll meet you in the cemetery at sunup."

"Zella sends her love," he calls as I leave.

Love goes a long way. I stride down the street.

IN WHICH
I Get News of Alice

We leave the Catskills behind north of the cemetery and enter the Helderbergs. I know we are in them when the forest trees change. Maples and hemlocks are replaced by yellow birch and the northland's black spruce. Dark bogs pock the mountaintops. We sink up to our calves in one of these, so avoid the others by checking the map and plotting a course around them.

As we bushwhack along, the mountains themselves

tell me we have arrived. The Helderbergs are made up of layers of limestone and shale, through which underground streams and rivers have carved miles of caverns. Some near the surface have caved in, leaving gaping sink holes in the land. Others are walk-in caves.

These are magnets, and we explore each one we come upon. Deep in them we can hear subterranean rivers rushing off through the netherworld, and our voices echo and reecho through the halls. We see a dimly illumed underground waterfall and climb down to it for a dark thundering shower.

We spend the night by a cavern and before sunup are jogging along toward the 4-H Club fair. I am concerned about Alice's using the name Van Rensselaer. I can sense an Alice-scrape coming up. Imposters are not appreciated, not even yellow-headed ones.

Shortly after sunrise we come down the steep road into Livingstonville, a small town of no more than forty houses and stores cozied at the confluence of the Catskill and Lake creeks.

Virtually no cars pass us; the sidewalks are empty, and the homes, which were built many years ago, stand gray or paint-chipped behind walls of lilacs and groves of stately trees. Modernizing is not fashionable in Livingstonville. Even the store is an old grocery-gas-hardware-feed store and luncheonette–post office that dates back to the twenties, Bando says. It's a wonderful town.

We enter the all-purpose store and sit down at the

luncheonette counter. Only four people are here, which is the right number for any store as far as I'm concerned. Bando picks up the menu.

"Coffee, homemade sausage sandwich, and strawberry-rhubarb pie," he says to the woman behind the counter. She also seems to be the postmistress, for she is sorting mail as well as listening to Bando's order.

I stare at him. We've just finished a breakfast of fish chowder and sow-thistle leaves, and here he is eating again. No wonder he has a paunch! Or he did have one. He's walked it off, I see.

"Sam," Bando says. "What do you want to eat?"

"Nothing," I reply. "I'm stuffed."

When Bando's breakfast is set before him, I turn to the burly man beside me.

"Sir," I say to the stranger, emboldened by the comforting shelves of canning jars and bins of nails and feed. "Can you tell me how to get to the Livingstonville fairgrounds?"

"Fairgrounds?" His voice is so low it vibrates. "Ain't no fairgrounds in Livingstonville."

"There aren't? But there's supposed to be a 4-H Club fair in Livingstonville." I'm devastated as Alice slips away again. We just can't ever quite catch up with her. The postmistress finishes sorting the mail and brings me a glass of water.

"I just happened to overhear you," she says, pushing back her gray hair. "I'll bet you're looking for that hog show."

"I am," I reply.

"It's at the Monroe Farm, a piece up Hauverville Road toward Rensselaerville."

"Is that what you're looking for?" the man beside me asks. I nod. "Mammie's right. The hog show's up there on that farm. Lots of kids. Nice kids. They like pigs."

I impatiently wait for Bando to finish his meal so I can go outside and talk to him without being overheard. I know why Alice took the name Van Rensselaer. The postmistress unwittingly gave me the answer. I nudge Bando. He picks up the newspaper lying on the counter, sips his coffee, and reads. He's not ready to leave.

I count to one hundred slowly, then watch the postmistress read a postcard before putting it in a box.

"Here's a news story on the 4-H Club fair," Bando says. I count tractor tires. He turns the page and reads on.

"This note in the personal column ought to interest you. 'Skri. Hacking falcons at Huyck Preserve, 6:00 P.M., 25th of June. Check R library for final arrangements.' "

"That *is* interesting," I say, leaning over his shoulder to read this item.

I ask the postmistress where the Huyck Preserve is.

"Just this side of Rensselaerville," she answers, and I thank her and get right to my feet. Bando is still reading, so I look at the jelly jars. My clay ones are nicer.

Finally he lays down the paper, pays his bill, and we leave.

"Bando," I say as soon as we step on the sidewalk. "I know why Alice used the name Van Rensselaer."

"You do? Why?"

"She's telling me her destination."

"You're kidding. Where *is* she going?"

"To Rensselaerville."

"How do you know that?"

"Let me look at the Rensselaerville quadrangle map," I say and open it on the hood of a truck.

"Yep, there's a waterfall there. It drops about a hundred feet."

"She sent a message by changing her name?" Bando says incredulously. "That's pretty farfetched. She doesn't even know we're following her."

"She sure does."

"Come on, Sam. She's been at least twenty miles ahead of us ever since we left."

"But she's playing On the Track."

"So?" He throws up his hands.

"I should have known when I found the compass on the sand spit. We always begin with a directional guide. I was so sure she was off to find her own home that I forgot about that game pretty much."

I go on. "I didn't realize the name Van Rensselaer was a clue until the postmistress mentioned Rensselaerville. Then I knew Alice was telling me where she was going."

"You two sure make life complicated for yourselves up there in the woods."

"Lively," I reply. "Look here." I point to the map. "I'm right. Near the town is a waterfall and lots of acres for a pig to forage."

"Desdemondia," Bando says under his breath. "Well, if you are right, we should skip the pig farm. Alice won't be there."

"She won't. I'm sure of that. She's at that falls right now, climbing up a cascade or sitting in an air pocket under an overshoot."

We pack up the map and head for the road to Rensselaerville.

"I think we should stop at the pig farm, anyway," Bando says after a while.

"I'd rather go on," I say. "I'd like to find her before she's fined for having a pig on a nature preserve. The waterfall's on the Huyck Preserve. And we're tracking her to keep her out of scrapes, aren't we?"

"Nevertheless," Bando says, "I think we should talk to Hanni. It'll only take a minute to ask her if Alice told her where she is going. Hanni should still be there. The paper said the fair would last four days."

"Okay," I agree. "Maybe she left another clue with Hanni." We trek along in silence for about a mile.

"Sam," Bando suddenly says. "Want to watch the hacking tonight after we find Alice?"

"You bet I do," I answer. "Maybe there'll be some young peregrine falcons at hack."

The thought of seeing falcons on the wing lightens

my feet, and I step up our pace through the rugged farmland.

Along the way we talk about the weather and about the poor crops to our right and left, and finally we stop talking. Bando's brow is wrinkled, which means he's troubled. We walk on.

The uphill road plunges through a quaking aspen grove. A brown thrasher sits on a twig imitating all the birds in his area. I name them as he sings, "bluebird, cardinal, yellow-throated warbler." Then I whistle Frightful's name several times. It would be fun if he added that to his repertoire. There would be a bird in the Helderbergs who could call her name. I shake my head at the idea. I miss Frightful so much.

Around a bend, we see a large white farmhouse with Greek pillars, a barn, a silo, and a fenced yard where a dozen or so pickup and farm trucks are parked. Kids my age are everywhere.

"The Monroe Farm. Spotted Poland Chinas. Breeders." I read on the gatepost, then pause. A sumac bush has been deliberately cut and bent toward Rensselaerville. In the break is an acorn.

"Bando, I'm right," I say, pointing to Alice's woodland signature. "She's going to that falls."

We walk to the pig yard. A boy and a girl about my age are leaning on the fence, chatting, and I look down on the prettiest, cleanest pigs I've ever seen. I could almost like them.

I exchange hellos with them and ask for Hanni.

"She's in the first hog barn," the boy says, pointing. "Right over there."

"Come on, Bando."

"I'll stay here," Bando says. "You should talk to her alone. I'll study the pigs. I've never been this close to real pigs before."

I go in the barn where, after my eyes have adjusted to the dim light, I see a tall girl with bangs and shoulder-length soft brown hair crouched over a pig. She hears my steps and looks up.

"Hanni?"

"Hi."

She's pretty.

"Is Alice here?" I ask.

"Oh, you must be Sam." I nod. Her very blue eyes smile into mine. "She was expecting you, but she had to leave before you got here. She told me to tell you she was going ahead with the original plans you two made. She said you'd know what that meant."

"Oh, yes. The original plans," I say out loud while crying inside. What original plans?

"Good," I add, then take a deep breath, wondering if this is another Alice-clue.

"Did she take Crystal?" I ask, grasping for something to say.

"No, Crystal's here. Mr. Monroe will take care of her until Alice comes back."

"Oh, that's nice." I'm surprised to hear this *and* delighted. It's the first real news I've gotten. She's coming back to this farm.

"Where is Crystal?" I ask, trying to sound appropriately eager to see her. "I'd like to say hello. She's a neat pig." I think of Huck Finn again and feel myself blush.

"Crystal's in the third pen. Go talk to her. She's so lonely without Alice. Alice talked about how much you liked Crystal." Hanni looks smack into my eyes and smiles mischievously. There is a bolt of honesty skipping between us. She knows Alice likes to tell tall tales about me. I smile. I like her in her 4-H Club green shirt and trousers even if she does like pigs, or hogs, as they call them here.

"I'll be with you in a minute," she says.

I look in the third pen in despair. There are three pigs here. Which one is Crystal? I decide to leave before Hanni finds out I don't know, but she joins me.

"Sam," she says. "Pet little Crystal. Look at her, she's so sad." In vain I study the three spotted pigs to see which one is sad. They all have turned up mouths and seem to be completely happy.

"You *are* sad, aren't you Crystal?" Hanni says. I glance sidewise to see which pig she is looking at. Her lashes are so long I can't tell where her eyes are focused. I shift nervously from one foot to the other. I can't keep up this hoax much longer. I'm about to spoil Alice's story about my liking Crystal and come out with the truth when a pig with a white nose and black spots on her snout sniffs the air and runs toward me. I take a chance that she is recognizing the odor of her human family like all pets do—even members of the family they've never met. To all animals, even pollywogs, the family has a distinctive aroma, as distinctive as a clan plaid.

"Hello, Crystal," I say and pat the pig with the nose spots, hoping I'm right. The pig grunts expressively, and I scratch the bristly head. Hanni is smiling and watching the happy reunion. I am right.

Two other kids join us, but they are not interested in Crystal. They are staring at me, smiling, almost in deference. I am flattered, until I remember who I am, and when I do, want nothing more than to escape.

I back away, and just in time. Crystal is showing the tips of her tusks in warning. Having recognized the Gribley odor, this clever pig now knows something else about me. She knows I don't like pigs.

"Hanni," I say. "It's been nice to meet you. I want to thank you for all you did for Alice."

"It was fun, Sam Van Rensselaer," she says, and her eyes twinkle. She lowers her voice. "Did you understand the message? Do you know where she's going from here?"

"Yes," I reply. She tosses her hair with a flip of her head and smiles her beautiful smile. I wish it were for Sam Gribley, not Sam Van Rensselaer.

Then she winks and her eyes shine softly. She knows who I really am. The smile is for Sam Gribley.

With a couple of lilting strides, I join Bando. We take to the county road.

"Does she know where Alice is going?" he asks.

"Yes," I say, then stop stone still. I look at him sheepishly. "I forgot to ask her. She asked me."

"What did you say?"

"That I knew." I am blushing. I start off again.

"She *is* very pretty," Bando chides and sets his pace to mine.

"I did learn something," I tell him defensively.

"What's that?"

"Alice is coming back here."

"Good. We can take it easy," he says and slows down.

IN WHICH
The Dawn Breaks over Me

As we near Rensselaerville, we sit down in the shade of a white ash and plan what to do next.

I will go to the falls to see how Alice is. Bando will go to the library to find out where the hacking will be held on the vast preserve. That decided, we arise and I start off. Bando holds me back.

"You know, Sam," he says, "I've been thinking about

this hacking business in the paper. There's something strange about it. First of all, six o'clock in the evening is a bad time of day to hack a bird. My friend, Steve, at the peregrine mew, puts the fledglings out early in the morning so they'll have all day to look around and learn the environment before they fly off.

"And secondly, the news of the hacking wasn't on the front page like the pig show. It was in the paid personals. I think it was paid for because it's a message for one man, Skri, whoever he is. He was probably told to watch the newspaper for the date and place to meet."

"To hack birds?"

"I don't think they're hacking birds. I think it's a cover-up for something else. But I don't know what."

Bando turns to go, his black eyebrows pulled together in puzzlement.

"I'll meet you at the library," he calls.

"Okay," I reply, and, eager to see Alice, take off at a run down a dirt road, then cut over to Tenmile Creek, passing through a forest of yellow birch and maples. I follow the stream to the falls, a beauty that splashes down an eighty-foot staircase. The water hums, whispers, and spins white threads before pooling at the bottom.

This is it, I say to myself, this has to be where Alice is.

I jump down the rock staircase, pausing on ledges to look for signs of her camp, and come upon the ruins of

Alice's camp

an old mill. I poke around briefly, then go on to the bottom of the cascade. Finding no clues, I am on my way back up the falls when I see it.

"Alice's castle," I say, clambering up to a ledge where a stone wall with stones placed one on two, two on one, protects a natural cave from rain and wind.

I crawl in and give out a whoop. I've found her at last. Who else would make a bed of boughs and put a rabbit-skin pillow on it? Who else would have a container made out of two huge sycamore leaves sewn together with wild grapevine thread and filled with daylily buds?

My heart is beating as fast as a bird's. Alice is here, but she's also not here. She must be out foraging. I'll sit on the ledge and wait for her.

Now that I've found her what do I do?

When I started tracking her, I was only going to make sure she didn't get into a scrape. Since I know she's playing On the Track and we're supposed to find each other, I think I'll just hide until she comes back and say "Boo!" like she does when she finds me. Then I'll hug her.

To wait out of her sight, I climb into a young hemlock with limbs that hang over the falls and sit among the dense needles. From here I can see the creek, the gorge, and a pine plantation. From whichever direction Alice comes, I'll spot her.

As I settle in, I note that the sun has crossed the meridian. A yellow-shafted flicker chisels for an insect in a tree, and a kingfisher alights on an aspen bough. Alice has still not come back.

Suddenly the kingfisher screams his alarm note, and the forest becomes still. Wild eyes join mine, looking for the danger. Into the clearing below me slips a large eastern coyote. Gray as a wolf and almost as big, her movements are agile and swift. She lifts her head to inspect a scent on the wind. Her eyes are yellow fire.

I can't see her too well, but I can make out a large bird in her mouth.

This is the first eastern coyote I've ever seen, although Miss Turner said that this nearly extinct animal is making a comeback. Before the first settlers arrived in America, the big gray coyote of the woods lived and hunted all over the Northeast. With the cutting and burning of the forests for farming, its habitat was eliminated. Without the forest foods of ruffed grouse, turkeys, raccoons, and wood rats, the eastern coyote almost died out. Only a few lived on in the Adirondacks and the Catskill Mountains.

Then things turned around for woodland creatures. Like my mountain, the tilled land eroded and grew stones, not crops, and the farms were abandoned. The forests returned and the forest animal community returned with them, including the eastern coyote, which now ranges from Canada to the Bronx in New York City.

I sit perfectly still. Miss Turner said the eastern coyote is a clever hunter. Perhaps I can learn something from her.

The kingfisher keeps screaming his alarm cry but from a safe distance. The coyote ignores him, then moving so effortlessly she seems to float, she stops directly under me and drops the bird she is carrying. She teases it with her nose.

I lean forward and a branch snaps. The coyote vanishes, gray into green. Bird feathers ride the little whirlwind her passage stirred.

Annoyed at myself for scaring her, I settle back again and wait for Alice.

The shadows grow longer. A crow flies silently into a tree across the stream and, after checking the land and sky, drops to the ground near the coyote's prey. Cautiously it walks up to it and pecks. Suddenly there's a gray streak of coyote, a jaw snap, and the crow is dead.

She *is* a clever hunter. That bird was a trap.

Well, if that isn't neat. I'm going to do that, too. I take my sling and a stone from my pocket and move to a limb where I can swing my arm if another creature comes to the bait. I see the bird pretty well and it puzzles me. I come down lower. On its legs are jesses, swivel, and leash. Dropping to the ground, I pick up a sharp-shinned hawk.

The trappings are very professional, the bird fat and in good health. I wonder if this was one of the birds to be put at hack. It can't be. It's an adult. Only juveniles are hacked. It must belong to one of the hackers. He's brought her along to fly and exercise her.

I backtrack the coyote by following feathers and find that she killed her prey in a clearing not far from the falls. Feathers are scattered everywhere. I circle the area.

Whoever was here left sometime today. The dirt that put out the fire is still warm. I look around for a hacking board. There is none, nor is there any indication that there ever was one. But there *have* been birds of prey here. There are holes in the ground, and a mark where a perch fell and was dragged, probably by the coyote as she went off with the sharp-shinned. All the perch holes are circled with claw marks. A tethered raptor will make marks like these. When frightened or restless, they fly to the end of the leash, drop to the ground, and tear the earth with their talons. Frightful made such a circle around her perch before she felt comfortable with me.

I find the clinching proof that raptors have been here. Falcons, hawks, and owls swallow fur, bones, and feathers as well as meat, then regurgitate, or "cast," the unused parts in tidy pellets. There are castings near the perch holes.

This has to be the site of the hacking, but why isn't anyone here? Did the coyote scare them off? I guess so. I'd sure move if a coyote killed one of my birds.

I go back to the falls. Alice is still not here. I'm beginning to think she's gone fishing or berrying and will not return until dusk. It's about four o'clock. Time to find Bando.

Putting the jesses, leash, and ring in my belt pouch, I follow Tenmile Creek to the bridge and climb the abutment. At the top I get my first look at Rensselaerville.

It's pretty, but more so is a working water mill right across the road. Eagerly I circle it. The waterwheel itself is housed in a huge shed built against the milling room, which is two stories high.

Boy, can I learn a lot here! A huge, wonderful, operating water mill. As I round the building I find an old millstone. That tells me this is a gristmill, not a sawmill, and it tells me the mill is old. The stone is dressed with circular furrows, a design that hasn't been used for more than a hundred years. The furrows move the ground flour out into the vat.

I walk around the mill again then go to the front door, certain I'm going to be disappointed, for I have not seen a person or heard the wheel turn since I arrived. I am right. A sign on the door reads: HOURS: 12–5 SAT–SUN, MID-MAY THROUGH LABOR DAY. GRIST MILL 1789.

"It's Tuesday," I say to the door and knock anyway. No one answers. It's just as well. I haven't time for this right now. I've got to tell Bando that I've found Alice's camp and a site where falconers, if not the hackers, have been.

I hurry down the main street, which is lined with wooden houses painted white, yellow, blue, and red. Some look to be as old as the mill. Behind them rise the steeples of several churches. Enormous maples and spruces shade the sidewalks. Like Livingstonville, this is a very quiet town. There is no one but me on the street.

I come to a Tudor town house with RENSSELAER-VILLE LIBRARY AND READING ROOM hand lettered under the gable. I open the door.

Bando is at an antique reading desk, engrossed in a book. I slip up quietly and sit down beside him.

"Find out about the hacking?" He startles and looks up.

"Not yet. I've been wandering around town waiting for the library to reopen. It's not a busy place. The hours are eight to eleven and four thirty to six. The librarian just opened the doors again."

"I've found Alice," I whisper.

"You have?" His face lights up.

"Well, yes and no. I've found her camp. She wasn't there, but she'll be back. She's made a fine stone-walled camp. Quite permanent."

"In that case," he says, closing his book, "let's celebrate by going across the street for an early dinner. At the grocery store where I stopped for a newspaper, I heard that the chef is marvelous."

"Aw, come on Bando," I say. "I don't like fancy places. Besides I have dried venison and horse sorrel for dinner." He's unmoved. I try another temptation. "Let's eat by the waterfall and wait for Alice."

"I can wait more patiently over good restaurant food." He shoulders his packbasket. "We won't be long."

"I haven't got any money."

"My treat. You've treated me all along the way. Now it's my turn."

"I found where the hackers have been. Don't you want to see?"

He looks interested when I say that.

"Are they there?"

"No."

"Then I'll see it later."

Reluctantly I follow Bando to the library door. As I pass the checkout desk, I stop. A book entitled *Goshawk,* by T. H. White, is in the return box. I thumb through it, for although I have read it many times, I can always read it again. It's about the training and manning of the spirited, fighting goshawk.

"Would you like to take the book out?" asks the librarian, a scholarly looking man who is settling down in his chair to work.

"No, thank you," I say. "Not today."

"There's been quite a bit of interest in hawks and falcons around here lately," he says.

"Any particular reason?" Bando asks.

"There have been falconers around," he says, stroking his beard. "Just a few weeks ago two men offered my son, Eric, a couple of hundred dollars to locate a sharp-shinned hawk nest for them."

"Did he do it?"

"No, he was afraid they would harm the birds. The conservation officer, who is rooming across the street this week—he moves around from town to town—told Eric there was a renewed interest in hawks and falcons since some of them have been designated endangered species.

"They're precious, and precious things are worth a

lot of money—like the nearly extinct white rhinos of Africa. Poachers make fortunes selling their horns. Terrible." Bando is moving toward the door, but the librarian is not finished.

"Look at this," he says and walks over to the community bulletin board.

"Two men put this up when I opened this morning." He points to a card.

"Skri," it reads. "Hacking moved to Beaver Corners, dawn of the 26th. Go to church. Bate." In the left-hand corner are some Arabic letters.

"That's interesting," comments Bando.

"See that," the librarian taps the letters. "That was put there just before eleven. A well-dressed man drove up in a green car and came in. He read the note and signed it."

"Hmm," Bando says. "Probably acknowledging he's read it."

"He was chatty," the librarian goes on. "Talked to me for quite a while—said he was from Saudi Arabia. He thumbed through the goshawk book, too. Said the sheik he worked for had a goshawk.

"The Arab sheiks prize falcons," the librarian continues. "They've been practicing the art of falconry for thousands of years. I understand they'll pay more for a falcon than a racing car, especially since that pesticide DDT got in the food chain and wiped out so many of the birds of prey."

"They'll pay high prices?" Bando says.

"Selling falcons to Arabian sheiks," the librarian goes on, "has always been a big business, even when Jesus lived."

Bando opens the door. "We're going across the street to the restaurant. If you hear or see anything more about the hacking, we'd sure like to know."

"All right. I think the two men will come back to see if their note has been read and signed. And by the way," he goes on, "the men who put up the note are the same ones who wanted Eric to find them a sharp-shinned hawk nest. They're in town. Eric and I saw them as we came down the road just now." He looks at me. "You were at the mill, and they were walking up the creek, of all things."

Bando reads the posted card once more and shakes his head.

"Let's dine," he says. "I need to think, and I think best over food."

"Okay," I say, "but I sure want to surprise Alice when she comes home. Let's eat fast."

As I enter this restaurant, I am prepared to shrink into the furniture, but it's nice. The room is bright and pleasant. One wall is a grocery store, where coffee, canned soups, bread, and pancake mixes are stacked on shelves. The kitchen is on the other side of a large, pass-through window. Two young men in chef hats are consulting over the stove. It's early, around 5:00 P.M., but there are already two couples at a table near the window. The food must be good. I sit down and pick up the menu.

"Squab with sorrel sauce," I read aloud. "Smoked eel on a bed of wild asparagus."

"Desdemondia," groans Bando. "Wouldn't you know I'd hit a restaurant that specializes in game and wild foods. I'm back on the trail again."

One of the chefs, a large man with rosy jowls, comes to our table and introduces himself as Mr. Milo, the head chef and owner of the restaurant.

He addresses Bando. "The Cajun opossum with wild rice is superb."

"I have my heart set on filet mignon," Bando states. "Don't you have steak?"

"Well, yes," he answers reluctantly. "But the leg of wild rabbit with tarragon sauce is much better." Bando rolls his eyes and orders the steak.

"I'll take the wild rabbit," I say, then add, "have you ever tried it on a bed of daylily buds?"

"Daylilies? No, I've never even tasted them, but I hear they're a great delicacy."

"I have some with me if you would like to try them." I take a leaf bag from my belt pouch. "Moisten them in egg and roll them in flour—preferably acorn flour—and fry them."

"Thank you very much," he says and sniffs their tart odor.

"Mr. Milo," Bando says. "If you're interested in wild

delicious

Daylily

foods, speak with my friend Sam here. He's an expert."

"He is?" He turns to me. "Can I talk to you later?"
I nod and he writes down our orders.

"I'd like that steak very rare," Bando says, and Mr.
Milo turns to go, then leans down to me.

"I have mulled sumac tea," he says. "Would you like
some?"

"I sure would."

When the marvelous meal is consumed, we step out
of the restaurant and into the late afternoon light just as

a pickup camper pulls up to the library. A man gets out and hurries inside, leaving another man sitting at the wheel with the motor running. They must be the two men the librarian suspected would be back to see if their note on the bulletin board had been read and initialed.

We are crossing the street when the man comes out of the library.

"Bando," I say, pointing. "That's Officer Longbridge!"

"That man?" he says. "He's not Leon Longbridge." The man hears us, looks up, and jumps in the pickup. The door slams and the car speeds off.

"He *is* Leon Longbridge," I say. "He's the man who confiscated Frightful. He has one blue eye and one brown eye."

"He may be the man who confiscated Frightful, but he's not Leon."

I feel sick. I went to Delhi to find out if the conservation officer was named Leon Longbridge, but I didn't think to look at him.

"Sam," Bando's voice is urgent. "That man has Frightful, and he's about to sell her. He's no hacker. Let's find the conservation officer and get to Beaver Corners now."

"I'm not coming," I say.

Bando spins around and stares at me. "Don't you want to get Frightful back?"

"Yes, yes," I answer. "But Alice camped near those

hackers and the librarian saw them going up Tenmile Creek a little while ago. I'm going back to find her."

"Yes, do!" he says forcefully. "Go find Alice."

I borrow the Westerlo and Altamont quadrangle maps and we separate, planning to meet at Beaver Corners at dawn if all is well.

IN WHICH
I Am On the Track

I run down the street, vault over the bridge railing, and climb down the abutment to the creek. I take off my moccasins and, wading into the cool water, splash upstream toward Alice's camp.

I'm a tug-of-war inside. I want to look for Frightful with all my heart, and with all my heart I want to find Alice. But the battle, my head says, is already won. I've got to find Alice.

Some things become clear as I run. Frightful was stolen from me. And Bate, who must be that blue-and-brown-eyed man, is going to sell her to Skri at Beaver Corners. Hacking is just a code word that means Bate has birds to sell.

What isn't clear is Alice's situation. Did the two men find her? Did they harm her? I run faster.

With the beginning of twilight darkening the falls, I splash up to Alice's camp.

She should be here, but she's not. Where is she? Feeling prickles of fear running over my skin, I crawl into her stone home and sit down.

I am paralyzed. I can't seem to act. I don't know what to do. Should I wait? Or should I get the police? In anguish I roll over and bury my face in her rabbit-fur pillow.

It crackles. I snatch it up and find a letter. Crawling out on the ledge, my hands trembling, I lay a small pile of pine needles and twigs, then, taking out my flint and steel, strike a spark and start a fire. As the flame flares up, my heart thumps like a plumping mill. Why is she writing me a letter? That's not part of On the Track. She must be in trouble. I unfold a sheet of paper with the Monroe Poland China Farm crest on it and see it is dated this morning. The letter was here when I arrived before noon, but since I didn't lie down on the pillow I didn't find it.

"Hi, Sam," I read. "Isn't this fun?"

Fun? Are you crazy? I am worried to death about you, Alice, and you think this is fun. Don't you know that dangerous men are around you? I hold the letter closer to the fire and read on.

"There were falconers here in the woods. I saw them. They left about an hour ago, soon after the nice woodland coyote killed one of their birds.

"I have some good news for you. But I can no longer wait for you to get here to tell you. You're too pokey. I'm off to the Helderberg Escarpment."

She's gone. She departed after the men left the woods and before they came up the creek. She's all right. Maybe they didn't even see her. I breathe a sigh of relief and read on.

"There's a leaf bag of hickory nuts on the ledge above the bed. Help yourself. The coyote has puppies under the rhododendron bush by the old mill. Let's get a coyote puppy; they're adorable. Signed,

"Your friend, Alice Van Rensselaer. Ha. Wasn't it fun having everyone bow and scrape because they thought you were a Van Rensselaer? People-clues work when you give them to nice people like Mr. and Mrs. Van Sandtford and Hanni. Hanni's neat.

Alice."

I groan and smile at the same time. "You're impossible."

Now that I know she's all right I'm angry at her. I haven't got time for her little games with sun compasses, pigs, Van Rensselaers, and coyotes. I've got a sawmill to tend and food to gather for the winter.

Alice, will you ever grow up and think of someone besides yourself?

But I am on the move. Alice is safe. I should have

known when I saw that eight-hundred-foot drop off the Helderberg Escarpment that she was headed for that falls from the moment she left her tree house.

Now, to go to Beaver Corners and get my beloved falcon back.

I stamp out the fire, bury the charred twigs, and sprinkle the burned spot with dirt. As the full moon comes over the tips of the hemlocks in the east and the sun goes down in the west, I climb down the falls and splash toward the bridge.

A dark mass to my left attracts my attention; something dull in texture is floating on the surface of the darkening stream. I wade to it.

"Oh, no," I wail.

It's the mother coyote. That's what the men were going to do when they headed up the creek, kill the coyote. They came back to seek revenge. Near the mother floats a puppy, and I can look no more. These men are cruel—and they have Frightful.

I splash down the creek, climb to the bridge, and put on my moccasins.

I don't even glance at the gristmill, but go straight to the restaurant.

The evening diners, a well-dressed group, are chatting and waiting to be served. I walk as casually as I can to the kitchen, where Mr. Milo is checking a dish in the oven.

"Mr. Milo," I say, trying to be calm. "Where's the police station?"

"There's no police station in Rensselaerville," he says. "Why? What's up?"

"Two men are about to sell my falcon to an agent for an Arab sheik. They're at Beaver Corners near East Berne and should be arrested. It's a felony to hold endangered species, and it must be worse to sell them."

"The nearest police are about twenty miles from here in Altamont," Mr. Milo says, his eyes wide. "I'll call Sean Conklin, our conservation officer. He's been staying in town. He can make arrests."

Mr. Milo dials his number and gets no answer.

"Good," I say. "He and Bando must have gone to Beaver Corners."

"Anything I can do?" Mr. Milo asks. "My buyer is going there in the morning to purchase red raspberries from a farm. He can give you a ride."

"No, thanks," I say. "It's only about twelve miles and there's a full moon tonight. I'm on my way."

"Suit yourself," he says and I hurry off.

At the last streetlight on the road out of town, I take out the map with the Helderberg Escarpment on it. Alice is probably already there. I study the contours and names. Most likely she's near the Indian Ladder where Outlet Falls plunges off the cliff. Miss Turner said that once the Indians felled a tree against the escarpment. The stumps of its branches, which they had trimmed away, formed the rounds of the ladder they climbed to the top. Now, she said, wooden and iron steps take its place.

I start off for Beaver Corners in the last light of day,
happy that Alice is far from the men who have Frightful, but keeping an eye out for piled stones or corncob
arrows to say for certain that she is.

The road winds through farmland that looks like a
rough quilt in the glow of the rising moon. Lights go off
in a lonely house at the end of the macadam, and I'm on
a dirt road.

Bats swing over my head and nighthawks cry as I
hurry along. The freshness of the countryside and the
knowledge that Alice is safe sends me whistling on my
way to find Frightful.

Almost all the lights are out in the little town of
Berne as I come down a steep road to its main street.
One streetlight is burning above a historical marker
and, knowing I don't have to reach Beaver Corners
before dawn, I stop and read it.

"The Anti-rent War began here in 1839. The farmers
of the Helderberg Mountains declared they would no
longer pay rent to the Van Rensselaers and honor leases
which bound their land forever and forever, for an annual payment, to a landed aristocracy.

"The rent was ten to fourteen bushels of wheat, four
fat fowls, and one day's service each year with team and
wagon. The tenant had to pay the taxes and build and
maintain the roads. The patroon reserved all water
and mineral rights. After two hundred years without
being permitted to own the land they had opened and

worked, the tenant farmers rebelled. Dressed as Indians, they harassed the Van Rensselaer agents and the
state militia when they came into the mountains to collect the rent. The militia fought back. The war went on
for thirteen years, the legal struggle for ownership for
another twenty-four. Finally, one hundred years after
the Declaration of Independence, the Supreme Court
ruled against the Van Rensselaers."

The rent seemed like a lot to me, if the land was anything like Great-grandfather Gribley's. Ten to fourteen
bushels of wheat would have been most of his crop.

As I cross a bridge and head toward East Berne,
which is about two miles from Beaver Corners, I see the
ruins of an old water mill. It, too, is illuminated by a
streetlight. With only a couple of hours of walking
ahead of me, and it being hours before dawn, I take time
out to look at the mill. There is not much left of it. The
stones in the crumbled walls (they must not have been
laid one on two, two on one) are soft with moss. There
are no millstones around. It must have been a sawmill.
That's neat.

I look for rusty machinery, shafts, and bolts that I
might use, find none, and turn to go when an out-of-
character structure on the sluice wall attracts my attention. It's a pile of stones two on one, one on two. Alice,
I say. She's passed by. All is well. She's left me a message at a place she knows I'll stop—an old water mill.

Alice's sundial

I smile. On the Track is very satisfying—when it's going right.

The moon shines on her structure, and I get down on my knees to try to figure out what she's saying. Two large rocks support a thin triangular stone in an upright position. Thirteen pebbles are arranged in an arc. It's a sundial. She's telling me what time she was here. I look closer. A stick is laid on the two-hour. The sun was up. She was here this afternoon at two. Good, I say. She's sleeping by the falls right now.

I'm about to start off again when I decide to use the moon and Alice's dial to find out what time it is. When the moon is full, which it is tonight, it is directly opposite the sun, so the shadow it casts will give me the correct time. I look down. It's eleven o'clock.

I'm about six miles from Beaver Corners, and the men won't be there until dawn. I think I have time to grab a little sleep before I go on. I'm pretty tired.

Several hours later, I awake in alarm—have I overslept? I jump up, look at Alice's dial, and am relieved to see it's only 3:00 A.M. The moon is beginning to slide west. I orient myself by facing it. My right arm points north. Beaver Corners is northeast of me. I start off in that direction, set a swift pace, and cover the four miles in a little more than an hour. Two to go.

East Berne is a smaller town than Livingstonville. It doesn't even have a gas station, and the post office is a trailer. I like it but do not linger.

I take the road to Beaver Corners, pass several dark houses and a church, and then I'm out in the wilds again. Miles of dark swampland lie to either side of the road. Frog songs and owl calls hang like a sound blanket over this lowland. I jog along, watching for bobcats and beaver—even black bear.

I arrive at Beaver Corners as the eastern sky begins to lighten. There's not much here, a crossroad, woodland, and an abandoned church that looks like it's ready to fall down. I don't see Bando or the conservation officer's car, but recalling the note on the library wall, I cross the road to the church.

As I walk, I whistle for Frightful, a birdlike call in the night. If she's here, she'll answer me.

She does not.

I round the abandoned church and find Bate's pickup. They're here, but not in the truck. I peer through the camper window. Frightful's not there, either, but I do see falcon perches, leashes, and hoods. She's near. I run around the church. She's not staked out, so I look for her in the woods. As I come down a slope, I see a green car parked in the tall grass near a beaver dam.

It must be the agent's car. I look through the side window but see only seats.

I despair. Maybe the coyote killed Frightful before she killed the sharp-shinned. Alice didn't mention Frightful at all. I poke my head in the church and wonder why they ever decided to meet here. The place is falling in and very dangerous. Boards creak and the floor is ripped up and gaping. Where are the men, where are the birds? They're around here somewhere.

I walk deeper in the woods in search of them, give up the hunt, and return to the other side of the road to wait for Bando and Officer Conklin.

I see nothing but nature and hear nothing but nature.

When it's light enough to read the maps, I take out the Altamont quadrangle and look at Beaver Corners. There's a cave marked on it, just about where I am sitting. Maybe that's where the men are.

Poking around, I push back some tall rushes and find a path leading right up to the cave.

The entrance is narrow, the cavern black. I climb a

pine and knock off an old limb stub rich in resin. On the ground I start a small fire with my flint and steel and light the knot. When it flares up, I slip between two huge slabs of limestone and sidle down the tight tunnel. Suddenly I am in a high, narrow room. This is great. Water trickles down the walls; a bat comes in for the day and hangs upside down on the pointed ceiling above me. I hold my torch high and see three long, narrow passageways leading into the dark underworld. This doesn't look like a good meeting place, but a cave is a cave. It screams out to be explored, and I go on. Walking down one of the tunnels, I turn a corner and am looking out on the beaver dam and the agent's car. The cave has two entrances. I go back and take the middle passage. It ends.

I might as well go down the last passage. Bending low, I inch along. The pine knot flares and throws off so much black smoke I do not see a fourth passageway on my left. I pass it. The tunnel I'm in dwindles to two feet, and I turn back.

As I return, I see the tunnel I missed minutes ago. It is wide and high enough for me to walk in upright. I ease myself along, intrigued by the smooth, waterworn walls.

Far ahead a light shines. This is not the blue white light of day but a yellow electric light. Walking toward it, I see that it is coming through a crack in the boards of a big door. I hear voices. Quietly I approach and peer through the crack.

I can see only half of a basement which, I judge from the distance I've come, is under the church. A man steps into my vision—it's Bate. He's holding a leash in one hand, and probably Frightful in the other, but I can't see that hand. My heart beats so hard it shakes my shirt. Let it be Frightful. Let it be Frightful.

I move slightly so I can see the other half of the room—and my spirits sink. Bate is holding, not Frightful, but a prairie falcon. Bate's driver is standing beside him. Seated on a barrel is the man who must be the agent, Skri.

"We made a deal for a peregrine falcon," Skri says. "I won't pay fifty thousand dollars for a prairie falcon. No. No. And where is the sharp-shinned?"

I have seen and heard enough. Biting my lips to keep from crying, I pick up my pine knot and return to the road and the dawn.

Something terrible has happened to Frightful. I don't even care if the men are arrested or not. She's dead; I know.

A car drives up, stops, and Bando jumps out.

"Hi, Sam." he says. "Officer Conklin and I came here last night, but no one was around."

"There is now," I say as Officer Conklin comes around his car and introduces himself. He is a tall, bony-faced man with a mustache and a lot of red hair. He carries a revolver on his hip. The work of an environmental conservation officer is serious.

"Where are they?" he asks, looking around.

"In the basement of that church," I answer. "But you can't get there through the church; it's falling down. The cave across the road leads into it."

"The old Tenant Hideout," he says in surprise. "The farmers of the Helderbergs went into the church basement and hid in this cave when the rent collectors and the militia came after them. Not many people know about it now. Just local kids and a few spelunkers.

"I'll hide my car off the road in the woods," he says, "and we'll wait in the bushes for the men to come out."

"It's no use, sir." I say. "You can't arrest them. They don't have my peregrine falcon. She's dead."

"If they are selling hawks and falcons, I can arrest them," Sean Conklin replies. "Birds of prey are protected by three different laws, one of which is a multinational treaty endorsed by 103 members. Fines run up to $250,000.

"I've been after these fellows for a long time," he goes on. "They are not licensed falconers and should not be keeping these birds, and for sure not selling them."

We walk around the church to the pickup, and I show him the green car by the beaver dam. Bando tells him that the librarian saw the man called Skri drive off in such a car.

Officer Conklin puts a foot on the steps of the church. Boards rattle and creak.

"They surely won't come out this way," he says. "Let's wait by the cave entrance."

Hardly has he spoken than we see Bate and his friend coming across the road toward us. They have no birds at all. Conklin can't arrest them. They're going to walk away free.

"Hello, Conklin," Bate calls jauntily.

"Hello, Bate."

Helpless to act, he watches them go around the church to their pickup. Then I think of the cave.

"Don't let them get away," I say. "Bando, come with me."

I dash through the woods to the green car just as Skri, carrying the hooded prairie falcon on his fist, comes out of the beaver-dam cave exit and runs to his car. I swing my sling over my head, aiming for the car door, and strike it a thundering blow. Skri jumps. The bird flaps.

"Stop where you are, mister," Sean Conklin calls. "You're under arrest." Seeing the revolver, Skri quietly walks toward him.

"It's his bird," he says, pointing to Bate.

Officer Conklin turns to Bate. "If that is so, you'd better come with me, too. You are not on the roster of licensed falconers."

"Where is my peregrine falcon?" I cry. "What did you do to her?"

He does not answer.

"You didn't take her to the university, did you? She's dead, isn't she?"

He does not answer.

"The man's not going to talk, Sam," Officer Conklin says. "He'll incriminate himself."

I turn away in despair, and Bando slips his arm around my shoulder. I shrug him off and walk to the edge of the woods. Sitting down, I put my elbows on my knees and my chin in my fists. I swallow hard. I had been so sure I would find Frightful here.

After a while Officer Conklin walks over to me.

"Sam," he says. "We're taking the men to Altamont to book them. Do you want to come?"

"No, no, I don't, thank you," I answer. "I'm going to the Helderberg Escarpment."

"Let me shake your hand," he says, extending his right hand. "Your quick thinking saved the prairie falcon."

I look up. Bando is holding the hooded falcon and smiling at her. She is a beauty.

"Sam," he says. "Sean Conklin needs me to carry the falcon while he drives these men to Altamont. After he has booked them, he and his son will take the bird to New Paltz. There's a licensed falconer at the university who will ship her to Boise, Idaho, where another falconer will meet her. He'll hack her back to freedom in her native habitat."

I am listening intently.

"He says there is a network of falconers who use their knowledge to keep these birds flying."

"That's what falconry is today," Officer Conklin

adds. "Falconers working for the birds of prey, not the birds of prey working for falconers."

"Are you sure you don't want to come along? Then we can start home."

"I'm going to get Alice," I say. "She's at the big falls on the escarpment. We'll be there if you decide to join us."

With my hands in my pocket and my head bowed, I take the road to the Helderberg Escarpment and to the water that spills eight hundred feet.

"The goshawks," I say, breaking into a run. I had forgotten all about them. It's the end of June. They'll have young. The eggs hatch around the first week in June, and the nestlings are ready to fledge in early July. During this time the parents are very dangerous. Their parental instincts are at their height, and they defend their offspring with strikes and slicing talons. Frightful's parents were docile compared to these birds, and they were fierce enough. They nearly knocked me off the cliff.

I run faster, for as sure as my name is Sam Gribley, Alice will climb that tree to see the nestlings. And as sure as her name is Alice Gribley, she'll end up on the ground or badly cut or both.

IN WHICH

A Bird Talks to Me

The sun is just hitting the tops of the trees when I find a well-marked trail to the big falls and take off along it.

I hear the cry of a goshawk and look up. Recognizing the female by her great size, I stop running to admire the silver gray body streaking through the sky. She is carrying a rabbit home to her nestlings in her taloned feet.

I keep her in view as I follow her toward the falls. Suddenly she screams the alarm cry of the goshawk. Her mate appears in the sky, seemingly coming from nowhere, and dives straight down at me. I must be near the nest.

I am. High in the spruce tree in front of me is a large nest of sticks and—climbing up toward it—Alice.

There she is. Her yellow hair sticks straight up as she lifts a wiry leg and places it on a limb.

The female goshawk climbs, positions herself above Alice, and dives.

"Alice!" I yell. "Duck."

With her wings snapping to gain speed, the great bird aims for Alice, who ducks her head just in time. The female shoots over the treetops, turns, and comes screaming back. The gleaming scimitars that are her talons slice the air just above Alice's head.

"Alice," I shout again. "Get down here."

"Sam!" She looks down and laughs happily.

"You're going to get hurt!" I holler angrily.

"She can't hit me," Alice answers and leans out to see me better. "There're too many limbs." The spruce tree is densely limbed and needled, but what Alice doesn't know is that a goshawk can maneuver a maze.

The frantic hawk speeds upward and, catching a downdraft, hurtles herself at Alice again.

"Here she comes!"

Alice pulls a limb across her body. The hawk dodges it and flies off. Once more Alice leans out to look down at me.

"Sam, hi. I knew you'd find me."

"Alice, get down here. That bird is dangerous."

"I'm okay. I won't let her hit me." She brandishes a spruce branch to show me how she fends the bird off.

"Please."

"Not yet." She climbs higher. The female screams an alarm which is answered by the tercel, who instantly appears and dive-bombs Alice.

Three crows hear the alarm and fly out of the woods to harass the goshawks. Cawing frantically, the crows pursue. To them, any bird of prey must be harassed, but goshawks must be unmercifully bedeviled. They caw without letup.

The tercel ignores them and climbs, it seems to me, into the very stratosphere. Somewhere out of sight he turns and comes into view, plunging straight down at my sister. She flattens herself her against the tree. This is crazy.

"Come down, Alice!"

"No."

Concerned now, I take a running start, jump, grab the first limb of the spruce, and find myself kicking wildly to fend off the female goshawk.

Alice climbs higher. I climb after her. The red eyes of the tercel flash as he comes at me. I pull down a branch. He veers, screams, and speeds off. After wiping spruce dust out of my eyes, I look up to see Alice practically in the nest.

"Sam, come look at the babies."

I can't believe what she's doing. Miss Turner told her what happened to people who went near goshawk nests.

"Get down before you're knocked down," I shout and climb faster.

Alice doesn't come down. I can barely see her for the dense limbs, but I do see the parent goshawks. They scream and dive, but do not hit her.

I watch and wait, not daring to climb any higher. The limbs that hold the nest are too small to support both Alice and me.

The nestlings call their wheezy notes. The parents swoop. Finally, Alice starts down, and I lower myself on the ladder of limbs, looking up as I go to make sure she's coming. Through the needles, I see three baby goshawks peering over the side of the nest. Their mouths are open in fury.

The tercel circles the tree and grows calmer as we descend.

I drop to the ground, followed by Alice. The female alights on the top of a dead tree, panting from fatigue and fear. Her beak is open, her tongue thrust out. She lowers her wings to attack again. What courage.

I pull Alice across the clearing into the shelter of the forest understory. Out of breath, we stop and look at each other.

"Where have you been?" she asks.

"Where have I been? Alice—!" What can I say? "You've got a cut on your head," is all I can think of, so I say it.

Taking out some leaves of the horse sorrel I had picked for last night's meal, I wipe away the blood. The Iroquois Indians used the leaves and roots of this plant to stop bleeding and purify cuts. The bleeding does stop.

"You look like a war veteran," I say, throwing my arms around both her and her pack.

"Be careful," she says, pulling away.

The goshawks have located us and are circling above the trees. I take Alice's hand and pull her to the edge of the escarpment, where I had seen a ledge about ten feet down. I scramble to it and reach up to help her. She slides to my side.

We find ourselves on a ledge under an overhang. I push Alice far under it.

"Get back there where the birds can't see you," I say, urging her deeper into the cavelike shelter.

"Be careful," she snaps. "You're jabbing the baby."

"What *are* you talking about?"

Taking off her pack she opens it and gently lifts a screaming, fighting baby goshawk.

"What are you doing with that?" I shout.

"Sam, don't be mad." The fierce nestling clenches her talons on air. "I got her for you. When I read your note saying Frightful had been confiscated, I cried. Then I remembered the goshawks Miss Turner had told us about. So I got you one."

"Oh, Alice." That's all I can say.

I have accused her of everything from being selfish to stubborn. I have even wanted to send her home. And now she has gotten me this priceless gift. I take the wild-eyed hawklet in my hands and, holding her feet-out, bury my face in her sweet birdy-smelling feathers.

"Oh, Alice, she's beautiful."

"*Eeeck,*" cries the bird, turns her head, and clamps her hooked beak on my hand. Alice pulls her work gloves from her pack and hands them to me. She took them, I now see, to handle a goshawk. She gave a lot of thought to this adventure.

Putting on the gloves, I hold the screaming warrior at arm's length.

Alice's gift

"What a present, Alice. What a wonderful present."
Gently rolling the little goshawk on her back, I stroke her breast to hypnotize her and calm her down. She looks at me. I look at her and fall in love. She has large eyes, a Persian beak, and gray silver feathers. Her eyes are just turning red like her parents'. Wrapping her carefully in my T-shirt so she can't see, thrash, and hurt herself, I place her far back under the overhang where she can recover from the scare of being handled by people.

"I'm going up for water, Alice. The little bird is thirsty." She hands me our leather carrier.

"You rest," I say. She nods and sits down grinning happily but apparently glad to obey for a change.

I climb to the top of the escarpment. Not far away a stream flows out of a limey cave, rushes to the edge, and plunges off. I watch its breathless descent.

Maybe Alice wasn't coming here to see this waterfall, I say to myself as the wild stream shoots off into space, but I'm sure glad she did. I stand and admire it in silence and am soothed by the sight of the falling water.

I fill the water bag and am starting back when a squirrel runs over the leaves. I load my sling and, twirling it above my head, let go of one string. The animal falls dead.

At last, victory on the first shot. Maybe Alice and I *can* survive on my mountain after all. I pick up the squirrel and a brown paper bag dropped by a hiker, then look around for a meadow environment. I find it, a clearing made by campers. As if I am in a familiar grocery store, I look along the meadow edge until I see what I've come for—the delicious leaves of the lamb's-quarters. I also check out a moist pocket by the stream for groundnuts and am rewarded with a string of three-inch nuts on the roots of one plant. I take the nuts and replant the roots.

I am rich again. I have Alice, a squirrel, groundnuts, and greens. I climb down to our camp. Alice is hugging her knees and looking out over the valley below.

"Sam," she says. "Let's stay here a few days. It's beautiful. Look at the view." Needless to say, I hadn't noticed the view, but out before us lie mountains, villages, and rivers. The Adirondacks rise like a jagged blue cutout in the far distance, and off to the right Outlet Falls shoots out over the ledge and spins a white trail to the rocks below.

Groundnut

"Good idea," I say. "It's the perfect place for you and me. I'm close to a goshawk's nest, and you're next to a mighty waterfall."

After making a small fire, I cut the paper bag with the scissors in Alice's Swiss Army knife and fold it into a box. In it I put the lamb's-quarters and water and place

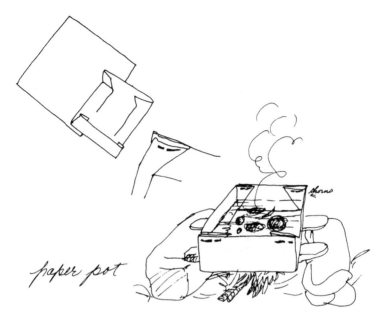

paper pot

it directly on the fire. The paper won't burn, because the water keeps it below its kindling point. You can do this with leaves too. The squirrel I cook on a spit.

"Alice," I say after we have eaten. "We have to return the little bird."

"No, Sam, no."

"It's illegal to have her."

"No, it's not. It's a hawk, not a falcon."

"Goshawks are protected by law, too. Sean Conklin, the conservation officer, said all the birds of prey are protected under the International Migratory Bird Treaty. They belong to the world."

"Oh, Sam, no. I came so far to get the little bird for you."

"I know it," I say. "Boy, do I know it." I look at her.

Mother was right to let Alice stay on the mountain. Living with nature teaches you to give. Alice would not have thought of doing something for me when she first came to my wilderness home.

"Please, don't take her back," Alice pleads. "Not now."

"Well, not right away. We'll enjoy her until dark. Tonight, when the goshawks can't see, I'll return her to her parents."

Alice shakes her head sadly.

"You'll feel good," I tell her, "knowing the little bird will take her place in the wild scheme of things."

"No, I won't. I want you to have a goshawk."

I uncover the quiet nestling, who, small as she is, picks a battle with me, a giant. She stabs and grips the glove. Carefully unlocking her strong talons, I place her on the ground and offer her a drink and a squirrel part I saved for her. She eats ravenously, and sadly I think of Frightful when she was this age. Then I cover the little bird again and put her far back under the over-hang. Thrilled by the privilege of just holding a baby goshawk, I step lightly to the edge of our hideout.

"Creee, creee, creee, car-reet."

I grab Alice's arm.

"Did you hear that?"

"Frightful!" she gasps.

We scramble to the top of the escarpment. Shooting across the clouds like a crossbow in the sky speeds a peregrine falcon. No other bird has that profile.

"Creee, creee, creee, car-reet." And no other bird but Frightful knows my peregrine name.

"Frightful," I call. I can barely see her for the mist in my eyes. She is coming toward us, pumping her wings with quick, strong strokes. Three feet from my face she calls my name again, swoops up, and "waits on" just above me.

"Creee, creee, creee, car-reet." Frightful drops lower, hovers in front of me, then climbs away. She goes higher and higher until she is out of sight.

"She's free, Alice, she's free."

"I knew that."

"What do you mean, you knew that?"

"I told you in my note that I had some good news for you, didn't I? Well, that's it. I set Frightful free."

"You did?"

"I found her in the Rensselaerville woods. I cut off her jesses. That's better than her going to the university, isn't it?"

"Tell me again. What did you do?"

"Cut her jesses."

I whoop in joy, sweep her up in my arms, and hug her.

"How did it happen?"

"Well, while I was foraging near the Rensselaerville falls, I walked into a clearing where there were three tethered falcons. One of them was Frightful. I recognized her by the jesses and leash you made. No one was there, so I cut her free. That's all."

"Alice," I close my eyes in thanks.

"Then," she continues, "while I was standing very still, watching her on the top of a tree getting her bearings, the coyote slipped up and killed one of the other birds. I stood perfectly still. She didn't see me because she was too busy trying to carry the bird off. It was tethered and she couldn't run off with it, so she sat down and looked at it. Then she got up and dug under the perch until it fell. She picked up the bird and walked away. The ring slipped off the fallen perch, and she dashed into the woods. Clever isn't she?"

I am shaking my head and grinning at Alice.

"I was going to let the prairie falcon go, too," she goes on, "but a pickup with a camper on it came into the woods and I ran behind a big tree. Two men got out, saw that Frightful and one other bird were missing, and cursed a lot.

"They were real mad. When they saw the coyote tracks they decided she had killed both Frightful and the other bird. I guess they were afraid she would kill the last one, because they packed her up, gathered their gear, and left. I don't know who they were."

"They were thieves and they went to Beaver Corners, not far from here. The conservation officer arrested them this morning."

"They were arrested?" Her eyes are wide open and sparkling. "Well, that's good. I didn't like them."

"What's more, they killed the coyote and her pups."

"Oh, no, Sam," Alice puts her fingertips in her mouth, bites them, and takes them out. "Oh, no. The coyote was so nice. I wanted a puppy. What's the matter with people?"

"Some humans think we have the right to be the only predators on earth."

Frightful spirals down from the sky, throws up her wings, and hovers above my lifted hand. My heart pounds.

"Creee, creee, creee, car-reet."

"Hello, yourself, Frightful. Hello, hello."

She wants to come back. I can have her again. All I have to do is whistle her name and she will alight on my fist.

"Call her, Sam," Alice cries urgently. "Call her. Call her."

I purse my lips to whistle. That's all it will take—one whistle of three notes, down, up, down. I want her so much. Frightful "waits on," listening for her name, the signal for her to drop to my hand.

"Call her, Sam. Please, get her back."

I press my lips together. Frightful spreads her tapered wings and catches a rising thermal of spiralling air. She circles up and up and up. All I have to do is whistle. She's waiting for me to call her. She needs me as much as I need her.

She's at the top of the thermal, a speck in the sky.

She waits. I don't whistle.

She tarries a moment longer, then peels off, and speeding like a falling star, shoots off into a cloud and is gone.

"Oh, Sam," Alice cries. "Why didn't you call her? She would have come back."

"Because," I answer softly, "she can breed. I saw her flirt with a tercel last spring. She will have young.

There will be wild peregrines on the cliffs again."

I take Alice's hand and squeeze it. "Thank you, for setting her free."

We stand on the escarpment for a long time, staring up at the cloud through which Frightful sped to freedom.

After a while we let ourselves down to our ledge and campsite. I sit on a rock with my head in my hands.

Alice hugs her knees. "Well, here we are," she says. "We don't have a peregrine, and you won't keep the baby goshawk, so it's a good thing I took Crystal with me."

"What do you mean?"

"When I started out to get the goshawk, I decided I might as well take Crystal. Mrs. Strawberry once said that the Monroe Farm near Livingstonville breeds Poland Chinas. Since the farm was on the way to the Helderberg Escarpment, I decided to drop her off."

I swallow hard as I recall the placard on the Monroe Farm.

"To be bred?"

"Well, we don't have Frightful anymore."

"Alice, that means piglets."

"Of course," she snaps. "She's not going to have falcons, that's for sure."

"I hate pigs, Alice," I say. "You know that. They rout up the forest floor and destroy the plants and the animals that live among them. They're smelly. . . ."

My tenderness for Alice is fading. I see my wilderness home muddy with wallows and stippled with pig bristles.

"Oh, Sam," she says. "I wouldn't bring her up on the mountain. I'll be keeping her in Mrs. Strawberry's empty pigpen."

"Thank you, Alice," I say and sigh.

Kneeling before the fire, I pull apart the coals and place the groundnuts in them.

"Hall-oo, the house!"

"Bando!" I shout and climb up to the top of the escarpment to greet him. The female goshawk drops down from her nest and, feet outspread, bombs Bando.

"Hey," he yells, dropping to the ground. "She's a wild one."

"Come down to our ledge where she can't see you," I say and lead the way.

The goshawk brushes me with her wing as I throw my legs over the escarpment and scramble down to our camp. Bando is close behind.

"Alice!" he shouts. "Where have you been? We've been looking all over for you."

"You should have known where I'd be, what with Frightful confiscated," she says sounding miffed, and then I know why. She starts telling him about the baby goshawk and how I won't keep her after all the trouble she has gone to.

"Sam's right," Bando says, and she sits down in a huff.

Eagerly I ask him what happened in Altamont.

"Bate, his buddy, and the Arab are free on bail pending trial," Bando says. "And the prairie falcon is on her way to Idaho.

"How's that for a happy ending?" he asks and takes a sandwich from his packbasket.

"We have a happier one," I say.

"What is it?"

"Frightful is free."

"She's what?"

"Free. Alice found her in the woods by the Rensselaerville waterfall and cut her jesses."

"You did?" he says, taking her hands in his. "Alice, you're wonderful." He looks at me.

"Do you think she'll survive?"

"I sure do. She was here only fifteen minutes ago, fat and beautiful."

"Frightful was here? How do you know?"

"I know all right," I say, looking at the sky. "She called my name."

Bando is grinning.

"That *is* the perfect ending," he says and, sitting down, looks out across the beautiful valley and mountains.

I pull a groundnut out of the fire, let it cool, peel it, and hand it to him.

"Here we go again," he says and, hesitatingly, takes a bite.

"Hey, this is darned good. What is it?"

"Pignut," I say, "for one of its many names." He laughs and takes another bite.

Later, as we all watch the sun slide down the western edge of the great escarpment, we sit in thoughtful silence. The stars come out. The moon is just rising, but it is so dark a daytime bird can't see. I get to my feet.

"It's time to take the little goshawk back." I put on Alice's work gloves and pick up the nestling.

Stroking her softly, I place her in Alice's backpack and scramble to the escarpment top. Gingerly I climb the tree, trying not to jar the little bird too much. Then, high above the waterfall, the woods, and the great wide valley, I nestle her among her siblings. They murmur a greeting and rouse. I think of the wild forests, the cliffs, and the meadows over which they and their offspring will reign, I hope, forever. Then I climb down.

The return of the little bird was as uneventful as her capture was frenzied. The parents, who were sitting in a nearby tree, did not move. They never saw me in the dark. I hope they can count to four. It would make them happy.

I drop back to our ledge, to find Alice balled up like a little caterpillar and sound asleep. Bando is stretched out on his back, his hands under his head, looking out at the stars.

"You know, Sam," he says when I sit down.

"What, Bando?"

"There's a miller in Rensselaerville who knows how to convert a water mill to electricity." He rolls his head my way to watch my reaction.

I see Frightful peeling off and vanishing from sight. I see the little goshawk cuddled against her siblings. I see the stars in their places and hear the waterfall shooting to its destiny out over the edge of the escarpment.

"I'll look into it," I say. "Zella and Alice would like it."

"What about yourself? Would you?"

"Yes. I'm ready. It will make them happy. Besides, I'm going to be very occupied. I'm going to speak to the conservation officer about getting a falconer's license."

"But Frightful's gone."

"You said your friend Steve needed people to raise and hack peregrine falcons. I'd like to do that."

"You're certainly qualified, and he's often said he would like to have someone raise the birds in a natural setting. He thinks they would adjust to the wild more easily." Bando frowns and turns to me. "But, Sam, won't it be hard to come to love them as you will, and then have to let them go?"

"You ask that, Bando, because you don't know what it feels like to set a peregrine falcon free."

Frightful's Mountain

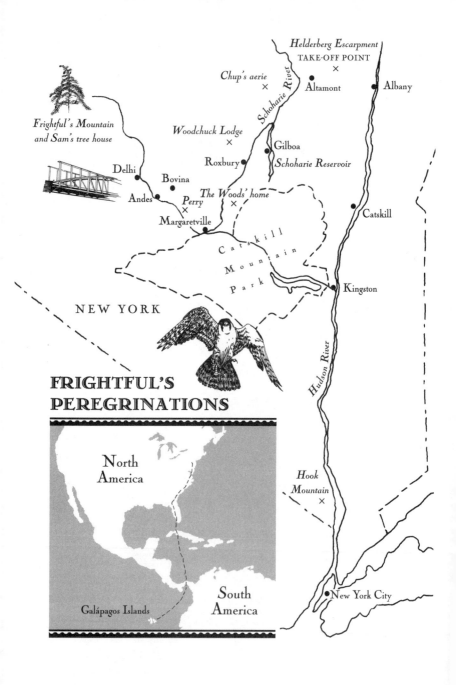

Frightful's Mountain
and Sam's tree house

Delhi

Andes

Bovina

Perry
×

Margaretville

Chup's aerie
×

Woodchuck Lodge
×

Roxbury

Gilboa

Schoharie Reservoir

The Woods' home
×

Helderberg Escarpment
TAKE-OFF POINT
×

Altamont

Albany

Schoharie River

C a t s k i l l

M o u n t a i n

P a r k

Catskill

Kingston

NEW YORK

Hudson River

**FRIGHTFUL'S
PEREGRINATIONS**

North
America

South
America

Galápagos Islands

*Hook
Mountain*
×

New York City

Frightful's Mountain

written and illustrated by

JEAN
CRAIGHEAD
GEORGE

With a Foreword by
Robert F. Kennedy, Jr.

DUTTON

CHILDREN'S

BOOKS

New York

Library of Congress Cataloging-in-Publication Data

George, Jean Craighead, date
Frightful's mountain / written and illustrated by Jean Craighead George.
— 1st ed. p. cm.
Summary: As she grows through the first years of her life
in the Catskill Mountains of New York, a peregrine falcon called Frightful
interacts with various humans, including the boy who raised her,
a falconer who rescues her, and several unscrupulous poachers,
as well as with many animals that are part
of the area's ecological balance.
ISBN 0-525-46166-3
1. Peregrine falcon — Juvenile fiction. [1. Peregrine falcon —
Fiction. 2. Falcons — Fiction. 3. Wildlife conservation — Fiction.
4. New York (State) — Fiction.] I. Title.
PZ10.3.G316Fr 1999
[Fic]—dc21 99-32932 CIP

Published in the United States by Dutton Children's Books,
a division of Penguin Young Readers Group
345 Hudson Street, New York, New York 10014
www.penguin.com/youngreaders

Designed by Sara Reynolds
Printed in USA
First Edition
4 6 8 10 9 7 5 3

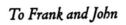

To Frank and John

Contents

Foreword

In 1986, I met Jean Craighead George at a friend's home in the upstate New York town where we all live. I grew up admiring the Craigheads, a family of naturalists, whose adventures I followed in *National Geographic* magazine, where they always seemed to be attaching transmitters to grizzly bears, banding bald eagles, or paddling canoes and fiberglass kayaks on first descents down the best western white waters. Always, there were flocks of children participating in every adventure and experiment. I thought the Craigheads might be the only family in America that was having more fun than the Kennedys. Obsessed with falcons as I was from birth, I read *My Side of the Mountain* in 1964. When I met Jean Craighead George that day in New York, she reminded me about the letter that I had written her, at age eleven, politely inquiring if she knew where I could find an occupied kestrel nest. The following year, my father finally bought me a pet-store red-tailed hawk. I manned her to my fist although I still lacked the tutelage to train or hunt her.

But in the autumn of 1968, I entered Millbrook School in upstate New York, drawn by its informal falconry program. At Millbrook, just across the Hudson from Delhi—where Sam and Frightful had had their adventures—I found a small cadre of students who not only shared my devotion to the birds, they had mastered the sport of falconry. That autumn, we captured and trained red-tails and kestrels, immature birds on their first migration. We used bow nets, bal chartris or harness pigeons, and contraptions that bristled with monofilament snares and nooses which we found diagrammed in Beebe & Webster's *North American Falconry and Hunting Hawks* or described in the classic writings of Frederick the Great.

By the time the leaves fell in the third week of October, we had trained the birds to come when we called and to follow like dogs, but high in the canopy flying from tree to tree over our heads. We beat the bush below them for cottontail and pheasant, worked the corn stubble for giant Belgian hare and the forests for red and gray squirrels. We flew falcons and goshawks but mostly wild red-tails, pioneering many of the game-hawking techniques still used by American falconers.

I don't think any of us realized how unusual our success in training red-tailed hawks to hunt was until we all made a pilgrimage to see Al Nye the following Thanksgiving in Falls Church, Virginia. Nye, one of the fathers of modern game hawking, flew peregrines and goshawks, the classic choices of traditional Asian and European falconry. Nye showed us his prized European goshawk, Suzie, and boasted that the bird had already taken a dozen cottontails that season. When we told him we'd taken around the same number with our red-tails, he reacted skeptically. Convention considered the North American red-tail to be at best an inferior hunting tool. European falconers dismissed them contemptuously as "buzzards." We told Nye, "We have the pelts to prove it."

We talked about hawks every spare moment—at meals, between classes, and after chapel. At night, we fashioned hardware, hoods, jesses, and gauntlets and bewits out of tough, pliant kangaroo hide. We marked in our memories the raptor nests we found during our daily winter hunting excursions when no leaves obstructed our view of the upper canopy. In the spring, we climbed up to those nests to band baby red-tails, crows, and owls. We learned to use ropes and climbing spurs to scale the tall oak and ash trees where the large raptors nested. I also learned taxidermy and basic veterinary skills, how to determine disease, check for worms, give injections, and diagnose a range of illnesses and parasites that afflict raptors and other animals. We even began a raptor breeding project, one of the first in history, and were partially successful, persuading a golden eagle and a red-tailed hawk to lay eggs in captivity.

Since my years at Millbrook, I have flown hawks nearly every autumn. These days, I am flying a pair of Harris hawks. I have flown my hen, Cuchin (a superb hunter), for fourteen years. I continue to trap, band, and release hawks every migration on Orange County's Schunnemunk Ridge—a vantage from which, on a clear morning, I can glimpse the Catskill peaks around Delhi. On a good day with a south wind, we trap upwards of fifty hawks: peregrines, Cooper's hawks, sharp-shins, red-tails, goshawks, merlins, and golden eagles. I maintain breeding aviaries for hawks and owls at my home in Mount Kisco, New York, a few miles from Jean George's home. I breed quail, pheasant, and occasionally turkeys, and I operate a wildlife rehabilitation center, with state and federal licenses that allow me to rehabilitate orphaned and injured raptors. My experience as a young falconer accounts in large part for my lifelong devotion to raptors and my continued interest in natural history.

Our time as falconers left its mark on my schoolmates as well. All of them have chosen careers in the natural sciences or as environmental advocates with exceptional records. For each one of them, reading *My Side of the Mountain* was the formative inspiration of their falconry experience. My years as a falconer helped drive my own career choice as an environmental lawyer and advocate. The knowledge and experience I acquired from falconers have marked my life and made me a far more effective advocate on nature's behalf. I have to assume that thousands of other children outside my immediate circle were also inspired to varying degrees of ecological stewardship by their exposure to Sam Gribley's adventures in *My Side of the Mountain*. It's my hope that this wonderful sequel, *Frightful's Mountain*, will inspire thousands of new kids.

ROBERT F. KENNEDY, JR.
July 1999

Frightful's Mountain

Frightful, the peregrine falcon, could not see. A falconer's hood covered her head and eyes. She remained quiet and calm, like all daytime birds in the dark. She could hear, however. She listened to the wind whistling through pine needles. This wind music conjured up images of a strange woods and unknown flowers. The sound was foreign. It was not the soft song of wind humming through the hemlock needles of home.

Frightful was a long way from her familiar forest. Suddenly an all-invading passion filled her. She must go. She must find one mountain among thousands, one hemlock tree among millions, and the one boy who called himself Sam Gribley. The one mountain was her territory; the one tree was Sam's house; the perch beside it, her place. And Sam Gribley was life.

Frightful Takes Off

Frightful had not been quite two weeks old when she first saw Sam Gribley. He had lifted her from her nest on a cliff. Small as she was, she had jabbed him with her already powerful talons as he carried her to the ground. "I'm going to call you Frightful," he had said. "You are a raving beauty." Then he carried her to the gigantic hemlock tree on the mountain and into its hollowed-out bole. This was Sam's home.

He fed her four and five times a day. He carried her on his gloved fist and talked to her. Before long, Frightful thought of him as her mother. He nurtured her like a peregrine falcon mother would.

When she was older, Sam made a perch for her and placed it outside his tree. He taught her to fly to his hand. When she was full-grown, he took her hunting with him. By now, the memory of her parents was pushed far back in her mind. Sam was her family.

At night and on winter days, Sam brought Frightful inside the huge old tree. She perched on his rustic bedstead and warmed herself by the clay fireplace. On spring and summer days, she would sit on her perch outside and watch the birds, the butterflies, and busy Sam. Patiently she waited for him to take her hunting. It was her greatest pleasure. She loved the sky. She loved the updrafts and coiling winds, and she loved "waiting on," hovering above Sam until he kicked up game. Then she stooped, the wind singing in her feathers.

Frightful was an excellent hunter who rarely missed. The food was shared. Their lives depended on each other. She must find Sam again now.

Frightful crouched to fly. She could not see. She folded her gray-blue wings to her body and straightened up.

Hooded and tethered, she had traveled with two strange men for several days.

One of them had taken her from the perch beside the big hemlock tree. He had a deep jerky voice and a face like a condor's. She looked intently at him before he slipped the falconer's hood over her head.

Sam had begged and pleaded with the man not to take her away, but he had pushed Sam aside and carried her down the mountain to a pickup truck. A leather perch had been presented to her feet. She had stepped up on it as Sam had taught her to do. A door had closed, and she was inside a camper on the truck. The motor rumbled, and she was moving. A falcon bell tinkled nearby. A sharp-shinned hawk had shifted his feet. A prairie falcon called out a single note. They, like herself, were sensing the direction of the moving pickup—east, northeast, east, then straight north.

Several feedings later, the second man put Frightful on a perch in the pine forest. The prairie falcon and the sharp-shinned hawk were there, too. She could hear their bells tinkling. Although they were birds who would readily attack her, she was not afraid of them.

Frightful was a peregrine falcon. She was faster and more agile than any other bird or beast the world around. Her long pointed wings; wide shoulders; and strong, tapered body were sculpted by the wind, the open sky, and the nature of her ancestral prey—swift birds.

Frightful sat calmly under her hood, turning the sounds in the pine forest into mental images. A song sparrow caroled. A cardinal chirped. They told her she was in a forest clearing edged with bushes where song sparrows and cardinals lived.

A northern waterthrush trilled. Frightful envisioned a dashing stream shaded by a majestic forest, the summer home of the northern waterthrush. She heard the stream in the distance. It had many voices as it spilled down a stairway of rocks.

Suddenly the cardinal screamed an alarm. A predator was approaching. The songbirds stopped chittering. The forest became silent. Even the insects ceased stridulating. Frightful pulled her feathers to her breast. The enemy was low and coming toward her.

The sharp-shinned hawk flew off his perch in terror. His bell tinkled. He was stopped by his leash, which was knotted to a steel ring at the base of his perch and to the jesses on his legs. He jumped forward, fell back, and beat the earth with his wings.

A killing snarl colored the air red.

An eastern coyote had killed the sharp-shinned hawk. The killer, bird in her mouth, ran toward her pups in the woods. With a jerk, she, too, was stopped by the leash. She turned back and dug at the base of the perch until it toppled and fell. The next sound Frightful heard was the clink of the ring at the end of the leash bouncing over the ground. The sounds faded into the woods.

A wind twisted Frightful's silky pantaloons of pinstriped feathers, which hung down over her enamel-shiny legs. Her tail flicked. She was nervous.

Human footsteps approached.

Their sound did not conjure up the image of the men she had been traveling with. Wary, she lifted her wings to fly.

A hand touched the front of her legs, and she stepped up onto it as Sam had taught her to do.

"Hello, Frightful." Her name; but not Sam's voice. The tone was soft, like the call of a mourning dove.

"What are you doing here?" the voice asked, and Frightful recognized Alice, Sam's sister. In her mind's eye, she saw a rosy face with sea-blue eyes and yellow hair. Frightful relaxed. Alice was family.

She liked Alice, who ran and jumped. She also darted. Frightful liked movement. A spot in her eyes that connected to many nerves gave her an instant focus on movement. Running, leaping Alice was a member of Frightful's home forest. Sam must not be far away. Frightful eased her grip on Alice's bare hand. She lifted her talons.

"Frightful," Alice said softly. "You've got to get out of here." The young girl's voice brought back images of the one mountain among thousands of mountains, the one hemlock tree among millions of trees—and Sam.

"I'm cutting your jesses," she whispered. "You are surrounded by enemies! Fly, fly far away.

"Fly away, Frightful! Sam is not allowed to have you. He has to have a falconer's license, and he's too young to get one. Fly, Frightful! Fly far!"

A quick slash of a knife, and Frightful's jesses and leash dropped away. The hood was flipped off.

And Frightful could see.

"Fly!" Alice urged.

Frightful saw the clearing before her and the leaves on the bushes, even the shiny needles at the tops of the pine trees. Her eyes were endowed with incredible vision.

Alice tossed her into the air.

Pulling on her powerful wings, Frightful sped to the top of the tallest pine and alighted on a slender twig. Her large, black-brown eyes observed the forest, the cascading stream, a town tucked into a steep valley, and rolling mountains as far as she could see.

She turned her head almost all the way around, but could not see or sense the one mountain among thousands of mountains, the one tree among millions of trees. She must get higher. She flew. Strong wing beats carried her into a thermal, a column of warm air that rises from the sun-heated ground in a spiraling bubble. She got aboard and circled upward a thousand feet.

The view was still unfamiliar. To the northeast the rolling mountains ended in a steep escarpment. A waterfall plunged down it, falling two hundred feet to the ground. Beyond the escarpment stretched a valley almost obscured by industrial haze. Rivers threaded through it. Directly northward the rugged Adirondack Mountains stood in a green haze above the land.

Frightful had not been fed for ten hours. She was desperately hungry. Her first act of freedom would be to hunt for herself.

But the forest was not the habitat she knew. Sam had trained her to hunt in abandoned fields. She circled and waited for him.

He did not appear. Frightful flew higher. A movement on the ground caught her eye. Alice was walking on a road that wound through the pine forest. Frightful pumped her wings once and plummeted earthward. When she was twenty feet above Alice's head, she scooped her wings, dropped her secondary feathers, and braked herself. She hovered, "waiting on" for the girl to kick through the fields and scare up the game as Sam would have done.

Alice did not look up. Her eyes were on the road. Presently she came out of the forest into open farmland. Frightful's eyes sought movement. This was the kind of country she and Sam hunted. Tipping one wing, she moved effortlessly over an abandoned field. She waited on for Alice.

But Alice did not come into the field. She stayed on the macadam, where nothing lived. She was in a hurry. Breaking into a run, she dashed around a bend, just as a yellow-white-and-brown dog with long ears and droopy eyes left his hideout in a culvert. He saw Alice run past him. Crouching, he pulled his tail between his legs and dropped out of sight in the daisies. He had been beaten as a pup and was terrified of people. He was thin, but not skinny, for he lived quite well on the mice and rabbits in the field. The farmer who saw him from time to time called him Mole. Every time he lifted his gun to shoot the dog, Mole disappeared in the ground. The man had Mole pegged for the killer of his chickens.

Mole slipped silently through a thistle patch. A pheasant burst up. Frightful rocketed earthward. She struck the bird a mortal blow and dropped with it to the ground. Instinctively she covered the food with her wings to hide it from other predators. She plucked but did not eat. She was waiting for Sam.

Mole smelled the dead pheasant and lifted his head above the thistles. Alice was gone and, seeing no other humans, he followed the scent of the game. Suddenly he burst upon not just a pheasant, but also Frightful. He stopped. Frightful lifted her feathers and threatened him. Then, holding the heavy bird in one foot, she beat her wings and skimmed over the thistles. She gained height and sped away and up.

Like a lightning bolt, a red-tailed hawk swept under her and, upside down, grabbed the pheasant in his talons. Frightful was pulled a short distance before she opened her feet and let go of the food. Four crows flew out of the woods and chased the red-tailed hawk.

Two crows saw Frightful. They turned away from the red-tail and, cawing frantically, dove at her.

Frightful flew into the leafy shelter of a maple tree growing along a fencerow.

"Come harass the falcon," the raucous crows called to each other. The message traveled swiftly, and crows came flocking to the tree. Two dozen gleefully pestered their enemy.

Frightful ducked the black bombers until she could stand them no longer. Taking flight, she sped around the barn and into a pine tree at the edge of a woodlot. She alighted close to the tree trunk, where her dark back feathers and striking black head would blend with the bark. The crows did not see her and returned to their nests.

The excitement of the hunt and chase had tired Frightful. She rubbed her head on her broad shoulder, fluffed her breast feathers, and rested. Her lower lids moved up over her eye and met the upper lids. The image of the one hemlock tree among millions filled her mind's eye and then faded. She was asleep.

Frightful awoke as the morning sun brought color to the tops of the trees. Still ravenously hungry, and growing weak from lack of food, she left the pine and circled above an alfalfa field.

A mouse came out of its den and chewed on a grass seed. Frightful threw up her wings and dropped. She never completed the stoop. The male red-tailed hawk shot out of the woodlot. Wings pumping, he was on a bullet-straight path for Frightful. His mate sped to his left.

Frightful saw the hawks coming, maneuvered her wings, and shot herself up into space like a rocket. High above the red-tails, she looked down. Now she had the advantage. She was above them. To all birds anything overhead is a threat. The hawks beat a fast retreat to the woods. The female lit on a bulky stick nest where four nestlings huddled. Frightful had been in the territory of two devoted parents who were defending their young against a falcon.

Frightful put distance between them by climbing higher. A mere speck in the sky, she took a reading on the polarized light of the sun. The rays vibrated in lines that told her the direction. She sensed the one mountain among thousands, the one tree among millions—and Sam. She must go there.

Mindful of the red-tailed hawks, she flew north to get beyond their territory before heading for the mountain. In moments she was looking down on the escarpment and waterfall. They touched a memory of the right world for a peregrine, a memory as old as her species' time on earth. Drawn to the cliff and the waterfall, she flew lower and lower.

On the top of the escarpment stood Alice. She was under a spruce tree, staring up at it.

Frightful soared toward her.

Two goshawks, the lions of the woodland birds, suddenly dropped out of the trees and dove at Alice. They skimmed over the blond head and climbed skyward. In the top of the spruce tree sat four young goshawks. Alice was discovering, even as Frightful had, the fury of parents protecting their young.

Alice shinnied up the tree trunk, grabbed a limb, and climbed toward the nest tree. The female goshawk rose, dove, and rose again, her huge feet with their black talons poised to grab her flesh. Alice swung an arm and fended her off.

"Alice! Duck!" Sam's voice.

Frightful's world was suddenly right. Sam was here. The two would go hunting. She would catch their breakfast, and he would hold her on his hand and feed her. He would talk and whisper to her.

She waited for his three-note whistle that meant, "Come to me." There was no whistle.

"Come down, Alice," Sam shouted.

"No," Alice shouted back.

The girl climbed on. She broke off the dead limbs, pushed back live ones, and wiggled upward. Near the nest the male goshawk struck Alice's backpack a powerful blow, nearly knocking her out of the tree. Sam leaped to the lowest limb and climbed. The huge female goshawk dove at him. He held out his foot to fend her off. Her talons slashed his moccasin.

Frightful swept down from the sky and perched in an oak tree, waiting for Sam to go hunting.

Alice climbed into the bulky nest. She picked up a baby goshawk and tucked it into her backpack.

"Sam can't have a falcon," she said to the bird. "But you are a hawk. You'll love Sam."

Quickly she scrambled over the edge of the strong, revamped crow's nest and started down the tree. Sam saw her coming and climbed down too. He jumped to the ground. A moment later Alice dropped beside him. The raging goshawks attacked again.

Sam pulled Alice into the shelter of the woods. The goshawks followed screaming, until the two enemies disappeared under a clump of mountain laurel.

Then the goshawks saw Frightful. They attacked her head on. She twisted, confusing them, and climbed swiftly out of their reach.

When Sam and Alice came out of the woods, the winged lions bombed them again. Taking advantage of this, Frightful dropped over the edge of the escarpment. The goshawks did not see her.

She landed on a rock that stuck out from the cliff and shook the excitement out of her feathers. Behind her was a cave. She walked into its shelter, then out. It was comfortable and safe, but she was too weak from hunger to stay there. A day and a half had passed since she had eaten. Stepping to the edge of the rocky overhang, she looked for food.

She saw movement on the cliff. Sam was standing under a jutting overhang not far from her. With one powerful stroke of her wings she was above him.

"Creee, creee, creee, car-reet," she called. This was her name for Sam Gribley.

"Did you hear that?" Sam exclaimed to Alice.

"Frightful," she shouted.

"No other bird but Frightful uses my peregrine name." He stepped to the edge of the ledge and looked up.

"Frightful!" he called.

She scooped her wings back then forward and hung above him.

"Creee, creee, creee, car-reet," she called.

"She's free, Alice," Sam cried. "She's not dead. I was sure she was dead."

No whistle told Frightful to alight on Sam's hand. She waited for this command, sculling her wings. An updraft carried her higher. She looked down. Still Sam did not call her to his hand. And because he had trained her so well, she could not alight without his whistle.

Confused, she let herself ring upward on a thermal, peeling off at a great height. Then she flew out over the valley. She must hunt for her life.

But she could not. Sam was her mother. She needed him. He needed her. She turned back.

This time she hovered before his face.

"Creee, creee, creee, car-reet," she called.

"Hello, yourself, Frightful. Hello, hello."

"Call her down, Sam," Alice screamed. "Whistle for her."

He did not.

Frightful flew higher—waiting.

Another draft of warm air swept up the escarpment, struck her open wings, and ringed her up again. She rode this thermal to the top, where the air was cool and could not lift her any higher.

Closing her wings to her body, she dropped headfirst almost a thousand feet, braked, and waited ten feet above Sam.

Again he did not call her.

A strong wind gusted. Frightful tipped one wing steeply, turned, and glided with the flow out over the valley. Above the Schoharie River turbulent air waves tossed her up, down, and sideways. She closed the slots between her flight feathers and maneuvered the bumps like a mogul skier.

"Cree, cree, cree." One of her own species was calling her. She turned her head and saw a male peregrine falcon. The tiercel caught up with her, then passed beneath her, flying upside down. He was so close she could hear his contour feathers buzz in the wind.

"Chup, chup," he sang. Frightful slowed down, instinctively recognizing the love song of the male peregrine falcon.

"Chup, chup." He flew on his back again. He rolled in loops, then once more on his back. He took her talons in his.

"Chup."

Although the time of peregrine courtship was over, and other males and females were feeding young, this male was seeking a mate. Frightful found herself responding to him. Holding her wings steady, she followed him on a steep descent. Vortices of air spiraled out from her wing tips, sending golden hemlock pollen twisting in circles.

Then she saw Sam at the top of the spruce tree. He was returning the little goshawk to its nest. Frightful turned back.

Chup chased her. He made an awe-inspiring loop and cruised upside down beneath her. Gently he held her talons again, and a new feeling brightened Frightful's mood.

"Chup, chup, chup," the tiercel called as he flew ahead of her. This time Frightful caught up with him. They flew in tandem above the Schoharie Valley.

I N   W H I C H

Frightful Goes to Falcon School

Chup led Frightful higher and higher, to the misty bottom of a fair-weather cumulus cloud. Frightful left him. The fuzziness of clouds, even thin clouds, was distracting to her. She liked clear air.

Soaring back toward the escarpment, she scanned twenty miles in all directions for the one mountain where the one gigantic tree grew. She did not see the mountain.

From out of nowhere bulleted the female goshawk.

Frightful shot up into the protection of Chup's cloud. The goshawk turned back.

"Chup!" The tiercel appeared in the mist, flew close to her, then dove earthward at a steep angle. Again his "chup" touched some deep peregrine memory in her, and she followed the daring tiercel.

Seconds later he thrust out his feet and landed on a cliff ledge. Frightful thrust out her feet and came down not far from him. She was on a stony rampart above the Schoharie River. The cliff and the river spoke to her of her first home and her parents. She held her wings to her body and stacked her tail feathers. She was agitated. The scene was familiar and unfamiliar.

Chup walked toward her, lowering his head in deference to the greater size and power of the female peregrine. "Cree," she responded, and relaxed.

But for size and Frightful's almost black head and cheek straps, Frightful and Chup looked alike. Both had large black-brown eyes, set deeply under flat foreheads. Their beaks were ebony black with saffron-yellow nares. White throats and cheek patches shimmered above pale breast feathers stippled with black flecks. Their wings were long and graceful instruments of speed. They sat erect. They held their heads high. Their beings were lit with an inner flame and, at the same time, the cold stillness of ice. They were the royalty of birds.

Frightful quickly took in her situation. The cliff was about sixty feet high and set back from the river. The land below was bottomland, where red maples, trees of the wetlands, grew. Geese and ducks paddled among cattails and sedges that lined the river's edge. Bank swallows popped in and out of nest holes on the far riverbank. Directly below the aerie was a pine tree where two blue jays had built a stick nest. In it were four scrawny nestlings. Chup let them live. They were part of his aerie community, like the flowers and the huckleberries.

Frightful had arrived in perfect peregrine habitat. She was only vaguely aware of this. Almost her whole life had been spent with Sam on a mountain. Sam and his forest and abandoned meadow were her habitat.

She looked at Chup. He bowed his head to her. His respect awoke Frightful to action. She stretched her neck high. She lifted her feathers to look larger and therefore more beautiful to the tiercel. With this feather talk she told Chup she was bonding with him. She felt a closeness to this pleasant member of her species.

Then a slight movement provoked her to peer behind Chup.

Three young peregrine falcons stared at her. The eyases sat on their bums, legs stretched out in front of them. They were very young, no more than a week old. Their plump bodies were covered with white down; their beaks and feet were gray like the rocks. They were huddled on bare earth in the middle of a garden of pink blazing-star flowers.

"Psee psee," each one cried. "Feed me." The sound stirred a new feeling in Frightful. She leaned down as if to

pluck food, then, not knowing what came next, she stared at Chup.

Chup picked up a half-eaten duck and delicately snipped off a small bite. Folding his talons under his toes, he walked to an eyas and placed the morsel in her open mouth. He pulled off another bite and then another, feeding the chick until she was quiet. When the other two called "psee," he fed them morsel by morsel, patiently, devotedly.

Frightful watched, her own terrible hunger mounting.

When the wobbly eyases stopped eating, Chup broke off a bite of duck and offered it to Frightful. She swallowed ravenously and waited. She was back in her pattern with Sam. When Sam fed her she waited to see if he was going to give her just a bite and take her hunting again, or carry her home to feast and rest. Chup was not part of this routine. He offered no more bites, nor did he take her hunting. Instead he left. He flew off to do as the peregrine tiercel must do—hunt for his mate and young, until the chicks were well feathered and could keep themselves warm without being brooded. When that happened, the female mate would join in the hunt.

Not Frightful. She looked at the duck Chup had left. According to Sam's training, it was hers. Gingerly at first, then ravenously, she fed herself. Death by starvation comes quickly to a bird of prey, and strength returns as quickly. With each bite her eyes began to glisten with energy, and, like a flame, she soon flickered and stood tall.

Vitality restored, she lifted one wing and stretched it as far as it would reach. Then she stretched the other, wiped her beak, and sat contentedly.

Two days ago Chup's first mate, mother of the chicks, had flown out to stretch and exercise after days of inactivity. She had not come back. When several hours had passed and the chicks were screaming, Chup knew she had been killed. That afternoon he searched for another mate. The eyases must live. He called the love song over cliff and river. No female appeared.

That night he brooded the eyases. He fed them in the morning. He hunted at noon when the air was slightly warmer and he could leave them unattended. As he hunted, he looked for a mate.

High above the escarpment he saw Frightful hovering above Sam Gribley. He called her, but she paid him no heed. When, however, she rode a rising thermal and passed near, he rolled and danced for her. He flew upside down for her, touched her feet. When she began to notice him, he lured her toward his motherless young, but she was not easily won. Once more she turned and flew away. On the third attempt he succeeded.

With Frightful at the aerie, Chup's world was right again. His chicks had a mother.

But all was not perfect.

Frightful, who for most of her life had been raised by Sam—not by peregrine falcons—had much to learn.

She did not know what to do with three eyases that looked like wobbly birds, not like Sam. When Chup left, she stared at them curiously. They stared back. The smallest one, a tiercel, shivered. His chilled wings beat the earth like a drummer's stick. Frightful tilted her head, the better to see Drum's movements. They were telling her something.

"Psee," he cried in peregrine baby talk. The sound reached down into Frightful's early memories of her mother. She drooped her wings. Drum cried again. Instinctively she turned under her piercingly sharp talons, and stepped over the shivering eyas. He trembled. She raised her feathers and sat down. Drum wiggled into her warmth. Feeling his little body against her brought her into the brooding mode of the birds. When the other two nestlings crept into her feathers, she went into a trance. A goshawk flew overhead; a rock fell off the cliff and bounced past the blazing-star flowers. Frightful did not move.

"Psee," Drum called. After he had been brooded and warmed for an hour, he was suddenly voraciously hungry. He looked up at Frightful and screamed for food. With a start she came out of her trance, stood up, and shook her feathers.

"Pseeee, pseeee." Drum screamed louder. His open beak was bright red and rimmed with yellow. It was a bull's-eye that guided a parent to the mouth. Frightful saw the target and was inspired to tear off a small bite of duck. She held it in her beak, not knowing what to do next. Drum was too young to reach up and take it, and she did not lean down to put it into his mouth. She held the food in her beak above him. He did not take it, and after a short time she swallowed it.

"Psee, psee, psee." Now all the chicks were calling. They pressed up against her, their red and yellow mouths wide open, their wings fluttering. Frightful was overwhelmed by demands she did not understand. The one hemlock tree among millions came to mind, and she lifted her wings to fly.

Chup appeared in the distance. She recognized him a mile and a half away, although a mere speck. He grew larger and larger until he landed, full size, with a soft rustle beside her. In his feet was another duck. He presented it to Frightful and waited for her to do what came next—take it to a plucking perch away from the aerie, defeather it, then feed it to the eyases; the loudest, most aggressive first.

But Frightful did not carry it to a plucking perch or pluck it. In her past, Sam had prepared the food.

She did sense from Chup's stare that she should do something. So she preened her flight feathers, wiped her cheek on her shoulder, and walked under an overhanging rock. She hid from the screaming chicks. Chup waited patiently for her to do her part. She put her head in her shoulder feathers and closed her eyes. The eyases screamed. Chup could wait no longer. He carried the bird to his own plucking roost and prepared it.

"Psee, psee, pseee," the chicks screamed as he returned with the food and dropped it at Frightful's feet. He must hunt. She must do the feeding.

Frightful did not. She looked at the duck and then away. The eyases cried relentlessly, their eyes wide, their necks trembling from hunger.

That message reached Chup. He leaned down and snipped off a tender morsel. Lady, the largest of the two female chicks, bolted to him, stepping on Drum in her rush. She opened her mouth, and Chup fed her bite after bite. Then her sister, Duchess, pushed her aside and begged for food. Chup fed Duchess, too.

When the little females were satisfied, Drum reached up to Chup. At that moment a movement in the valley caught Chup's attention, and, good provider that he was, he left the aerie to catch a pigeon. Feeding was not on his agenda anymore.

Frightful saw Chup capture the bird in midair. She was interested, but when another pigeon flew by, she did not go after it. Sam had trained her to hunt the rabbits and pheasants that lived in the abandoned fields on their mountain. She turned her back and ate duck.

Drum screamed and screamed.

Frightful knew she should do something. She held food for the tiercel again. Drum opened his mouth and reached up. Brooding the fuzzy, white eyas had calmed him down once. She opened her feathers to him and sat down. He nestled up against her and stopped screaming.

Frightful felt his warmth against her body like a messenger of love. Ill-equipped as she was to be a mother, she called softly, "Cree." *I love you.*

Hours later she got to her feet and walked to the duck. Drum hobbled behind her. When she stopped and leaned over the food, he wedged himself under her. She tore off a morsel. Her head was low and he snatched the bite from her. She did not mind. Frightful plucked another bite for herself. Drum took that bite and the next until he was satisfied. Then she ate.

For the next week Chup fed Lady and Duchess and

hunted for the whole family. Drum had learned to get food from his strange mother.

The eyases grew their second, heavier coat of natal down when they were about fourteen days old. With that development they could regulate their temperatures. That was the signal for Frightful to go hunting. She did not. She kept brooding the chicks and letting Drum take food from her. Chup fed Duchess and Lady.

Despite their unorthodox lifestyle, all five peregrines prospered.

The chicks grew rapidly. As their flight feathers appeared, their white down disappeared. By the time they were four weeks old, they were almost full-grown and testing their wings. They needed food, lots of it, and Chup could not fulfill their demands. The eyases screamed and yelled constantly. It was time for Frightful to hunt.

On a late June day when the cliff side was green and yellow with chickweed, Chup caught a passing starling on the wing. Frightful was excited by his victory and flew out to get the bird. Chup winged above her and dropped it. She turned upside down and caught it in her talons.

The feat awoke a deep instinct in Frightful. She carried the bird back to the aerie and plucked it. But she did not feed the chicks, nor did she eat it. Not being hungry herself, she left it at the scrape and flew to a rock ledge above the aerie.

Drum ran to the bird. He tore it open and ate. His sis-

ters ate. Despite their new mother, the timetable of peregrine development was taking care of them. The young
peregrines were old enough to feed themselves—and to
attack their parents.

Frightful moved out of the aerie to a pine stub. Left
alone, the eyases explored the flowers, the rocks, and the
crevasses in the cliff. Lady picked up a feather in her beak.
Duchess took it from her. Lady rocked back on her rump
and threw up her feet. Duchess threw up her feet. They
locked talons and pulled. Drum jumped on a moving
feather and tossed it into the air. As it spiraled downward,
he rolled to his back and snagged it in his talons. Frightful
watched them curiously. They were playing peregrine falcon games she had never learned. High on her stub, the
young fed, Frightful pulled one foot up into her feathers
and sat quietly.

From a distance Chup saw that Frightful was not going
to hunt. He flew back and called her. His voice was insis-
tent. Frightful flew to him.

Chup led her out over the valley, saw a duck, and
plunged. Frightful sensed she should hunt ducks, but could
not. Chup was gone. She rode a strong wind eastward, her
wings outstretched, her feet pressed against her tail, the sun
shining through her feathers.

She was over the escarpment and waterfall. Recalling the
goshawks, she changed her direction. As she flew over the

woods, she saw the young goshawks with their parents. They were chasing crows and adroitly maneuvering among the tree branches. Their broad, short wings were designed to speed them in and around trees and branches. Frightful was a bird of the open sky. She climbed high above them.

The landscape passed swiftly under her, and in mere moments she was above the pine forest where she had been a captive of the two strange men and where Alice had set her free. Frightful searched the macadam road for the girl and was over the abandoned field.

Mole slid out of the culvert and sniffed his way along a small mammal trail. Frightful flew above him and waited on. This dog, like Sam, scared up game.

Mole wove through the grasses. A rabbit leaped up, and within seconds Frightful was on the ground, game in her talons. But Mole was there, too. The falcon and the dog looked at each other. Mole dropped down on his belly and snarled. Frightful covered the food with her wings.

Mole lunged for Frightful. In a flash, game in her talons, Frightful and the rabbit were in the air. She flew several hundred feet before coming down. Mole, keeping low and out of sight of the farmer's gun, sneaked up on her. Again he lunged. Frightful took off, hit a strong updraft, and was lifted over the field and barn.

She heard Mole barking irritably as his food went flying away.

She did not see the farmer come out of his house with a shotgun, nor did she see Mole dash into the culvert. Frightful was over the goshawk nest, and she was flying hard.

Frightful set her wings and glided above the waterfall and cliff to the Schoharie Valley. She descended gracefully to her aerie with food for the eyases.

I N W H I C H
The Eyases Get on Wing

Drum, Duchess, and Lady glanced at the rabbit. It was not part of their food vocabulary, so they kept right on screaming. They were hungry for waterfowl or land birds.

Frightful ate the rabbit while the eyases watched, twisting their heads from side to side and calling "pseee" when she swallowed. Duchess walked up to her, screaming in earsplitting decibels. Then the eyas lifted her wings and attacked. Frightful backed off a few steps and stared at the young falcon. Lady and Drum lowered their bodies horizontally and charged Frightful. The eyases had become dangerous. They were practicing for the competitive world they would soon face. Frightful wanted no part of this schooling. She lifted herself into the air, fanned her wings, and flew to her tree stub.

Chup came home. He brought no food to the eyases. Duchess charged him, mouth open, feathers lifted. He sat still and panted in the sun. His feathers were rumpled and he held his head low. Chup had not eaten for a day and a half. He was weak. That did not matter to Duchess. She attacked him. Chup, like Frightful, was forced to leave.

Alighting on the dead limb of an oak, he looked down and saw the rabbit. Without hesitating, he dropped down onto it and ate, fending off the eyases. He could still dominate them.

Chup had catholic tastes. He was nine years old. Each winter he migrated to South America. When the El Niño rains changed the balance of nature and birds were scarce, he dined on mammals and iguanas. Rabbit was food, and he was hungry.

Lady and Duchess stopped screaming. Chup was eating rabbit; it must be food. Painfully hungry, Lady led a raid.

She sneaked up to Chup. When he covered the food with his wings and body, Duchess reached in from the rear and snatched the rabbit. She tore off small bites but did not like the taste. She shook her head and sent the meat flying against the rocks. Chup finished eating and flew off.

Drum, who had now seen both parents eat this new food, dragged what was left under the overhang. Taking a bite in his beak, he swallowed. It was not delicious, but it was satisfying. He plucked another bite, then another. Drum was a survivor.

When he was satisfied, Duchess and Lady tried the strange food again. They ate gingerly, partially satisfying their hunger.

By sundown the peregrine family was fed if not full, but more importantly the family had a new housing arrangement. The eyases were now old enough to attack anything in sight, including their parents, and with that, their parents had sensibly turned the aerie over to them. Frightful and Chup did not return to the nest site. Frightful slept on the stub of the pine tree, Chup on the dead limb of his oak.

That evening they all watched orange and pink clouds float against a turquoise-blue sky. Chup felt restless. His offspring could not only eat on their own but also defend themselves. Just before sundown he spread his wings and soared out over the valley. He climbed high, he spiraled down, he skimmed along the river. With quick wing pumps he shot up and out of sight of Frightful and the eyases. Just before the sun set, he sped earthward, landing lightly on his dead branch. He heard the eyases chittering, saw Frightful sitting erect on her stub, and let his nictitating membranes slip across each eye. His lower eyelids closed upward and cut out the last of the daylight. The cliff side was quiet. The peregrine family was on schedule with summer. The eyases were completely feathered, feeding themselves, and aggressive, and the parents were perched alone.

With the help of Mole, Frightful now regularly brought food to the eyases. Each morning she flew southward to Mole's farm and brought back strange but nourishing foods, which she dropped to the youngsters. Chup, who had gotten thin doing the job of two parents, began to put on weight.

Mole also gained weight. The old hound had the canniness of a wolf. It didn't take him long to realize he had a hunting companion who was quicker on the pickup than he. The first two times Frightful went off with the game he had flushed, he could do nothing but bark. Then he learned that she didn't like groundhogs. She had tried one and abandoned it to him. She also didn't like skunks or rats. He chased them all. She got the rabbits and pheasants. He got the rest.

Mole and Frightful went hunting almost every day. When they had harvested the most conspicuous and abundant animals of the farm fields, Mole led her to more distant fields. The animals they left behind would breed, and their offspring would breed, until there were too many for their food supply. Then the two hunters would return and adjust the numbers again.

When the fields yielded little game, they worked the barnyards and farm gardens. Together they kept the rabbits and groundhogs from eating the farmers' crops and the rats from eating the corn stored in cribs and bins.

And so Frightful hunted with Mole, as she had hunted with Sam, and became the provider Chup and the eyases needed.

The eyases grew properly. At five weeks of age they were as big as their parents. Only a few bits of down on their heads and shoulders and their brown-gray color told how old they were.

On a hot day in early July, Duchess sat at the edge of the aerie, her wings lifted to keep her cool. A wind blew over her. It moved more rapidly over the top of her wings than under them and created lift. Up she went. She hung above the ledge for a moment, became confused, and stalled herself out by moving her wings and changing the wind flow. She fell back to the aerie.

Lady faced the wind, lifted her wings, and was airborne. She, too, fell back. She sat on her heels. Something new and wonderful had happened to her. She had been in the air with space between herself and the cliff. She and the wind had managed this wonder, which had changed her sense of who she was. She was a bird. She must fly.

A few minutes later, Duchess flapped her wings. She was lifted up and over Lady's head like a bit of thistledown. She alighted on a rock, where, somewhat astonished, she looked down on Drum and her sister. From them she looked into immeasurable distances—above, below, and to all sides—then nervously preened her feathers.

Frightful came home with a rabbit and dropped it in the aerie. Duchess jumped to get it, fell, spread her wings, and sailed. Quickly closing them to her body, she dropped down on the aerie. She ate what was now delicious rabbit to her.

That afternoon a thunderstorm darkened the river valley. Chup came home from his hunt. Retreating to his dead limb, he watched the lightning buzz around the cliff. Frightful flew from her stub and walked under an overhang near the aerie just as rain poured out of the clouds. The eyases crouched against each other, holding their feathers at slight angles that shed the water in rivulets. They shook, cleared water from their eyes with their nictitating membranes, and listened to the thunder boom.

When the storm passed and the sun came out, Chup set out over the valley, not to hunt, not to check on populations of doves and ducks, but simply to fly. He coasted on downwinds, rode like a water skier on turbulent winds, and soared on light breezes.

Frightful followed his flight with her keen eyes until he disappeared in a cloud. Then she left the rain shelter and returned to her tree stub. She sat quietly.

From the aerie, Drum, Duchess, and Lady watched everything that moved. The ocular pectin in their eyes had developed. They could see the movements of an ant walking as far away as the distant river. They studied and noted and memorized. They collected visual memories that would serve them for the rest of their lives.

Drum, fascinated with his acute vision, walked to the edge of the aerie to watch young swallows in their nests in cliff holes across the river. A wind struck him from the side; he flapped his wings to keep his balance and he, too, was flying. He soared along the cliff and landed with a crash on a ledge about a hundred feet away. Elegantly he folded his wings to his body and stood tall. He watched the rainwater fall from the leaves of the forest below and a tree frog vibrate his throat with song.

Suddenly Frightful plummeted out of the sky and landed beside him. Drum called, "Pseeee," and opened his beak to be fed.

Chup, who was soaring under the purple-blue cloud bottoms, saw Frightful with the fledgling and flew down to his dead limb. He called her away from Drum. The fledgling must survive on his own. Once again Frightful's early training did not help her with peregrine protocol. She heard Chup scolding her, but remained with Drum. Companionship with Sam had colored her concept of life. Young, old, bird, boy, girl, dog—companionship was comforting.

Early the next morning she flew off to hunt with Mole. Drum awoke and stared at the valley. Crows winged past, calling out messages to family members to stick together. A leaf spiraled toward him on an updraft. He did not try to fly again. Mother would come back.

Frightful did return to Drum with a rabbit late in the morning. Drum did not eat it. He had not cast a pellet this morning. Birds of prey eat meat, bones, feathers, and fur. They absorb the nourishment and cast out the indigestible parts in a tidy pellet. They cannot eat again until the pellet is cast. Drum sat quietly, food before him, waiting for his body to go through this cycle.

Duchess and Lady saw Frightful bring food to Drum and set up such a screaming demand that Frightful picked up the rabbit and carried it above the aerie. She dropped it to them. Chup watched her.

Frightful saw the food fall onto the blazing-star leaves and seedpods, then flew to a tall hemlock at the top of the cliff. Sitting among the lacy needles, the image of the one mountain among thousands, the one tree among millions, and Sam came to mind. She scanned the horizon for her home, then forgot it. Duchess now had her attention.

The young falcon was running to the rabbit with outstretched wings. The air flowed over them and under them, and before she could stop herself, she was off the ground and in the air. She flapped and sailed out over the red maples. High above them she stalled out and fell, landing in a treetop, her wings spread across leaves and twigs. She hung there for a moment, her shiny legs dangling. One foot found a sturdy limb, and then the other. Awkwardly folding her wings to her body, Duchess stood upright on the tree limb and shook out her rumpled feathers. When she was comfortable, she looked around. Food, companions, and parents were out of reach. She must fly to survive.

Meanwhile, Lady went over to the rabbit and stuffed herself. She napped in the noontime heat, opening her beak to pant and perspire. Upon awakening she played with a feather, then a stick. Feeling restless, she stretched her wings. The air picked her up, and Lady was flying, too. She flapped to the pine tree where the blue jays had nested, landed, and lost her balance. Thrashing her wings, she righted herself on a limb. Spellbound, she began to stare at the silver river. It moved.

Out of reeds and willow trees sped a flock of red-winged blackbirds. They flew up and circled around her. Tiny, fearless birds, they screamed and dove. They skimmed by

her head. They struck her with their wings. Duchess
ducked and dodged and finally decided to leave. Flapping
her wings uncertainly, she jumped off the limb and headed
for the aerie. The blackbirds cried louder and dove at her
like pellets of hail. Not far from the cliff face, Duchess lost
her lift and fell down through leaves and twigs. She came to
rest on a royal fern. It bent under her weight and lowered
her into the fern bed. The red-winged blackbirds could not
see her and flew back to the reeds along the river. Duchess
sat in peace, but also in fear. How would she get airborne
again, buried down in the windless and wet fern bed?

Drum, who had finally cast his pellet, eyed the rabbit in the aerie and set off to walk the short distance for a meal. He flapped his wings to help himself over a bramble bush and was flying. He hit a thermal and went up. Holding his wings firmly outstretched, he spiraled high above the cliff. The air was cold at the top of the thermal, and the warm bubble vanished. Drum fell earthward. He hit the ground, spreading his wings and tail to cushion his fall.

Drum got to his feet and ran to a bush. From the bush he flew to a cedar tree, and from the cedar tree to an oak at the edge of the cliff-top woods. He flew, hopped, climbed to its crown, and looked down on the vast valley the river had carved. He saw Frightful on her stub and let out a wild call for food.

Chup answered from above. He dove, scattered a flock of ducks, and brought one back to the aerie. He dropped it without slowing down, then flew over the cliff, over Frightful, over Drum, over the woods, and out of sight.

I N   W H I C H
The Wilderness Tests the Eyases

Frightful watched Chup wing over her pine stub at the edge of the cliff. She had no desire to follow him.

Her attention was riveted on the fledglings. Duchess

was in a red maple, Lady was out of sight in the fern bed, and Drum was perched in an oak tree behind her. Not one could reach the food she and Chup had dropped in the aerie—unless they flew.

No peregrine instincts told Frightful how to get the fledglings on wing. She sat and waited until it became too dark to see.

Lady awoke hungry. She was cold and wet. She shivered as she shook the water from her body and wings. Flapping hard, she struggled to fly out of the fern bed.

Duchess, on the other hand, did not seem to care if she ever flew again. She was comfortable. A dove flew past her. She focused on it with keen interest. A robin sang. She stared at it, then settled dreamily on her limb.

Drum had another agenda. Seeing his mother on the pine stub, he called pitifully, "Pseeeee pseee." She did not look at him. Desperately hungry, he jumped toward her, spread his wings, and was sailing like a paper airplane toward the ground. He hit the grass and stopped, *kakak*-ing in fear. Frightful heard him but did not answer. An ancient peregrine instinct was finally guiding her—do not feed the fledglings.

Drum hunkered down where he was for most of the day. As evening approached, he lifted his feathers to keep warm. A damp, cold wind rolled along the ground and over him. Drum hopped into a huckleberry patch at the edge of the cliff and lay down on his stomach.

Frightful closed her eyes. The flatness of the stub under her feet reminded her of her home perch. She could see her mountain, the hemlock, and Sam. Her mothering was coming to an end.

At dawn the next day she looked about. She preened, then touched the gland near the top of her tail and lubricated her dry feathers with its oils. She glistened.

A heartfelt "pseee" from the cliff top reached her ears. Drum thrashed out of the brambles into view. He saw Frightful and cried again. She stared and sat still.

Drum's "psee" became an angry "kak, kak" that tripped him into action. He beat his wings and took off. He dropped—down, down, down. He alighted on the aerie, scattering the seeds of the blazing-star flowers with the blast of air from his wings. With a hop and two flaps, he was upon the rabbit.

Duchess saw Drum eating. She spread her wings, soared out of the red maple, and landed with a thud close to him. He lifted his feathers to scare her, but she was bigger, and bigness is boss in the peregrine's world. Duchess grabbed his food. Then she saw the duck. She preferred bird to mammal and jumped on the duck. Running, covering, walking, she took it behind the blazing-star garden and ate ravenously.

Lady, who was at the foot of the cliff, was cold and losing weight rapidly.

"Psee," Lady called over and over. Neither father nor mother came to her rescue. She fluffed her feathers to warm her body and sat still to conserve energy.

When Drum had eaten his fill, he walked toward Duchess. She lifted her wings and chased him to the edge of the aerie. She screamed, "Kak, kak, kak," and he took off. He soared over the trees, tilted one wing, and found himself headed for the cliff. He pulled up on his tail, down on his wings, and was climbing. He came over the top of the cliff and steered to his oak tree. Drum was flying.

Duchess, alone and full of food, sat in the clumps of blazing-star flowers and stared down on the blue-green landscape. Her sharp eyes widened. Far away she saw a gray fox. He was walking along a tree that had fallen across a meandering stream. The slender animal stopped at a limb, then walked down it and jumped to the ground. He disappeared in the fern garden.

Duchess looked away from the fox. He was too big to be food. She walked to the edge of the aerie. Suddenly she spread her wings, was lifted by an updraft of wind, and spiraled skyward on a warm thermal. As she balanced herself with wings, feet, and tail, she felt the new and wonderful sensation of flight.

The thermal collapsed, and Duchess fell landward, alighting on the limb of an enormous sycamore tree near the river. Birds were all around her—on the water, in the reeds, in the trees and sky. She stared at the different kinds. Each species moved differently. Ducks ran on the surface of the water to get airborne. Pigeons banked and turned en masse in the sky. Swallows dipped and darted. Rails kept low in the marshy river edges. Cranes flew laboriously, then swiftly.

She chased the birds but could not catch any of them. After many hours, she flew home to the aerie and food.

Following Lady's scent, the gray fox located her exact position with his nose and leaped. She was gone. He looked up. The young falcon was climbing the cliff, beating her wings, taking hold of rock cracks with the hook of her beak and her talons. She scrambled and flopped. The fox climbed after her.

Frightful suddenly appeared above him. She dropped headfirst, pumping her wings close to her body, and hit the fox with her talons. She was going twenty miles an hour. He yelped and leaped. Too heavy for Frightful to hold; she let go.

The fox fell, lit on his feet, and ran into the woods.

Frightful returned to her stub.

Lady struggled on up the cliff. With a last effort, she pulled herself over the aerie ledge and flopped down on her breast, wings out. She rested with her beak on the ground. She was exhausted.

"Psee," she cried weakly, unable to reach the remains

of the rabbit. Frightful saw her struggle, but she did not help. Lady was out of the nest. She must make it on her own.

Hours passed. The young falcon grew more feeble. She was near death.

Chup sped into view. He dipped above Lady and dropped a pigeon. At the sight of the food falling her way, Lady felt a powerful desire to live. She flipped to her back and snagged the pigeon before it hit the ground. She rolled to her belly and tore off small bites. Energy rushed through her body, and she lived.

Three young peregrines had survived their first flights.

By the end of August the juvenile peregrines were catching almost all of their food. They wandered farther and farther from the aerie.

On a sunny day Lady flew far down the river valley. She lit on the tower of a church in a small town. Along the street were elegant Victorian homes. An elderly man emerged from one, walked to the churchyard, and scattered birdseed. Down from the trees, window ledges, and rooftops flocked many pigeons. They dropped to the man's feet and ate.

Lady did not go back to the aerie. In the days that followed she grew strong and fat.

Drum stayed near the river. He was a stunning juvenile

tiercel. He had his mother's dark head and his father's pale, blue-tipped body feathers. Like his father, he hunted the traditional food of his species—ducks and other waterfowl.

One evening, flocks of terns came to the river marshes. They were down from Alaska and Canada, migrating ahead of a cold front. In the few days they lingered in the Schoharie Valley, Drum grew fat on them. Then one dawn the birds took off for the south, and Drum went with them. His food was migrating; he must follow. In less than two days he and the terns and willets reached Delaware Bay.

When the September winds blew the downy milkweed seeds to new soil, Chup was gone, too.

A week later Duchess sensed another cold front bearing down from the northwest. She took a reading on the sun's rays and, pointing her beak south, she, too, departed. With her went little cedar waxwings and juncos.

Lady sensed the high pressure of the same front and she, like Drum and Duchess, began the long pilgrimage of the peregrine falcon to warmer climates.

Frightful was alone, the only peregrine falcon in the Catskills who had not migrated. She was thin. She had not put on the extra layer of fat birds need before instinct tells them they are ready to go. She lingered at the aerie, hunting the nearby fields. At night she returned to her stub.

Without the fledglings to feed she grew heavier, but weight alone was not enough to start her migrating. There were three signals she must feel: the fitness of her body, the rightness of the environment, and the chill of the atmosphere. She felt none of these.

Three weeks later, when orange, yellow, and purple leaves were showering down from the trees, Frightful was fat. Food was now scarce, and snow was in the air. She faced south. All the signals said go. But she did not.

Time passed; snow flurries came and went. Thousands of birds flew south. She watched them, lifted her wings to migrate with them, then folded them back in place. She could not go.

Early one morning a cold wind sent shivers through Frightful. She got aboard a thermal and ringed up. On it was a lone red-shouldered hawk. At the top of the bubble the hawk snapped its wings and shot south. Frightful hung there. She was looking down, not southward, searching for the one mountain, the one tree, and Sam. They were not to be seen. She got off the thermal and dropped back to her stub.

She dallied another two weeks. The window of the fall migration is open for only a few months. Once closed, the messages from body and environment shut off, and it is too late to go.

For Frightful that would be disaster. There would not be enough food for her to survive in the frigid northern winter.

I N   W H I C H

Frightful Peregrinates

When a light snow covered the Schoharie River Valley, Frightful's bird sense urged her one last time to leave or die. She took a reading on the sun's rays, listened to her internal compass, and started south.

She covered only ten miles before she turned back. She was hungry. She would find Mole.

When she was over the pine woods where she had been held captive, she flew faster. Mole's farm was ahead. Speeding swiftly, she overshot the farm. It had changed. The weedy fields where the game lived had been leveled and their black soil turned over in neat rows. The dense bushes along the fences, where many birds lived, had been clipped. She circled the culvert. It, too, was changed. The bushes that covered its entrance were gone. The culvert was a round, bare hole.

"Creee, creee, creee," she called.

Mole did not come out.

Frightful circled the farm again but did not find the yellow hound. She flew to the silo. The air was bumpy where warm currents met cold. She rode the waves to the ledge of the silo and stepped under the jutting roof. The veins of her flight feathers were split and dry. She oiled them, then snapped them back in line by running her beak down the shafts from base to tip. She let go with a flick that triggered the veins to fall neatly into place. This done, she was sleek and ready to hunt.

Frightful surveyed the landscape. Even the woods were different. The leaves had fallen, and the red-tailed hawk nest was empty. The parents and young had migrated to warmer lands.

Weak from hunger, she left the silo and flew back over the culvert. She waited on for Mole. The wind tossed her. She matched each burst with a twist to stay in place, but Mole did not come out.

Behind her, purple-red and blue-gray clouds forecast rain and wind. It was urgent that she find food. Swooping along fencerows to scare up game, she searched intently. Nothing stirred.

Twilight sent her back to the silo ledge, her hunger raging.

Hours later she was awakened by thunder shaking the old silo. The dark night was lit by flashes of lightning. With each flash she saw dancing trees and wild water pouring across the barnyard. It gushed out of Mole's culvert. The flashes became almost continuous, then stopped. The rain pummeled, swished, pattered, and was over. She went back to sleep.

At sunrise the sky was white-yellow and pale blue, the colors of a rain-cleansed day. The woods and farm sparkled with freshness. Frightful flew over the culvert and waited on. Mole did not make an appearance.

She was growing weaker. Spotting a distant harvested cornfield, she flew to a tree at its edge. She waited for something to move. Finally she caught a mouse. The storm had driven the bigger game into their shelters and burrows. In the late afternoon Frightful flew back to the culvert.

Out of the sky plunged a bald eagle. He aimed right at her. She back-flipped, and he missed. The eagle beat his wings and got above her for another strike. He dove. She rolled to her back, threw up her feet, and raked him with her sharp talons. He flew up to strike again. Frightful dropped to the ground and, as the eagle dove once more, ran into Mole's culvert. He lost sight of her. He climbed, circled the culvert once, then boarded an air current that carried him off toward the Hudson River. He would spend the winter fishing there.

Safe inside the culvert, Frightful panted from fright, then quickly became calm. Bird emotions are intense but short. She glanced at her surroundings. The gushing storm water of last night had slowed to a trickle. She drank. Refreshed, she walked to the mouth of the culvert, saw no eagle, and sprang onto her wings. She climbed high and fast over the tilled field.

When she was high enough to feel safe, she leveled off. An undulating wind rocked her southward over a brushy meadow. She came down on a fence post and watched for food. She was growing feeble as hunger weakened her.

Suddenly she was in deep trouble. The sun was setting. In mere minutes the light would be too low for her to find a roost. She flew up into the last light. It illuminated the bell tower of the abandoned church at Beaver Corners. She headed for it.

Winging to its weathered and rotting peak, she landed gracefully. The churchyard was thick with weeds. A farm and a woods lay nearby. She had been here. She shifted her weight nervously as the condor face of the man who had taken her from Sam flashed into her visual memory. She felt fear, but it was too late in the day to move on. She forgot him.

Snow patches lay under trees where the sun did not fall. A migrating Cooper's hawk dropped into the nearby woods for the night. Like Frightful he, too, was late.

The sun set. The sky turned a twilight purple. Frightful could see only light and dark shapes. She flew down to the sill of one of the four glassless windows in the church bell tower. Lifting her wings, she walked into a square, moldy room and jumped up onto a rusted bell lying on its side. Every window was black with night. She shook her feathers and, weak from hunger, fell into a restless sleep.

Last night's thunderstorm had preceded a cold front. The temperature dropped below freezing, and the migration of the birds stopped. The robins and wood thrushes and other small birds that navigated by the stars at night fluttered down into the trees. They sought the warmth of the wind-breaking woods to wait for the cold front to pass.

At dawn they tittered among the trees. They called to each other and ate insects numbed by the cold.

It was also too cold for hunger-weakened Frightful to fly on her way. She must eat.

She took off from the tower and flew out over a weedy meadow. A rabbit jumped up and ran toward a thicket of spiny hawthorn trees. Hunger sharpened her skills, and Frightful was upon it before it reached the fortress.

No migrating eagle passed overhead; no barred owl saw her. She ate, her strength returning quickly. The leftovers she carried back to the bell tower.

The cold did not let up for days. Frightful and the thrushes stayed on at Beaver Corners.

In the middle of one night the warmth returned. Wings rustled like taffeta as the birds lifted themselves out of the woods and continued their migration. Frightful opened her eyes. Ribbons of birds were flying across the yellow face of the moon. The birds were navigating by the shining light of stars.

In the morning the haze of an Indian-summer day erased trees, fields, and roads. Frightful could not see well enough to fly. She shifted her feet restlessly. The one mountain among thousands, the one tree among millions, and Sam were coming more vividly to mind the longer she lingered.

On an unusually warm day in early November, she stepped to the open sill of the bell tower. She had caught no food for two days. She must move south.

Frightful tried to read the angle of the sun's rays, but a gray-blue haze cut them out, and she could not get their message. She turned her head from right to left. She felt tiny iron particles in her brain lining up with the earth's magnetic field. She needed both the sun's rays and the magnetic field to plot her course. She had only one.

She took off anyway.

Frightful headed southwest.

She flew over the town of Berne and the steeples of North Blenheim. She chased a night heron up the Schoharie River, lost him, pursued a mallard duck, and lost her. She was not trained for birds. She stopped chasing them and came down to rest on a spruce tree on the banks of the Schoharie Reservoir.

The air was dense with moisture; clouds thickened and darkened the sky. Around noon they let go. Rain poured down. Tree trunks became rivers and spruce needles waterfalls. Frightful was her own tent. Water ran off her head and shoulders, her beak, and her tail. No wetness seeped through her feathers. When the rain blurred her eyes, she cleared them by flashing her nictitating membranes like windshield wipers. She sat calmly in the deluge.

A lost great blue heron took shelter on a limb below her. Frightful looked at it only because it moved. The bird was too big for her to take.

A wind hit the forest in strong gusts in the afternoon. Clouds circled clockwise. The edge of the last tropical storm of the year had twisted up from the south and was drenching the Schoharie Valley and Reservoir.

Rain fell for two nights and three days. Frightful

dropped lower on the spruce tree and waterproofed her feathers with the oil from her tail gland.

The deluge slowed, the clouds circled counterclockwise, and a flock of spotted sandpipers blew in from the coast. They ran the shore edges like windup toys and snatched minute bits of food. Frightful turned her head away. Her natural prey, the waterbirds, still did not interest her. Sam's training had faded somewhat under Chup's menu, but game from the upland meadows was still very much her idea of food.

The sun came out. Frightful flew to the top of the tallest spruce. Although the day was windy, all the guideposts she needed to orient herself were readable. She found the longitude of the Atlantic flyway, the migrating route of the birds of the east, and the magnetic field of the earth. She flew. She was going away from the one mountain among thousands, the one tree among millions, and Sam. She was going south to warm weather and food.

Catching an air current that took her up and over a mountain, she looked down on acres of open fields, meadows, and grassy clearings. Here lived the food she liked. She coasted down to the roof of a small cabin. It was Woodchuck Lodge, the mountain home of nature writer John Burroughs. Before Frightful could gather her wits, a chipmunk, abroad on the nice day, snatched some grass seeds and ran under a mammoth boulder and was gone.

Around the rock were drifts of snow, now sodden from the tropical storm. A plaque marked John Burroughs's grave.

Frightful brought herself to attention. She must eat. Concentrating, she looked at every twisting grass blade and bobbing seed head. Suddenly she drew in her feathers and stretched her neck. The mountain laurel by the lodge was shaking. Frightful lowered her body to strike.

Out from under the porch came Mole. His ears and coat were plastered with autumn's burrs and Spanish needles. Around his neck was a collar. Mole had been on an adventure.

The adventure had taken him far from the culvert.

While Frightful was watching the young peregrines learn to hunt, Mole's run-down farm had been sold. The new owners were aunt and uncle to Hanni and Hendrik Van Sandtford, friends of Sam and Alice Gribley. Hanni and Hendrik had come over to Altamont to help their relatives restore the neglected farm. They had cleared brush, tilled the abandoned fields, and leveled the overgrown fencerows.

Their work done, they were driving home in Hendrik's pickup when they saw a dog slinking along the side of the road. He wore no collar to say he was a pet. Hendrik stopped the truck, and Hanni jumped out. Mole vanished into a culvert. After many kind words and tasty food offerings, Mole finally trusted Hanni enough to creep into the cab. He cringed at her feet all the way back to the Van Sandtford farm.

At the farm, Hendrik combed the burrs from Mole's hair and gave him a bath. Mole was embarrassed. He put his tail between his legs and hung his head. Next Hendrik put a collar around his neck, snapped a leash to it, and dragged him, protesting, all the way to the barn. A bed of sweet straw, water, and ample food were put down. Mole dug under the straw and hid. He refused to eat. Hendrik sat with him late into the night, talking softly.

Mole heard "good dog" many times and then his new name, General. He listened to the kindness in Hendrik's voice and finally ate and fell asleep as the sun was coming up.

Two nights later he chewed through his leash and jogged west. He crossed the bridge at Gilboa and climbed into the forested mountains.

He hunted, slept, and came out of the trees at Woodchuck Lodge. The layout looked good to Mole. Weeds, briers, and the grasses told him there would be rabbits, pheasants, woodchucks, and mice. He sniffed around the lodge, found no scents to say the house was occupied by people, and squeezed under the porch. Near the chimney base he clawed out a cozy wolf bed and settled in.

Although Mole was happy to be away from people and bedded down in his own home, he was faced with a problem. The cold had sent the woodchucks into their burrows for the winter. After a few days of fruitless searching, he trotted across the field, headed for the town dump he had passed on his way up the mountain.

"Creee, creee, creee."

Mole stopped. Sniffing the air, he looked up. Frightful was sitting on top of the lodge, feathers shining in the autumnal light. He stared at her.

She cocked her head and stared at Mole. She did not wonder at finding him again, just opened her wings and flew out over the field. Mole broke into a run and, nose to the ground, worked the grasses and dead goldenrod spikes. A rabbit burst up. Swift as light, Frightful was upon it. She pumped her wings and carried it away without coming down to the ground. When she was almost to the lodge, a great horned owl saw rabbit and falcon, sped silently out of the woods, and sank her talons into the food. Thrown off balance, Frightful fanned her flight feathers, regained her equilibrium, and went after the owl. Owl and rabbit vanished into the woods. Frightful, a falcon of the open skies, did not follow. She pushed down on her wings and up with her tail and came to rest on the porch railing of Woodchuck Lodge. Mole was right behind her.

The two looked at each other, then the old hound turned and went back to his hunting field. On the second try they caught a pheasant. This time Frightful scanned the sky for thieves before flying with it to the rooftop. Daintily she ate choice pieces.

Mole sat on his haunches, looking up at her, his tongue hanging out, his mouth drooling. He wanted his share of that food. Suddenly he growl-barked so viciously that he scared Frightful. She took off, leaving the food behind. The bird rolled down the shingles and fell to the ground. Mole picked it up and, tail wagging, carried it under the lodge. There he feasted.

Frightful had eaten enough to bring back her strength. She flew to a tall tree and perched. The bright sun was warming the fields and meadows, creating a twisting and invisible bubble. On it rode a lonely peregrine tiercel. He circled up and up. Frightful opened her wings. Lift took her into the thermal. She spiraled to its ceiling. The tiercel peeled off and shot south like a missile.

Frightful was next. She circled the top of the bubble, tipped her wing, and spread her tail. Everything was right—the angle of the sun's rays, the wind, the temperature, and the magnetic field of the earth. She ripped through the sky like a meteor.

Her wings spread in glorious flight, she looked down on the vast landscape.

And there it was. The one mountain among thousands of mountains, the one tree among millions of trees, and somewhere there, the one boy.

Frightful turned abruptly west and in minutes was over the mountain. Snow lay on its highest levels. Food would be scarce here.

She flew back to Woodchuck Lodge. There the last weak messages from the environment pointed her southward again.

But she had seen the mountain.

Confused, she *kakak*-ed in distress and flew into the spruce tree for the night.

I N   W H I C H

Frightful Finds the Enemy

The next day was cold. Sleet and rain fell on the Catskill Mountains. The air currents dropped steeply earthward, making it difficult for Frightful to fly. She flew above the trees but could not get high enough to see her mountain again.

Chilled and tired, she came back down to the spruce tree near the lodge to wait for the ice storm to pass.

Mole holed up under the house. The sleet had driven the game birds and animals into retirement, and he knew it was useless to hunt. However, unlike Frightful, Mole had another option. Around noon he trotted off to the town dump. At dusk he returned refreshed.

For the next few mornings Frightful watched Mole leave the lodge and return in the evening. His tracks were soon covered by snow and icy rain, erasing all signs of the hound's travels.

One evening Mole did not return from the dump. Frightful spent several days hunting without him. She caught a mouse running over the snow and a squirrel that had ventured from its leaf nest.

When Mole finally came back, he was limping. His left ear was torn and bleeding. He had lost a fight for a female Labrador on a farm down the mountain. He squeezed under the porch and did not make an appearance for several more days. When he did emerge, he eagerly hunted the Burroughs fields, and Frightful joined him.

The sleet, snow, and cold kept Frightful confined to the mountaintop at Woodchuck Lodge. Finally the air currents stopped dragging her down, and she flew high enough to locate her mountain, but the entire western horizon was swathed in clouds. She went back to the spruce tree.

At last a high-pressure bubble brought sunshine to the icy Catskills.

Frightful shook out her feathers and preened and oiled them. She lifted her head. Her large, round eyes searched for the indicators that would guide her on her way. She found none. The window of migration had closed for Frightful. She was a winter bird, one who cannot go south.

Like all winter birds, Frightful's life was threatened.

But the day was clear. The sun sparkled on the ice and snow, and the wind blew the last clouds away. Frightful left the spruce tree and climbed up and up. When she reached two thousand feet high, she saw at last the one mountain in thousands. She flew straight for it.

Gliding over densely wooded White Man Mountain, her eyes pinned on Sam's mountain, her position fixed, she heard a familiar cry.

"Cree, creeee, creee."

She dove down and skimmed the tops of the trees. Duchess was somewhere below.

"Cree, creeee, creee." The call directed Frightful's eyes to a perch on the ground. On it sat Duchess.

"Cree, cree, cree," Frightful answered from a leafless maple.

Duchess wore a falconer's hood. She was jessed and leashed. Her juvenile feathers were rich brown in color. She was fat. Duchess was living well.

"Kak, kak, kak." Two goshawks sat on perches not far from Duchess. Beyond the birds was a small hunting cabin set back in a grove of young hemlocks. Near it stood a pigeon cote and a duck house.

The cabin door opened and a man stepped out.

"I thought I heard a wild peregrine," he said, lifting his binoculars. He wore camouflage pants and a sheepskin vest filled with pockets. Around his neck hung a falconer's whistle. Frightful knew the man. One eye was brown and the other eye was blue. He had a condor face. This was the man who had taken her from her perch beside Sam's hemlock tree. This was Bate.

"Spud," he called. "Come here." The door opened, and Spud came out. He was portly and wore a dirty ski jacket.

"What's up, Bate?" he asked.

"We just got real lucky," said Bate. "There sits twenty-five thousand dollars." He pointed to Frightful. "Twenty-five and twenty-five makes fifty thousand. Let's get her."

"Come on, Bate," Spud said. "We ain't got time. Skri's waiting for us. Let's sell these birds before the bird cop finds us and we go back to jail."

"Leon Longbridge is never gonna find us here," said Bate.

"Could," said Spud, peering around. "I saw that falcon guy from Roxbury driving along the lumber road down below."

"Who's he?"

"The guy who came to the sheriff's office and took the prairie falcon and the sharp-shinned to the falconer in New Paltz. He was lookin' hard up-mountain."

"That don't mean nothin'," said Bate. "You can't see this place when you're ten feet from it."

"Well, let's get out of here anyway. He knows we were in jail for selling falcons and hawks to wealthy Saudi Arabian falconers. That's a federal offense. Remember?"

"They let us off light."

"Yeah," said Spud, running a thick hand through thinning hair, "but a second offense is federal prison, and that's a long stay. Let's go."

"We can catch this bird in minutes," Bate said. "Her crop is empty. She's hungry. Probably lost on migration.

"Twenty-five thousand is a lot of dough." He focused his binoculars on Frightful again.

"Go get the mist net," he said. "I'll get a duck for our pretty duck hawk. That'll get her in the net in two seconds."

Spud hesitated.

"Get goin' if you want to get out of here so bad," Bate said.

Spud hurried into the cabin for the net. Bate walked quietly to the duck house.

"Creee, creee, creee," Frightful called again. This time Duchess recognized her voice. She turned her hooded head almost upside down, then sideways as she listened.

"Pseee, pseee," Duchess answered in baby talk. "Pseee, Pseee," she repeated. Frightful sat quietly. What little instinct she once had had for feeding the young was entirely gone. The nesting season was over. But the baby call brought a feeling of comfort to Frightful. She was a winter bird and a lonely one. She listened quietly.

Bate and Spud, moving like midnight bats, left the cabin and darted through the trees.

Frightful watched them. She closed her wings to her body and pulled her tail feathers together one upon the other. She did not fly.

"Pseee, pseee." Duchess again called the hungry nestling cry, reminding Frightful that she herself was very, very hungry.

She looked for movement. Her eyes went to the men. They were the only action. She watched them stretch a long mist net between trees. It rippled, then went taut and almost disappeared from sight.

Bate took out a duck from his vest pocket and, holding her in his arm, stroked her breast until she was hypnotized and calm. Then he tethered the Muscovy on the other side of the net from Frightful.

"All set," he whispered to Spud. "Follow me." He led him in a wide arc away from Frightful and back to the cabin.

"She's still there," Spud said as he opened the door. "I'll stoke up the woodstove while we wait. It's chilly."

"Don't bother," said Bate. "As soon as the Muscovy flaps, that falcon will dive and hit the net."

"I hope so. I don't like this."

The Muscovy came out of her trance and shook. Frightful saw her. She tensed to dive.

Bate watched through his binoculars.

"There she goes! We got her," he said.

"Not yet," said Spud. "Let her get real tangled in the net. We've waited this long; a few more minutes won't matter."

Frightful straightened up. Ducks were not prey. She was still Sam's falcon. Waterfowl did not interest her.

"Cree, creeee, cree," Duchess cried. The Muscovy heard the falcon cry and flapped in terror.

Calmly turning her back, Frightful took a bearing on the sun's position and beat her strong wings. She flew straight for the one mountain among thousands, the one tree among millions, and Sam.

I N   W H I C H

Disaster Leads to Survival

The wind carried Frightful speeding down the side of White Man Mountain. As she came over a logging road, a man walked out of the leafless November woods. He was dressed in a tan jacket and pants and strode with a gait as free as Sam's.

"Creee, creee, creee, car-reet." Frightful called Sam's name.

With a swift wing beat she alighted above a transformer on an electric utility pole. The man was not Sam. She lifted her wings to fly.

A wind gust knocked her off balance. She tipped, spread her flight feathers like fingers, and braced herself against two wires. Sparks sizzled and burst upward. A powerful electric current shot through Frightful. Her feathers burned. She could not move. The electricity held her prisoner.

She passed out.

Jon Wood saw Frightful get zapped. He grabbed a fallen branch, climbed a boulder under the utility pole, and tried to knock her off the wires. He brushed her, but could not dislodge her. Taking the long branch in both hands, he swept it back and forth. Frightful's left wing was pushed from the wire. The circuit was broken. She fell to the ground.

Jon Wood picked her up and folded her wings to her body. He looked at her burned flight feathers. He saw her cloudy eyes.

"A fabulous and rare peregrine," he mumbled, "and she's dead." He stroked her still-warm breast.

"Another utility-pole disaster," he said to himself. Then went on, "I get so angry about this. It doesn't have to happen."

Smoothing Frightful's seared feathers, he opened a large pocket in his jacket and placed her in it. He would report her death to the U.S. Fish and Wildlife Service in Albany. They kept records of the endangered peregrine falcons. The birds, once down to zero in the East, were gradually making a comeback, thanks largely to a falconer, Heinz Meng. He had bred the first peregrines in captivity and, using an ancient technique called hacking, had been able to free them to the wild. Other falconers learned from him, and the peregrine began to recover.

Jon thought of Heinz as he stood on the mountain road.

First it was DDT and other pesticides that killed the great peregrines, he mused. Now it's death on utility poles.

His warm brown eyes narrowed.

"This does it!" he said to himself. "All the utility companies have to do is lower one wire so the birds can't touch those two parallel hot lines and complete a circuit. One little adjustment—that's all—and thousands of these great birds would live."

He opened his pocket and peered down at Frightful, thinking, I've written the utility-company manager so many times, my fingers hurt. Today I'm calling the company president.

He strode on down the mountain to the road where he had left his car. Saddened and angry, he drove home, parked near his barn, and walked to a large bird mews.

"Hello, Sammy," he said to a magnificent bald eagle. Sammy was recovering from an accident with an automobile.

"Kak, kak, ka, kleeeek," the bird replied. Jon smiled and looked from the handsome eagle to his own home. He was proud of it. As a young man he had built it himself on acres of field and forest deep in the Catskill Mountains. The house was dug into the hillside to conserve heat. It was shingled with handmade shakes. Jon had trained a falcon to hunt with him. He had planted his own vegetables. When his land was flourishing, he went back home and married a young woman named Susan. He took her to his mountain with some apprehension. "Do you like it?" he had asked. "I want to live here all my life," she answered.

As Jon worked the land and flew his falcon, he saw how important the raptors were to the environment. Some kept the excess birds under control; some kept the rabbits from destroying his garden; others cleaned up the rats, mice, and voles. He studied and became a master falconer with a license from the U.S. Fish and Wildlife Service. He taught his raptors to fly free and come back to the lure, and the next thing he knew, he and Susan were visiting schools with their birds to tell the children of the importance of the birds of prey.

Jon Wood paused before opening the door to his house. He looked out over the silent white mountains and braced himself to tell Susan the bad news.

"Susan," he said as he walked into the kitchen, where she was feeding an owl. "Another zapped peregrine." He reached into his pocket. "Hey!"

Frightful was moving. Astonished, he lifted her up and rested her on the palm of his hand. She looked at him out of bright eyes. Jon grinned in disbelief.

"Susan," he said. "She's not dead. I can't believe it. She was zapped, burned, fried on a utility pole."

"Oh, Jon," said Susan, coming closer. "She looks awful. We should take her to the vet."

"Let's wait," he said. "She looks amazingly perky. We'll jess her and I'll check her out."

Susan opened a cabinet and took out a pair of leather straps. They were jesses. Falconers for three millennia in Asia and Europe had put the exact same kind of straps on the legs of their falcons, hawks, and eagles. The jesses were held in the fingers or clipped to a leash to keep the birds from departing.

Jon stroked Frightful's wings and breast, then held her feet in his hand and her body along his forearm. Taking first one leg between his fingers, then the other, he gave her jesses, then pulled on a falconer's glove. Gripping the jesses, he flipped her upright on his hand.

For a moment Frightful looked around. Finally she roused, shook her feathers, and sat quietly. She was in a house. Gone were the mountains, the woods, and the Schoharie Valley. Unperturbed, she then stared at Jon Wood. He smiled and lifted her close to his face.

"How do you feel?" he asked by making soft peregrine calls.

"Creee," Frightful said, expressing her comfort.

"A peregrine," Jon said to Susan. "A fierce and noble

falcon right out of the wilds of White Man Mountain, and look at her—sweet as a baby."

"She didn't even bate," said Susan. "I've never seen a wild bird that didn't try to fly, get stopped by the jesses, and hang upside down. She flipped up on your glove like a trained bird."

Jon twisted his fist to examine Frightful's breast, then her back and wings. He touched her seared feathers and feet.

"She looks okay," he said, smiling. "I can't believe it. No flesh burns, no broken bones from her fall—nothing. A few blackened feathers. She should be fried black."

Susan moved toward Frightful with the gentleness of a mother bird.

"Hello, lovely lady," she said. "I'm so glad you're all right."

Frightful sensed in Susan the same love that emanated from Sam, Alice, and this man who held her. She roused to express her contentment, then shook. Several burned feather tips fell to the floor. She observed her surroundings. A prairie falcon called softly from another room. A snowy owl clapped his beak and hissed. She saw rooms, tables, stoves, and daylight coming through windows. This was not Sam's hemlock-tree home, but it did not frighten her either.

Jon brushed away a loose feather from her head and put his hand on her breast. Her felt her crop, the upper portion of the gullet where the food first lodges after swallowing. It was empty.

"You're awful thin," he said. "It's late for you to be up north here."

Susan stroked the quiet bird.

"What are you going to do with her?" she asked.

"We'll fatten her up and let her go."

"But not until spring."

"Not until spring," he assured her. "She wouldn't make it." He held Frightful close to his face and chirped at her.

"What are we going to do with her tomorrow?" he asked. "We'll be gone for five days. We have appointments to show our birds at seven elementary schools."

"Maybe Anthony would drive down from Altamont and feed her," Jon suggested. "You know he's an apprentice falconer."

"I have a better idea," Susan said. "We'll take her with us. We'll show the kids what utility poles do to birds."

"Yes," Jon agreed wholeheartedly. "They should see her."

Susan looked in Frightful's dark eyes. Frightful looked into Susan's eyes and on beyond.

"You're mysterious," she whispered. "The migration is over, and yet you're here. You're a wild bird, and yet you're tame. Where did you come from? What do you know?"

Susan tilted her head to delve the mystery, could not,

and turned back to the job of packing canvas carriers with food, hoods, and jesses for the eagle, hawks, owls, and falcons.

"By the way, Jon," Susan said, checking the list one last time, "what were you doing up on White Man Mountain in the first place?"

"Oh, my gosh, I nearly forgot." He dashed to the phone and dialed the number of the conservation officer for the Roxbury area.

"Hello, Peter. This is Jon Wood. Yesterday I saw smoke rising about where Jebb Harper's hunting cabin is. He hasn't used it since he got rheumatism, and he never lends it out. I went up to check it today."

"Trouble?"

"Yes," he answered. "I didn't go too close because I heard a peregrine falcon call near the ground—then men talking. I was unarmed."

"Hmm, what do you think?" Peter Westerly asked.

"Well," Jon answered, "that man Bate and his friend are out of jail, you know. Last spring they were selling falcons to an Arabian agent, and I haven't heard yet that they've reformed."

"True," Peter Westerly said. "I'd better get Leon Longbridge from the Delhi area and go up there. He's been worried about those two ever since he learned that the Arabian agent, Skri, was back in the area. Sounds like they're up to it again. You heard a peregrine falcon, huh?"

"And a goshawk."

"Oh, boy. Here we go."

Jon hung up and told Susan that the falcon poachers were at work again.

"Are you going to help catch them?" Susan asked.

"I wish I could," he answered. "But we have a long day tomorrow and all the rest of the week. Leon and Peter are the ones to do the job anyway."

When Frightful had eaten until her crop was round and full, Jon showed her a perch. She jumped to it, shook her feathers, and settled down. Jon scratched his head.

"She sure is cooperative," he said.

Frightful sensed she was among people who shared Sam's spirit. She turned her head and tucked her beak behind her shoulder.

On her way up the stairs to bed, Susan stopped and contemplated Frightful.

"You know, Jon," she said, "I have the funniest feeling that our guest is a trained falcon."

"I've been thinking that, too," he said. "She's so relaxed. But where did she come from? I'm the only falconer who can have a peregrine in this part of the state."

"What about Roger Hartzbeen?"

"He's still an apprentice falconer," Jon said. "He won't be able to have one for five years."

"Maybe she got away from someone in Canada," Susan offered.

"But she's not name-tagged. Falconers tag their birds in case they get lost and someone finds them."

"She's a very beautiful bird," said Susan, admiring her dark head and large eyes. She came back down the steps and leaned over Frightful.

"I wish you could talk," she said. "I think you have a destiny to fulfill.

"That's it," she said softly. "I believe I've just spoken your name. You are Destiny."

The next day Jon Wood carried Frightful to a large mews on the hilltop and unsnapped her leash, holding onto her jesses. He opened the door.

"Stay here for a little while," he said. "When we all come back from our school trip, this will be your home. It's big enough for you to get some exercise and catch your own food." He turned his fist until Frightful faced him.

"When the birds return in spring, and food is plentiful, I'll let you go. You can fly home." He peered into the calm eyes. "Wherever that is."

Jon talked to Frightful just as he talked to all his birds of prey. They felt his affection for them in his voice and responded to it with lifted feathers and soft sounds. As Frightful listened, Sam came to mind. She called, "Creee."

Jon held her against a padded board that stretched from one side of the mews to the other. She jumped up onto it and looked about. Three sides of the big mews were wooden. A high ledgelike shelf was built into one corner. It somewhat resembled a peregrine's favorite nesting site—a cliff. Frightful did not fly to it. She stayed on the board.

A ceiling protected the mews from rain and snow, but more importantly from the wild hawks and owls for whom anything that moves is fair game.

Sunlight streamed through steel chicken wire on the fourth side. Frightful did not try to fly through it. Jon observed that.

"Susan's right," he said to Frightful. "You have done all this before. Every other new bird I put in here flies into the wire before it learns it's not free."

Frightful shook her feathers, stretched one wing, and glanced out at the mountains. She was facing home and Sam. She pointed her beak in his direction.

Jon went from one mews to another, hooding each occupant and carrying it to his tour van. He picked up a big, fluffy snowy owl and put his nose into the sweet, dense feathers on his head.

"You're going to have fun, Mr. Freeze," he said. "Kids will hug you to death. And that's what you like best of all."

Presently Susan arrived.

"Hello, Destiny," she said, and added, "Creee, creee, creee."

Frightful heard her own language, lifted the feathers on her head, and drew herself up tall. Susan smiled, stepped

into the mews, and took Frightful on her gloved hand. She carried her to the rear of the van and put her in a carrying case. Frightful did not resist.

"Destiny," she said. "You didn't even struggle. You are a wonder." Carefully she latched the holding case, then peeked in at her.

"You are going to change many lives. That's your destiny."

Taking off her falconer's glove, she picked up Mr. Freeze and climbed into the front passenger seat. Mr. Freeze, who had been hatched in an incubator and had never known any mother other than Susan, cuddled in her lap.

The van, with its beautiful cargo, drove off.

At the bottom of the hill, Jon stopped. A state highway maintenance truck was parked across from his drive. Two men were unloading equipment on the side of the road.

Jon stuck his head out the window. "What's up?"

"Bridge repair," shouted a wiry man in an orange helmet. He crossed the road to the van.

"Bridge repair?" Jon asked. "There are no bridges around here."

"Yeah, there's a little one back toward Roxbury. You probably never noticed it. It's just a flat span over a seepage area."

"The potholes need more repairs than that thing does," Jon said.

"Yeah, but we've got orders to repair every bridge in the state, big and little. Governor's decree. No exceptions. New policy since those people died when the hundred-year flood collapsed the Schoharie Bridge. Big political issue— safety."

"When do you start?"

"In a few days," he said. "After that we go on to Margaretville, and then the iron bridge at Delhi. That'll be the first week in May."

"What's the matter with the Delhi Bridge? It's practically new."

"One of the pilings is crumbling from water erosion. But really it's the same thing—governor's decree."

"Well, I guess it's a good idea," said Jon. "But this equipment is an eyesore. I hope you finish in a hurry." The man shrugged and crossed the road to help his fellow workers.

Susan looked at Jon's scowling face.

"It is a good idea, Jon," she said. "The Schoharie Bridge was falling apart for years and years, and no one did anything about it until it killed five people."

"I know. I just hate to have to look at all that industrial equipment at the end of my beautiful road. This is my Eden."

"Creee, creeee, creee."

Jon thrust his head out of the window and looked up.

"Another peregrine falcon!" he said. "What's going on?"

"Creeee." Frightful answered Duchess from inside her box.

I N   W H I C H
Hunger Is Frightful's Teacher

The first visit was a middle school in Roxbury, not far from the Woods's home. Jon and Susan arrived quite early. Jon brought the van to the shipping entrance and carried the hooded falcons and hawks into the auditorium. He put the owls in hollowed-out tree stumps on the stage. Round-eyed, they peered silently out of round holes. When all the birds of prey were in place, Susan let some of the students hug Mr. Freeze. The owl chuttered in pleasure, and the kids oohed.

Then the learning show began. Jon held up Sammy, the bald eagle. He spread his seven-foot wings. The kids gasped. Sammy was breathtaking.

Jon named all the birds and flew the prairie falcon from one end of the auditorium to the other. Holding her high, he talked about the important role of birds of prey in nature.

Finally Susan took Frightful out of her carrying case.

"This is Destiny," she said. "She is a peregrine falcon, or a duck hawk, as these wonderful birds were once called.

"She was late in migrating south this year and came over White Man Mountain on a chilly day. She alighted on a utility pole that held a transformer. She lost her balance, spread her wings, and completed the circuit between two wires. She was shocked with electricity.

"She couldn't move. The electricity froze her to the wires."

Susan went on to say that Jon had flipped her off the wires with a branch and carried her home in his pocket, thinking her dead.

"Suddenly," she said to her wide-eyed audience, "Destiny moved in Jon's pocket. She was alive. We could not believe it. The jolt had not killed her, just burned her wing tips. Jon took her in his hands, smoothed her feathers, and jessed her. Then, with all the grace of the peregrine falcon, she flipped herself up on his fist and looked at us."

Susan held her high. "She is a survivor and she is alive. She wears burns that tell about the dangers of utility poles for our wild birds." The children stared at Frightful, and some said they could smell the acrid scent of her scorched feathers clear at the back of the auditorium.

Jon then told the story of how one of his falcons was electrocuted on the wires of the transformer in his field.

"Ahhh," murmured the kids.

"Once a month I write to the utility company and ask them to lower one wire—that's all—just lower one wire one foot. That would do it. Then the birds couldn't touch the two wires and complete the circuit. Thousands of eagles, hawks, and beautiful owls like these could be saved.

"Not getting any reply," he went on, "I telephoned the management. I got the old runaround. 'Push one to speak to Miss Jones; push two for billing; push three to talk to customer service'—and on and on."

A small girl with dark hair and blue eyes raised her hand and stood up.

"Mr. Wood," she asked, "can we write to the utilities president and ask him to fix the poles?"

"Me, too," said the boy next to her. "I write good letters."

There was a clamor of voices. A teacher put up her hand.

"Do you have a name and the address we could write?" she asked. "This would make a wonderful project for us."

"Creee, creee, creee," Frightful called.

"Destiny wants us to write," piped another little girl, and took out her notebook and pencil.

"Creee, creee, creee."

Jon picked up a sheet of poster paper and wrote:

Mr. Lon Herbert, President
New York Electric Company
Albany, New York 10579

He propped the poster against Frightful's perch. The students bent over their notebooks.

Dear Mr. Lon Herbert,

How would you like it if you were walking a wire, slipped, touched another wire, and was zapped—fried so your mother wouldn't even recognize you?

Well, the birds don't like it either.

Here is a drawing of how to change the wires on a transformer so eagles, owls, hawks, vultures, even blue jays don't get zapped.

Sincerely,
James

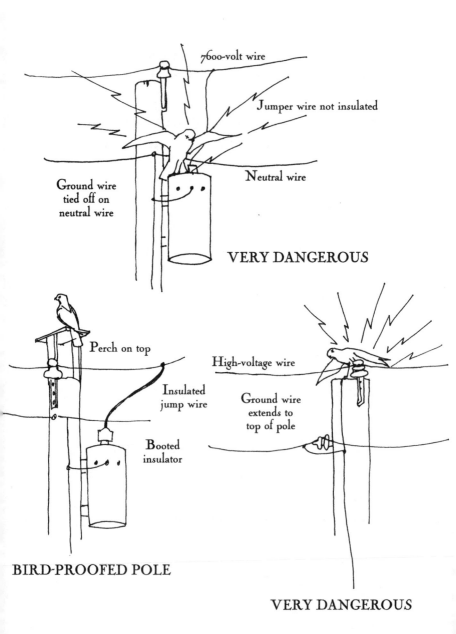

7600-volt wire

Jumper wire not insulated

Neutral wire

Ground wire
tied off on
neutral wire

VERY DANGEROUS

Perch on top

High-voltage wire

Insulated
jump wire

Ground wire
extends to
top of pole

Booted
insulator

BIRD-PROOFED POLE

VERY DANGEROUS

Dear Mr. Lon Herbert,

Birds have rights, too. People cut down the trees and put up electric poles that zap them. I think they should be able to sue you. A bull hit my dad and he sued the farmer and my dad wasn't even dead.

I am going to be a bird-defense lawyer when I grow up. Andrew.

Dear Mr. Lon Herbert,

We are studying civil rights. The falcons and owls and eagles have no civil rights because you discriminate against them.

Sincerely,
Maria

Jon and Susan carried the letter idea to all the schools they visited, and when the week was over, six hundred were in the mail.

"You know, Susan," Jon said when they were driving home, "those letters just might help."

"Of course they will," Susan replied.

As they came to their drive, they glanced at the bridge-repair equipment, looked the other way, then drove up the long dirt road to their house.

By late afternoon the Woods had returned all the birds to their perches and mews. Jon carried Frightful to hers. He tossed her off his fist and smiled at her.

"Good girl, Destiny," he said. "You just might have saved a lot of birds." He paused. "I hope so." He closed the mews door and walked to the pigeon cote to refresh the pigeons' water.

"Creee, creeee, creee."

Duchess swooped over the cote and climbed up into the sky.

"Creee, creee, creee," Frightful answered.

Jon looked up.

"It's another peregrine falcon," he said. "What is up with you birds? Peregrines in November. Something's out of order."

Duchess circled overhead, then dove over the pigeon cote, sending the birds into panic.

"You're hungry," Jon said as Duchess climbed for another swoop at the pigeons. He was about to release one for her, but changed his mind. He and Susan raised these pigeons for their hawks and falcons to chase and perfect their skills. They were smart pigeons. They always got away. They knew how to dodge their pursuers with twists and turns and disappear in the woods. They would fly around the countryside for a day or two, then return to the cote. Falcons and pigeons both enjoyed the game.

Jon got a rat instead of a pigeon.

He walked into the field, calling to Duchess in peregrine talk. She appeared overhead, prepared to take another swipe at the cote. He tossed the rat. It ran only a short distance before Duchess struck and carried it to a tall spruce behind the barn. She ate for the first time since Bate had turned her loose. He had unsnapped her jesses when he saw Leon Longbridge and Peter Westerly approaching the hideout.

Jon released another rat in Frightful's mews. She watched it dash to the chicken wire and squeeze out.

"Hey," he said. "Don't you know what a rat is?

"Well, Miss Destiny, the rat crop of New York practically supports our wild raptors now that we've wiped out most of their natural food. And a good thing, or we'd be overrun with rats." He peered up the statuesque figure sitting quietly on the padded board. "And that's a big help to humankind.

"So, I'm going to teach you about rats. You'll need to know all about them when you're on your own." He went back for another. Frightful let it escape, too. It wasn't a rabbit or a pheasant. It wasn't even a waterfowl. She turned her back on the next one.

"I guess you're not hungry enough to learn," Jon said, and gave the friendly call note of the peregrine.

At sunset a fine snow fell. It covered the mountains and roads, the fields and the mews on Jon's mountainside. The owls watched it seep into their homes. The daytime birds slept.

At dawn the Catskill Mountains were white and silent. Frightful opened her eyes on a changed landscape.

The snow fell for two days and nights, and Jon did not feed Frightful all this time. He did come to speak to her and check her burned feathers. The breeding season was over, and she was molting. New feathers were replacing the burned ones.

Susan came to Frightful's mews one day.

"I know you're hungry, Destiny," she said. "But you're being trained. And hunger is your teacher."

She pulled on her falconer's glove and stepped inside the mews.

"Rats are good," she said. "Taste this." Frightful flew to her hand and gulped a large bite of rat. She looked at Susan and called for more.

"I can't give you more," she said, placing her on the padded board. "You learn by being hungry." Susan returned to the house.

The bite of food perked up Frightful. The red-tailed hawk in the next mews moved, and Frightful flew at her, hit the wire, and dropped to the ground. A movement on the sumac bush outside caught her eye, and she flew at a blue jay. The wire stopped her.

That evening Jon opened the mews door and stepped in. He released a rat. Frightful struck it before it had run a foot. She carried it to the padded board. There she deftly used the nick in her beak to cut the spinal cord. It died without pain.

And Frightful ate rat.

Two more weeks of school visits, and several hundred more letters were sent to Mr. Lon Herbert.

Susan called her friend at the local radio station.

"These kids have written incredible letters," she said. "You ought to read them on the air."

The friend was also a bird lover. The following Saturday he asked several of the kids to come to the studio to read their letters. A New York TV station liked the story and sent a cameraman to Jon's house to film the children with Frightful.

The next day three linemen arrived at Jon's door.

"We're here to change the wires on your transformer," said the heavier of the three men, smiling pleasantly. "Also to insulate exposed wires."

"That's just wonderful," said Jon. "But how about changing them all over the state? Changing one isn't going to do much good."

"Three," said the pole climber. "We've been told to change three. Which ones do you want changed?"

"That one on our hill," Jon said, pointing to the pole that had killed his falcon.

"And the one by the Roxbury Elementary School," Susan said. "In fact, it would make a lot of children happy if you fixed all the utility poles."

"Three," said the large man. "Our orders are to fix three."

Frightful Finds Sam

In early March the first of the migrating falcons and hawks returned to the Catskill Mountains. Frightful was in her nuptial plumage. She had molted completely. The scarred and broken feathers were gone. The white on her tail and under her chin was as bright as new snow. Her back was thunderhead blue, her rose-tinted breast had the brightness of cloud tops. Her head was almost black. She was healthy, and educated in rats and pigeons.

She knew the pigeons and their flight patterns especially well. Her mews faced the cote, and she watched the birds long hours. She saw how they dodged Jon's young falcons with twists and turns. She saw them return home to the cote on smooth, slow glides.

Jon noted Frightful's interest in the pigeons and rats, and on a bright but chilly morning he carried her to the top of his mountain. Susan hurried behind him, jumping patches of soggy snow.

Frightful cocked her head as Jon took off her jesses. She stood free but did not fly. Drawing herself up tall, she mapped the direction to the one mountain among thousands, the one tree among millions. No spring force pulled her north with the returning falcons. She was home, and not far from Sam.

Jon touched her beak with his finger. Susan hugged her arms to her body and watched wistfully. She loved and hated the moment when they set birds free.

"Good-bye," Jon said, and cast her from his hand with a

strong thrust of his arm. Frightful bulleted into the sky and opened her wings.

Susan called, "I'll miss you, Destiny." She moved closer to Jon.

"Oh, why do I get so involved with these birds?" she asked. "It's so hard to tell them good-bye."

Jon nodded and concentrated on the disappearing speck.

"I wonder why she's going toward Delhi?" he finally said. "That's the last place in the world for a peregrine falcon to nest. No cliffs over there."

Frightful knew exactly where she was going. She sped into the wind and covered the thirty miles to the one mountain among thousands in less than ten minutes.

She dropped down onto the one hemlock among millions and came to rest.

"Creee, creee, creee, car-reet," she called.

There was silence, then, "Frightful!"

Sam put down the plumping-mill crossbar he was repairing and jumped to the rock by Baron Weasel's home. Frightful peered at him through lacy hemlock limbs.

"Frightful!"

She dropped down three limbs.

"Frightful." Sam's voice lowered to a whisper. "You came back."

She hopped down to the next limb and looked for her perch. It was not there. But the plumping-mill crossbar was. Frightful alighted on it.

"Creee, creee, creee, car-reet." She was home.

Sam leaped from the rock and walked slowly toward her. His blue eyes looked into hers. His suntanned face creased with his big smile of wonder.

"Now, what do I do with you, beautiful bird?" he asked. "I can't keep you. The Feds say I'm not old enough to have a falconer's license." Frightful tipped her head and focused an eye on Sam.

"If I keep you, the Fish and Wildlife Service will just take you away from me. Maybe even jail me. You're an endangered species. I can't harbor an endangered species. I've learned that much!

"But," he said, leaning closer to her, "if I don't jess and leash you, you're not a captive bird.

"Will you stay anyway?"

Frightful made soft noises and flew to the Baron Weasel rock. The plumping-mill stick slipped and fell to the ground.

It hit with a force that scared Frightful. She flew to the lowest limb of the hemlock. Sam sat still.

"I missed you," he said. She lifted her feathers and softened her eyes. His words held the sounds she recognized as human love and affection. He chatted on.

"I'm pretty good at getting squirrels now, Frightful," he said. "I had to learn to hunt them after they took you from me. I use the same kind of sling David used to kill Goliath. It's accurate and packs a wallop. But it's not like hunting with you. We were a team, and we shared such good food. Tasty rabbit for you, rabbit stew for me; good pheasant liver for you, pheasant pot pie for me. Squirrels just don't quite make it."

Frightful bobbed her head and listened. Sam talked on.

"Alice and Mrs. Strawberry eat pork. Alice bred Crystal, her pet pig, and she and Mrs. Strawberry raised the piglets. They sold several of them for lots of money. They butchered one. It's pretty good. They saved three for breeders.

"I go down to the farm several times a week to help Mrs. Strawberry with her crops and garden. She can't do the heavy work anymore, and Alice is busy with the pigs and livestock. I like the work. I learn from the land and the sun and rain."

Frightful bent her knees to fly, but Sam spoke on, softly and rhythmically. She straightened up and listened.

"And Bando. Bando's making Adirondack furniture out of twisted forest saplings and limbs. They're wonderful pieces. People come from New York and far out of state to buy them.

"Zella's gotten so she likes their cabin. That is, after Bando and I got the waterwheel generating electricity. She has an electric stove and washing machine now. And—"

Footfalls in the woods alerted Frightful to danger, and she flew for the sky. Seconds later Alice came running up the path.

"Alice," Sam shouted. "Stay where you are."

"Why?"

"Frightful's here. You scared her." He circled the big hemlock, looking up among the limbs for his friend of the mountain.

"How do you know it's Frightful?" she asked.

"Creee, creee, creee, car-reet," Frightful called from overhead.

"Oh, Sam." Alice sucked in her breath and stared up at the hemlock. "It is Frightful. She called your name."

Frightful flashed her wings and flew over the trees.

Sam whistled the three notes, "Come to me," and ran to the bare rocks at the top of the mountain. He searched for her.

She was beyond his sight, cruising above the West Branch of the Delaware, looking for rats. She glided past the library and came to rest on the top of a handsome iron bridge. It was a bowstring truss seventy feet high. On each side of the span were iron bows. They were braced in place by a horizontal girder, to which iron columns and webs were riveted. The ends of the bows were embedded in cement pilings.

From the top of the downstream bow, Frightful saw the pigeons of Delhi. They wheeled up into the sky, broke apart, came together, and disappeared among the houses.

Frightful did not chase them. She had found the moun-

tain, she had found the tree, and she had found Sam. But a plumping mill was not a good perch. The bridge top was excellent. She dropped from the upper bow to the wide, horizontal girder.

She walked the girder until she came to a plate that joined the girder to the webbing. It was flat and roofed by the bow. She walked under it and looked out on the river and the valley. She liked this spot.

Frightful rested and pulled a foot into her breast feathers. The sun dropped low. Below her, red-winged blackbirds clinked good-night songs as they retired among the tall rushes. The cars that drove over the bridge trembled it as if they were wind in the trees. Some deep peregrine instinct told her this was where she belonged. Not in the forest. Not in a mews. She preened her feathers and watched the sun set. Night came.

In the morning she was hungry, very hungry. She flew up and down the river, saw nothing moving, and returned to the one hemlock.

"Creee, creee, creee, car-eet."

Sam burst through the deerskin door of the tree. He pulled on his deerskin jacket and waved his gloved hand.

"Okay," he called. "Let's go hunting, old friend." Whistling and swinging his arms, he ran down the trail to the meadow.

Frightful knew exactly where he was going and flew ahead of him to their old hunting ground. She waited on while Sam kicked through the weeds and grasses, still covered with snow. A rabbit jumped up, but so did a wood rat.

Frightful struck the rat. She covered it with her wings. The sky was full of thieves. Sam ran to her.

"Well, I'll be," he said. "A rat! Think I'm going to eat rat?" He laughed as he picked up both rat and Frightful in his gloved hand.

"Well, I'm not," he said. "You've got the whole thing to yourself." He smiled while Frightful ate. When she had consumed the parts she considered her share of food, she stopped eating. Sam took the food from her, and she rode home on his fist, free and unjessed. He talked happily to her.

"This might work," he said. "Both of us free."

As they approached the hemlock forest, Frightful looked up. Chup was overhead. She recognized his wing beat and shape. She opened her wings and flew from Sam's fist.

"Creee, creee, creee," she called.

"Thanks for the rat, Frightful," Sam called, but she was out of earshot. Still talking to her, he held up the rodent by the tail. "And just what do I do with this? Huh, Frightful? Pâté de rat?"

Wings rustled, talons dropped like a jet's landing gear, and a red-tailed hawk snagged the rat. She flew off.

"Well, that answers that," he said. "As Bando always says, 'Ask nature questions, and you will get answers.' "

Sam strode home over a forest floor spangled with flowering partridgeberry plants. He whistled and smiled.

Frightful maneuvered bumpy winds as she descended to the river and her bridge. She landed on the bow with a soft thud and looked up. Chup was flying straight to the cliff above the Schoharie River. She called. He heard but did not turn back. He was a smart missile aimed for a predetermined destination. Every March for ten years he had made this plunge from high above Sam's mountain to his aerie on the cliff.

Just before he flew over the road to Roxbury, a crew of

men in orange vests loaded equipment onto a yellow tractor-trailer. The materials had lain all winter at the end of Jon's road. A crane operator drove his awkward-looking vehicle off the grass onto the macadam and waited for instructions.

"The Margaretville Bridge is next," Joe Cassini, the foreman, said. "Then Delhi."

Although Frightful knew where Chup had gone, she did not follow him to the Schoharie cliff. Like many birds, the birds of prey mate for life, but Frightful had two forces keeping her where she was—Sam and the iron plate under the arc of the bowstring bridge. In a very few hours the bridge had become her aerie. It was home. And up the river on the mountaintop was Sam. She could hunt with him when she could not find food on her own.

Not only did her love for the iron plate and Sam keep her from going to Chup, but so did a new feeling deep inside her. She wanted to lie down. She scratched the plate with her talons several times, then lowered herself to her breast. She got up and scratched again. Frightful was making a scrape, a peregrine falcon's nest, which is nothing but bare earth or, in Frightful's case, an iron plate where she wanted to sit.

The more she scraped, the more content she became with her aerie, and the more Duchess, Lady, and Drum returned to her visual mind. That night she slept on her breast. She had never done that before.

The next day Frightful took inventory of the food of

Delhi. Pigeons were bountiful, and there would soon be more. Pairs were nesting in the rococo architecture of the churches and Victorian houses. Males and females took turns brooding the eggs and flying to the courthouse park to feast on seeds and bread. The food was scattered by two elderly sisters, who argued every day about which pigeon liked which sister the best.

That morning Frightful watched the ladies open their bags and scatter the food on the ground. A flock that had been waiting for the two women to arrive winged down from trees and cupolas, fighting each other for first place. Frightful caught a loser in midair. She carried it back to her iron aerie and stood over it. She did not eat it. She was waiting for the "psee" cry of baby falcons, or the "good girl, help yourself" words from Sam. Hearing neither, she finally ate.

That afternoon Frightful toured the backyards, the tumbling buildings in town, and dumps at its edges. Rats moved in and out of bags and boxes and auto parts. She saw whiskers twist, eyes move. When the rodents saw her, they disappeared deep in the debris.

Frightful circled wider, looking down on fields and farms beyond town. Female cottontails were preparing nests in the snow-matted grasses. There would soon be an abundance of young, and the young would have young. When they were all rushing around fighting for the limited food supply, Frightful would find them easy to catch. Like all predators, Frightful hunted the most abundant prey. She would take them until the rewards were not worth the energy spent to find and catch them. Then she would move on to other large populations, leaving the survivors to multiply.

Frightful returned to her bridge in the late afternoon. She walked along the broad horizontal girder, feeling in sync with her world. There was an abundance of food in and around Delhi. With Sam's and Jon's training, she had become a peregrine falcon of the twenty-first century. Her native taste for ducks and shorebirds had been replaced by an appetite for the pests of humankind.

She was hardly back from her tour when Chup flew over the bridge. He called to her. He cut love arcs before her eyes. She flew out to meet him. She spiraled in a sky roll with him. She copied his aerial loop-the-loop, then flew in tandem with him down the river. She was following closely when Chup suddenly sped toward the Schoharie River. Frightful followed reluctantly.

Over Gilboa, she braked by pulling down on her secondary flight feathers and tail. Turning in the air, she caught a northeasterly wind and went back to the West Branch of the Delaware. She skimmed up to and lit on the graceful bow of the Delhi Bridge.

In the late afternoon she grew very hungry and flew up the river to Sam's mountain and the one hemlock. She worked her way down through its dense limbs almost to the ground. Her old perch was back up. She hopped down onto it.

"Creee, creee, creee, car-reet," she called.

Sam poked his head out of the stone water mill he had built with the help of Bando and his wife, Zella, Alice, and the town's public librarian, Miss Turner. Bando looked out, too.

"Did I hear right?" Bando asked Sam.

"Yes, you did. Frightful's back. And," he said, "she's sitting on her perch."

"Desdemondia," Bando gasped, and grinned.

"Yesterday we hunted together. Just like old times," Sam said.

"She hunted with you?" Bando loved rabbit stew.

"Don't get excited; she hunts rats now."

"Rats?"

"Got any good recipes for rats?" Sam asked.

"Hmm," Bando said. "The wildest of all our falcons, the one most intolerant of human beings, has discovered rats. She will be an enormous asset to Delhi."

"Well, she's not helping me," said Sam. "I'm not going to eat rats."

Sam and Bando walked to the round stumps Sam had cut from the bole of a tree and sat down to watch Frightful.

"Wonder where she's been," Bando whispered. "Do you think she went south?"

"She looks as if she's been living in a palace," Sam answered in a low voice. "Her feathers, her posture, her demeanor say she's in wonderful condition."

"She came back to you," mused Bando. "That must mean she is imprinted on you—thinks you're her kind of critter. She probably won't mate."

"I'm not sure just how deeply she is imprinted on me," Sam said. "I got her when she was ten days old. Frightful knew her parents. That's not like the falcons that were incubated and nurtured from day one by people. They never mate with their kind. Frightful has a good chance to discover she is a peregrine falcon, find a fine mate, and have young."

"That'd be nice," said Bando. "Imagine having Frightfuls flying above the mountains and rivers of the Catskills again."

The two friends lapsed into silence. Bando leaned on the stone table; Sam wrapped his arms around his knees.

"She's back," mused Bando.

"I hope she mates," Sam said. "We sure need peregrine falcons. They're so important in the balance of nature."

The silver rays of twilight slanted through the hemlock needles in dusty streams. The kinglets, who were just back from the south, sang their vespers. Frightful was quiet. Sam and Bando were quiet.

Presently Frightful flew from her perch, wove her way up through the dense tree limbs to open sky, and returned to her bridge. She walked to her scrape. As night came to the Catskill Mountains, she pulled one foot into her breast feathers and closed her eyes.

The lengthening hours of daylight worked their spring magic on the birds. Their reproductive organs responded to the light, and they began to build nests. For her part, Frightful slept on her scrape, her breast against the iron plate. Despite blasts of cold winds, rain, and snow, Frightful felt the peregrine falcon spring.

She awoke at dawn to hear Lady calling and glanced up. Lady was headed home to the cliff above the Schoharie River where she had been raised. She had survived the winter in the traditional peregrine way by migrating to South America. She had lived on ducks and shorebirds, and she had ingested DDT. Banned by the U.S. Congress because it killed millions of birds, fish, and amphibians after World War II, the insecticide called DDT was still being used in South America. Lady got her share of the poison when she ate the birds who had eaten the DDT-killed insects in Chile. Each winter she would accumulate more of the poison in her body tissues. The shells of her eggs would be thin and eventually smash when she tried to incubate them. She would not live to be ten or twenty-five years old, as some peregrine falcons do. She would tremble and die after a few winters in South America.

Frightful watched Lady until she was out of sight. She did not see her come down on a sycamore tree near the

Margaretville Bridge. Men in orange coveralls were working there. Standing on platforms, they were painting the webs and cords sage green. A cement mixer churned. This was no place for nervous Lady.

She took off for the Schoharie River. Near her birthplace she flew into Chup. Recognizing her, he chased her away. Offspring do not come home. Lady sped east. When she had put forty miles between herself and her first home, she was over the upper Hudson River. Swinging back and forth across the great waterway, she searched for a cliff like the one she had been raised on.

No sooner was Lady out of sight than Frightful forgot her. She flew up and down the river, looping and spiraling; finally she turned and flew to Sam's mountain. She alighted on her perch. Sam was building a fire to cook his breakfast of wild cereal grains he had collected.

"Creee, creee, creee, car-reet."

He straightened up, saw Frightful, and his eyes twinkled.

"Good morning, beautiful bird," he said, taking her measure. "Guess we won't hunt today. You're fat and full of rat."

"Creee," she called softly.

After eating his porridge, Sam got a bowl he had chipped out of stone and filled it with chunks of pine resin. He put it in his stone oven and threw on more wood. The resin melted; he dipped a stick into the goo and worked it into a crack in the plumping-mill box. When it cooled, he poured water in it. The box no longer leaked.

Frightful looked out at nothing as she listened to old, familiar sounds on the mountain. Behind her the downy woodpecker drilled into a dead tree with a special beat she recognized. He had been a resident of the hemlock grove ever since she had lived there. A flock of ruby-crowned kinglets alighted in the top of the big hemlock. They called to each other a twittering farewell, as they did every year at this time. Sam's mountain was their last rendezvous on their trip north. From this forest they would fly off by twos to their ancestral breeding grounds.

"The kinglets are here," Sam said to Frightful. "It's bird springtime in the Catskills, snow and all." He looked up at the walnut-sized birds flitting among the tree limbs.

"Time to build a nest, Frightful," he called.

Frightful stretched one beautifully gray-spangled blue wing, then the other. Bending her knees, she pushed off and wove awkwardly upward through the trees. She was no forest goshawk.

Clear of the last twigs, she trilled a soft tribute to wings and flight, and dove freestyle down the mountain to the river. She was leveling off to land on the bridge when a male peregrine joined her. They landed simultaneously on the top of the arch of the bowstring truss.

"Chep, chep, chep," he called. Frightful jumped down

to the large horizontal web and walked to her scrape. He
followed for a few steps, then stopped. Frightful was a third
larger than he. He bowed to show his respect. An alu-
minum Fish and Wildlife Service band ringed his leg. He
had been raised in captivity and released to the wild by
Heinz Meng. The number 426 was visible on his band.

Frightful looked at him. She did not attack. He held a
tasty bite of food in his beak and presented it to her. She
accepted it. He bowed again, then shook out his feathers,
which were ruffled and bent from travel. 426 had spent the
winter in Ecuador and was now looking for a roost like the
one he had known in the breeding barn of the falconer.
Coming over Sam's mountain, he had seen Frightful and
followed her to her aerie.

The coming of spring was affecting Frightful. She
glanced at 426, leaned down, and scraped the iron plate.
426 came closer.

She lifted her feathers to him. He hurtled himself into
the air, bulleted down the river valley, made a two-circle
loop, climbed, and sped back to the bridge. Frightful
watched his spectacular sky dance twice more, then she flew
off the bridge and traced the same design in the air. She
climbed, looped, and finally, in a graceful maneuver, held
on to his feet as he flew upside down beneath her.

For three days Frightful and 426 danced above the river
and mountains. They flew so high they could see the Hud-

son River. They flew so low they scared the nesting red-
wings. Upside down, they called to each other.

Then Frightful led 426 to the one mountain.

"Creee, creee, creee, car-reet," she called, and landed in
the hemlock tree. 426 came down beside her.

Sam whistled their hunting tune.

Frightful left 426 and flew to the mountain meadow.
There she waited on, watching Sam run through the laurel
and seedling hemlocks to their field. Just as he arrived, 426
swooped under her, took her feet in his, and swung her in
an arc up into the sky. High above Sam they opened their
wings and flew in tandem down the mountain over the river,
up into the clouds and back to Sam.

Laughing, crying, Sam watched them disappear again.

"Frightful, you've got a mate!" he exclaimed, and
climbed the nearest tree as swiftly as a marten. Near the top
he saw Frightful and 426 drop out of sight in the river valley. Suddenly they reappeared again and, looping side by
side, flew straight toward Delhi.

Sam noted their direction. He lined up the top tree on a
mountain with the weather-vane rooster on the peak of a
distant barn and scrambled down.

He ran full speed downhill for the West Branch of
the Delaware, looking at rocks and trees for white streaks
of bird excrement that marked a peregrine falcon aerie.
He saw no such marks, absolutely none, then remembered

that Leon Longbridge had told him no peregrine falcon would nest near Delhi—no cliffs. The bridge was high, and he recalled that peregrines had learned to nest on bridges. Running hard, he took his Peaks Brook trail to town.

When Sam reached the bridge, Frightful was playing with 426, sliding and gliding on the winds at fifteen hundred feet.

Finding no telltale marks of an aerie on the bridge, Sam walked up Elm Street and stopped in the library to get a book on farming wild edible plants. He was returning when Frightful and 426 came back to the bridge. She saw Sam. He did not see her, and she did not call his name.

It was evening. Eighteen miles and sixteen minutes away as the falcon flies, the repair work on the Margaretville Bridge was nearing completion. Supplies were loaded onto trucks and flatbeds, and orders were called in for air compressors and movable work platforms.

"The bowstring bridge at Delhi is next," Joe Cassini said on a cellular phone to his boss at the Department of Transportation in Albany.

The following dawn the sky was pink and orange with May's morning light. Frightful and 426 mated. Fifty hours later she retired to the scrape. Sitting down, the wind from the river brushing her face, she laid a pale cream-and-pink egg. It was mottled with rich red-and-brown splotches. Thousands of tiny pores in the shell allowed oxygen to enter and water and carbon dioxide to escape. A thin cuticle glistened on its surface. This would prevent bacteria from getting through the shell. The egg was a masterpiece.

Frightful did not incubate it. She and 426 perched nearby, looking at it and feeling new interest in the bridge and the river valley. Then they took off together, a synchronized pair, looping and diving in the sky.

There Are Eggs and Trouble

Two days later Frightful laid a second egg. Again she did not incubate it. Without her warmth, the embryos could not develop. Nevertheless they needed attention, and she turned them every three or four hours. The turning twisted the ropelike chalzas attached to each end of the yolk and to the shell. This twisting tightened the chalzas and kept the yolks suspended in the middle of the albumen so that they did not stick to the inner shell.

Frightful pulled a feather from her breast and watched it blow off on a wind. Before she lay the first egg, both she and 426 had lost so many feathers on their breasts that these areas were naked and bare. These were brood patches.

Both parents would brood the eggs. Warmer than feathers, the bare skin would raise the eggs to seventy degrees Fahrenheit. At that mystical temperature, life would start.

The day Frightful laid the second egg was cold. Nevertheless, she and 426 left the eggs and flew off to the courthouse cupola. 426 saw the pigeon ladies come out of their house and the pigeons flock to meet them. He dove. The pigeons scattered. Frightful watched from above the trees. She saw a bird fly away from the others in confusion, dove at it, and missed.

Later that day they were successful in their cooperative hunting. Frightful caught a rat.

That night was very cold. Frightful stood over the eggs, not sitting on them to start incubation, but protecting them from the freezing air. She let her long breast feathers and pantaloons make a tent around them as she stood. Her brood patch was swollen and soft with a jellylike fluid.

Three days after the second egg was laid, Frightful laid a third. When she stood up to look at the rich colors and exciting shapes of her clutch, her knees bent. She sat down. Her brood patch fit gently around the eggs like a soft hotwater bottle. Long feathers that had developed around her brood patch dropped around the eggs like a down comforter. They kept the warmth in and the cold out.

Around noon the peregrine eggs reached seventy degrees. Miraculously, inside each egg one cell became two,

two became four, then eight. Life was exploding in its various and complicated ways. Frightful sat tight.

That afternoon 426 became provider and helper. He flew off alone and came back with food. He fed her, then she stood up. He sat down and brooded the eggs. Frightful flew up and down the river, then winged over the one hemlock, calling to Sam. When she was well exercised, she returned to the scrape. 426 got up. Frightful sat down on the precious eggs.

Around six o'clock the next morning 426, who was sleeping near the top of the bridge against a vertical web, awoke. He checked Frightful and flew off to hunt.

Sam saw him go. He walked onto the bridge and whistled. Frightful did not answer.

"I know you're there," he said. "I've been watching you from Federal Hill."

Frightful was quiet. The longer she incubated, the more deeply she went into the trance of incubation. Only 426 could bring her out of it, and only to eat and fly briefly.

Sam whistled again. Still no answer. He grinned. Frightful, he knew, was now incubating.

"Good girl," he said aloud; then to himself, "At last I know for sure that she is not so deeply imprinted on me that she could not mate and raise eyases. I am so, so glad. I did not destroy her wildness after all."

Whistling, Sam swung off the bridge and dropped to the water's edge, where he walked gracefully upriver, jumping stones and skirting marshes. He arrived at the path to Mrs. Strawberry's farm. Today was the day to plant her rye. The maple leaves were flowering.

On May 8 a diesel truck, pulling a flatbed of lumber and roadblocks, crossed the Delhi Bridge and parked on the town side of the river. Workmen placed detour signs and orange cones on either end of the bridge, tied orange ribbons to webs, and conferred with their boss, Joe Cassini.

The café owner, Betty Christopher, drove up in her car and poked her head out the window.

"What's all this about?" she asked Joe Cassini.

"Bridge repair," he answered.

"About time," she said. "The last couple of floods just about tore out the pilings. Gonna fix them, too?"

"Yeah," Cassini answered. "The pilings are first."

"I've been expecting them to go any day," said Betty Christopher, "and dump everyone on the bridge into the river. I'm glad you're here."

"They're not that bad," laughed Joe Cassini. "But we're repairing this bridge and every other bridge in New York State. Even ones that hardly need it."

"How am I going to get to work?" she asked. "I live on the mountain side of the bridge, not the town side."

"We're setting up a detour. Turn around and cross on the lower bridge."

"Gotcha," she said, and drove off.

A week later the workmen finished the crib that would

support the bridge while they replaced the pilings. No sooner was it up than a diesel truck with air compressors pulled onto the bridge. Men with ear protectors picked up their jackhammers and tested them. Blasts shook the bridge.

Frightful stood up.

"There's a peregrine's nest on this bridge." It was Sam's voice below. She sat down.

"So?" said Joe Cassini.

"Well, peregrines are an endangered species," he said. "They are protected by law."

"We ain't going to shoot them," Joe Cassini said.

"But you'll scare them away," Sam replied. "Isn't there another bridge you could work on till the end of June?"

"There are a lot of other bridges. But the Department of Transportation says we do this one—now."

"Tell them peregrine falcons are nesting here. I'm sure when they hear that, they'll want to wait until the nesting season is over. These are very special birds."

"You tell them," Joe Cassini said. "I don't know anything about that stuff." He gave orders to a man who was standing beside the piling and turned his back on Sam.

Sam looked up at the long horizontal girder, then down at his body. He measured his body width against the width of the girder.

"It ought to work," he said, and ambled toward the mountain side of the bridge. Walking to the bottom of the bow, he glanced back. The repair crew was busy. Grabbing the bow in both hands, he ran up it like a spider. At the fifth vertical from the mountain shore, he eased onto the wide horizontal girder and lay down. He was out of sight on his belly. He inchwormed to Frightful. She was tucked under the bow, her eyes calm and broody. Sam pressed his lips together and chirped.

"Car-reet," Frightful answered, and stood up. She turned the eggs to keep the developing embryos from sticking to the shells.

Leon Longbridge, the conservation officer, and four kids walked onto the bridge. Sam watched Leon. A little less than a year ago Sam had thought Leon Longbridge was the man who had confiscated Frightful and taken her from him. Sam had been dead wrong. The culprit was a falcon thief named Bate. Leon Longbridge was Delhi's conservation officer and a truly fine man, as the town kids had discovered. Leon's favorite bird was the peregrine falcon, and last summer when a boy named José Cruz and a girl named Molly came to his office to ask about peregrine falcons, he had expounded with beautiful stories about their courage and swiftness. They wanted to hear more, and it was not long before he found himself taking them on early-morning bird walks.

Only last evening, Molly, who was ten years old with black bangs and a pigtail, had called him.

"I think two peregrine falcons are nesting on the bridge," she had said. "And the workers are scaring them."

"Good for you," he had said. "You're right. There is a pair on the bridge, and I am sure all the noisy equipment will drive them away. I'm going to ask the foreman if he can't work somewhere else the first thing in the morning."

"Can José and I come with you?" she had asked.

"Sure," he had said.

"And Maria and Hughie?"

"I don't see why not," he had answered. "The more the better."

Now Sam, flattened out on the girder, was watching them walk toward the foreman.

"Off the bridge," Joe Cassini shouted. "The bridge is closed. Get off."

"Peregrine falcons are nesting on this bridge," Molly piped.

"We've come to ask if you could stop work," Leon Longbridge said. "Could you work somewhere else for a month or so?"

"Get off the bridge," Joe repeated. Leon Longbridge nodded and led the kids to the riverbank.

"Let's hold a meeting," Molly said, and sat down on the grass.

Leon told them the endangered species were protected by the federal government. He said he had notified the U.S. Fish and Wildlife Service in Albany that the birds were in trouble. The Feds seemed to think the birds would be all right.

"Anyone know the governor?" Leon asked. "He can stop the repairs."

"Not me," said José, and slapped his black, curly head with both hands. "I wish I did."

"By the way, Molly," Leon asked, "how did you happen to see the falcons?"

"My bedroom looks out on the bridge," she said, and pointed to a Victorian masterpiece at the bottom of the mountain, directly in line with the bridge.

"What can we do?" said Maria, a sturdy little girl in white overalls. "The workers are going to scare them away."

"What about writing letters to the governor?" Molly asked.

"Yeah," said José. "When Jon Wood showed us a peregrine falcon that had been electrocuted on utility poles, we wrote letters to the company."

"And they fixed three poles," said Molly.

"Move on," Joe Cassini called. "It's dangerous here."

"Let's go back to my office," said Leon, getting to his feet. "I have papers and pencils there."

As they jumped to their feet and hurried off, a crew member put on his ear protectors, picked up his jackhammer, and pushed the start button. The powerful tool roared. He attacked the piling, the jackhammer shaking and spewing dust. The noise bounced off one hundred iron webs in an earsplitting exchange of sounds.

The kids and Leon Longbridge looked back to see the falcon fly in terror. She did not.

Stretched on his belly, Sam spoke gently to Frightful.

The constant vibrations from two jackhammers trembled the huge horizontal web, but Frightful stayed with her eggs. When two more hammers joined the mayhem, she came out of her incubation trance. Her eyes widened in fear.

"Pseee," Sam called, squeezing air between his teeth to make a bird sound.

Frightful stood up.

Softly, softly Sam whistled to her. She cocked her head. The jackhammers stopped. She did not fly.

"Car-reet."

"It's all right," Sam said. "It's all right."

He reached out his hand to her.

The four jackhammers blasted again, sending sound waves bouncing around the webs and girders that held the bows in place. The waves banged out every possible note known to iron and air.

"Car-reet," Frightful called softly.

Sam lay perfectly still, his hand inches from her. Relaxed and smiling, he whispered over and over, "It's all right, Frightful. It's all right."

She pressed the precious eggs against her warm brood patch. She settled down but was still alert.

For the three hours that the jackhammers blasted, Frightful watched Sam. He transmitted calmness. Despite the din, she slipped into the trance of incubation, this time more deeply than before. She saw and heard nothing beyond her scrape.

At twelve o'clock the work crew put down their tools and ambled to the river's edge to eat their brown-bag lunches. The bridge was quiet.

Sam stood up, touched his toes, and stretched. He backed up against the next vertical iron web to keep out of sight of the workers and glanced at the river far below.

"I feel like a bird way up here," he said to Frightful. "What a super thing it must be to fly."

Frightful did not stir.

426 dropped out of the mist of a low cumulus cloud, where he had been nervously circling. He landed on the top of the bow with food for Frightful. He saw Sam and flexed his legs to take off, but did not. 426 had been hacked to the wild by a motherly human. If frightful was at ease with Sam, so was he. Sam did not move a finger.

426 shifted the bird in his talons to his beak, and dropped down to Frightful. He called the peregrine note to awaken a mate from the incubation trance. Frightful brightened and looked at him. Glancing at Sam, who was tree still, he tore off a bite and presented it to Frightful.

A jackhammer blasted. 426 swallowed the offering and took off in panic. Frightful was ready to follow him. But the eggs had power over her. Feeling them beneath her, she settled back to mother them.

"Frightful," Sam said. "This is going to be a problem. 426 is not going to feed you with those blasters around." He took his penknife from his pocket and cut off tender bites. Frightful took the food from him until she was satiated.

"I wish you could exercise," he said. "I can feed you, but I sure can't sit on the eggs."

At five o'clock the noise ended. The work crew drove away, and Sam got to his feet.

"You're a brave bird," he said. "Hang in there. I'm going to catch and cook me a fish.

"Then I'm going to make a camouflage. Somebody is

going to look up here, and if they are standing at the right angle, they'll see me. With a burlap bag and some reeds woven into it, they'll think I'm windblown debris.

"When I go down, I'll leave it up here. Hopefully all the falcon watchers will think it's the nest.

"And something else. I'll get Alice to buy some orange material. She and Mrs. Strawberry can make a vest I'll wear, like the workers. There's a hard hat in Mrs. Strawberry's barn. If anyone sees me climbing up the bow to the nest, they'll think I'm a crew member." He looked down on the broody Frightful. "You and I have got to get these little birds in the sky. The rivers and valleys need them."

He whistled softly.

"Sleep well. I'll be back in the morning."

IN WHICH
The Kids Are Heard

For fifteen days Frightful, with Sam's help, sat through the blasts of the jackhammers and the rumble of trucks. 426 bravely brought food to her at noon when the bridge was quiet, but he could not drive himself to take his turn brooding.

But he did not abandon his family. He watched Frightful during the day from the big sycamore tree on the riverbank and at night from the top of the bridge.

Frightful slowly adjusted to the noise of the jackhammers. Sam was nearby. She listened to his soft whistles and words when the noise was the worst. 426 was too terrified to come to the nest and feed her, but he dropped food onto the girder. Sam took his place and fed it to her.

Each day as she felt the chicks develop, Frightful heard less of the commotion.

On day eighteen of incubation, Joe Cassini looked up and noticed sticks and reeds where the fifth vertical met the bow.

"There's that nest everyone's so riled up about," he said to Dan Martin, a Mohawk Indian whose balance and fearlessness on high girders made him one of the most valuable bridge workers. "Looks perfectly fine to me."

Dan studied the sticks.

"Yeah," he said. "Messy bird." Then he thought a minute. "I never knew peregrine falcons made nests. They like bare ground."

"I guess we learn something every day," said Joe Cassini.

Dan Martin wasn't convinced. He kept an eye on the nest as he carried lumber to the men who were building a form around the ravaged piling. As he worked, he wondered about a peregrine falcon and a stick nest.

On day twenty the jackhammers stopped. The cement mixer drove onto the bridge, and blasts were replaced by grinding and tumbling sounds. Frightful barely heard them.

She could feel the chicks move inside the eggs. The yolks had transformed into embryos, complete with tiny blood vessels, and they had grown heavier. This sent her deeper into the incubation trance. Even a dynamite blast on day twenty-two did not frighten her.

With the jackhammers silent, 426 fed Frightful again and nervously sat down and brooded the eggs while she exercised. Sam watched, ready to help out if 426 became frightened again.

One day when the tiercel was brooding the eggs and Frightful was looping and gliding, she heard Sam whistle from the mountain that rose above the river. The three-note call had a new ending, a "yippee" note that said, "All is well."

Sam was in a lean-to he had constructed on the mountainside. It was eye level with Frightful's aerie. Out from it he fished and gathered wild tubers and greens. After dinner he would lean back against the base of an old chestnut oak, put his hands under his head, and watch the aerie. Now and then he whistled to Frightful.

On this evening Frightful answered his call with "car-reet," and he smiled and remembered how she had saved his life by catching food for him in the wilderness.

"We'll get through this, too, old girl," he said. "Only nine days to go."

When the sun set that night, Sam cut one more notch in

a stick to keep track of the thirty-one days of incubation. He wondered why Leon Longbridge had not been successful in stopping the repairs. Leon wondered why the birds had not deserted. Relentlessly, the bridge work went on.

Sam now went up the iron bowstring bridge to feed Frightful only if the equipment on the bridge indicated it was going to be another noisy day. 426 had not adjusted to that. On these days Sam climbed to Frightful before the kids came by on their way to school to check on the falcons. They would look, smile, and leave a little before the school bell rang and the work crew arrived. In this interval Sam had time to climb down the bridge and disappear without being seen.

One morning when Sam had finished feeding Frightful and was on his way down, Molly arrived. She saw him. Quickly he stepped to the horizontal girder and walked to the middle of the bridge, his orange vest catching the sunlight. He inspected the bolts in the web joints and made notes without pencil or paper. Then he turned and walked past the nest, grabbed the iron bow, and backed down to the bridge floor. With Molly still looking at him, he dropped over the bridge, grabbed the form around the piling, and climbed down to the river shore. He vanished in the cattails.

That day, as Sam had anticipated, was an extremely noisy one. 426 stayed away, and Sam didn't get back to Frightful until after five. She was ravenously hungry. He fed her until her crop was full. Satisfied, she arose and turned the eggs.

The next morning just after Sam arrived, Frightful heard the voice of her winter friend, Jon Wood. He was on the bridge with Leon Longbridge. The two had been consulting about how to save the peregrines of the Delhi Bridge.

"We aren't getting anywhere with the Department of Transportation," Jon said. "They won't stop the work for any reason at all. None."

"That's what the Department of Wildlife Conservation is telling me, too," said Leon Longbridge. "My boss has been trying to stop them; but the order is—make these bridges safe. The Feds don't think it's a problem yet."

"I had hoped the kids' letters would get some action," Jon said. "They got the utility company to fix several poles. Molly told me they've written the governor about the peregrines. He controls the Department of Transportation."

"Yeah," said Leon Longbridge, "but they are only getting form letters back; 'thank you, but . . .' " He studied the aerie.

"I think we ought to move the eggs," Jon finally said. "She's been incubating long enough to be so deeply attached to them that she'll follow them anywhere. We can put a box in that sycamore tree by the river and transfer the eggs to it. She ought to go right to them."

"I know songbirds will go to nestlings when you move

them," Leon said. "But I've had no experience with moving eggs."

"Well," said Jon, "sometimes it works, sometimes it doesn't. Let's give her a few more days. She seems to have adjusted."

"I just can't believe the female didn't leave the first day the work crew blasted off their jackhammers," Leon said. "She had hardly finished laying. Most females would have deserted this nest and found another site. She had plenty of time to lay again."

"Something we don't understand is holding her there," Jon said.

When the first workers arrived, Jon and Leon left the bridge.

"I don't get it," Jon said, shaking his head. "Peregrine falcons—two of the mere thirty-four in the entire state—and the bureaucrats won't stop this work for them."

"NASA held back on a rocket launch to save a nest of egrets," said Leon. "But New York can't save endangered falcons."

They walked to their cars in silence.

"By the way," Leon said as he unlocked his door, "tomorrow before school the kids are going to hold a parade to save the falcons."

"That's great," Jon said. "But they'd be more effective in Albany."

"I don't think anything will change Albany," Leon said. "The orders to go forward with the repairs are written in stone."

Jon looked up at the bridge.

"At least the jackhammers have stopped," he said. "The Transportation Department said it would only take a few more days to finish pouring the cement for the pilings. Then we can relax if . . . if she's still there."

"I think we ought try to move her," said Leon. "I made a scrape—an open box with a narrow strip of wood to keep the eggs from rolling out. I'll put sand on the bottom."

"Hmm," said Jon, glancing up at the aerie.

"Can you help me put the box in that big sycamore?" Leon asked. "I think we ought to try something."

Jon started his van. "I still can't believe the female hasn't deserted," he said. "Only that serene falcon Susan named Destiny would put up with this."

Suddenly he jumped out of the van and lifted his binoculars to his eyes. "Hmm," he said to himself. "She did fly toward Delhi. Hmm."

Leon studied the aerie again.

"There are sticks near the nest," he said. "They've been there for about two weeks. What do you make of that?"

"I have no idea," Jon said. "Sometimes the tiercel will bring a stick or two to his mate out of love, but not that many—I don't think. Still, there must be some explanation. There are a lot of mysterious things about that nest." He shook his head, got back into his car, and drove off.

Sam was stretched out on the wide girder, under the burlap camouflage. The cool air from the river had carried the voices of Jon and Leon to his ears.

He had not expected anyone to question the sticks and reeds. When he looked at them from the ground, he could believe that either a tiercel had brought them or maybe even an osprey. The big fish hawks put sticks in many places during the breeding season. Suddenly he was worried. Maybe, he thought, it really is time to move Frightful and her eggs. If they don't, I will.

Belly flat on the girder, he watched the workers pick up their equipment and put on their hard hats. When they were busy, he slipped out from under the burlap and straightened his orange vest. He pulled himself to the bow and backed down to the bottom like a veteran engineer. No one paid any attention to him. He walked off to his lean-to and removed his vest and hard hat.

Before sunrise the next day, Sam hurried down-mountain to the big sycamore, jumped for the lowest limb, and swung hand over hand to the trunk. He climbed, examining limbs and forks. When he could go no farther he whistled to Frightful. They were about eye level.

"Creee, creee, creee, car-reet," she answered wistfully, and stood up then, turned her eggs.

"How do you like this spot?" he asked. She was brooding again.

He was about to climb down when he saw kids gathering at the public library. They were waving handmade posters. Hughie Smith, the middle-school drummer, beat his drum, and the poster carriers strode down Elm Street, headed for the bridge.

PEREGRINES EAT RATS.
SAVE OUR TOWN.

PEREGRINES ARE NOBLE.
WAIT ONE MONTH TO REPAIR
THE BRIDGE.

IT TAKES ONLY THIRTY-ONE DAYS
FOR A BABY FALCON TO HATCH.
IT TOOK MILLIONS OF YEARS
TO MAKE THE FALCONS.
STOP THE BRIDGE REPAIRS.
SAVE THE PEREGRINES.

WE HAVEN'T FALLEN IN THE RIVER YET.
POSTPONE THE BRIDGE REPAIRS.
LET THE FALCONS RAISE THEIR YOUNG.

SAVE THE PEREGRINE. SAVE US.
WE ARE NATURE, TOO.

By the time the parade reached the Delhi Bridge, there were about thirty youngsters. Beaming parents and curious townspeople stood on the sidewalks, watching.

Joe Cassini had been warned about the parade and had come to work early. He stepped out to meet the protesters.

"Go on home or you'll be arrested," he said, shooing the kids away with gestures.

Molly stepped forward, trembling but determined.

"We just want you to stop repairing the bridge until the end of June," she piped.

José was emboldened by her courage. "That's all the time the falcons need to grow up and fly away."

Hughie beat out a roll on the drum.

Cassini crossed his arms on his chest. "Go home," he repeated.

"I can't believe you don't care," said Molly, backing away. "These are endangered falcons. And they are going to have babies."

"It ain't my decision," the foreman stated firmly. "Orders come from Albany. Tell them."

"We did," said Maria Carlos, who was wearing a peregrine T-shirt she had designed. "They don't see any problem."

"Neither do I," said Cassini. "The bird is still up there, isn't she? We haven't scared her off. What's the big deal? Now, get going." He walked toward them.

"No," said Molly.

Leon Longbridge came running up to her.

"Come on, Molly. This way, Hughie," he said. "Let's go into town. We'll march down Main Street."

Glad for the suggestion, the kids turned around and walked up Elm Street to Main. Cars slowed; pedestrians stopped. Parents confessed to strangers and each other that they never had the least interest in falcons until their children told them about the peregrines of the Delhi Bridge. They were furious that the state wouldn't stop work until the little birds got on wing. The crowd wasn't large, but the police chief recognized an awakening "situation" when he saw one. He called for more officers.

Then he led the parade to the park in front of the courthouse and let the falcon lovers wave their signs at passing cars.

"Save the peregrines," shouted José. A TV cameraman and a newswoman jumped out of a van, looked over the kids, and walked up to José.

"What is your name?" the newswoman asked, holding the mike close to his face.

"José Cruz, first baseman on the school team. I am ten years old and I am in the fifth grade. I want to grow up and become a falconer."

"Thank you. You've answered the first question fully. Now the big one."

"What is it?"

"Do you think it's more important to save a peregrine falcon nest or mend a dangerous bridge?"

"Save the peregrine falcons," José answered clearly. "Save the peregrine falcons!" a cluster of nearby kids echoed.

"But what about people? Aren't they important?"

"They have a detour," José said. "Save the peregrine falcons," he repeated. The other kids cheered and stuck their posters in front of the camera.

"Thank you very much," said the interviewer and turned to a jackhammer operator who had come to the park to fill his water bottle.

"How do you feel about this problem?" she asked.

"Save the peregrine falcons," he said in a loud, clear voice.

A gleeful roar went up from the poster wavers. Cars coming off the detour slowed and stopped. Horns blasted.

"What's going on?" an out-of-town driver asked.

"Keep moving, keep moving," ordered a police officer, stepping into the road and waving the car on. "You're backing up traffic. Keep moving."

The courthouse clock struck 8:30 A.M.

"School," said Molly. "Let's go." Hughie Smith rolled his drum, and the police officers stopped traffic to let the kids cross Main Street.

Sam, who was watching from the sycamore tree, decided this was a good time to feed Frightful. She hadn't eaten this morning.

He was pulling on his orange vest when 426 dropped out of the sky and lit on the aerie near the scrape. He bowed to Frightful and called the note that broke the incubation trance. She got off the eggs. He took her place—and brooded.

"Wow, good," Sam exclaimed. "We may get little chicks yet."

Sam returned to his mountainside camp and ate a breakfast of nuts and dried apples from his root cellar on the mountaintop.

Things continued to go well the next few days. The cement pouring ended. After that the noise level dropped to tolerable. A few days later Molly borrowed a spotting scope from the Audubon Club, and she and her friends set it up in her room with its perfect view of the nest. Frightful and the scrape filled the lens.

"They'll be hatching soon," Molly said, and let Hughie Smith take a look.

"It seems," he said with a wistful smile, "that despite everything, the peregrines of Delhi are going to have chicks." He turned and looked at Molly. "The mom is fidgety like a hen hatching eggs."

At that moment Frightful heard the chicks cheeping inside their shells. She listened, not hearing the workers below or Sam Gribley, who was creeping along the girder to her.

"Frightful," he said, disbelief in his voice. "Now they're going to paint the bridge!"

There Are Three

At dawn the next day Leon Longbridge wedged the
wooden scrape into a fork in the sycamore tree and
wired it in place. He climbed down and hurried to his car
to watch what came next. Frightful was too broody to notice
what was going on below her, but not 426. He sat on the

bridge top in the cold dawn, watching Leon climb down from the tree and Jon Wood grab the iron bow and climb toward him.

When Jon was too close, 426 took off with a loud snap of his wings, climbed high, and dove at the man. Jon ducked and climbed on.

Sam in his lean-to was also watching.

"That ought to work," he said to himself. "The eggs are so close to hatching, she won't abandon them."

Frightful snapped out of her trance when Jon Wood swung down to the horizontal girder. She got to her feet.

"Hello, Destiny," he whispered. "I'd know you anywhere."

Frightful recognized him.

"Psee," she called, and stepped back over her eggs.

He inched slowly toward her.

426 screamed the alarm of the peregrine. The penetrating call touched Frightful's survival instinct, and she flew off the eggs.

The air was cold. Jon carefully wrapped the warm eggs in bubble plastic and lowered them onto a hot-water bottle in his backpack. He shouldered the pack, grabbed the bow, swung up onto it, and backed down its curved slope to the bridge.

Frightful flew back to her scrape. Her eggs were gone.

"Kek, kek, kek," she cried. 426 answered her distress

call and dropped down beside her. The empty nest stunned and confused them.

Movement at the foot of the sycamore caught Frightful's eye, and she saw Jon Wood. She screamed and dove. He was the one who had taken her eggs. He saw her coming and covered his head with his hands. A talon scraped him. Quickly he scaled the tree to the artificial scrape and, fending off Frightful with one arm, he gently lay the eggs in the box. He climbed down, ran across the bridge, and joined Leon Longbridge in his car.

Frightful circled and swooped to a limb in the sycamore tree. 426 joined her.

Sam watched. Leon and Jon watched.

Minutes passed. The air was cool.

Frightful flew from the tree back to the bridge. She circled once and flew back to the tree.

She cried her worried call.

426 answered. Agitated, he flew over the town. Frightful followed him.

An hour passed. The pair did not come back.

"Okay," said Jon Wood. "This isn't working. The eggs have been uncovered for sixty minutes, and at forty-five degrees Fahrenheit, that's not good. I'm going to put them back."

He climbed to the box, wrapped up the eggs once more, and returned them to the scrape on the bridge.

He was backing away when Frightful lit on the girder and, putting one foot in front of the other, ran to the eggs. She sat down and pressed her brood patch against them. She stood up. The eggs were cold. She sat down again.

An hour later she got up and walked away. The chicks in the shells had not moved. She walked back, turned, and snuggled them against her brood patch. She called wistfully.

Dan Martin arrived early for work. He looked up at the gray-blue sky and put on his rain gear. Seeing Leon Longbridge and Jon Wood, he asked about the falcons. Jon told him they had tried unsuccessfully to move the eggs.

"We've got to somehow postpone the bridge painting," Jon said. "I guess there is nothing you can do. I'll try calling Albany again."

The rain was beginning to fall when Joe Cassini arrived. Dan Martin greeted him as he got out of his car.

"We can't paint today," he said. "Bad rainstorm coming."

"We can sandblast," Joe Cassini said. "Is there any reason why we can't start cleaning up rust spots in the rain?"

"No," said Dan Martin. "Rain shouldn't make any difference."

Then Joe Cassini turned to Dan and put his hand on his shoulder.

"When we get to the webs," he said, "I want you to

paint the ones near the nest. You seem to know something about peregrine falcons."

"Enough to ask this: Do we still have to go ahead with the work? The bridge won't fall down now."

"We still have to go ahead," Joe Cassini said. "I checked with Albany myself. The governor is relentless. Said the tourists were beginning to come to the Catskills, and he wants the work done on time."

"I've just been talking to Leon Longbridge and Jon Wood," Dan Martin said. "They tried to move the eggs to another site this morning."

"Yeah?"

"It didn't work. They had to put them back before they froze."

Joe Cassini glanced at the aerie. "Funny," he said, "but I like those birds. They're real spunky."

Two hours later, when Frightful again turned the eggs, there was still no movement.

426 arrived with a pigeon. He pulled off a morsel to feed Frightful. The sandblasting machine started up. 426 dove onto his wings and sped away.

Sam left his lean-to and walked partway down the mountain. Frightful had not eaten for eleven hours. The high-pitched noise of the sanders had driven 426 away. The tiercel, he knew, wouldn't come back until the workers went home. And that was too late.

Frightful had to be fed, but how? The crewmen were all

over the bridge, hanging work platforms and blasting rust. There was no way he could climb to the aerie without being seen, and he did not want to be seen. Not now. He had worked with Frightful for two weeks, and he didn't want to be stopped. Best to keep out of sight. He was known in Delhi to a few people—Miss Turner, the librarian; Leon Longbridge; and some of the kids. They referred to him as Thoreau, the boy who lived on Peaks Brook Mountain. That was just fine, but climbing a bridge made him obvious, and that was something Sam didn't want.

Just before noon, the rain poured down in torrents. The crew got into their cars or ran to the café. Sam's deerskin jacket repelled water like a nor'easter coat. He lifted his binoculars.

Frightful was off the eggs. She was standing on the food 426 had brought, eating heartily. When she was satisfied, she brooded again.

"She must have brought the eggs back to temperature," he said. "Even in this rain. What a noble bird."

Sam walked down the mountain, crossed the river on rocks, and took the long trail to his hemlock tree. He lit a fire in his fireplace and stretched out on his bed.

"Four or five more days," he said. "I wonder what else can happen?"

At that moment Frightful felt the chicks move vigorously inside their shells. A burst of rain struck the bow and rushed down the vertical webs. Water spilled on her. She sat calmly, a tent over her precious eggs.

Day twenty-nine dawned cold. A snow flurry powdered the mountains and dropped white crystals on the town. Frightful cocked her head and stood up. One egg was vibrating. Inside, the chick's neck was twitching spasmodically, then its little body stiffened. A sharp egg tooth on the top of its beak pierced the inner membrane, and its nostrils pushed into the pocket of air at the top of the egg. The chick's lungs filled. It breathed.

"Cheep."

Frightful lifted her body so that she had very little weight on the hatching chick. Her warm feathers fell around it. As the chick breathed, the oxygen inside the egg was replaced by the chick's carbon dioxide. The gas twitched her muscles. The head wobbled, the body stiffened. A fragment of shell lifted, and fresh air rushed in. The chick lay still. Hours passed. The other two chicks went through the same ordered sequence of hatching. Each step was vital to their safe entrance into the world.

After struggling another day, the first chick cut a larger hole and thrust her beak and egg tooth into the air. She breathed freely.

She rested, letting her lungs became fully functional.

While she was quiet, Frightful stepped off the eggs and 426 stood over them.

On day thirty-one, the chicks' heads were circling inside their shells, cutting through them.

The sandblasters screamed below; work platforms clanged in the wind. Frightful and 426 heard nothing. They were hatching the chicks.

The little female cut through two-thirds of the shell top, then pushed the cap with her shoulders. It popped open. She stuck her head out.

A cherry picker rolled out onto the bridge and lifted Dan Martin to the top of the bow. He sanded the rust by hand, checking to make sure he wasn't disturbing the peregrines. Frightful was on the nest, her feathers draped around the hatching chicks.

Once her head was out, the first chick, a wet little female, easily kicked herself free of the shell.

A peregrine falcon was born. She was Oksi, the wide-eyed.

Frightful let her feathers fall over Oksi while the little bird rested from her great struggle. 426 perched quietly by.

In about an hour the chick was dry and fuzzy white. Her wings were stubs, her eyes closed. Her beak and feet were enormous. She wobbled.

Finally the workers quit for the day. The other two chicks hatched to the peaceful sound of wind playing on the webs of the Delhi Bridge.

That second day of June was cold. Snow clouds hung over the river and valley. The mountain laurel tightened their leaves, and the apple blossoms froze.

Frightful did not feel the grip of the arctic cold. Her

chicks were under her breast feathers, nestled against her brood patch; her wings were around them like insulating blankets.

Sam was back in his lean-to. He put down his binoculars. "Good girl," he said.

Below him in the Victorian house, the falcon fan club was peering through the spotting scope in Molly's room.

"Three babies," Molly said. Her eyes twinkled. "I saw them when the mom stood up."

"Lemme see," said Maria, and adjusted the focus on the scope. "Aw, phooey, she's sitting on them."

"Three babies!" said Hughie. "They can't paint the bridge now."

"Wanna bet?" asked José.

"No," Hughie answered, "I don't."

"Let's write the governor again," Maria said. "We'll tell him about the babies. He loves babies. He said so."

"Tell him we'll name them after his kids if he stops the work," said Molly. "That might do it."

"Wanna bet?" asked José.

Over the wind that was piping among the webs of the bridge, Frightful heard Sam's whistle. It came from the mountainside. She turned her head his way but did not answer. The three chicks were nestled under her. She was part of them. She moved as they moved. She slept when they slept. For the first time, Frightful felt the all-consuming oneness of motherhood.

The bridge was quiet. 426 flew in and perched near Frightful.

The three eyases did not eat.

The kids in Molly's room worried. Sam worried.

Frightful did nothing about it. She bellied up to the little peregrines and looked admiringly at each individual.

Oksi, the falcon and the first hatched, was bigger than the two tiercels. Her eyes were large and penetrating.

"Pseee," Oksi called late in the afternoon. 426 pulled off a tiny bite of meat and fed her. The chick was still living on egg-sac food and did not need the morsel of liver, but it started her digestive tract working.

"Kak, kak, kak, kak, kak." This call came from Screamer. Frightful fed him a bite.

Before dusk, Blue Bill, a spunky tiercel with an unusually dark beak, called to his parents, and a snip of liver started his system working.

Sunday the bridge was quiet. Sam planted potatoes for Mrs. Strawberry and went back to his home in the hemlock tree.

Frightful mothered her chicks. The fumes from tourist traffic rose as the sun warmed the roads. Frightful blinked as it burned her eyes, but she did not leave.

Around noon, 426 circled over the courthouse park,

eyes on all movements. A child wheeled his tricycle down the sidewalk, sending the pigeons into the sunlight like water-splash. 426 swooped, caught one on the wing, and brought it back to the aerie. He gave bites to Frightful, who, ever so precisely, placed the bites into the open mouths of the eyases.

On Monday morning, Joe Cassini and Dan Martin arrived at the bridge early.

"The Transportation Department still says I must go ahead with the painting," Joe said to Dan. "So the plan is this: First we'll paint all the webs but number five. Then we'll do the big horizontal girder and the bow. By the time we get that far, the babies'll be about ten days old."

"Then what do we do? They can't fly then, can they?"

"No, not according to Leon Longbridge," Joe Cassini said, looking up at the aerie. "But he did say that when they were ten days old and pretty well feathered, he could move them to the box in the sycamore tree. Said their parents will feed them for sure."

"Maybe this mother won't do that," said Dan Martin. "She's a funny bird. She's not too motherly when she's not on her aerie. I've seen her flying off toward that mountain upriver and staying a long time."

"Dan," Joe Cassini said, "you get up there and paint the webs, but don't scare them away. I've got a soft spot for that family." Joe Cassini looked at the top of the bow. "I'll give you a cherry picker if you need one."

"I don't," Dan said, and walked along the bridge to study the complex webbing.

A dark-green pickup truck pulled up to the roadblock on the town side of the bridge, and a lean man in a green uniform got out. He surveyed the webs and bow of the bridge, then walked over to Joe and Dan.

"Good morning," he said. "I'm Flip Pearson from the U.S. Fish and Wildlife Service."

They shook hands.

"I understand you have a peregrine falcon nesting on this bridge," Flip Pearson said.

"Yeah," Joe Cassini answered. "A pair."

"I've been sent by Washington to move the eyases to another site." A second man got out of the pickup and joined him. "This is Dr. Werner, our peregrine expert."

"Pleased to meet you," Joe Cassini said. The doctor nodded but did not acknowledge the greeting. His dark hair almost covered thick black eyebrows that shadowed a thin face. He did not even speak.

"It's important to save those birds," Flip said.

"It sure is," said Joe Cassini. "There's an awful lot of opinion around here to do just that."

"Think you can move them?" Dan Martin asked. "The state tried once. But it didn't work."

"That's what I understand," said Flip Pearson. "But they moved eggs, not eyases." Dr. Werner glanced up at the bridge.

"Eyases are a whole different ball game," Flip Pearson went on. "Once the chicks are hatched, the parents will take care of them wherever you move them."

"Are you going to put them in the sycamore tree?" asked Joe Cassini.

"No," Flip answered. "That's too low. No peregrine would come that low and that close to the traffic."

"Is that so?" said Joe Cassini. "I guess the conservation officer didn't think of that."

"That's why the falcons didn't come back to the eggs," Flip said. "Too low."

"Well," said Joe Cassini, "what can we do to help you?"

"The faster we move, the better," said Flip Pearson. "Could you bring the cherry picker up to the nest?"

"Dan," said Joe Cassini, "you can operate the cherry picker, can't you?"

"Yeah," he said. "But won't it freak them out?"

"The quicker we take them, the quicker the birds will adjust," said Flip. Dr. Werner nodded a strong affirmative.

"There'll be some panic," Flip said. "But when we relocate the eyases, the parents will calm down."

"You sure?"

"Yes, I am."

Dan Martin started the cherry picker and drove it under

the aerie. He lowered the bucket; Flip got in and was hoisted to the nest.

Molly was watching from her bedroom window. She focused the spotting scope on the door of the green pickup. "U.S. Fish and Wildlife Service," she read, and got on the phone.

"Hughie," she said. "Call the kids and tell them to come down to the bridge right away. The U.S. Fish and Wildlife Service is finally doing something about the peregrines."

"What?"

"Moving them, I think." She hung up.

Frightful did not see the cherry picker until Flip's head and arm came up over the horizontal girder. She took off in panic. 426 followed her. They climbed above the bridge and swooped down on the man. Frightful struck his head as he reached into the scrape and grabbed the eyases.

"Lower away," Flip yelled when he had the little falcons in a canvas pack. Dan Martin brought the cherry picker back to the ground. Flip climbed out and hurried toward the pickup truck with the pack.

"Let's see the babies," Molly called from the bridge barricades. Hughie was standing beside her with his mouth wide open. Maria arrived, then José. They pushed toward Flip.

"Can we see the babies?" José asked excitedly. Flip held the bag against his chest and shoved the kids back. Joe Cassini stepped up to him.

"Let them take one peek," he said. "These are the kids

that have been holding parades and writing letters to save the peregrines."

Flip Pearson looked at the falcon expert. He nodded but still said nothing.

"Okay," said Flip. "Step close, and I'll let you see."

He opened the bag. Molly looked in.

"There're only two," she said.

"That's all there were—two."

"I saw three," insisted Molly.

"Mortality is high during the first few days of a bird's life," said Flip. "There were only two."

Screamer let out a terrible cry, and Flip closed the bag.

"Okay, kids, back off," Flip said angrily. "We've got to get these birds to their new home before they die, too." He followed Dr. Werner to the pickup. Molly was close behind.

"Where are you taking them?" she asked.

"I can't tell you," Flip said. "Against regulations. These birds are protected by federal law." Dr. Werner started the motor.

The truck pulled away and sped down Elm Street, turned right at the T, and disappeared behind the bank and the café.

"Where's Leon Longbridge?" Hughie asked suddenly.

"Didn't you call him?" Molly asked.

"I thought he would know. The Feds must have told him they were coming."

The kids looked at each other. Their eyes widened.

"You see Leon Longbridge?" José asked Joe Cassini.

"Not this morning," he said.

"He'll sure be glad to know someone finally moved those birds," said Dan Martin.

"Wanna bet?" said José as he started running for Leon Longbridge's office.

The school bell rang.

"Cree, cree, cree, kak, kak, kak."

High above the Delhi Bridge, Frightful screamed and spiraled, her pointed wings cutting frantic patterns in the sky.

I N   W H I C H

Sam Takes Charge

Sam was at his lean-to, his elbows propped on his knees, his binocs pinned on the green pickup. He had watched the two U.S. Fish and Wildlife Service men rescue the peregrine eyases of the Delhi Bridge. He was grateful to them. The bridge painting was becoming intolerable.

Sam studied them closely. The dark-haired man seemed familiar, but he didn't know any Fish and Wildlife Service people. He turned his glasses on Frightful. She zoomed out of nowhere and landed on the scrape.

Why wasn't she following the Feds and her eyases? She was not even looking in their direction. And then he saw why. An eyas appeared and nestled into her warm breast feathers.

"What the heck!" Sam said aloud. "She's feeding!"

He put down his glasses and whistled his "come here" notes to Frightful.

Frightful turned her head but did not answer. She was mothering Oksi and calling a worried "kak, kak" to 426. He came down from a height where no human eye could see him, landed on the girder, and took off again. The man in the cherry picker had so terrified him, he could not force himself to sit on the bridge. He caught a wind and was sped up the mountain. He came to rest on a large maple near Sam's lean-to and flattened his feathers to his body. His eye pupils were pinpoints of fear.

"Kak, kak, kak." 426 yelled the distress cry over and over.

Sam lowered his glasses to the bridge span. The men on the paint crew were swinging the work platforms under the fifth web, getting ready to paint the seemingly empty aerie. Down on Elm Street, Molly, José, and Leon Longbridge came on the run.

They joined Joe Cassini and Dan Martin at the cherry picker.

"Good news," Joe said. "The Feds moved the little birds."

"No, they didn't," Leon said. "They stole them. Those men were not from the U.S. Fish and Wildlife Service. I checked on them when Hughie called me. And they weren't from the state, either."

"Who were they, then?"

"Poachers—a special kind of poacher," said Leon. "They'll raise the eyases and sell them for tens of thousands of dollars."

"Did you get their license plate number?" Molly asked Joe hopefully.

"No," he answered. "Never occurred to me they weren't legit. But they should be easy to find. They were in an old green Chevy pickup with an official insignia on the door."

"What'll we do?" José asked, tugging Leon Long-bridge's sleeve.

"I've already called the police," he said. "Also Jon Wood. He suspects some poachers are hiding out in a cabin on White Man Mountain. Maybe we should begin there."

"Can we come?" Molly asked, clapping her hands.

"No," Leon said forcefully. "Those guys are dangerous. Now, run along to school. You're late."

When Leon went back to his office, Joe Cassini and Dan Martin looked up at the intricately webbed bridge that had been a home for the peregrines. Its crisscrossed grid was a huge silver tapestry in the gray spring light.

"Well, Dan," Joe said, "the falcons are gone. We'll sand-blast the aerie. Nothing to stop us from painting now."

"Except that thunderstorm hanging over the mountain," Dan Martin answered. "I'm going to sit this one out. I don't want to be caught in a thunderstorm on an iron bridge." He closed his paint bucket and returned it to the supply truck.

Joe Cassini was checking the sanding job on the bridge railing when the first peal of thunder rumbled. He called the men down from the work platforms and sent them to the safety of their cars. In his own car he took out a thermos of coffee, drank several gulps, then leaned back and closed his eyes.

"How was I to know wildlife officials from poachers?"

he asked himself. "Well, I hope they get caught. I got real fond of those birds." Lightning flashed like fireworks.

Oksi pressed up against Frightful and crawled deeper into her feathers. Both sat still and waited. The falling air pressure foretold a severe storm.

Sam felt the warning, too, but he planned to take advantage of it. He walked down the mountainside to the road and sat under a large rhododendron bush. The clouds rolled over Delhi in blue-black boils, their bottoms illuminated by white flashes. A few large raindrops splattered down onto the rhododendron leaves, then many. A fork of lightning opened a cloud. It closed with a thunderous boom. Water spilled down in sheets.

When he could no longer see Joe Cassini's car for the rain, Sam crawled out from under the bush and ran to the bowed arch. Barefoot, using his hands and feet, he went up it. The rain poured off his hair and down his face. Lightning danced over the bridge and town. The thunder became a continuous boom. When he got to where the bow met the fifth vertical web, Sam whistled three notes.

There was no response.

Dropping to the horizontal girder, he flattened out on his belly.

"Frightful?" he whispered. "Are you there?" The rain deluged, flooding the girder and running into the aerie.

"Creee, creee, creee, car-reet."

"Hey, Frightful," he said. "I'm going to take the little falcon to our home. Follow me." He slipped his hand under her. She did not move.

"Lift up. Pssst, psst. I love you. It's all right."

Sam wormed forward until his hand closed over a small, warm body. Frightful *kakak*-ed and flew into the rain.

He put Oksi inside his shirt against his chest, then tied a leather thong around his waist so that she wouldn't fall out. He backed down the bow.

A jagged white lightning bolt hit the steeple of the church near the courthouse. A boom of thunder as loud as a cannonade shook the bridge.

"Too close," said Sam. "Let's get off this thing."

He jumped to the ground, glancing back to see if anyone had noticed him. Not much chance. The rain was falling so hard that he could barely see the cherry picker in the middle of the span. Picking up his moccasins, he crossed the road and went up the mountain.

He did not stop at his bivouac. Moving quickly, he took a deer trail to the long path that led up the one mountain to the one tree. He hurried. Little falcons needed constant food.

From time to time he glanced up through the rain, hoping to see Frightful above them. The deluge was too heavy to see anything beyond gray streaks of water.

"She'll know where I'm going," he said, and ran on up the trail.

When he stepped into the ancient hemlock, Oksi was still warm and dry inside his shirt. He put her on the floor. Oksi sat back on her heels and screamed without letup while he changed into the new suit he had made from the hide of a road-killed deer. He lit a fire and sat on his bed. The eyas screamed on.

"Your mom," he said softly, "will find you as soon as the storm stops. This is her first home."

Oksi cried louder, opening her beak to be fed.

Outside, the rain kept falling.

"Kak, kak, kak"—the peregrine worry call.

Sam grinned and poked his head out the deerskin door, expecting to see Frightful. He saw only rain bending the branches of the hemlocks and running in rivulets down their trunks.

"Where are you, Frightful?" he called. "Your eyas is very hungry. I don't want to feed her. She will imprint on me and think she's a person. Then she will never mate with her kind."

"Kak, kak, kak."

The frightened peregrine falcon called again. "Let it be Frightful," Sam said, squinting up through the big hemlock limbs at an erect, broad-shouldered bird near the top.

He whistled. The bird shook off the rain.

"Too small to be Frightful," Sam mused. "It's her mate. But he's not much use. He won't feed the eyas at this stage of the game. She's too old. We've got to find Frightful." The eyas screamed so hard that Sam's ears rang. He found Frightful's old hood and deftly put it over Oksi's head. She immediately stopped screaming.

Dashing out through the rain, Sam entered the mill house and picked up a box he had made with boards Bando had cut for his furniture and discarded. The box had five sides. If the box that Leon Longbridge had used was a model, Sam's needed one more thing. He picked up a slat of wood about three inches wide and bored holes in it. Next he bored holes at the edge of the box opening. With his penknife he whittled sticks to make pegs and fastened the board to the box with them. The board was just high enough to prevent the eyas from falling out. He had a home for Frightful and her baby.

When he was done, the rain had stopped, and the thunder rumbled down the valley. Sam returned to the little falcon and took off her hood. She screamed for food. Hoping she was hungry enough to eat on her own, Sam took a deer mouse out of the pocket of the rain-drenched suit.

"I trapped this at the lean-to," he said to Oksi. "A guy never knows when he'll need a mouse in this life." Oksi fluttered her fuzzy white wings and screamed louder. She was frantic and close to the first stage of starvation.

"You've got to eat this by yourself," Sam said, and threw the mouse on the ground. She did not even look at it, just up at him, and screamed continually.

Sam put the hood back on her head and went outside. He strapped the nest box to his back and, gripping the lowest limb of the hemlock, swung hand over hand to the tree trunk.

"Kak, kak, kak."

Sam looked up. 426 flew out of the hemlock, circled, and disappeared.

"That *is* Frightful's mate," he said. "I recognize the broad band on the tip of his tail."

He whistled for Frightful, but she did not appear, and he climbed on up, limb by limb.

"Where is she?" he asked himself. "She should have been right above me—even in the rain. Did I put too much faith in our friendship? I thought she knew I was taking her eyas to our tree. I was so sure she would follow me.

"I was wrong."

Sam stopped where two limbs made a secure brace for the box and tied it to the trunk and both limbs. He tested it several times for stability, then climbed down.

"If this doesn't work," he said aloud, "I'll have to feed the little eyas. That will change her whole life.

"I also might be jailed for harboring an endangered species."

I N   W H I C H
Sam Battles Bird Instincts

Frightful had completely panicked when Sam reached under her in the thunderous storm. She flew into the drenching rain and gained altitude, ready to strike him with all the force of her speeding body.

A powerful gust of wind caught her wings and swept her upriver. Its downdraft pulled her toward the water. She fought wind and rain to get back to the bridge, but the storm was the master. She gave up and dropped into a calm eddy of air behind a bank of willows.

"Creee, creee, creee," she called from a dead stub. Lightning burned streaks in the sky, and thunder cannonaded.

"Creee," she called once more, then pulled her head down between her shoulders and let the rain run off her body.

Through the storm she listened for 426. She had last seen him swooping down on the man in the cherry picker.

"Creee."

There was no answer from 426.

She waited in the willow tree until her fear subsided. It was short-lived. In moments she was quietly listening to the rain slap the leaves around her.

After a long time, the deluge stopped.

In less than two seconds, Frightful was back on the horizontal girder of the bridge. She walked to the wet scrape, turning under her talons so as not to injure the young.

"Creee," she called. No eyas answered, nor did 426.

At recess Molly and José came splashing through big puddles to the bridge. They stood before it, looking up at the webs and the graceful bow.

"The bridge has changed," Molly said. "It's dead."

"Yeah," said José. "No peregrines. Not even a coat of red paint can make it fun again."

The two walked along the bank and watched frogs jump into the river until the bell rang at the end of recess. They started back. Leon Longbridge pulled up beside them.

"Listen to this," he said, waving a paper. "It's from the governor."

"Read it. Read it, please," said José.

"It's addressed to me and the students of Delhi Middle School." He began:

Thank you for your many well-written letters concerning the peregrines of Delhi Bridge.

I am pleased to inform you that I share your concern. Work will stop on the bridge on Route 28 until the young peregrine falcons are fledged.

Although the bridge repair is urgent, our endangered

species, once gone, cannot be brought back. Therefore I have told the head of the Transportation Department of the State of New York to work on Bridge 92 at Gilboa until the little family is on wing.

My administration actively protects the environment of New York State, and I am happy you are in favor of this policy.
Sincerely,
Governor George Marki

"Too late," Molly whispered, tears in her eyes.

"For lack of understanding," Leon Longbridge said, "we've lost three beautiful eyases."

"Can I read the letter?" Molly asked.

"I've made you a copy," Leon said, handing her a paper. "And one for you, José."

After rereading the letter three times, José folded it and put it in his pocket.

"We've got to catch the poachers," he said. "We've got to get the babies back." He turned hopelessly to Leon Longbridge. "How can we do that?"

"The state troopers are looking for them right now," Leon said, "and the Department of Motor Vehicles is checking the ownership of all the Chevy pickups. So far nothing."

Molly put the letter in her book and, without another word, walked back to school. José walked silently behind her.

Frightful stared into her empty scrape.

Restless and upset, she flew to the park, caught a pigeon, and carried it to the cupola of the courthouse. She ate and watched for 426.

When she was comfortably full, she carried the remains back to the scrape and tore off an eyas bite. There were no open beaks to fill. She peered at the girder, waiting for the little falcons to thrust up their heads. They did not. She swallowed the food.

Frightful did not leave the aerie. Her mothering instincts were strong. She still felt the presence of her chicks. But as the hours passed and her eyases did not appear, the feeling began to fade. Without her young to inspire her, it would not take many days for the nurturing instinct to die.

In the early afternoon, Frightful left the bridge and flew over the town, the river, the mountains, in wider and wider circles.

Eventually she flew over 426, perched on the one hemlock on the one mountain. In seconds she was beside him.

A movement below caught her eye. She tipped her head. Sam had stepped out of the tree.

"Creee, creee, creee, car-reet," she called.

"Frightful!" he cried joyfully. "Where are you? I hear you." He whistled and stepped back.

"Oh, Frightful," he said when he saw her. "I have your little eyas. She's right here. Follow me."

Sam put Oksi into his soft backpack, shouldered it, and

started climbing. 426 cried out the peregrine alarm and sped off. Frightful stayed.

When Sam reached the nest box, she was only ten feet above him. He held up the eyas.

"Here she is. You must feed her. She's hungry."

He placed the downy chick in the box and hurriedly climbed to the ground.

Frightful watched him.

Sam watched her.

There were no hunger cries from Oksi. She was too perplexed by the box. She sat still, waiting for her mother. Oksi could not see Frightful from inside the enclosure, and Frightful could not see Oksi from where she was sitting. She must hear the eyas call to locate her.

Sam paced and watched from below. The little bird needed food and needed it right away. A few hours without eating at this time of Oksi's life would put hunger streaks in her feathers. Weakened, they would break when she was old enough to fly.

Sam got his falconer's lure from the hemlock house. It was a chunk of deer hide with pheasant feathers tied to it. He spun it around his head on a long line. In action, the lure looked like a bird—food. Frightful had once been so well trained, she came to the lure even when she was not hungry, but that was long ago. She cocked her head and looked with interest at the whirling lure. Sam whistled.

She sat. Finally Sam tied the mouse to it and swung it again.

Frightful saw the mouse. She dropped swiftly, hit it, and went with it to the ground. Sam picked her up.

"Frightful, gal," he said, blowing out his breath in relief, "you've got a job to do. The eyas is in that box in the tree. She's in trouble. She needs you."

Frightful did not understand the words, but she did understand Sam's worried mood. She sat on his hand and looked at him.

"I'm going to climb the tree with you," he said. "No, you'll fly if I do that. I'd better jess you first."

Sam carried her into the hemlock tree.

"Creee," she called, recognizing the cozy interior of the one tree on the one mountain. She roused and sat contentedly.

Sam cut two thin pieces of deer hide, made three holes in each, and, tucking ends inside holes, he fastened jesses to her legs with the falconer's knot, the knot that never binds.

Frightful felt the jesses go taut as Sam gripped them between his thumb and forefinger. It was a familiar feeling. She wiped her beak on his fist and sat erect. He walked outside.

"No one had better see us now," he said with a chuckle. "I'd be hauled off to jail for practicing falconry without a license." Frightful fluffed. Sam started climbing.

His maneuvers around limbs were jerky, and Frightful thrust out her wings to keep her balance. Twice she tried to fly.

They finally reached the box. Sam placed her in it.

"Pseee," called Oksi.

Frightful heard the feeble cry of her chick. In her eagerness to reach her, she struck the box hard with her wings. The hollow sound was terrifying. She took off.

"Oh, no," Sam gasped. "You're wearing jesses. I'm in real trouble if anyone sees you." Then he added, "But I don't care. You know where the eyas is. You'll come back and feed her."

Frightful screamed as she flew around the mountaintop in wider and wider circles. She calmed down, remembered the hunger cry of her eyas, and dove gracefully toward the tree.

Suddenly, a red-tailed hawk grabbed Frightful's jesses, mistaking them for food. He pulled her downward, then let go before they both fell into the trees.

Catching herself on her acrobatic wings, Frightful skimmed up through and over the trees. She flew down the mountain like a hurtled rock and alighted on the Delhi Bridge. Panting, she gazed at the river until she was calm.

The painters were back at work.

A car screeched to a stop, and the driver pinned his binoculars on Frightful.

"I'll be darned," said Perry Knowlton, a falconer. He picked up his car phone and called his friend Jon Wood.

"Lose a peregrine?" he asked.

"No; why, you see one?"

"Yeah, and she's wearing jesses," Perry said.

"Where are you?"

"I'm at the Delhi Bridge. There's a jessed falcon on the bow. What do you make of that?"

"There was a pair of wild falcons nesting there," said Jon, "but they didn't have jesses. Call Leon Longbridge; he might have heard about a lost falcon. I can't come help you. I've a week of school shows coming up."

"I'll try to follow her," Perry said, and hung up.

Frightful dove into a flock of pigeons wheeling out over the river, snatched one in the air, and flew on.

Perry watched her as he drove along the riverside highway. When she flew up-mountain he parked, jumped from his car, and kept her in sight until she disappeared. Then he picked up the car phone and dialed Leon Longbridge. His answering machine went on.

"This is Perry, Leon," he said into the machine. "There's a jessed peregrine flying around here. Jon Wood doesn't know anything about her. She's just gone up the river toward Treadwell. I'll drive along that road and ask the residents if they know anyone who has a falcon around here." He thought a moment, and went on, "Would you call your boss in Albany and inquire about licensed falconers in this area? I don't know of any except Jon Wood and me; but there may be others."

Frightful was over Sam's mountain, hovering above the one tree, searching for her eyas. The roof of the box prevented her from seeing inside. She flew to a large oak. This was a familiar tree. On its broad limbs sat the wigwam Sam had made for Alice. Alice was not at home.

Frightful bobbed her head and twisted it as she stared at the box in the hemlock. Oksi was there. As much as she disliked flying through forest limbs, she must. Hopping from oak to maple to hickory to tulip tree, the pigeon still in her talons, she made her way to the top of the ancient hemlock.

"Kak, kak, kak, kak." Frightful cried the alarm call of the peregrine and dove at a monsterlike creature in the tree. She did not scare it. It moved closer to Oksi.

The bulky thing had a tanned chicken—feathers, head, comb, and all—for a head. A burlap bag hung down from it. The head moved into the box. In its beak was food. Oksi snatched it and ate. The monster withdrew and returned with more food. Oksi gulped.

The ogre disappeared, and Oksi came to the edge of the box. She peered down at this strange mother. The head wiggled as hands stuck food into the chicken beak. Then the monster mother climbed back to her. Oksi ate. She ate until her crop stuck out and she could eat no more. The monster mother went down the tree to the ground.

Sam Gribley took off the burlap bag on which he had affixed Alice's whole tanned chicken skin. He looked for Frightful.

"I scared her badly," he said aloud, "but at least her eyas ate. She didn't see my face, so she won't imprint on me." Then he thought about what he had done and chuckled. He spoke aloud.

"You had better come back and feed her, Frightful," he said, "or she'll be imprinted on a monster chicken."

Sam drove a stick into the ground and drew a line along its shadow. The shadow would move away from the line as the sun moved. He could tell by the distance it traveled how much time had passed. At this time of year, it would move three and one-half inches each hour.

"The little eyas is good for maybe three hours," he said to himself. "If Frightful doesn't come by then, I'll have to be a chicken monster again." He grinned and went inside his tree to write in his journal.

"I think I gave Frightful an awful scare," he wrote.

The hours passed. The stick shadow moved ten-and-a-half inches—three hours. Frightful sat motionless on a tree stub above the West Branch of the Delaware. She was still afraid but, at the same time, pulled to her chick in the one tree.

The sun shone on her blue-gray shoulders and gleamed in her large eyes. Her feet gripped the dead limb more and more tightly. She could not relax.

Hunger finally forced her to move. She flew up the river valley, spotted a rat moving along the side of a farm silo, and took it. She carried it to the courthouse cupola.

Tenderly she plucked a bite and held it in her beak, waiting for an eyas to take it. None did. She swallowed it.

Suddenly Frightful's need to return to her eyas overwhelmed her fears. She spread her long, tapered wings and flew toward Oksi, rat in her talons. A soft wind carried her swiftly up the mountainside. She circled the one hemlock. No monster with a chicken head hung in the branch. Frightful landed on the tree.

The box and the eyas were gone.

"Creee, creee, creee, car-reet," she cried.

"Not the tree," Sam called from below. "The eyas is on the roof of the mill house. I put her out in the open where a peregrine's aerie should be."

Frightful saw Oksi.

She sped down, food in her talons, and landed on the floor of the box.

Oksi screamed.

Sam watched, his fists clenched, his body tense.

Frightful tore off a morsel and fed Oksi.

"Phew!" Sam let out a long, long breath.

IN WHICH
A Pal Finds a Pal

O ksi was six days old on that eventful day. She was a ball of white fuzz with huge shining eyes rimmed with saffron. Her beak was pale blue. She had two needs: food and Frightful's warm brood patch, and now, at last, she had both. She crawled into her mother's breast feathers and sat quietly.

Sam closed down the waterwheel early and carried wood to his stone oven to make a fire. The oven sat a few yards away from his table and the four tree-stump chairs. All were in the umbra of the magnificent hemlock. When the fire was lit, he wrapped cattail tubers and trout in two large may-apple leaves and placed them in the oven. Then he rested his elbow on the table and scratched his head.

The dark-haired man came back to mind. Sam jumped to his feet.

"Skri! Bate!" he said out loud. He thought a moment. "It's eyas time. The poachers are at work for that Arabian agent again." Sam remembered how Sean Conklin and he had caught Skri leaving a cave at Beaver Corners last June. With him was the man called Bate and his friend.

"That's it; Skri and Bate took the eyases." He sat down again. "But where are they?"

While his supper cooked, his mind ran over all the possible answers to his question.

"Bate won't be at his home in Altamont—too risky. They all know him." He thought harder. "Seems he goes incognito," he recalled. "He told me he was Leon Longbridge, and he told Joe Cassini he was a government official. He's got to be someplace where he can act like somebody else and get away with it. Where's that?"

The sun went down, and the troublesome day was over. Alice came up the twilit trail with a basket of sweet wild strawberries from Mrs. Strawberry's field. She sat down on a log stump at the table and decapped one.

"I have a dog," she said, handing Sam the strawberry.

"A dog?" said Sam, popping it into his mouth, then poking a stick into the trout to test its doneness. "I thought you were a pig girl."

"Pigs are best," said Alice, "but this dog is special."

"Where did you get him?"

"Remember Hanni?"

Sam blushed and smiled.

"Of course I remember Hanni. What about Hanni?"

"Well, she and Hendrik found this dog over near the Helderberg Escarpment and took him home. He was so terrified of people he chewed his leash and got away. Last week when Hanni was visiting the John Burroughs lodge, she found him again."

"What was he doing at the John Burroughs lodge?"

"Denning under it and living off the land, like he does."

"Smart dog." Sam smiled. "I like his spirit."

"Except there were two Park Service rangers there who were trying to shoot him for catching game. That's dumb."

"Maybe. What happened?"

"Hanni told them the dog was hers and took him home again."

"She and Hendrik brought him to me. Hanni thought I could bring the love of people to him, like I did to Crystal, my pig." Alice smiled. "The dog's adorable—a yellow cur with long ears; big, sad eyes—and the best rabbit chaser I've ever seen."

"What's his name?"

"Hendrik and Hanni named him General, but their aunt and uncle said the people they bought the farm from called him Mole. He lived in a culvert. I like the name Mole."

"So do I. And where is Mole?"

"Down at the farm with Mrs. Strawberry. I'm going back. I just want to get some rawhide from you to make him a special collar. I want to braid it into a tough band so he can't get loose."

"Sure he won't eat it?"

"He can't reach it, silly," Alice said.

"Alice," Sam said, taking his supper out of the oven, "did you say Hanni talked to two rangers at the John Burroughs house?"

"Yes; you know, the Park Service owns it."

"But the Park Service doesn't own it. It is owned by descendants of the John Burroughs family. There're no rangers on duty there. Bando and I camped there when we were looking for you last spring."

"Well, whatever—two men were going to shoot him."

Sam shared his meal with Alice. The trout was tender, but the cattail tubers were tough. When they had finished their meal with the delicious strawberries, Sam got deer hide from the mill house and cut off long strips for Alice.

"Thanks," Alice said, and put them into her pocket. "I'm off now, to bring love to Mole."

Sam was out of bed early the next morning. Barefoot and lacing up his deerskin shirt as he stepped outside, he looked over the pond into Frightful's nest box. He had placed it so that the opening faced him. Frightful was far back in the corner, mothering. Although all seemed well, it was not. There was no tiercel. Sam would have to bring food to Frightful until 426 came back. The eyas was still too young for Frightful to leave her and hunt.

While Sam cooked cornmeal mush for breakfast, Frightful came to the front of the box and scanned the skies, looking for 426. Oksi was screaming to be fed. The air was chilly.

She called for her mate. He did not answer.

Around noon, when the air had warmed, Frightful gave the little eyas the last bites of the rat. Then she sat down and brooded her.

Sam whistled that he had food for her, but she did not fly to him. Oksi was shivering. She needed her mother's warmth.

Several hours later, Frightful stood up and walked to the edge of the box. She called for a new mate. She called over and over again.

Then down from the clouds, over the feathery tips of the hemlocks, came Chup. He circled the mill house and dropped onto its stovepipe.

"Chup, chup," he called, and flew to the box. 426 was dead. He would not have permitted another male in his territory had he been alive.

"Creee," she called.

Chup also was single. His mate had not returned to their aerie one morning, and he was forced to be mother and hunter to three eyases again. This time he had been unable to call in a mate, and his chicks had not survived.

The day they succumbed to starvation, he flew down the Schoharie gorge and up over the mountains of Delhi. He cried in distress. Gliding over Peaks Brook, he heard Frightful calling for a new mate. He folded his wings and dropped down onto the mill-house roof. He jumped up to the nest box and bowed to her. Frightful looked at her mate of last spring as if it were perfectly natural for him to be there.

Chup looked at Oksi and without even a signal from Frightful, walked to Oksi and dropped his feathers over her. Frightful flew off to hunt. She sped to the abandoned meadow, now pale green with raspberry and young hawthorn leaves. She hovered, watching for game.

A rabbit jumped up and darted away. Frightful stooped and did not miss.

She was on the ground with it when she heard a dog woof. She covered the food with her wings, then looked around. Peering through the bushes at her was Mole, his head twisting in curiosity. He recognized Frightful. Frightful recognized him. He came toward her. He wanted some rabbit.

This was no time to share. Frightful clutched the food in her talons and beak, and with deep wing beats was airborne. She gained altitude, maneuvered, and steered through the trees to the mill house. She and the rabbit landed with a thud in the box.

Only Oksi's tail feathers showed beneath Chup. He stood up and without making a sound, flew to the top of the hemlock. Frightful fed the eyas.

Sam was dipping a water bucket into the millpond when he saw Chup leave the nest box.

"Hey, that's Frightful's mate!" he exclaimed. "Great—I'm relieved of my tiercel duties, and just in time."

He hurried to the root cellar and packed his rucksack with enough nuts, venison jerky, and big potatolike Jerusalem artichoke roots to feed himself for three or four days.

He was adding dried apples when he heard a suspicious noise, and moved a sack of dry corn.

"Jessie Coon James," Sam exclaimed. "Where have you been all these months?" He rolled his tongue, imitating a raccoon purr, and held out his hand. His old friend waddled up to him, ears down in deference.

"Got a family?" Sam asked. "Must not, or you'd have them with you and I would be foodless."

Jessie Coon James took an ear of corn in both forepaws and chewed.

"Give me that corn, you bandit," he said and, laughing happily to see his old friend again, picked her up and hugged her. Jessie grabbed the corn tighter.

"Oh, all right," he said. "You can have one ear." Jessie took it in her teeth and dropped to the floor. Sam watched her. Jessie departed through a tunnel she had dug under the door.

"Aha," he said. "I'd better fix that before I go, or I won't have any food when I get home." Then he added, "Speaking of fixing things, I'd better remember to remove Frightful's jesses. I don't want anyone to come by here and see her with those on. They'll fine me for harboring an endangered species."

An hour later, when the hole was mended and Frightful's jesses removed, Molly and José were walking across the Delhi Bridge. Molly looked up at the empty nest site.

"José," she said, "we've got to find the baby falcons."

"How?" he asked helplessly. "Leon Longbridge has the police looking all over three counties, and they can't find them. How can we?"

"By remembering things." She rubbed her forehead. "Last spring the newspaper said the sheriff arrested some falcon poachers in a cave at Beaver Corners. I'll bet they are the ones who stole the eyases, and I'll bet they're right there now."

"And just how do we get there?"

"We tell Leon Longbridge. He'll take us."

"He might," said José, then beamed. "I hope so. I love caves."

Leon Longbridge, they learned, had already checked the cave and found nothing. Molly and José went back to the bridge to think some more.

At that moment Sam was walking across his mountain meadow when he heard the clinking of a chain. He scanned the field and forest edge. A hawthorn bush trembled. He stole up on it.

"Well, who are you?" he said to a dog, whose broken chain was wrapped twice around the hawthorn. The dog wore a braided leather collar.

"You're Mole," Sam answered himself. "That's who you are." Mole wagged his tail.

"You should be named Houdini. You get out of every leash, collar, and barn you're put in." Smiling broadly, Sam got down on his knees. "And here I am getting you out of this mess." Carefully he unwound the chain, then gripped it firmly in one hand. He took Mole's chin in the other.

"You've got a lot of beagle in you," he said. "You can be a big help to me on this trip. How about coming along? You can sniff down food for the two of us—and maybe a criminal or two."

Sam started off. Mole wouldn't budge.

"Come, Mole. Come." He yanked on the leash.

Mole pulled backward, ducking down his head to slip his collar.

"I'm sorry," Sam said. "You don't want to come with me. Of course not; you don't know me. Here," he said, and held out his hand. "Let my odors tell you all about me."

Mole sniffed. Rising strong and sweet from Sam's hand were informative scents. They told Mole that Sam was a young adolescent, nonviolent, and that he liked wild foods. Mole also learned that Sam was related to Alice and that he lived in a hemlock tree. Mole finally decided he liked what he smelled and licked Sam's hand.

With that, Sam sat down and rubbed Mole's big ears. He talked to him softly, then kissed the top of his nose and told him what a good dog he was. He hugged him close.

Mole nuzzled his head under Sam's chin and whimpered softly.

"Thanks," Sam said. "I love you, too. Can we go now?" he asked.

Mole's droopy eyes sagged. Sam got up and tugged on his leash, but Mole would not move. He braced all four feet and pulled backward.

"Oh," Sam said, "I hear you. You don't like to be tied up." He took off the collar and leash and threw them into the bushes. Mole wagged his tail. Sam patted his head.

"Now, can we go?" The happy dog bounced down the mountain, sticking close to Sam's side. When the blissful pair came to the dirt road that led to Bando's house, Sam stopped.

"It would be great to have Bando along," he said, glancing in the direction of his friend's cabin. "But there's no use even asking him. He's not going to leave Zella. She's going to have a baby pretty soon."

At sundown Sam and Mole camped by an abandoned barn on the side of Mount Warren. Mole caught a feral chicken, and Sam cooked it on a small and smokeless fire.

He was an expert at making fires no one could see. When, at ten o'clock, the temperature dropped sharply, they moved into the barn and dug into a straw pile.

The next thing Sam knew, a rooster was crowing to the dawn. Sam jumped up so fast he frightened a hen. She flew off her nest, squawking and clucking, and sped out of the barn. She left behind feathers and twelve eggs. Sam helped himself to four. He boiled them hard and shared them with Mole. After washing his face in the farm spring, he and Mole resumed their trek into the dense forests of the Catskill Mountains. Later in the morning, they came to the mowed meadowlands under the power lines.

"Creee, creee, creee, car-reet."

"Desdemondia," said Sam, using Bando's respectable expletive. "That's Frightful. Only one bird calls my peregrine name."

Frightful hovered above them. "How did you find us?" he said, eyes twinkling. "Took Mole and me a day and a half to get here."

Mole dashed into the grasses and weeds. Nose to the ground, weaving in and out of young goldenrod and raspberry plants, he flushed a pheasant.

Before Sam could see whether it was a male or a female, Frightful was carrying it off toward their mountain.

"Hey!" He whistled for her to come to his hand; she flew on.

Mole barked.

In four minutes Frightful covered the air miles to her mountain. She plucked the bird on the roof of Alice's wigwam and carried the meal to the box where Chup was brooding Oksi.

Suddenly a tall, angular man stepped out of the woods. Chup gave the alarm cry and took off. Frightful sat still.

Leon Longbridge lifted his binoculars and focused them on the wooden box. "Well, I'll be," he said to himself. "There sits the falcon of Delhi Bridge. I'd know that dark, beautiful head anywhere." Then he saw the eyas.

"Wow," he said aloud. "I don't know how the two of you got here, but you're free—and that's all I'm concerned about."

He glanced around and realized he was at Sam Gribley's home. He had heard about it through young Matt, a newspaper reporter. Matt had told him that Sam had a "cool" home in a huge hemlock on a mountain. He said that he had a falcon and homemade fishhooks and fishing rods. He never told him where. Leon studied the mill house, the oven, and the stone table.

"I would sure love to live like this," he said wistfully.

Although he was curious, he did not step inside the hemlock home. He respected Sam's privacy. And so, glancing once more at Frightful, he strode down the trail, wondering how the peregrine of the Delhi Bridge and her eyas had ended up in a box on Sam's mill-house roof. He was smiling.

"Hmm," he mused. "Matt did say the kid was a falconer." He whistled a bright bird tune and thought about the bridge. "How did that kid get the eyas down from there?" he asked himself. "That must have been some act."

It took Sam and Mole until noon to reach their destination—the woods behind the John Burroughs lodge.

Sam put down his gear in a dense grove of young hemlocks.

"Stay," he said to Mole. "I'm going to climb that big tree and see what's going on. Park Service rangers at the John Burroughs Woodchuck Lodge? Humph. Some story."

Mole did not "stay." He knew perfectly well what the word meant, but he also knew where he was.

While Sam climbed the tree, Mole took his favorite fern trail to the lodge. He slipped under it, sniffing. Wood rats and a skunk had almost immediately taken over his old bedroom. He set upon the wood-rat burrow, digging downward, sending the earth flying. The rat family exited by another tunnel.

He rested a moment. The skunk must be handled differently. The den entrance was right beside his own bed at the base of the chimney. He lay down and woofed into it.

His presence should send the skunk or skunks out their back door.

Suddenly he stopped. Men were talking in the room above him; their voices vibrated the old wooden floor. His terror of people returned. Mole put his tail between his legs and slunk out from under the lodge, into the bushes. He returned to Sam's pack in the hemlock grove and lay down.

Sam jumped down from the bottom bough of the tree and hurried back to Mole.

"Good boy," he said, taking the dog's head in his hands and kissing the bridge of his muzzle. "You didn't run off." Sam rubbed Mole's big ears, then his own.

"Listen to this, Mole," he whispered. "There are two men here. I saw them through the window. I was too high to see their faces—only their feet.

"Also, there's a rabbit hutch by the toolshed." He crouched down. "Falconers raise them for falcon food.

"And down by the county road is a huge rhododendron thicket. I think I saw a green vehicle parked in the middle of it. Let's take a look.

"Come quietly, Mole." The dog rose and followed.

Sam took a circuitous route through the woods to the county road. He walked south on it, then turned onto the dirt lane that led to the lodge. The rhododendron thicket was about twenty feet back from the Burroughs's lane and about a quarter of an acre big. Sam pushed back branches and looked around. There sat the green pickup with the U.S. Fish and Wildlife Service emblem taped to its door.

"Park Service rangers don't hide their pickups," he said to Mole, and walked noiselessly around the thicket until he found where the bushes had been cut down to let the green pickup enter. He walked to the Chevy. In it were three animal-carrying cases.

"These cages don't tell me much," Sam said to the dog. "They could carry rabbits or falcons or cats or even you, Mole."

Mole began sniffing.

Sam memorized the New York license plate, then walked to the cab and looked in.

"Oh, boy," he said. "Whitewash—bird excrement. Falcons? Could be pigeons." He looked further. "A half-empty box of bullets. I don't like that, Mole."

Mole began to snuffle, sucking gobs of air over the hundreds of scent glands in his nose. Then he wagged his tail at a gray pellet on the ground.

Sam looked down.

"By golly," he said and picked up a casting from a bird of prey. He examined it carefully. It was mostly fur.

"Rabbit," he said. "The rabbits I saw are for food, and they are being fed to a falcon, an owl, a hawk, or maybe a raven." He noted the roundness of the pellet. "I say eyas—peregrine eyas."

Sam put the pellet in his pocket and walked back to the hemlock grove the way he had come. Seating himself on the ground behind the biggest tree, he cut a piece of venison jerky and gave half to Mole. Chewing on the other half, he stretched out on his back and wondered what to do next. He had to get the birds without the men seeing him. They were armed. Mole lay down beside him, the skunk on his mind.

"Looks like we've found Bate and Skri," Sam said, "and it looks like we've found the eyases."

Sam rolled over on his belly. Mole put his head on Sam's shoulder.

"We've got to be careful, old friend.

"I've got a plan," Sam said, more to himself than to Mole. "Frightful's little falcons are in the lodge. I'll get one of the rabbits and let it go in front of the lodge." Then he addressed Mole. "You'll chase the rabbit and yip so loud that the men come out to see what's going on. Then I'll go in the back door and get the eyases. I'll be up the mountain by the time Bate and his friend can get their rabbit back. You'll have to follow my trail and catch up with me.

"Got it?" Sam looked into the hound's sad, droopy eyes. "I'm not so sure you do, but I do know you'll chase anything that runs or flies."

He patted Mole's head. "Okay, this is it," he said, and headed for the rabbit hutch. He never got there.

Mole caught a whiff of the skunk and in seconds was under the lodge. He bore down on the skunk at the entrance to his den. Seeing Mole, the skunk calmly waited, then looked at him, aimed his rear end, and let loose a jet stream of musk. It burned into Mole's nose and eyes. He yiped in pain and ran around the lodge. The scent instantly seeped up through the old floor boards. It penetrated the kitchen in a yellow mist.

"Phew!" Sam recognized Bate's voice. "Skunk. A dog got hit by a skunk." His eyes burned and smarted. He could not see. Knocking over chairs, he and his friend ran to the front porch.

"Smart Mole," said Sam, and dashed through the kitchen door.

"I stink!" Bate bellowed from the front porch. Sam

clutched the eyas box. Bate roared on. "I'm going for a can of tomato juice to wash in."

Sam didn't expect that. Bate was stumbling toward the kitchen. Sam was trapped. He put down the eyases. A big box for firewood stood near him, so he opened the lid. The box, as he had hoped, was empty. Into it he went—one second late. Bate was in the kitchen. Sam crossed his fingers in the darkness, hoping Bate's eyes were burning too much to have seen him. He sat perfectly still.

"You're under arrest!" Sam heard a new voice say. "You are stealing falcons." Sam lifted the lid high enough to see not one but two police officers in the doorway. They were facing Bate.

"Where is Skri?" one of the officers asked.

"I didn't steal those birds," Bate said. "The guy you are looking for is in that box. I came in to look around this famous lodge. I found him here with two falcons." He rubbed his smarting eyes. The officers rubbed their eyes, and Sam pushed up the lid of the wood box and stood up.

"Who are you?" an officer asked in surprise.

"Sam Gribley. I live down by Delhi. I came here to get these two chicks and bring them back to their mother. She is nesting near my house."

"That's a likely story," said the other officer.

"He lies," snarled Bate, backing toward his gun on the

sink drain board. In the din of the accusations, a third man entered the kitchen. Sam breathed a sigh of relief. There, in his camouflaged fatigues and hiking boots, was Sean Conklin, the conservation officer of Albany County. He and Sam had tracked down Bate, who, posing as Leon Longbridge, had stolen Frightful from Sam. Sean Conklin would speak up for him. He would let him take the eyases home to Frightful. Sam climbed out of the box, smiling from ear to ear.

Off in the distance Sam heard a car door slam.

"That's Skri," Sam said, "the Arab agent. He's getting away in the pickup."

"Don't worry, Sam," Sean Conklin said. "He won't get away. My assistant, Henry Ryan, removed the spark plugs from the truck."

One of the police officers snapped handcuffs on Bate.

"Let me out of here," Bate snarled. "I'm no thief. I'm a citizen."

"You're no thief, all right," Sam said. "You are worse than that. You're a traitor—an environmental traitor. These little falcons belong to North America."

"I'm a citizen," Bate said, his face growing red with anger.

"Yes, you are," said the officer, "but that doesn't give you the right to sell endangered species. Let's go see the judge." He steered him to the door.

Bate looked back over his shoulder. "I stink," he said. "Can't I even get some tomato juice?"

"I can't smell you anymore," the police officer said. "That's the best part of skunk spray. After a short while, you can't smell yourself—or anyone else who's been doused in it." He chuckled. "But wait till I get home to my wife!"

Sam sniffed himself. He did indeed think he smelled clean. The police officer was right. He sniffed again, then picked up one of the little eyases.

"Hello," he said to the bright-eyed bird, now showing the tips of his wing feathers. "Want to go home to your mom?"

Blue Bill looked at Sam and sat very still, eyes wide.

"He likes you. He sits still even if you do smell," said Sean.

"I wish that were true," said Sam, stroking the downy head. "But the truth is birds can't smell much. He's just scared."

Henry Ryan came in the back door.

"Those two are on their way to jail again," he said, and grinned happily. "This time I hope the judge keeps them there."

Sam picked up the eyas box.

"I'll feed the little birds," he said. "They're restless. They're getting hungry. Then I'll take them home."

"I'm afraid you can't do that," said Ryan.

"Why not?" Sam was astonished.

"You're not a licensed falconer."

"But . . . these are wild birds."

"Not now. They've been registered in Albany. These two little birds are quite famous and are under the protection of the United States government."

"Who is going to raise them?" Sam asked. "They'll never fly free if people raise them."

"A falconer near Delhi is going to raise them—Perry Knowlton. He'll hack them back to the wild. They can learn to be free."

Sam shook his head. He had never heard of Perry Knowlton. He leaned over the box and whispered in falcon talk to the little birds.

"You really should give them to me," he said.

"And why should I do that?" Henry asked.

"I have their mother," Sam said. "She nests in a box at my home on the mountaintop. And she is free."

"Are you kidding?" Henry asked. "Tell me." Sam told Sean Conklin and Henry Ryan the story of Frightful and the Delhi Bridge.

"You say the third chick's in a nest box on your property and its parents are taking care of it?" Henry asked in disbelief.

"Yes," Sam answered. "Frightful would take the little

eyases right back. And that's the best thing for everyone."

"It is," said Henry, "but we can't do that. Too much red tape. The eyases would be grandparents by the time we got through all the bureaucratic loops."

"With every day that passes, they're more deeply imprinted on people," Sam said. "They need their own kind."

"I know that," said Henry. "But we can't turn them over to you."

Mole came into the kitchen. His eyes were still smarting from the direct skunk hit. He sought comfort from Sam.

"Get that dog out of here," said Sean Conklin. "He smells terrible."

"I don't smell him," said Ryan.

"I'm going out on the porch," said Sean, and departed. Ryan followed.

Blue Bill gave a hunger cry. Sam found falcon food in the old refrigerator, picked up the eyas box, and went out to the porch.

Mole wagged his tail and trotted after him.

"Stay," Sam said. "And I mean stay right here. I'm going to try once more to get the little eyases. I have one more trick up my sleeve." Mole hung his head, put his tail between his legs, and sat down.

On the porch, Sam and Henry each fed a little falcon, then rocked back on their heels and looked at them.

"Suppose," Sam said slowly and deliberately, "you two had to go to town. And when you got back, the eyases had disappeared?"

"I'd be fired," Henry answered promptly. "And I've got two kids."

"You know we can't do that, Sam," Sean Conklin said.

"Okay," Sam agreed. "But I really don't understand. Everyone wants to save the peregrines, but no one will do what it takes to save them—from stopping work on a bridge to returning chicks to their parents."

He leaned over the eyases, who were now back in their box, full and sleepy.

"Pssst," he squeaked through his tightened lips. "Psst."

The downy birds lifted their heads and turned their huge black eyes upon him. "Creee, creee, creee," he cried, imitating Frightful. The eyases screamed the mother recognition call. Sam touched them gently on the beaks. Then he stood up.

Sean and Henry stared at each other. They had just seen a boy who could talk to peregrine eyases. They knew he was the one person in the world who should have the little birds. And they knew there was no way they could arrange this.

Sam backed down the steps, found his pack in the hemlock grove, and whistled for Mole. Together, they crossed the field in the direction of the mountains.

The two men saw them stride along.

"I think we should have gone to town." Henry said.

"We're not free to do anything but what we did," Sean answered, watching with no little longing the young man who walked to his own inner music.

I N   W H I C H

Frightful and Oksi Run the Show

The sun was held back by rain clouds the morning Frightful saw Sam and Mole come home from their wanderings. Sam whistled hello, but she did not reply. She was concerned with Oksi. This day had dawned cold, Chup was out hunting, and she had to brood the eyas.

Just as Sam and Mole went into the tree house, Chup came home to feed and brood Oksi, and Frightful took off. She sped with the air currents into a thermal that spiraled her high above Delhi. At the top of the warm air bubble, she peeled off and dove straight down. She landed on the cupola of the county courthouse.

Frightful drew herself up tall. The courthouse pigeon flock was winging into sight. She knew each pigeon personally. She knew the healthy and quick on wing. She knew the dumb and the clumsy. And she knew those with the highly contagious pox virus. She selected one of these and struck. The virus died with the bird, and she carried it back to Oksi.

When Frightful returned with food that day, Chup was freed from his nest brooding. Oksi was old enough to be left alone while Frightful hunted. He flew from tall tree to the tallest, spread his wings, and soared far from Frightful's Mountain. He had never been comfortable in the forest. He was a bird of the cliffs, open river valleys, and the bottoms of clouds. Spread-winged, he rode an air current to a cliff in Catskill Park, a three-minute falcon flight from Oksi. He was still concerned about her.

While Sam and Mole were away, Oksi had changed. The tips of her flight feathers had grown in, and she could stand and walk. She jumped on leaves that blew into the box and watched every bird that flew past. But the greatest change of all was that she jabbed a foot at Frightful when she came into the box with food.

Chup returned to the box one day to find no food at the aerie. He flew down to the river and brought back a duck. Alighting on the box, he was met by Oksi's two yellow feet and black talons. He left the food and took off.

As she grew and changed, the wooden box intrigued Oksi. It was far different from her first home. It did not look out on a vast landscape, but on a hemlock forest. From it she did not see ducks, but frogs and songbirds. The winds around her did not jet, but swirled and bumped.

Instinctively she disliked it, but because her parents fed her here, she became accustomed to it.

Sam would sit at his table at mealtimes and watch Oksi. He knew the box in the forest was all wrong for a peregrine, and so he would wonder what would happen when it came time for her to pick her own nesting site. Would she choose a cliff, a bridge—or, he mused almost longingly, would she pick a beautiful hemlock forest like this? Was she imprinted on Frightful's Mountain?

He was watching Oksi through the binocs one evening when Jessie Coon James came up to him and begged for a handout. Sam laughed and gave her his leftover rabbit stew. Ordinarily he gave it to Mole, but Mole was chasing a fox, and that could take all night. Jessie ate voraciously, then climbed the old hemlock and draped herself over a limb. She closed her eyes.

"Are you sleeping out tonight, Jessie?" Sam asked. "That's a good idea. Think I will, too. It's a balmy night."

A breeze rocked Jessie on her willowy limb.

Sam spread his deerskin sleeping bag on the big stone table and, after completing his chores and writing in his journal, he lay down and watched the stars come out.

Sam listened to the night sounds. A screech owl awoke and called, the barred owl by the mill house hooted, and from far away, he heard the lugubrious voice of Mole reporting his progress in a game of "catch the fox," a game both animals thoroughly enjoyed. After Mole found the scent and began the chase, the fox took great pleasure in tricking him. When Mole got too close, the fox would splash into a stream and wash away his trail, or he would sit in a scented wintergreen patch and watch Mole run right past him. Sometimes he fooled Mole by running the tops of fences or turning around and going back over his own trail. Before dawn, they both understood, the game ended. The fox would slip into his den, and Mole would go home, panting happily.

This night it was Jessie Coon James who had the game

plan. When Sam was asleep, she stole down the tree and circled Baron Weasel's den. Moving quietly, she swam across the millpond to the sluice and climbed up the wall. The shale bricks made perfect hand- and footholds.

She was headed for the roof but was stopped by the overhang. She backed down and tried climbing the down-mountain side of the mill house. Again she was turned back by the overhang.

While she puzzled, Oksi slept, Frightful slept, Sam slept, and Mole ran the top of an old stone fence, following the fox.

Jessie Coon James was not defeated. She walked to the up-mountain side of the mill house. She climbed again, and this time she reached the stovepipe. It was metal and slippery but was braced with steel bands. She caught a band with one front claw and was able to grab the overhang with her hind feet and, scratching hard on the shakes, pull herself up onto the roof.

Oksi awoke. It was dark. She could not see, but she could hear. Something was coming her way. She felt fear for the first time and backed into the corner of the box.

Jessie could see as well in the dark as she could in daylight. She approached the box, hooked eight front claws onto the rim board, and pulled herself in.

Oksi *kakak*-ed, threw up both feet, and sank her talons into the enemy. Jessie yiped a bloodcurdling scream, jumped back, fell, and slid down the roof, clutching with her claws.

Frightful awoke. Oksi was in trouble. She heard but could not see. She sat still.

Sam awoke. He heard Oksi screaming and dashed to the mill house just as Jessie came tumbling down the roof. Sam caught her before she fell.

Jessie's snarls so alarmed Frightful that, despite the darkness, she flew for the nest box. She struck the mill-house roof with a crash, spread out her wings, and lay still.

Sam saw her hit. He climbed to the roof and, taking a grip on the wooden shakes with one hand, grabbed Frightful by both feet with the other. She hung head-down quietly as Sam thrust her into the box. He climbed to the ground and waited.

With Oksi beside her, Frightful shook out her feathers and sat quietly. Oksi did not jab her.

Sam listened. No sounds of distress came from the box.

"Phew," he said, and was about to step on Jessie in the dark when she snarled.

"Jessie, what do I do now?" he asked the raccoon in exasperation. "No matter where I put Frightful and Oksi, in a tree or on a roof, you can get to them."

A silent gray missile sped out of the forest.

The barred owl hit Jessie a one-footed blow on the shoulder and flew up to strike again.

Sam picked up the stunned raccoon. The owl dove at them both. Sam ducked and ran up the hill and into his tree home. He put Jessie on the floor and lit the wick in a turtle shell filled with deer fat.

Light filled the warm interior of the old tree. It shone on the clay fireplace Sam had built from riverside clay. It lit up Frightful's falcon hood on a shelf and threw light on a stack of library books. Sam was preparing to take the high-school equivalency test.

He moved the turtle-shell lamp close to Jessie.

"You've got a mean slash on your shoulder, Jess," he said, then took out his knife and began cutting away the fur from the wound.

"That was Frightful's chick you were trying to eat," he said. "You like Frightful, remember? You never once attacked her, and she never once attacked you.

"You've got to be friends again." He bandaged the wound with sphagnum moss and strips of deer hide. Jessie lay in shock.

Sam talked on, feeling totally inadequate. Telling a falcon and a raccoon to be best friends was almost impossible.

But Jessie had already gotten the peace message. Not from Sam, but from the birds of prey. They had spoken clearly. The territory around the mill house, at the risk of death, belonged to the owls at night and the falcons by day.

Sam stopped talking and picked up his bandaged friend.

He carried her to Alice's tree house to recover out of sight of the birds of prey.

As soon as the sun came up, Frightful left Oksi and flew to the big hemlock. Undaunted by the night's scare, Oksi stood up and watched the awakening birds. She was absolutely intrigued by them at this time in her life and remembered every pattern of the flight of each species.

Suddenly she saw Sam's head coming over the edge of the mill-house roof. She lowered her whole body and ran at him.

"Kak, kak, kak," Oksi warned, and jabbed out a foot.

Frightful flew down from the tree and landed on the top of the box. She looked at Sam, who had reached the box.

"Terrible night, wasn't it, old girl?" he said. "Well, I'm going to fix things. I'm going to get a tall pipe and have Bando solder a metal plate to it. I'll fasten your box to the plate and erect it in the open, where a peregrine aerie ought to be.

"No raccoon can climb a steel pipe," he said, "and your eyas will be safe until she can fly."

"Kak, kak, kak, kak, kak, kak," Oksi screamed, and attacked Sam. When she thrust out her feet, he grabbed them and quickly hooded her.

"Jessie Coon James is laid up," he said to Frightful, "but

not the barred owl—and he can, and will, strike by day. I'm taking your eyas to our tree until the pole's ready."

Frightful called "creee" once. She did not call Sam by his falcon name.

"You are getting wilder, Frightful," he said. "The bond between us is breaking down. That's good. Good for you, sad for me."

Sam made Oksi comfortable inside the tree, then took the trail to Mrs. Strawberry's farm and her collection of pipes and lumber and wheels and scraps of metal.

On the way home he asked Bando for help, and before the sun set, they had put Oksi, unhooded, into the nest box and erected pole, box, and her in the clearing by the millpond. The box now had a porch, where Frightful could drop food without getting jabbed.

They stood back and admired their work.

"It's getting late," Sam said when the job was done. "Aren't you worried about Zella?"

"No," Bando said. "I've got a little gadget in my pocket called a cell phone. Zella will call if she feels any contractions."

"Wow," said Sam, remarking on Zella and the telephone.

Oksi walked out on the porch and *kakak*-ed angrily.

"Neat bird," said Bando, grinning.

"She really is," Sam said, and smiled broadly.

"She does seem a little accident-prone," Bando remarked. "It's been one crisis after another for that bird."

"Yeah," Sam mused. "Only three out of ten birds live long enough to raise their own young."

"Seems," Bando said, "she must be one of those three. She's somehow survived all the hazards of her first forty days."

Sam nodded as he gripped the pole to see if it was firmly planted.

"I'd like to see a raccoon scale that," he said.

"Looks Jessie-proof to me," said Bando.

"Do you realize this is the little eyas's fourth nest site?" Sam said. "I keep wondering what kind of nest she will choose when she grows up and looks for an aerie. She might be a Gypsy nester."

"That's proper," Bando said. "After all, she is *Falco peregrinus,* the pilgrim falcon." They exchanged serious glances. They knew it was important to show this eyas a peregrine's world, and they weren't sure they had done that.

Oksi was oblivious to this chatter. She had her own agenda with her world, and Frightful was the first to discover it.

The very next day Frightful landed on the aerie porch. She was leaning over to pluck a pigeon when Oksi charged her, beak open, feathers raised. She hit her full force. Frightful jumped onto her wings, left the food, and flew to the top of the ancient hemlock.

She shook out her ruffled feathers. Oksi had graduated from grammar school.

From that moment on, Frightful fed her not in the box, but on the wing. She dropped food onto the hacking porch and sped away. She did not perch in the hemlock to chaperone Oksi anymore, but flew over the mountain to the cupola on the Delhi courthouse. There she kept the pigeons of Delhi from spreading disease.

One morning she recognized Leon Longbridge standing on the sidewalk. With him were two children. She kept them in the corner of her eye while she watched the pigeons.

"That *is* our falcon," Leon Longbridge said, focusing his binoculars on Frightful. He grinned and handed the field glasses to Molly.

"How do you know?" Molly asked.

"She has a very dark, almost black, head," he said, "and her eyes are quite large—larger than most peregrines'. When you watch birds long enough, you see their differences. She's our bird, all right." He smiled but did not tell the kids that he had seen the Delhi falcon feeding the third chick in a box on Sam Gribley's mountain.

"Hey," exclaimed Molly. "She sure is our bird. She has little heart-shaped black spots on her breast feathers. I looked at them a million times from my bedroom window."

"You're a good observer," Leon said. Molly looked pleased and passed the glasses to José as Hughie Smith joined them on his way to his drumming lessons. Molly pointed out Frightful to him.

"Neat," he said, and looked up at the conservation officer. "Mr. Longbridge, when can we visit our chicks at Perry Knowlton's?"

"In about two weeks," Leon replied. "He doesn't want them to get comfortable with people while they're young. He's keeping them as wild as possible. He put them with a breeding pair that had only one eyas, and they've been taking care of them. They just might forget their early nurturing by people and become wild."

"I hope so," said Molly.

Leon went on, "Perry said I could bring you all over when he hacks the birds. They'll fly if they are afraid of you—and that's what we want them to do."

Frightful, who was tipping her head now and then to focus on Leon Longbridge and the kids, also had an eye on the courthouse pigeons. When they fanned out and came back together in a silvery knot, she dropped from the cupola, scattered them, and, reaching down with one golden foot, picked up the dumb bird who was flying the wrong way.

Frightful carried the food up over the West Branch of the Delaware.

"Where's she going?" Hughie asked.

"Let's find out," José piped. "Can we follow her, Mr. Longbridge? You're real good at that."

"I don't think we should," Leon answered. "We've given her enough trouble. Don't you think she needs some privacy?"

"Yes," said Molly emphatically, "or she won't come back next year. Peregrine falcons like privacy."

So they stood on the street and watched Frightful until she was too far away to see, which was in mere seconds.

Suddenly Leon Longbridge put his glasses to his eyes and focused them overhead.

"Look! There's her mate," he exclaimed excitedly.

"Cool," said Hughie. "Maybe they'll nest again. It's not too late, is it?"

"I'm afraid it is," Leon Longbridge said. "The tiercel is roaming away from the aerie. That means he's done nesting."

"What do we do now?" complained José. "We can't see the chicks, we can't follow the falcon—"

"There are some transformers up the valley, where our falcon went," said Molly.

"Oh," said Hughie. "Back to letter writing. Okay, I'm getting good at that."

Frightful flew high over one of the transformers Molly was speaking of. She found an updraft on the side of her mountain and rode it without beating a wing. She tipped and sideslipped around the big tree and dropped the pigeon. The bird hit the porch, bounced, and went over the edge. Oksi jumped for it, spread her wings, and was flying. She flapped, shot ahead, and crashed into the ancient hemlock. Grabbing at limbs with her feet, she fell several yards before she got a good grip and flapped herself upright.

Oksi saw the bird. It lay on the ground by Baron Weasel's door. She was very hungry. She dropped down on it, clutched it, then flapped her wings to get airborne. Beating them hard, she skimmed forward but could not get off the ground. At the edge of the millpond she stopped and looked behind her. She had lost the bird.

A bullfrog moved; she thrust out a foot and snagged it. This was not her kind of food, and she let it go. She realized she was on the ground and became nervous. She opened her wings. There was no breeze to give her lift. Frightful's Mountain was a poor place to get airborne. She ran—wings open, pantaloons fluttering—and jumped up onto the stone table.

She sensed a silence around her. Mole was asleep on Sam's bed in the tree. Jessie was down at Peaks Brook. Baron Weasel was in his burrow. The barred owl was perched on a limb halfway down Frightful's Mountain. Only Sam was watching, and he was inside the mill house.

"Accident-prone Oksi," he said to himself. "She's going to get killed if she stays out in the open like that.

"I should grab her feet and toss her onto a wind. No,

that's not right. She's going to have to find out for herself."
He put his elbows on the windowsill. "It's sure terrible," he
mused, "to be a parent knowing that there are eagles and
goshawks lurking everywhere in these mountains."

Sam stood still and watched. Oksi remained on the
table. She was uncomfortable there. Once more she spread
her wings and once more she got no lift. There was no wind
to help her fly.

Mole woke up, smelled Oksi, and pushed open the
deerskin door. His nose directed his eyes, and he ran at her
as he ran at pheasants to flush them up.

He never reached her. Frightful dropped from the sky
and hit Mole with the force of a jackhammer. He yiped and
rolled into the millpond, stunned. His head went under,
and he gulped water.

Terrified, Oksi beat her wings with all her strength and
flew. She flew above Sam, who had waded into the
millpond to save Mole. She came to rest on the mill-house
roof.

Sam pulled the drowning dog to shore.

"Your mouth's too big for mouth-to-mouth resuscita-
tion," he said. "I'll try the Heimlich maneuver." He
pressed down on Mole's chest, then let go. Mole spluttered
and breathed.

He rolled his eyes at Sam.

"Frightful got you," he said. "You can't mess with her

eyas. She's a winged lioness." He helped Mole to his feet. "You and I had just better stay in the hemlock tree until Frightful gets this kid on wing and out of here, or someone is going to get killed."

He helped Mole, who was dripping and coughing, up the slope and into the hemlock. Mole lay down on the floor. After a short while, he breathed normally and thumped his tail.

The talon cut on his head was bleeding profusely. Sam washed it with cold water, saw it was not severe, and patched it with jewelweed leaves to stop the flow of blood. Then he gave Mole a deer bone for consolation and went to his desk. He opened a book.

"As long as we're stuck here," he said, "you might as well learn something. I'll read to you."

He began:

" 'With his first trip to France in 1781, a five-year period began in which Thomas Paine used his skills to work more openly on behalf of the United States to insure that his liberal-republican ideals were implemented.' "

He glanced at Mole. The dog's eyes were closed. "We're on page one hundred thirty-one in Jack Fruchtman Jr.'s book called *Thomas Paine*," he said.

Mole opened his eyes and thumped his tail. Sam went on reading.

Frightful Feels the Call to the Sky

Atop the mill house, Oksi turned her head almost all the way around in one direction and then the other. She saw trees, boulders, the millpond, and, high above them, a bright glimpse of blue sky. The sky captivated her. She sensed she should be there. She flapped her wings. Nothing happened. The air was still. No wind gave her lift. She closed her wings to her body and flicked her tail in frustration. She needed to be in that sky.

Frightful watched Oksi from Sam's tree. Her eyas had taken her first flight. She was no longer a nestling but a fledgling, a flying member of bird royalty—the family Falconidae. But Frightful was not about to join Chup wandering free on wing. She had still another duty—to provide food until Oksi could catch her own.

Oksi's mood changed from frustration to curiosity. She turned her head almost upside down to focus on a twisting leaf, a flying beetle, and a bird. Birds excited her. She lifted her wings to chase, thought better of it, and folded them to her sides.

Eventually she grew tired and put her beak in the feathers between her shoulders to sleep. The afternoon shadows lengthened and turned purple-blue. Up in the big tree, Frightful closed her eyes. From time to time she opened them and checked on Oksi.

Sam read on. Mole chewed on the deer bone.

Suddenly—"Sam, where are you?"

Bando was running toward the big tree, waving his arms. Oksi awakened and flapped her wings. A gust of wind rushed under them and lifted her off the roof. In seconds she was above the hemlock grove, on her way—somewhere.

Sam saw Oksi soaring to independence at the same time he heard Bando shout. "It's a girl! It's a girl! Her name is Samantha."

"Samantha?" Sam said, and Oksi was forgotten. "Who named her that?"

"Zella," said Bando as he caught his breath from running.

Sam couldn't speak.

"Now we have a son and a daughter," Bando said, putting his hand on Sam's shoulder. "Those are Zella's words."

Sam ran his fingers through his hair, trying to take in the wonder of having a namesake.

"I've got to get back to the hospital," Bando said. "I'll pick up my surprise for Zella and Samantha." He winked. "Think she'll like it?"

Sam still could not speak.

Bando's blue eyes shone under his dark eyebrows and prematurely white hair. His face crinkled around a big smile. He waited for Sam to say something, realized he was overwhelmed, and hurried off to the mill house.

"Samantha," Sam finally said as his friend of the forest and wilderness left the mill house, carrying on his head the exquisite wild-cherry rocking chair he had been working on for eight months.

"Samantha," Sam whispered to himself. "I have a new friend."

Frightful did not hear the excitement. Oksi had disappeared over the mountain, and she was speeding to catch up with her daughter. She finally took the lead and steered to Sam's meadow. She alighted on the limb of an oak tree. Oksi landed on a hickory stub.

Frightful scanned the meadow. Oksi scanned it, too.

A rabbit jumped. Instinctively Oksi dropped from her perch. She missed. She hit where the rabbit had been, not where it would be by the time she struck. The rabbit dove into a patch of greenbrier and Oksi flew back to her perch.

While she sat waiting for something else to run, Frightful flew back to the courthouse. She returned in the late afternoon but brought no food. Oksi, who had still not caught anything, ravenously attacked her mother.

Frightful dodged, climbed swiftly, and sped back to the cupola. In the morning she caught a pigeon.

Oksi saw Frightful flying toward her with the food when she was still a long way off. She waited, then attacked. Frightful dropped the pigeon. With a twist, Oksi caught it in the air and returned to the oak tree. She ate rapaciously.

Although she had never been taught this, Frightful was following ancient peregrine instincts. She was hacking her daughter—bringing her food when she could not catch her own.

Four miles away, on the side of Palmer Hill, Perry Knowlton was doing the same thing for Blue Bill and Screamer.

He carried Screamer to the hack board, a food platform on stilts. He had constructed it below his house on the far side of the pond. It was shaded by a tree. To keep predators like Jessie Coon James from climbing it, he had encased the stilts in tin sleeves. Carefully he removed Screamer's jesses and held him high.

Screamer saw the food on the hack board and flew to it. He was hungry. Perry had not fed him for a day to get him ready for this moment.

"So far so good," he said, and went back to the barn for Blue Bill. Perry held him high.

Blue Bill had imprinted on Perry more deeply than Screamer and was perfectly happy to sit on his hand and admire him.

"Go," Perry said, lowering his fist with a quick downward movement that forced Blue Bill to spread his wings. He flapped and he flew, too, but only as far as a tree limb— not to the hack board. There he sat.

"Ah, come on," Perry said. "You've been a mother's boy since I got you. Now, go join your brother and grow up."

Perry picked up the jesses, leashes, and falconry bells he had taken off the birds and walked the short distance to his bird barn. Blue Bill followed and sat on the roof.

"Ho-ho-ho." Perry bellowed the falconer's cry to encourage a bird to hunt.

Blue Bill turned his head upside down and observed the action until Perry opened the bird-barn door and stepped inside. Then he flapped his wings.

A bald eagle riding up the mountain on a rising thermal saw Blue Bill move and circled to strike.

Screamer, on the hack board, saw the shadow above him and instinctively crouched. He extended his neck and pulled his feathers flat. The great eagle, with its six-foot wingspread, did not see him. He was plunging toward Blue Bill.

Blue Bill saw him and shrieked the alarm cry. Perry ran out of the barn followed by Molly, José, Hughie, and Maria.

The eagle struck Blue Bill. Then he saw Perry and sped off. Blue Bill rolled down the roof and fell to the ground. Perry picked him up and put him under his shirt.

"Is he dead, Mr. Knowlton?" Molly asked fearfully.

"No, but plenty scared," Perry said. "His heart's beating as fast as a woodpecker drills. Let's go inside until he calms down."

The fans of the falcons of the Delhi Bridge trooped back into the clean, roomy bird barn and watched with great concern while Perry stroked the terrified falcon to calm him down.

José watched but was more interested in Screamer. He went to the window of the empty owl room.

"The other bird just flew!" he yelled. "He's going toward Bovina."

"Good," said Perry. "He's off."

When Blue Bill recovered his senses, Perry put him into a carrying cage and covered it with a blanket so that he couldn't see and beat his wings to get free.

"Aren't you going to let him go?" asked Hughie.

"Not today," Perry said. "I'll check him for injuries before I try again. After all, a bald eagle hit him."

"He thinks you're his mom, doesn't he?" Molly asked.

"Sort of," said Perry. "Two falcons raised him from about two weeks of age on, but he seems to have been more imprinted on people than his brother. Because of that, I may never be able to set him free."

"Oh, good," said Maria. "Then we can visit him often."

Perry smiled and opened the barn door.

"Hop in my van," he said. "I'll drive you all back to the courthouse."

"Maybe we'll find the other little falcon," José said. "The road goes close to Bovina."

"Oh, no," said Molly. "I hope he didn't go there. There are lots of transformers around Bovina. I found four when we were writing to the utilities company."

"Time to write letters again," said Hughie with a sigh.

Terrified by the eagle, Screamer had flown to an oak tree at the top of Perry's mountain. His fear died quickly, and he calmly looked around.

A flock of starlings swarmed past him, fanning out and coming back together. He found them interesting—they flew, they moved—they were birds. They swooped into the bushes and vanished. A red-tailed hawk soared by. Instinctively Screamer sat still until the hawk was out of sight. Then the starlings came wheeling back.

Screamer flew into their midst. The birds burst apart, exploding in all directions. He climbed high out of their sight. The birds turned and came back, re-forming their flock. One individual flew alone. Screamer bulleted down and picked it out of the air. He was on his way to independence.

That night he slept near the top of a red spruce. In the morning he followed the starlings that were streaming toward Bovina. They came down in a meadow. Screamer landed on a telephone pole, then skimmed the meadow, scaring the starlings into the air. He chased and attacked, but could not catch one.

Remembering Perry's food-laden hack board, he returned to it late in the morning, ate well, and departed. A few miles away, he stopped to rest. Screamer was outside Bovina again.

That same morning Oksi was sitting in Sam's meadow, hunting by sitting up high waiting for something to move. As the hours passed and she saw nothing, she changed her technique. She came down and skimmed over the tops of the knapweed and grasses to scare up the prey. A rat saw her and ran. She dove, missed, and headed back to the oak tree.

A small house sparrow came by, and she chased it. It dropped out of sight. A rabbit darted off through the weeds.

Oksi tail-chased the rabbit. It ran right, then left, right, left, its white tail warning the other rabbits to hide. Oksi chased right, then left, right, left, and speeded up to strike. The rabbit slipped under a pile of brush and was gone. Oksi flew back to the oak tree.

When Frightful returned to Sam's meadow the next day, Oksi chased her down the mountain. They lit on the bridge at Delhi.

Flocks of ducks and shorebirds had migrated down from the Arctic. They were swimming and eating below the two falcons on the West Branch of the Delaware. The ducks fled when they saw the peregrines. Oksi chased a group, missed them all, looped, and came back to the

bridge. She stood tall and alert. The water, the birds, the sky excited her. The open space felt right to her.

Before nightfall she had snatched a mallard duck that was dying from pesticide poisoning. She carried it to a gingerbread platform near the top of Molly's Victorian house. She ate and fell asleep.

In the early morning a "creee" awoke her. Blue Bill was circling the bridge. She recognized him, although more than a month had passed since she had last seen him. She flew to him, and together they rollicked above the bridge, tumbling on air currents that bounced and rippled like water.

Frightful saw Blue Bill and Oksi circling and diving. She flew to them, and the three falcons played on the invisible roller coasters of wind. When Frightful discovered what skilled flyers they were, she led them onto a rising thermal. They ringed upward and upward, wings spread, not flapping, just tipping now and then to keep them going up.

At two thousand feet they saw Chup far below, sitting on his dead limb above the Schoharie aerie.

Chup saw them, but he felt not one iota of paternalism. His duties were over. He was molting his flight feathers and chose to be alone.

For the next week, Frightful watched her offspring eagerly chase the migrating birds but could not share their excitement. She hunted from the cupola by day, and at night she flew back to the one mountain among hundreds, the one tree among millions, and Sam.

Screamer shuttled between Bovina and Perry's hack board for almost a week.

The day José mailed his letter complaining about the utility poles, Screamer came to rest on a transformer on a pole outside Bovina. A wind gusted; he tried to balance, contacted two wires, and fell to the ground. No one was there to pick him up.

Blue Bill and Oksi stayed around the good hunting grounds of Delhi with Frightful. They soared with her out over the countryside, learning to catch rats, mice, and pigeons. They became expert vermin hunters until Blue Bill found a cliff near the Pepacton Reservoir. Here thousands of migrating waterfowl came down to rest on the water. They were easy to catch, and when they moved on, he went with them. His early visual memory of life with Perry was forgotten. He followed the birds. He was not, after all, imprinted.

But Frightful was. She was held captive by her early training with Sam.

One day she watched a flock of doves disappear over the mountains. She followed them for a short distance, then flew back to the cupola on the courthouse. At dawn the next day she returned to her mountain and the nest box on the steel pole.

Sam was opening the mill sluice to start the waterwheel for Bando, now a busy father. He saw a shadow flash over the water and looked up.

"Frightful!" he shouted.

He held up his hand but did not whistle. Frightful hesitated, circled, and then did something she had never done before. She flew down to his hand without hearing Sam's whistle. Alighting as gently as thistledown, she curled under her toes to keep her talons from piercing his bare hand.

"Beautiful bird," Sam said to her. "Why do you honor me with this visit?"

"Creee, creee, creee," she called softly, leaving off the "car-reet" that said "Sam." He studied her. Her new feathers were darker and more lustrous than last year's. Her eyes were more brilliant and wide open. She was breathing regularly, and her breath was sweet.

"You're one healthy and beautiful bird," he said. "I thought you were here because you need me. But you aren't. Why are you here?"

Frightful faced south.

"Ah, that's it? You're leaving. You've come to tell me good-bye."

Slowly he reached out and stroked her gleaming black head.

"Creee, creee," he piped, but Frightful did not respond.

She looked up at the trees that closed off the sky, beat her wings, circled Sam's head, and climbed out of the forest.

"Good-bye," he called, and stopped. "Hey, what are you doing? You're flying the wrong way." Frightful was flying back to Delhi.

As she passed over Molly's house, she saw Oksi returning to her Victorian gingerbread roost for the night. The abundant pigeons in Delhi had kept Oksi from migrating.

As the light dimmed, the young falcon walked into her elaborate room with its curls and spindles and lay down. She got up, stuck her head out into the dusk, and lay down again. Something was happening to her, and she was restless.

The happening was migration. It was full upon the Northern Hemisphere. The shorter hours of sunlight and lowering temperatures were telling millions of birds to go south. The event had begun in mid-August. The loons, geese, ducks, and shorebirds had heard the message from the environment and had left the barrens of Alaska and Canada. A few days later the swallows and swifts felt the change and left the Northeast.

And now Oksi felt it. Kettles of northern peregrine falcons arrived in the valley. They picked out the weak and slow from the flocks of migrating birds and moved south when their prey moved south. The strong and healthy would survive to have strong and healthy offspring. The weak became life and energy for the falcons. Oksi watched, ate, and listened to the earth's atmospheric messages.

Frightful watched the migrating birds. Some flew west, some south; some migrated by day and some by night. She ate well and grew fat, until at last the shortening days and cold air urged her to go.

But the hemlock tree and Sam urged her to stay.

One chilly September morning, Oksi flew above Delhi, circling old haunts—the bridge, the cupola, and Frightful's Mountain. Near Bovina she got onto a thermal and ringed up and up. Spiraling with her was Chup. He peeled off at the top of the warm bubble and shot southward. Oksi peeled off at the top and joined the great North American bird migration. It was mid-September.

From the bridge top, Frightful saw her go. She lowered her body to fly, straightened up, and sat still. An hour later she returned to the hemlock. She bobbed her head up and down and nervously stacked and restacked her tail feathers. She flew back to the bridge. She flew to the cupola. Nothing was right.

In October she returned to Jon Wood's home. Alighting on the corrected transformer pole, she waited for Susan to appear with food. She saw only the boy who took care of the farm when the Woods were gone.

The pigeon cote was noisy, the rat cages were correctly smelly, but all were somehow wrong. She flew over the Schoharie Reservoir where she had weathered a storm. Frightening messages from the rays of the sun told her she was going the wrong way.

She flew back to the one mountain among hundreds, the one tree among millions, and Sam.

Mole was in the tree snoozing on Sam's bed, and Jessie

Coon James was in a hollow, dozing in winter lethargy. Sam and Alice were sitting around a small fire, cracking hickory nuts and putting the meats in clay tureens for the winter.

"Zella named her Samantha," Sam said. "Isn't that nice?"

"I know, I know," replied Alice. "How many times have you told me that? I saw her, and she's too little for such a big name."

"She'll grow up."

"They'll call her Sam, and then what?"

"That's even better," he said.

Alice stuffed a large piece of hickory meat into her mouth.

"Creee, creee, creee, car-reet."

Sam jumped to his feet.

"Alice," he said. "It's Frightful. She's here. She's not going to migrate. What do I do?"

"Call her down and keep her," Alice answered. "She would like that."

"I can't. Since I can't have her, I want her to be a wild peregrine falcon. She must go."

"Does every single, solitary peregrine have to migrate?"

"No," he answered thoughtfully. "There are some who have stayed near New York City all winter because there are so many pigeons. But they are not Frightful. She must be a one-hundred-percent pure peregrine, sailing blue skies, journeying to new worlds—and that means she migrates."

"Oh, Sam," Alice said, then thought a minute. "What makes birds migrate?"

"A lot of things, but mostly lack of food in the cold north. They follow the food supply."

"Then don't feed her if you are so anxious for her to be a pilgrim falcon."

"I'm not going to," he said, stepping back to try to find Frightful among the branches of the ancient hemlock, but primarily to keep Alice from seeing his great sadness. He wanted Frightful to stay with all his heart.

"I'm not going to," he repeated.

I N   W H I C H
The Earth Calls Frightful

And then it happened.

Frightful hopped from limb to limb until she reached the wispy top of the ancient hemlock. She turned her head slowly as she took a bearing on the sun's rays. She fixed on a longitude between ninety and seventy degrees. After many takes, the direction was indelibly printed on her brain. She pointed her head and body along the invisible line. She bent her knees and ankles. She lowered her wings.

"Alice," Sam whispered. "Frightful's leaving us!"

"How do you know?"

"Look at her. She has that southward concentration of migrating birds. I've seen it in robins and blackbirds."

Frightful flew. She did not look back.

"But she loves you," Alice cried. "She can't go. She doesn't know what to do without you."

"But she does," said Sam, watching her disappear. "She's flying south.

"Come back in the spring," he called, then added, "I'll be waiting."

Sam climbed the old hemlock, trying to catch one last glimpse of his beloved bird. She was already far away.

She rode the prevailing wind over the familiar mountains and rivers and beyond the Catskills into unknown territory. She did not hesitate or turn back. She memorized the landscape as she flew—forests, rivers, highways, and cities. In one hour she saw the Atlantic Ocean ahead. Its plantless expanse told her it was not the way to go.

She came down on a tor above the Hudson River and perched in an isolated ash tree. A Cooper's hawk and two red-tails were hunting not far away.

Frightful noted the moisture in the air, the clouds, the wind, and the other migrating birds passing overhead.

Blackbirds swarmed over the cattail swamp at the bottom of Hook Mountain.

In the morning the sky was clear and blue. She perched in the top of the ash, waiting for the earth to warm and the wind to rise and carry her on her way.

She took off about nine o'clock.

"Peregrine!" a man on the top of Hook Mountain shouted with gusto. He was seated before a spotting scope.

"That makes forty peregrines for the month," said a woman sitting on a camp stool. She put a check beside "peregrine falcon" in the raptor counting book. The tor top was speckled with men and women who came to Hook Mountain in the autumn to count the birds of prey. Each year these people, like thousands of others, tallied raptors along the four migratory flyways in North America—the Atlantic, Mississippi, Central, and Pacific flyways. They counted because the birds of prey were losing ground in the fight for survival. By comparing their numbers each year, the counters could tell whether or not their efforts to ban pesticides and pass laws protecting the birds were working. The birds of prey were vital to the health of North America.

The people on Hook Mountain cheered when Frightful went over. A peregrine was a thrill to see. The bird had been eliminated by DDT and pesticides in much of the

United States in the forties, fifties, and sixties. Even now it was still a rare sight—a beautiful rare sight.

Frightful's wings cut circles in the wind that sped her southeast toward the ocean. Abreast of New York City, she sensed she was off-course. Her internal compass and the increasing moisture in the air sent her westward. Rough air bounced her back and forth, but she found her longitude again over the New Jersey marshlands.

She dropped down to rest on the post of a duck blind. A shotgun blasted.

She took off, skimmed low over the tops of the sedges until she found a thermal, and rode it, ringing swiftly up, barely moving her wings as it carried her out of the range of the duck hunters' guns.

Soaring, tipping, circling at the top of the thermal was Drum.

"Creee, creee, creee," she called. Her first tiercel eyas answered with nestling talk, "Pseee," then adult talk, "Creee, creee, creee."

They sped out of the thermal together and started down the coast. They flew extremely high, keeping the ocean on their left. Drum had taken this trip last year. He picked smooth winds between towers of clouds as he led Frightful through the sky.

Frightful and Drum and several other birds of prey kept each other in sight. Traveling together, they formed a sky club. Before long they came to know each other and passed on information about the weather and the terrain. The experienced ones knew to come down early before a storm. Others sensed turbulence approaching and took detours around destructive winds.

Over Virginia a sudden gust of dry air pushed Frightful ahead of Drum. She had learned at Delhi that such a wind would be followed by a cold front. She flew faster to keep ahead of it. Six hundred miles from Hook Mountain, she came down on a utility pole on Cape Hatteras. Fifteen minutes later Drum joined her. Dropping out of the sky by twos and ones came the goshawk, the kestrel, the red-tailed, and the sharp-shinned—the bird club. They spread out over the vast wetland.

Frightful looked down on black ducks, mallards, blue-winged teals, plovers, godwits, yellowlegs, sandpipers—all the migrating birds that loved wetlands. At the sight of a peregrine falcon they vanished. Frightful did not chase them. She was looking for pigeons and rats but actually was not very hungry. She was living on her migratory fat. Perched on the pole, she oiled her feathers, which had become dry at the high altitudes. Drum oiled his on the mast of a sailboat that had been dumped in the marsh by a long-ago storm.

In the morning Frightful did not follow Drum southward. The wind was wrong. It was coming from the southeast, bending the trees to the northwest. She recalled the winds that had preceded the storm on the Schoharie Reservoir and flew inland to the little town of Plymouth, North Carolina. She landed on the bell tower of a church. She knew a church tower well, found one of the open windows, and walked in.

Drum had not gone far before he realized the winds were wrong. He back-flipped in the air and came down on a water tupelo tree about three miles from Frightful. The tree had grown great buttresses to support it in storms and in the watery soil.

Frightful in her church and Drum in his tupelo sat quietly through screaming gusts and dead calms. They preened. Frightful watched a duck fly into the reeds and a willet find shelter behind a dense clump of sedge.

The next day the winds were stronger. Lengths of clouds became stringy clusters of gray. Frightful stayed in her church tower, Drum settled closer to the bole of the tupelo tree.

Two nights later, windblown rain began to fall. First in light dribbles, then in gushes. The ducks and geese and herons hunkered down in the sedges and reeds. The warblers had gone inland to the pine forests. They pushed close to the tree trunks. The falcons and hawks sought shelter in forests and buildings. Those that had felt the lowering pressure of the storm, before Frightful and Drum had felt them, had flown west to get around it. They were sleeping in Kentucky and Tennessee.

Around two o'clock, Frightful's church tower vibrated

in the high wind. A shutter was torn from the rectory. It clattered down the street, breaking into splinters. The lights in the town went out. Frightful awoke from time to time, when the wind blew so hard it rang the church bells. She shook off the rain coming horizontally in through the windows, then put her beak into the feathers of her back and went to sleep.

Drum was not as comfortable. His tupelo tree lashed and coiled like a whip in the wind. He crouched, tightening his grip on the limb, and faced into the storm. Hours passed.

Just before dawn, a tidal wave six feet high roared across the marsh. It was seawater that had been lifted up into the center of the hurricane by the low pressure. It hit the base of Drum's tree and rose so fast that Drum was forced to fly. He could not see well, but he knew the direction of the forests. Beating his wet wings, he was carried, rolling and tumbling, low over the marshland. He crashed into a hill of groundsel bushes and wedged his way into their dense center. Then he climbed away from the rising water. Drum went lower into the bushes just as a 110-mile-an-hour wind struck. It ripped off every groundsel leaf, leaving the limbs bare. Gripping with all his strength, Drum faced into the storm, his streamlined body minimizing the wind.

Then came the calm. The eye of the storm passed through Plymouth at about two in the afternoon. Frightful was awakened by an all-encompassing silence. Drum sat still. This was no time to fly. Half awake, half asleep, he waited.

In the morning the eye of the hurricane was off to the north, and the far side of the storm struck the marshland. It was less forceful. The winds blew west now. Frightful stayed in the church tower. Drum stayed in the flooded groundsel bushes. The rain slowed, and the tide receded. By the end of the day the hurricane was off Cape Hatteras, on its way north. The sun came out.

Frightful caught one of several wet rats that had retreated to the church and crawled up to the bell tower. Drum shook the water from his feathers and flew inland. He climbed high, found a brisk wind, and sailed down the coast toward Florida.

Frightful took off around noon. She also climbed high. Although she had never seen the swamps and forests of Georgia and Florida, she sensed their place and recorded them on her visual mind. Navigating with her were members of the bird club. They had weathered the storm in trees and docks inland from the cape. Left behind were gaggles of ducks and geese. They had found their winter destination. The peregrine falcons flew on.

Two days after the storm, Frightful came down in a Florida sable palm and noted her global position again—eighty degrees longitude. She took off and flew over the tip of Florida. The club had dispersed. Each had gone on to its own ancestral wintering grounds. Two new companions joined Frightful, one an older peregrine falcon and the other a young tiercel.

The winds were light, and Frightful had to work hard to keep up her speed in the warm air below the tropic of Cancer.

She stopped overnight in Cuba and flew on the next day.

Immediately she was over the open water with no landmarks. She guided herself by the rays of the sun. When clouds piled up in the late afternoon, she came down on a key off the shore of Belize, caught food, rested, and went on.

She was alone now. She followed her directional line over the Caribbean Sea and caught up with Drum as they were approaching the Isthmus of Panama.

Drum looped in greeting. They flew in tandem to the palms and ficus trees on Barro Colorado Island and came to rest in black mangrove trees. They did not eat. A great urgency drove them on. In the morning they were over the Pacific Ocean, headed for Chile.

The winds changed from smooth glass to bumps. Drum recognized the edge of a tropical storm and turned east.

Frightful flew west. She also recognized the texture of the air and the color of the sky that foretold atmospheric trouble, but she chose to fly around the disturbance. Drum's course took him back to his wintering grounds on the Chilean shore.

Frightful flew for almost an hour to get around the storm before turning south. No land was in sight. She flew on.

In the late afternoon she held her wings straight out to glide and save energy. She dropped closer and closer to the surface of the ocean. She saw no resting place, not even a boat.

She flew all night.

At sunup she was still just above the water, her wings outstretched, gliding to find a badly needed bit of land. All was water.

As she looked and glided, a flock of storm petrels winged by. They wheeled in the orange sunrise. A flock of blue-winged teals flew with them. These were no birds of the ocean. They were birds of the land.

Land was near. Frightful summoned new energy and climbed into the sky. In the distance she saw a green-gray island.

With a last effort, she pumped her wings and flew straight ahead and came down on a *palo santo* tree on Española Island. Birds flew lazily above it. Male frigate birds with bright red balloonlike sacs under their chins cruised the shore. Not three feet from Frightful, seven little black

Darwin cactus finches were busily gleaning food. She waited for them to flee. All birds fled from her. The Darwin finches kept on hopping and eating. They did not know they should beware of predators. Frightful had arrived in the Galápagos Islands, six hundred miles out in the Pacific Ocean, where the birds and reptiles had lived for hundreds of thousands of years, perhaps millions, without predators. They were totally unafraid.

Frightful was unable to chase the friendly birds. They did not fly away from her, and because they did not, she was not inspired to chase them. She was exhausted and hungry amid friendly creatures. She was watching them, growing listless from hunger, when a wheeling flock of sanderlings and whimbrels from the continent flew past. They acted familiarly. They flew together and apart at the sight of a predator, and Frightful dove into their midst. She gave chase and finally ate.

Returning to the *palo santo* tree, she rested not far from a group of Galápagos mockingbirds. They were not as innocent as the little finches. They were attacking everything—iguanas, birds, other mockingbirds, and Frightful herself. They did not know she was a predator, but they did not like any other living thing in their territory. They swooped and dove and pestered. She returned the compliment. She swooped and dove—and they all stayed away.

From her perch she watched young sea lion cubs and

their mothers tumbling on the beach. The huge bulls were in the water. They roared and bellowed when another male came near their harem and offspring.

Something moved at the foot of Frightful's tree. She focused. A three-foot-long land iguana was chewing cactus fruits. His dragonlike spines and thick skin sent a strong message to her. He was not food.

For several hours Frightful bobbed her head and looked from one strange animal to another in this world of ancient survivors.

At sunset, clouds piled up like purple mountains, forecasting rain. Frightful flew to a shelter she had pinpointed on her arrival. She crossed the water to Gardner's Island and alighted on a steep lava cliff of cracks and niches. All were occupied by blue-footed boobies, big birds with startlingly blue feet. They chased her off their properties. She dropped to another shelter and was ushered out by Galápagos penguins. These perky, upright birds had been lost from the ice islands of Antarctica hundreds of thousands of years ago and, unable to swim back, had adjusted to the tropical heat. They cooled off by lifting their wings, panting, and jumping into the icy water.

Frightful left the penguins and blue-footed boobies to their caves and niches and rounded the island, looking for shelter. She came upon another cave on the western cliff, facing the oncoming storm. The cave was scoured by wind, sea, and water, and was deep enough for shelter. She walked into it.

That night a downpour pelted the cliff side. Frightful shook rain from her feathers without awakening. In the morning, bright sunlight turned the roughened water into patches of flashing silver. The clouds were gone. Frightful flew back to Española Island for food.

It was vacation time for peregrines, and Frightful sensed it. She flew for the sheer pleasure of flying. She winged out over the water to be rocked by warm sea winds. She climbed up into storm clouds and rolled out of them into sunshine. She turned loops and spirals.

Each morning for the next two months, she played with the air currents high above her rocky little island, then streaked to her *palo santo* on Española Island. When the daily tourist boats arrived around ten o'clock, she flew back to her island, leaving the sea lions, Darwin finches, marine iguanas—all the original residents—to entertain the people. They did this admirably, since they were totally unafraid of the two-legged mammals. Until three hundred years ago, no humans had come to these isolated islands, and the birds and reptiles had not learned to run from them. Their inherited memories covered one million years without people, and so the birds hopped close to tourists and fishermen. The sea lions did not move when photographers walked among them. Lizards challenged lizards while people

watched, and marine iguanas walked between human feet on their way down the beaches to feed in the sea.

On December 21, the day of the winter solstice, something happened to Frightful.

The image of the one mountain among thousands, the one tree among millions, and the one boy, Sam Gribley, flashed in, then out of her mind.

Three days later she left Gardner's Island. She stopped on Española for a week, eating well and putting on fat for the long flight ahead. She was going home. The sun had changed only a few seconds at the equator, but it was telling her body to migrate.

She pointed her beak south. In New York, shorter days had told her to go south. Here in the tropics the days were now growing shorter, and Frightful pointed her beak the wrong way.

She was ready to take off when a Galápagos hawk landed on a cactus in front of her. His feathers were dark brown, his eyes yellow. He flew into her face. Frightful fell backward, twisted onto her wings, and sped. Two other male Galápagos hawks came after her. They were a family of three males and one female. The males were defending their nest on a cactus not a hundred yards from where Frightful had sat. They all helped one female raise her chicks, each of which had a different father. The hawk family passionately attacked falcons from the north. Having sent Frightful on her way, the three males came after her, but Frightful's tapered falcon wings were faster than their broad hawk wings. She sped to the end of the island and rested on a lava rock.

Frightful was facing north. Suddenly the iron bits in her brain clicked a strong message to her—fly straight on. Her brain was feeling the pull of the earth's magnetic field, slight as it was.

Frightful flew north.

She flew along longitude ninety degrees, the longitude along which the Galápagos Islands lie. After a half hour's flight, she landed on a *palo santo* tree at the top of a dead volcano. She lingered uncertainly among complacent woodpeckers from the north. They confused her. They were busy being home lovers. Their ancient ancestors had found the Galápagos Islands so pleasant that they had not returned north. Frightful might have remained with them had not a flock of pintail ducks come down on the shore below. She chased them. Three left the island, headed north. She followed them, sensing that her inner compass had finally kicked in and was correct.

Frightful and the ducks came to rest on Darwin Island, the last outpost before El Salvador, a thousand miles away. Frightful was now north of the equator, but only about ten miles. She lingered on this bird-rich island to put on more fat.

In early January the sun's message was stronger. The days were several seconds longer—spring was coming to the north. She crouched low, straightened up, and bobbed her head. The one mountain among thousands, the one tree among millions, and the one Sam Gribley were pulling her home. She flew up the Galápagos longitude, headed straight for El Salvador in line for Wisconsin.

For many miles, she flew over the Pacific Ocean with a flock of red-rumped storm petrels. They dove for tiny fish. Around her, gulls screamed and pelicans flapped laboriously. Then the land birds vanished and she saw only birds of the open ocean, the albatrosses and snowy terns. Frightful sensed she was far from food and land.

The sun set orange-red on the ocean, and in seconds it was night. There is no true twilight in the tropics. The stars instantly appeared in the black sky, reflecting their light on a quiet ocean.

Alone in the starlight, Frightful flew on.

She breathed steadily as she followed her internal homing equipment. To save energy, she flapped her wings strongly, then soared for long periods on the errant winds.

She kept going.

In the morning she was on a clockwise wind that was carrying her east. She turned to get back on course when she saw land birds in the distance. She caught up and flew with them. They grew more numerous, then floating seaweed told of land not far ahead. Frightful held her wings outstretched and glided on the wind.

She put her feet down on a coconut palm on Cocos Island.

Sandpipers ran along the beach; gulls screamed and looped through the air. Migrating birds rested and gathered strength for the long flight north.

Frightful rested, then darted around Cocos Island for three days, eating and sleeping and gaining weight. When the sun had added another two minutes to the day, the mountain, the tree, and the boy appeared in her mind. Taking another reading on the sun's rays, feeling the magnetic pull of the earth, she flew north on the fateful ninety-degree line headed for Wisconsin.

Three hundred miles beyond Cocos Island, Frightful knew there was land to the east. She did not see birds or seaweed, but she felt the mass of a continent.

Ignoring the sun, she turned and flew east. After an hour manipulating bumpy winds, she arrived at the Isthmus of Panama.

Frightful flew directly to the mangrove tree on Barro Colorado Island where she had rested in the autumn.

She ate and slept. For three days she stayed on the island, looking northward from time to time, realigning her compass. When the rays of the sun and her magnetic sense lined her up with eighty degrees longitude, she was ready to fly. The one mountain in thousands, the one tree among millions, and Sam were straight ahead.

"Creee, creee, creee."

Drum slammed down beside her.

They exchanged soft noises of recognition, then swooped over the island, chased each other, ate well, and started home.

The trip progressed slowly at first. Frightful and Drum stopped in Cuba for ten days and along the northern coast of Florida for a week. As the days grew longer, they went faster. They lingered in South Carolina for only five days, flew over North Carolina, and came down for a day in Virginia. Cape May, New Jersey, was their next stop. On the narrow peninsula they met hundreds of other raptors going north to their aeries, their nests and scrapes. Frightful barely noticed them. No sooner was she rested than she took off for the one mountain among thousands.

Navigating now by the sight of familiar forests and rivers, she arrived home in three and a half hours and dropped into the one tree among millions.

"Creee, creee, creee, car-reet," Frightful called.

I N   W H I C H

Destiny Is on Wing

Frightful looked down on a snowy mountain. "Cree," she called softly to her nest box on the raccoon-proof pole. She recognized it under mounds of snow and ice and lifted her feathers in pleasure.

Other familiar objects caught her attention. There were the stone table and log seats. They had been cleared of snow. Baron Weasel's den was still under the rock. The snow around it was stamped with his footprints. The water-wheel was there, but not turning. The millpond was ice. A feeling of contentment settled over Frightful, and she rested from her long journey.

"Creee." Frightful looked up. Drum was overhead. He circled and called for her to follow him.

Frightful sat still. She was where she wanted to be—home with Sam. Drum dove toward her, called again, gave up, and went on. He was eager to get to his aerie in the Adirondack Mountains. On a steep cliff his mate of last year had laid eggs that had broken under her weight. Pesticide chemicals had accumulated in her body and weakened the eggshells. A week later she died from poisons she had accumulated in South America from eating birds that had eaten DDT-sprayed insects. Drum must find another mate this year.

Frightful swooped down onto the nest box. Snow splashed out in all directions. She jumped from the roof to the hacking porch, scattering that pile of snow. Leaning down, she peered into her old nest and walked far back into the cozy box. She picked up a windblown leaf in her beak.

After a long stay there, she flew to the stone table to look for Sam.

The deerskin door of the hemlock tree bumped open. Mole came out. He bounced through the snow, tunneled through deep drifts, surfaced, and ran down the trail.

Frightful flew after him, leaving her wing prints on the snowy table. She was hungry, and Mole, she sensed, was going hunting in the meadow where the rabbits and pheasants lived. She flew ahead of him and waited in the oak tree for him to arrive. He did not appear. Mole was tearing downhill to Mrs. Strawberry's farm for his daily treat from Alice.

A whistle from the mountaintop never reached Frightful's ears, nor did the words, "Frightful! You're back. You left your wing prints on my table! Where are you?"

Sam whistled the three notes that would bring Frightful to him, but she was out of earshot.

When Mole didn't show, she took to the air. Her hunger reminded her of the courthouse cupola and the pigeons. She skimmed down the mountain and followed the river valley to Main Street. Throwing out her yellow feet, she came to a gentle landing on the courthouse cupola.

The pigeon prospects were wonderful. Mrs. Dorst and her daughter, Ms. Sarah Denny, had fed the pigeons so well during the winter that they were already nesting and laying eggs. Without the peregrine falcons to keep them in check, they were so numerous that the courthouse windows and ledges were white with birdlime. Frightful had an endless feast before her.

Her biological clock was ticking rapidly toward nest-scraping time. This put her in a mood to check nest sites. Late in the afternoon she flew to the Delhi Bridge and walked to her old scrape on the girder. She did not remember the noise of last spring, but her visual memory was clear. She recalled trucks shaking the webbing, men on scaffolds and cherry pickers. She flew back to the courthouse. A visual image of the cliffs along the Schoharie was the next site to check. She watched the sky for Chup.

Molly came skipping down Main Street, spotted Frightful sitting erect and dignified on the courthouse cupola, and broke into a run. She dashed into the county courthouse building and found Leon Longbridge working at his desk.

"She's back," Molly cried excitedly. "The peregrine falcon of Delhi is back!"

"Are you sure?" Leon Longbridge was grinning.

"Definitely," Molly said. "Her head is almost pure black. Her breast is rosy white, and she's just beautiful. She's our falcon."

They stood side by side on the sidewalk across the street from the courthouse. Leon focused his binoculars.

"By golly," he said. "You're right. Not only is her head exceptionally black, but she's right in her favorite perching spot."

"Will she nest there?" Molly asked.

"Maybe. Falcons and most other birds come back to their old territories year after year," he said. "Some even return to the same nest sites."

"The bridge?" said Molly. "Will she nest on the bridge?"

"I don't know. Peregrine females are unpredictable."

"She has to. She just has to," said Molly. "That would be so cool."

Frightful cocked her eye and focused on a speck in the sky. She bobbed her head. Chup was speeding like a crossbow along the edge of a cloud. He was a mile away. She waited. He went right over Delhi and the mountain, heading for his cliff in the Schoharie Valley. Frightful was in the air before Leon Longbridge could say another word about female peregrine falcons.

"Chup, chup, chup, chup," the tiercel called. Frightful heard the peregrine love song. She caught up with him and flew at his side. They chased in and out of the misty edge of an ice cloud.

But Frightful felt she was going the wrong way. Her mountain was behind her. She tipped her wings, banked, and started back. The west branch of the Delaware, the town of Delhi, and the one mountain among thousands were where she belonged.

Chup came after her. He looped so appealingly that she looped in response. When she finished the aerial flip, she was flying close behind Chup, back to the cliff above the Schoharie River.

She landed on the ledge where she had helped raise Chup's motherless eyases. Lifting her tail and leveling her body, she walked to the abandoned scrape.

She straightened up—this was not right.

Chup, perched on the ledge of the aerie, watched her carefully. Frightful lifted all her feathers to make herself appear enormous. Chup backed up. The female peregrine was the power of spring. He bowed to her.

Frightful flew off. Chup followed her. Above Jon Wood's house, she located the tall silo and circled it. It had ledges for a scrape, and food abounded here. She landed just under the roof. Chup came down beside her. He did not like what he saw and flew back toward his cliff.

Frightful also found the spot not to her liking, but she

did not return with Chup. She flew directly to her mountain and landed on the wooden box. After a long wait, Chup joined her. She was the falcon. She made the nesting decisions.

Chup came as far as the ancient hemlock and stopped. He would go no farther. A nest box on a pole in a forest was totally wrong. He called to her and flew back to the Delhi Bridge. The span was relatively quiet. Sitting high above a river of ducks and waterfowl, Chup felt better. He waited for Frightful.

Atop the nest box, Frightful sat still—resolute. Presently she heard the voices of Sam and Alice as they came up the snowy trail from Mrs. Strawberry's farm. She fluffed her feathers. They brought pleasure to her.

"Well, what do you think, Sam?" Alice asked. "Isn't that exciting?"

"Yes, yes, it is," he answered. "I really would like to manage Mrs. Strawberry's farm for her."

"Not manage," Alice said. "She wants to give it to us when you're of age."

"We'll see about that," Sam said. "It should be yours. You've brought her prosperity with your Crystal and her Poland piglet offspring. And I have my own farm—my wilderness."

"I need your help," Alice said. "I can take care of the pigs, but not the fields."

Alice was quiet while they went on all fours up an icy hill.

"Besides," she at last said, "Dad and Mom and the kids would like the old farmhouse."

"They sure would!" Sam chuckled. "If Dad didn't have to plow rocks like he did up here, he would be happy all right." He thought a minute.

"You know, Alice," he said, "I have come to realize that I am a farmer already."

"You are," Alice said. "And so another farm would be perfect for you."

He tilted his head wistfully as he thought out loud.

"I am a farmer of wild foods—wild rabbits and pheasants, wild cattails and hickory nuts and walnuts." He was quiet, then went on.

"I sowed the abandoned field with plants the birds like and clover the rabbits like, and planted the clearings in the forest with wild bulbs and mountain lettuce. I've kinda made the Gribley farm produce what it is best suited for— wild crops."

"You sure did that," Alice said. "But with the Strawberry farm you can also have barbecued spareribs, and bread from the wheat crop."

The trail ended, and they walked to the root cellar. Sam brushed the snow off the door and thought about the evening's menu.

"Creee, creee, creee, car-reet."

He spun on his heel.

"Frightful!"

Sam whistled the three notes that had once brought her to his fist. She did not respond.

"You've been on a long trip, haven't you?" he said. "Your life is different now—all but your nest. You must remember raising Oksi here."

Frightful peered at him.

"You're one gorgeous falcon," he said. "Will you stay?"

"Oh, she has to," Alice said.

Still addressing Frightful, Sam went on, "Frightful, stay with me. I will manage Mrs. Strawberry's farm so you will never go hungry. I know how to increase the numbers of quail and pheasants and rabbits. Or do you hunt ducks and waterfowl now? I can increase their numbers, too. Come live with me on my wilderness farm."

Frightful hopped to the hacking porch.

"She must stay," said Alice, clenching her hands in excitement. "We'll have little eyases. They'll be free. No conservation officer can take them away."

"Chup, chup, chup."

"Creee, creee, creee," Frightful answered.

Chup was circling Frightful's Mountain.

She called to him. Chup circled in the sky once more.

He looped and flew upside down. He called the love song of the peregrine falcon.

Frightful hopped to the porch and took off.

She sped up into the cloud where Chup was cutting arcs and circles. She looped and spiraled.

In tandem they flew down the river valley. Near Delhi, Frightful took the lead. She went down Main Street, sped over Elm Street, and landed on the cupola of the court-house.

She scratched away the windblown leaves with her saffron-yellow feet and sat down.

She was home.

Chup knew it. He bowed to his mate.

Destiny's new life had begun.

A bowlike speck appeared over Frightful's Mountain. It grew larger and larger as it came toward earth. An instant later, Sam heard wind whistling through wing feathers. He looked up. Oksi bulleted down from the sky and alighted on the wooden box.

She called for a mate.

Afterword

If you go to Delhi, New York, you will not find the bowstring truss bridge over the West Bank of the Delaware River. I am a novelist, and I put it there for Frightful. A peregrine needs a high aerie with a beautiful view. However, nearby in the mountains you might find Jon and Susan Wood and Perry Knowlton. They are falconers who are urging the utility companies to make a simple adjustment on their transformers to save birds of prey. I invented their conversations and some of the incidents in which they take part, but I have truthfully represented their lives and work and their love of our birds of prey. They read the manuscript and agreed to be characters in this tale.

Heinz Meng is also a real person. He raised the first peregrine falcons in captivity and hacked them to the wild when everyone said it couldn't be done. A warm and extraordinary man, he asks no praise. His reward is sharing his knowledge with those who would help the peregrine falcons. Dr. Meng is a professor at State University of New York at New Paltz.

All the other characters are fictitious. The mountains are not. Ira Macintosh, who has climbed and camped in these beautiful forests, has checked out every name and slope for me.

Finally, this is also true: Peregrines nested on the Kingston-Rhinecliff Bridge that spans the Hudson River in New York State. When repairs began, no authority would stop the work to protect the endangered birds. Eventually the U.S. Fish and Wildlife Service moved the eyases, and the peregrines did get their young on wing. But the bridge-repair work never stopped for even a day.

JEAN CRAIGHEAD GEORGE